Fateful Knight

Knights of Kilbourne, 5

KEITH W. WILLIS

Rosewood Press

Where dreams and dragons take flight.

Fateful Knight

This is a work of fiction. The characters, incidents, and dialogues in this book are of the author's imagination and are not to be construed as real. Any resemblance to actual events or persons, living or dead, is completely coincidental. Any resemblance to actual dragons, living or dead, is completely intentional.

Published by Rosewood Press
14 Rosewood Drive, Clifton Park, New York 12065 U.S.A.

~ * ~

Third Edition 2026

Cover Art by Sevannah Storm

As always, to Patty. My light, my love, my friend, my inspiration, my fated mate.

Dear Reader,

Well met! I'm delighted you've decided to join me on another adventure to Kilbourne. Thank you so much for sharing your time with me. I know in my own busy life just how precious that commodity is. We only have so much time, and the knowledge you're spending it reading one of my Kilbourne adventures is overwhelming to a relatively unknown author such as I.

If you're reading this tale, odds are you've already read at least one of my previous excursions into this medieval, magical world. If not, while it's certainly not obligatory, I highly encourage it. Otherwise you may be just a bit at sea (and if it's the Thundermist sea, you may find yourself with a few extras...) as to just who these characters are and what's going on. Fair warning.

Fateful Knight is, in a sense, a return to the story of Morgan McRobbie. While I, like Morgan, adore Marissa, the last few books have somewhat neglected the erstwhile "Knight" of the titles in her favor, and I felt it only proper to give the good Knight-Commander a bit more scope in this outing. But don't worry—Marissa is still a major focus of the story, as is everyone's favorite dragon, Wyvrndell. In fact, Wyvrndell has become such an integral part of the series that I simply could not have told this story without him.

Please know that I absolutely love to hear from readers via email or through social media. I also am thrilled to meet you in person at the events I attend over the course of the year—both author fairs, and especially at the Renaissance Faires my wife and I attend (see my website www.keithwillisauthor.com for upcoming dates).

One last thing before you get to the important stuff—the adventures of Morgan and Marissa (and yes, Wyvrndell) and all their friends and enemies. If you enjoy this book, or even if you don't, I urge you to leave a review. Reviews and ratings are extremely important for authors, but also important for your fellow readers who may be undecided about whether to try a new author. It could be your review that helps them make that choice to join us in Kilbourne. So thank you in advance.

And now, let's get to the story. Dragons ho!
Keith W. Willis
Clifton Park, NY
December 2024

ACKNOWLEDGEMENTS

As I crawl muzzily out of the editing cave, covered in the red ink of slaughtered adverbs, bearing a half-filled mug of barely warm tea, and an extremely diminished plate of ginger biscuits, I realize it's time once again for me to say a few choice words of thanks.

First, to you, the readers and fans of the Knights of Kilbourne. You keep asking for more of Morgan and Marissa's adventures, and who am I to deny you that pleasure? It's an honor to know you enjoy the tales I tell, and I appreciate every single person who has purchased (or borrowed) and read my books.

To my friendly neighborhood fellow authors here in New York's Capital District, as well as all the amazing authors across the country and the world, who continually inspire me. I wish I could buy and read (and review) all of your amazing books.

To all the folks who put on the amazing Renaissance Faires we attend over the summers in order to bring you Kilbourne books in person—your hard work and dedication to these events are a true inspiration, and I'm grateful for the opportunity to be a part of them.

And to all the many faire-goers who took a chance on my books; and especially to those of you who came back for more. Support like that is simply overwhelming. I can only say, quite humbly, thank you.

And finally, with more gratitude than I can ever express—to Patty, my loving, supporting, and infinitely patient wife. My inspiration and my cheerleader. You not only put up with my obsession, but actively encourage it, and force me to do the most important task a writer can manage—get my butt in the chair and write. You read and reread; critique and offer brilliant suggestions; proofread more manuscript pages than anyone should ever have to (and haven't yet sent me a bill, and if that ain't love, I don't know what is...). I could not have done this without your love and support. You're amazing and I adore you and thank you from the bottom of my heart.

CHAPTER ONE
McRobbie House, Caerfaen

With a low growl, Duke Morgan McRobbie, Knight-Commander of the King's Legion, spun and hurled the dagger.

It struck the wall next to the door with a dull thud. The hilt quivered with a low buzzing like a hive of agitated bees. A moment later the door opened, and the wizard Sebastien peered out. He glanced at the dagger, inches away from his head, and an expression of mild reproof tinged his lips.

"Took you long enough, didn't it?" Morgan said, his voice husky with agitation.

The wizard raised his brows. "Hmm, perhaps. Duke Morgan, these things cannot be rushed." He looked again at the dagger and returned his gaze to Morgan, who was engaged in counting the holes in the wall made by his previous forays with the weapon.

Six. Damn it, he'd let his frustration get the better of him, and his duchess would not take kindly to his ruining the plasterwork of their new home. He didn't want an irritated wife. Or witch. He'd have to get this mess patched up right away.

"No, I suppose not," he said. "All this magical stuff is beyond me, you know." He shook off the tension that had been plaguing him, settling for a shrug combined with a glower. "So, what did you find? Did this exercise accomplish anything?"

Marissa emerged through the doorway behind the wizard, stretching her neck to and fro. Her dark hair was askew, and there were black circles under her gold-flecked brown eyes. After the events of the past weeks, along with Sebastien's intense examination today, Morgan found this no surprise. He was exhausted himself.

Before Sebastien could reply, she said to Morgan. "Well, I'm still a witch, for whatever that's worth."

Morgan slumped into a chair and closed his eyes. "And is this a good thing?"

"Yes," snapped Sebastien. "It is." He tempered his tone to say, "Better than the alternative, for certain. If she lost her powers altogether..." The wizard shuddered.

Morgan straightened and opened his eyes again. "I'm not sure I agree, Sebastien. If Marissa lost all her powers, those blasted bishops would leave her alone. She'd be safe. No price on her head."

"Is that what you think?" Marissa demanded, hands on her hips. "Imagine they'd say, 'Oh, no more witchy powers, eh? Well, all right, we've made a big mistake. Get along. Go in peace'."

The wizard chuckled. Morgan shot him a quick glare. That type of thing was no help at all.

Turning his attention to Marissa, he heaved a sigh. "No, of course not. Wishful thinking, I reckon."

"And anyway, my having magic means I may be able to help protect the women in the kingdom with powers. As foretold in that dratted prophecy." Her face twisted into an uncharacteristic scowl. "Not to mention, losing all my power might have resulted in... Well, you remember what Nardis said, when we were in Arvindir. When Azim was trying to steal my magic?"

It was Morgan's turn to grimace. "Yes," he said, in a voice so low it was barely audible. "I remember."

Oh, did he remember. What Nardis postulated, and Azim's sister, Saia, later confirmed, was the notion a magic wielder stripped of their powers would become little more than an empty husk, staring, vacant, and mindless. Not a pleasant prospect. Especially when the magic wielder in question was his wife of a few weeks.

Of course, over the course of their acquaintance, her magic had come in quite handy on more than one occasion. She'd been able to use it to save his life—both their lives, in fact—when Headmaster Rhenn and Kiera Northram plotted to murder the two of them. She'd tackled the demon which inhabited Chief Wizard Foxwent and sent it back to the netherworld. And she'd managed to vanquish Erkarna, the magic-obsessed dragon who'd intended to take her powers for his own in his scheme for world domination.

It had taken almost all she had left to save Morgan, herself, and Wyvrndell from Erkarna. The bitter memory flooded back: the acrid stench of the dragon's evil spells drenched his tongue, the crash of stones flung about in the battle thundered in his ears, and Marissa's limp form in his arms, spent and nearly drained of her powers, weighed heavy on his body. He shuddered at how close he'd come to losing her in that battle. But if it hadn't been for her magic, none of them would have made it out of Erkarna's cavern alive.

He ran a hand through his hair, forcing the memories to recede. There was more than enough to deal with without dwelling on the past. Ever since the rebel bishops declared a war on witchcraft and placed a price on Marissa's head, her power seemed more a bane than a boon. It wasn't by her choice magic flowed through her veins, he knew. Her powers were inherited from her parents, both puissant magicians themselves. But sometimes, damn it, he wished she didn't have it. Like now.

"Morgan?" Marissa's tone of long-suffering patience boded ill for marital harmony. "Why is there a knife stuck in the wall? And all these holes?"

Figuring a reply of "Trying to kill a spider" wouldn't be found acceptable, he grabbed his one opportunity to avoid this particular line of inquiry, like a drowning man latching onto a piece of flotsam. With a caginess borne of years of experience in Royal Council meetings, he ignored her question and instead asked one of his own. "How much?"

"How much wha—Oh, you mean how much power? I—Sebastien?" Her mouth tilted up at one corner and her eyes crinkled the tiniest bit. A sure indication the matter of knives and walls had been tabled for the time being, not forgotten.

Sebastien paused, seeming oblivious to the undercurrents swirling around him, and considered the question. "From what I was able to discern, nowhere close to what you possessed before. Though still quite enough."

"Interesting, if not particularly helpful." Marissa turned to Morgan. "Could you pour me a glass of wine? Sebastien's examination was exhausting." She flashed Morgan a wan smile.

"Of course. I beg your pardon, Marissa. I should have asked straight away." Morgan hastened to the sideboard and sloshed into a glass the first vintage he could lay hands on—a Vynfold red, one of her favorites. Striding to his duchess, he offered it to her. "Are you all right?" he asked. "Did Sebastien's probing hurt?"

She accepted the glass, took a sip of the wine, and closed her eyes for a moment. Once she'd opened them again, she drank some more and glanced at Morgan. "I'll be fine," she said. The color was returning to her cheeks even as she said, "No, it didn't hurt. It is disconcerting, though, having someone else wandering about in your head."

"I shouldn't wonder." Morgan nodded toward her glass. "More?"

"Best not or I'll be out like a snuffed candle," she said. Morgan led her to a chair, and she sank into it with a sigh. After another swallow of wine she regarded Sebastien. "So, tell us what you've learned from all this."

Sebastien claimed a seat and leaned back. Smoothing out the robe over his wiry frame, he steepled his fingers across his belly. "Very well. I've already stated, you are still a witch. Which is to say, you have an ample supply of magic ready to hand. However…" He closed his eyes.

"However?" she prompted when he hesitated.

"However, I don't think it's the magic you had originally."

"Oh." She cocked her head, considering the wizard's statement. Morgan squeezed his fists in an effort to prevent himself from doing, or saying, something stupid. Like, "Speak plainly, damn it, and get on."

"And you say this because…?" Marissa inquired.

The wizard opened his eyes again. "Your Grace, when I first discovered your magic, I was able to examine it. Not for a long period, I'll admit, but enough to become familiar with its characteristics. It was…well, orderly is the best way to describe it. Which was to be expected, considering the source of your magic."

"All right," Marissa said. "Go on."

"From my examination today, your magic feels different. Much more chaotic and less disciplined. Much…well, wilder."

"The Thundermist," Marissa breathed.

Morgan sucked in a breath.

The old wizard nodded. "The Thundermist. Somehow it infused you when you were on Fanshawe's ship, adding to your already substantial power. Well, the ritual devised by Erkarna appears to have stripped you of a good deal of your original magic. This leaves you with the powers bestowed on you by the mysterious Thundermist. There is no mention of this in the archives, at least from what I've been able to determine. So, a complete unknown. I'm not sure what effect it will have on you in the long run."

Marissa exchanged a glance with Morgan, who stood at her side.

He shrugged. "This is all beyond me," he said. "I'm merely the chap who happened to fall in love with a witch."

She threaded her fingers through his. "I'm delighted you did."

"Hmph," rumbled Sebastien, but a faint smile played across the wizard's face. "The point is," he went on, "your original magic, disciplined as it was, was able to temper somewhat the wilder power of the Thundermist. Without that counteracting force? Well, I don't know.

I don't imagine anyone does. I've searched the archives and found no mention anywhere of a similar situation."

"Princess Saia," Marissa said. Her eyes opened wide. "The Mist. It infused her, too, on our flight back from Arvindir. It was the same thing that happened to me. I think it's what enabled her to defeat Azim."

"What?" Morgan stared at her. "You didn't tell me."

"Well, with one thing and another," Marissa said. "Like Azim trying to murder us, then the confrontation with Foxwent, and Erkarna, and this whole nonsense with the Church… I guess it might have slipped my mind. Until now."

"Interesting," Sebastien muttered. "Is it possible you might convince her to allow me to conduct a similar examination?"

"I could ask her. Would it accomplish anything?"

Sebastien said, "Having a second sample—instance—well, whatever, you know what I mean—might give me a better insight into how the Thundermist magic acts. It could be important."

"All right, I'll ask the next time I see her. I can't guarantee she'll be willing to undergo an examination like I did."

Morgan cleared his throat. "Speaking of that, Marissa still has a considerable amount of magic available to her?"

"Enough to be getting on with," Sebastien said. "The problem is this: I'm not sure the royal enchantress here will be able to harness this wilder magic without a great deal more training. I'm afraid we're rather in uncharted territory."

"Bother," Marissa said. "Well, there's nothing for it. I'll have to contact Wyvrndell and ask if he can start our lessons again. I must say, while quite useful, I haven't missed them. But if I'm to fulfill the prophecy, though I'd much rather forget the whole thing, I'd better return to my studies."

Morgan furrowed his brow. "Any idea how you're to go about fulfilling it? I mean, a prophecy is all well and good, but some direction might be helpful, don't you think?"

Marissa gazed into her glass of wine. Seeking either inspiration or solace, he guessed. She'd made it clear she didn't like being the subject of this prophecy. At last she said, "No, there was nothing specific. The whole thing was too vague for my liking. So, short of blasting the rebel bishops with some dire curse, no. Which I don't know how to do anyway, and I don't imagine the king would approve if I did."

Morgan choked on a laugh. "No, I don't imagine he would. Even if you did, the whole thing has grown beyond the Church or rather the rebel faction of it."

"You're right. Unfortunately." Her gaze went distant.

Morgan was certain she was seeing the assassins who'd recently attempted to earn the bounty placed on her head. If not for the intervention of their resident ghost and his friends... *It might*, he glowered, *be nice to go a few days without anyone trying to murder one or the other of us.*

"Sebastien?" Morgan asked. "Any helpful suggestions from a wizard's perspective?"

The wizard rose from his seat. "No." He shrugged. "Not until we learn more about the Thundermist, and how it may impact the Duchess. And on that note, I'll bid you good evening."

Morgan walked him to the front door. "Is there anything else you can tell me?" he asked in an undertone.

"I've told you both all I've been able to discern," Sebastien replied. "If I come across anything new, I'll let you know straight away." He pulled open the door and stepped outside. "But I was serious about her current magic being unpredictable. If she tries any major workings, there's no telling what might happen."

"Marvelous," Morgan muttered. He closed the door behind the wizard and marched to where his duchess awaited him.

"About that knife..." she said.

~ * ~

McRobbie House, Caerfaen

"Wyvrndell?" Marissa called. "Can you hear me?"

"I hear you, Lady Marissa," the dragon replied.

The dragon's words in her mind felt comforting after so long an association with him. Unlike Sebastien's recent intrusion, which had muddled her for the better part of an hour afterward, she enjoyed hearing Wyvrndell's sonorous voice resonate in her head. He had explained, when he first became her tutor, how dragons are creatures of magic. *"As any with a bit of intelligence are aware,"* he'd said. *"Not having the necessary equipment for speech of your type, we have had to adapt to the circumstances. We have thus developed the ability to communicate by thought."*

Marissa returned her attention to Wyvrndell. "Oh, good. I'm sorry I've been so long in contacting you. Are you recovered...?" She fought to keep at bay the bitter memories of Erkarna's betrayal.

"From our encounter with Erkarna?" Wyvrndell said, and Marissa wondered if he was subject to the same nightmares. If dragons even had nightmares. *"I seem to have no lasting effects,"* he said. *"Well, except the one which gave me magic, thanks to you."*

She breathed a sigh of relief. Wyvrndell's acquisition of the power wrested from her made the whole debacle worth what she'd had to endure. That had been the point, after all. And better him than Erkarna, for certain.

"How does it feel?" she asked.

There was a pause, presumably while the dragon reflected. He was most deliberate in his thoughts, she had noted over the course of their acquaintance. He continued, *"It is a strange sensation to hold something no other dragon in recorded history has ever done more than dream of. To be able to perform some of the spells I have taught you. I imagine it will take me a while to get used to it."*

Marissa laughed. "I understand," she said. "I felt much the same way when Master Sebastien discovered my powers."

"If you wish to begin your lessons again, I am not sure when I will have time," Wyvrndell said. *"Things are fraught here in Ervantium, in the aftermath of Erkarna's betrayal."*

"Of course," she said. "But when you are ready, I'll present you with a new challenge."

"Indeed? What might this be?"

"Well, according to Master Sebastien, the power Erkarna stole from me, which ended up in you, is what my parents blessed me with. I've been left with that wilder magic given to me by the Thundermist. Sebastien thinks I will have a difficult time controlling it, and he insists I get back into training right away, to test its limits. Since you're my tutor, I hoped you might have some insight into the nature of Thundermist magic."

"I regret to say I do not," the dragon replied. *"To the best of my knowledge, Erkarna and I are the only dragons to have made any extensive study of magic at all, and he never mentioned Thundermist to me. Any knowledge he might have possessed has gone with him."*

She pondered this, then said, "Did Erkarna keep records of his research? Did he have books or histories which would provide some insight? I assume he must, for you said you studied with him for a long time. Might there be something in one of those?"

Wyvrndell was silent for so long Marissa feared she might somehow have offended him. When at last he replied, his voice was different, distant. *"Yes. He did keep records. He maintained a great library, with many books and scrolls. They are all in his cavern, where you defeated him. But the cavern is sealed, and none may enter."*

"Oh," she said, drumming her fingers on the arm of the chair. *I'd really hoped there might be something.* "Well, that's too bad. We'll have to muddle through without it. Let me know when you're ready to begin my instruction again. The wedding is over and done with, so I have much less to distract me from your tutelage."

The dragon's tone was dry as desert sands when he replied, *"I will admit, you did seem preoccupied at times."*

She laughed. "You mean you were forced to repeat yourself every other word. I'm sorry, Wyvrndell."

"Well, perhaps on occasion. I understand, it is a human trait, though I find myself sharing it, due to my constant association with you and Sir Morgan."

"Ah, we're becoming bad influences on you, as friends do. Wyvrndell, thank you for the gift of your continued friendship. I cherish it, and Morgan does too. I shan't keep you any longer. And I sincerely hope things settle down for you."

"Farewell," replied the dragon. Then his voice was gone, and Marissa was left alone with her thoughts for company, until her kitten leaped into her lap for ear scritches.

~ * ~

McRobbie House, Caerfaen

Marissa surveyed the tea trolley. Steam wafted up from the pot, filling her nose with the earthy aroma of the tea. Spiced cakes, redolent of cloves, cinnamon and ginger, the very essence of autumn itself, competed for her attention. It took all her self-control to keep from snatching one of the cakes and popping it into her mouth. *Soon.*

Briana, her maid, bustled by the doorway of the morning room to answer the rap at the front door. Marissa glanced at the clock and smiled. Right on time. In a moment, the Dowager Viscountess of Westdale—Lady Sybil, Morgan's mother—breezed into the room. She paused, then hastened to Marissa and encircled her in a tight embrace.

"My girl, it's a delight to see you," she cried. "You look marvelous. Morgan is treating you well, I take it."

"Splendidly," Marissa replied, hugging Lady Sybil in return.

She didn't think it the time to mention their more recent adventures. Stealing magical jewels, battling mad sorcerers, demons, and dragons, and almost being assassinated for being a witch, were not the topics of polite conversation with one's mother-in-law. And none of those things were Morgan's doing, so her statement was truth itself.

Instead, she said, "I'm so glad you're in Caerfaen. I've been dying to show you the house."

Lady Sybil, who was in residence at the McRobbie family estate in Westfyld, had sent a letter announcing her plan to visit the capital before the snows made travel inconvenient. Marissa offered—insisted, in fact—she stay at McRobbie House for the duration. After all, they had more room than they knew what to do with. Lady Sybil, ever independent, demurred, and declared her intention to stay with an old friend, also a widow. "She doesn't get out much," Lady Sybil had said in her last letter. "So I intend to drag her out to a play, several expensive restaurants, and carousing in a few dark taverns." Which, to Marissa's delighted amusement, was Lady Sybil through and through.

"I can't wait to snoop," her guest said, looking around the morning room. "This room is charming. Well done, my dear."

"Thank you. Here, have a seat, let me pour you some tea. And try one of Mrs. Brand's spice cakes; they're heavenly and sinful all at the same time."

Lady Sybil took the offered cup, set it on a small table by her chair, and helped herself to a spice cake. "Oh my," she said after savoring the treat. "Marvelous." She licked crumbs from her lips. "I adore this time of year, if only for the spices that come with it."

"Me too," Marissa agreed, helping herself to another of the cakes then passing the plate to her guest. "And don't worry about leaving any for Morgan. Mrs. Brand keeps him well supplied with ginger biscuits, so the cakes are all ours."

"Oh, I wasn't going to." Lady Sybil chuckled. "Morgan always had a weakness for ginger biscuits. One of the things he and Martin shared."

Marissa remained silent, staring unseeing into her tea. "Morgan misses his father," she said at last. "He doesn't talk about him much, but I can tell. I wish I'd known him."

Lady Sybil flashed a wan smile, and her eyes grew misty. "He would have liked you, I think. He liked girls with spirit. That you have and to spare." She cleared her throat. "All right, let's not go getting all maudlin here. On to more cheerful subjects. Tell me all the latest news."

"Well, let's see." She decided Lady Sybil would rather know their recent escapades than not. In all likelihood she'd heard some of them through her own sources. And she had, after all, been with Marissa when she'd been taken captive by the dashing pirate Captain Fanshawe. That sort of thing creates a bond, and Marissa realized at the time Morgan's mother was no delicate flower, by any stretch of the imagination.

"First off, right after the wedding…" Marissa launched into the tale of her and Morgan's adventures in Parthane, their escape on dragonback with Princess Saia, and the subsequent destruction of the Foxwent-demon. She segued into the encounter with Erkarna and the loss of a good chunk of her magic, and finished with the assassins who attacked upon their own doorstep, only to be foiled by Sir Jamie, the resident spirit of the home.

Lady Sybil stared in silent awe when the saga was completed. Marissa wondered if perhaps she'd been hasty in relating this epic tale. Perhaps her guest's sensibilities were more delicate than she'd thought.

Lady Sybil's mouth opened. Marissa waited, expecting chastisement or censure. Instead, the older woman emitted the loudest guffaw Marissa ever heard, her eyes streaming with tears of what she hoped was laughter.

"My god, you two do get up to things, don't you?" Lady Sybil crowed when she was once again able to speak.

"We…like to keep ourselves occupied."

"I should say. And now you're being pursued with ill intent by these blasted clergymen, eh? I'd like to give them a piece of my mind. Hounding women minding their own affairs and not hurting a soul. I never heard the like." Lady Sybil scowled. "I told the vicar he'd best not be party to any of this nonsense, or he'd have me to answer to."

"He was quaking in his boots, I'm sure," Marissa said.

"Oh, Ewen MacFarlane's a good fellow. I knew he wouldn't get up to any mischief. Still, best not to take any chances, eh? So, what are you doing about all this?"

"I'm open to suggestions," Marissa replied.

"Hex 'em?"

Marissa barked out a bitter laugh. "I wish it was quite so simple."

"Mmm. Yes, it would go against the grain, eh? Give legs to their argument of witches being evil."

"I'm afraid so. Also, I'm not sure I'd know how to do it even if it was justified." Marissa's mind was drawn to the grimoire she'd acquired, and the dark spells it had contained. *I'm sure I could have found something in that book of spells to deal with the bishops. But at what cost?* It was a good thing the grimoire had been destroyed along with Chief Wizard Foxwent. *Lead me not into temptation.* She forced her attention back to Lady Sybil and said, "My powers are a bit tenuous.

"Oh? Why do you say so?" Lady Sybil leaned forward in her chair, her gaze fixed on Marissa.

"I've probably said more than I should already." Marissa hesitated. But Lady Sybil was trustworthy and deserved to know how she'd been affected. "When Erkarna's ritual went awry—because he planned it that way—I lost a lot of my magic. Master Sebastien was here yesterday to examine me. He—well, do you recall, on Fanshawe's ship, how the Thundermist infused my magic, made it stronger?"

Lady Sybil nodded. "It's what enabled you to defeat Augustus Rhenn and poor, mad Kiara Northram when you hared off to rescue

Morgan from the black tower."

"Right. Well, what I lost to Erkarna was my 'normal' magic, if you will. What I've been left with is the power bestowed on me by the Thundermist. Which, according to Sebastien, is a complete unknown. So you see, even if I did try to do something major, like hex the rebel bishops, there's no telling what would happen. The hex might backfire, or cause something even worse to happen. I don't know and can't take the chance on it."

"I do see. You're like a chap in a brawl who's handed a sword and has no idea what to do with it. It could be helpful, or he could cut his leg off."

Marissa gave a most unladylike snort. "Yes, like that. I'm hopeful King Rhys will find a solution and I won't have to risk it. Speaking of swords…"

Lady Sybil cocked her head. "As one does."

"In the house of Kilbourne's Knight-Commander, as one does." Marissa chuckled. "More often than you'd ever imagine. At any rate, I've commissioned a new sword for Morgan. It's a belated wedding gift."

"Marvelous. Does he know about it?"

"No, it's to be a surprise. It'll be a surprise to me if the blasted thing ever gets finished. The smith says it's the most difficult commission he's ever undertaken, and he can't be rushed. I don't know why, it's only a sword…"

CHAPTER TWO

Ervantium

"Tell me," King Petrandius said. The old, black dragon's voice was quiet but compelling. "Tell me about magic."

Wyvrndell gazed at the ancient stones that formed the walls of the king's chamber, not seeing them, while he turned the question over in his mind. "Your Majesty," he said at last. "It is rather daunting being the sole dragon who possesses magic. And though I know the theory behind most of it, if I am honest, I have little I can put into actual use at the moment."

"Please explain, Wyvrndell."

The dragon king didn't sound angry or upset at his admission. Merely…curious. Wyvrndell fought down a hiccough and marshalled his thoughts. "It is difficult to put into words. The best way to explain is through an expression humans use. 'If a dog chases a cart and catches it, what will he do with it?'"

Petrandius eyed him, his gaze thoughtful. "Your adage presumes one understands the concepts of both 'dog' and 'cart,'" he said.

Wyvrndell started to explain, but the king held up a forestalling talon. "Which, fortuitously, I do. What you are saying, in this round-about fashion, is while you are in possession of magic, you do not know what to do with it."

Wyvrndell hung his head. "Yes, Your Majesty," he mumbled. "I am afraid so."

"Erkarna had very definite plans for it," Petrandius observed.

A flood of anger coursed through Wyvrndell at these words, like molten lava spewing from one of the volcanoes which dotted the far reaches of the northern mountains. "His plans," he said, "included killing me and my friends, and using his stolen powers to subjugate everyone: dragons, Dwarves, and humans, all to his will."

"So they did," the king replied. "And if not for you, my young friend, he would have succeeded, too."

"Not I," said Wyvrndell. "Lady Marissa defeated him to save me. And herself, and Sir Morgan…"

"Mmm, yes. The sorceress whose powers you bear, eh? It is interesting how this happened. It would, I think, be helpful to know more about it. Perhaps in time we will." The king paused, lost in thought. At last, he said, "Well, world subjugation is out. What options are left to us?"

"My hope, and what I always believed Erkarna intended, was to use magic for the benefit of dragonkind. Which sounds wonderful when you say it. It is the practical application that eludes me."

"Perhaps the quest," Petrandius mused, "was more about the challenge of seeking magic rather than the end goal of actually gaining it."

"I—" Wyvrndell hung his head again. "I am sorry, Your Majesty. I fear perhaps you are right."

"I generally am." The old dragon gave a chuckle. "However, like the dog in your adage, we—well, you, at any rate—by chance have managed to catch the cart. Is there naught you can do with it?"

"Oh, I can do spells," Wyvrndell said. "Watch." He held up his talons, muttered the brief words of the spell, and the little ball of light shone bright and crystalline, casting unruly shadows dancing into the corners of the chamber.

"So you can. What else can you—no, never mind, this is not the time. Tell me, Wyvrndell, was Erkarna's research focused solely on his scheme to rule the world? Or is there perhaps within his notes something which would serve to benefit the entirety of dragonkind?"

"I do not know. He never showed me much of his notes or research. He only talked in broad terms concerning his plan to harness magic. His cavern, I'm afraid, is sealed up tight. I did it myself."

"Quite right you were to do so. However, you will have to unseal it."

Wyvrndell shuddered.

"I know," Petrandius said. "You would much rather leave Erkarna's tomb, and those memories, locked away. Yet, if you are to complete your quest, I fear it is your lot to go there again."

"If you insist, Your Majesty, I will go."

"I do insist." The king said, his gaze fixed on Wyvrndell.

"However, you shall not go alone. Such an endeavor would, I fear, be asking too much of you."

Wyvrndell's spirits lifted at these words. "Will you accompany me?"

"Me? No, young one, not I. I will send two—no, three—others with you. Donathyr, chief of my guards. Also your sire, Wyzandar. And of course your young friend Aireantha. I believe with such companions, you will find your way."

Wyvrndell raised his head. "I will do my best, Your Majesty."

"Mmm, yes, I believe you will." Petrandius said, his tone encouraging. "Go and prepare yourself for this task. Entering that cursed place will not be easy for you, I know. I will summon the others and give them instructions."

With a bow, Wyvrndell departed from the king's chamber. While he walked through the dim corridors of Ervantium, he realized Petrandius's directive required him to search for the very information Lady Marissa wanted. Needed, if she was going to be able to make use of her magic. Perhaps there was something in Erkarna's notes to explain how Thundermist magic worked. This might, he acknowledged, be of double benefit.

Which didn't mean in the least he still wanted to do it. He would, he decided on a whim, go to the rocky ledge his father favored. There he could stretch his wings in the sunshine and prepare his mind and heart for the arduous task that lay before him.

CHAPTER THREE

High Street Watch House, Caerfaen

Harlan Jenks, captain in command of the High Street Watch House, jerked to attention when Sergeant Henry McGwyn pushed open the door of his office. Behind him, constables were scrambling to belt on swords, don helmets, and grab shields from their racks.

"Henry, what's going on? A riot?" Jenks cocked an ear, scanning for sounds of mayhem though the half-open window. All he heard was the normal hubbub of the city going about its business, and the annoying coo of a pigeon sitting on the sill. Jenks flapped a hand at the bird, which stayed put, glaring with a mad red eye.

"Might be, sir, if we don't soon get a move on," McGwyn said. "A couple of idiots have rounded up some witches. They're building a fire, sir…"

Jenks was already moving. Papers cascaded from his overloaded desk onto a floor littered with more reports, a spare pair of boots, and a half-eaten plum. He slammed his battered helmet on and buckled on his sword belt. "Where?" he demanded as a fire roared up within him, fueled by rage and exasperation.

"Over Long Bridge," McGwyn replied, following in Jenks's wake. They pounded down the stairs to the first floor. "In Avern Square. They can't do that, sir. Can they?"

"Not in my city they can't." Jenks hit the Watch House doors, shoved them open, and leapt down the four steps to the street. He turned to the left and ran.

Ahead, a clutch of constables pelted toward the Long Bridge. It spanned the River Tyree, which sliced Caerfaen in two. The stench of the river rose up, a heady mixture of mud, fish, and gods knew what various kinds of offal, assailing Jenks's nose. He tried to hold his breath while he crossed. It was to no avail, which was the normal course of things, and he ended up gasping in the mind-numbing cacosmia of smells. He sprinted across, choking on it.

The bridge was jammed with farm carts, merchants' wagons, people heading to or from the public market, and a great variety of animals. Donkeys brayed, cows lowed, and goats bleated as they were being driven to the market. Dogs yapped, chasing anything that moved. There was even the occasional cat, aloof to the hubbub, and the nastiest-looking raven Jenks had ever seen, perched on one of the bridge posts, muttering under its breath and watching him with a baleful eye.

"Clear the way, Watch business," Jenks called.

Which had little effect. If anything, the crowd clustered tighter. But he was used to this and oozed through the congestion like an eel, with McGwyn hot on his heels. Once they reached the far side of the bridge, things opened a bit, and Jenks put on speed once more.

He'd worked out long ago when he was a mere constable that there were four types of runners when trouble appeared. There were the spectators—those who ran toward the trouble to see what was going on, and enjoy the show. Or the fearful who ran the other way when they spotted trouble, so they didn't get caught up in it. Worse were the villains who ran because they'd caused the trouble in the first place and didn't want to end up in a cell or before a magistrate. And there were the resolute who ran toward trouble to try and stop it. Jenks vowed when he was a young rookie to always strive to be one of the latter. During his rise through the ranks, he'd done his best to instill the same drive in his constables and sergeants.

And here he was, once again, running toward trouble. This time, at least, he and his constables wouldn't have to chase after some thief or murderer trying to make a clean getaway. No, this time they were running to try and prevent stupidity from ruining some woman's day. To try, if it came down to it, to prevent bloody murder.

The throng of spectators hurrying to the square grew thicker by the minute, with more and more people joining the flowing tide washing toward the day's entertainment.

The smell of sweat and stale ale filled Jenk's nose. After the stench of the river, it was almost a relief. "Nothing like a good public murder to liven up the day," he grumbled sourly. His opinion of his fellow man wasn't good at the best of times. Things like this did little to bring up the average.

He entered the square a few steps behind the brace of constables.

McGwyn, puffing like a bellows, was still hard on his heels. Beyond the crowd, a plume of smoke was rising. With a muttered oath, Jenks pushed his way through the throng.

The spectators formed a large circle around a well-constructed pyre. Two women of indeterminate age and dubious witchiness were bound to the center pole. They were also gagged—no doubt to prevent the utterance of any dire curses upon their tormentors.

Two men of even more dubious intelligence faced the pyre. Each held a lit torch. One of the men looked to be in his mid-thirties, with an ale-flushed face and hard, cold eyes. The instigator, Jenks was certain.

His companion was younger, softer, and appeared to be beginning to regret what had started out as a lark and was turning into a nightmare. His face bore the expression of a man in urgent need of some place to spill the contents of his guts.

With nods and gestures, Jenks dispatched his men, sending them eeling around through the crowd, splitting into pairs in order to be less of an overt threat. The last thing Jenks wanted to do was spook one of these idiots into tossing his brand into the lovely, eager pile of tinder. The whole damned thing, women and all, would go up in a blazing twinkling.

Some of the onlookers were urging the two to get on with it. His constables, Jenks was pleased to see, were silencing them. Well, nothing for it. He stepped into the open.

"Hello, boys," he said, hooking his thumbs into his belt and rocking on his heels. "What's all this, then?"

The leader looked him over, decided despite the badge and sword he didn't present much of a threat, and deigned to growl, "Gonna burn us some witches."

The women struggled against their bonds.

"Nice day for it," Jenks observed, maintaining his position. "How come?"

"Church says so."

"Hmm." Jenks mused on this. "Church says so, eh? Tell me, if that's the case, how come you don't have a priest here?"

Hard Eyes shifted, an expression of puzzlement marring what were already unpleasant features. "Priest? We don't need—"

"Of course you do," Jenks said with the firm assurance of a man who'd done this sort of thing before. "If you're gonna do the job, lad, do it right. Gotta have a priest on hand to bless your work, eh?"

The two women ceased their struggling to stare at Jenks in abject, silent horror for this casual disregard of their plight. He turned his head enough so the two men weren't able to see and tipped them a quick wink.

While Hard Eyes was processing this new information, Jenks called out, "Henry. Scoot over to St. Basils, will you? Get Bishop MacFarlane. I'm sure he'll be happy to assist in this, um, noble endeavor."

"Right you are," replied McGwyn, hustling off toward the cathedral.

Jenks turned to his prey. "It's round the corner, won't take but a couple of minutes, right? When Bishop MacFarlane comes, you can get everything done nice and proper, like the church says. I can see you're both good and faithful followers. Oh, say, your torch is gonna singe your hand in a minute. Best put it out and light another, don't ya think?"

The instigator glanced at his brand, which was indeed burning close to the handle. Jenks eased his way closer to the men.

"Make way, make way," came McGwyn's voice. Glancing up, Jenks spotted his sergeant, with the bishop lumbering along behind, threading his way through the crowd.

"Ah, here's Henry with the priest," Jenks said. Both men were eying their diminishing torches. "So we can do everything like the church commands, eh?"

"Now, now, what's this, then?" rumbled the oversized man of God.

Jenks had forgotten what an imposing figure Bishop MacFarlane made. Jenks spoke up before the witch burners could get a word in first. He needed to keep them distracted and off balance a little bit longer.

"Father," he said, clasping his hands together in a show of delight. "So kind of you to join us. This pair of fine gentlemen—sorry, lads, I don't believe I caught your names…"

"Vern," offered the younger one, who appeared relieved at the delay in the proceedings.

"I'd be Angus," said the other, juggling his torch, which was going to scorch his fingers soon if they didn't get on with things.

Jenks continued to address the astonished bishop. "Vern and Angus have hearkened to the Church's call to burn witches, and—"

"What?" After taking in the scene, MacFarlane's eyes grew wide.

Jenks issued a brief nod and closed one eye.

The bishop, thank God, as one might under such circumstance and in the presence of an ecclesiastical personage, was quick on the uptake. "Um, yes, I see. Quite right to summon me, Captain. Well done."

Jenks said, "Your Excellence, before they get to it, I thought perhaps it might be appropriate for you to lead us in prayer." He'd managed, inch by excruciating inch, to edge close enough to Angus to touch his arm. *Not yet. But soon.*

"Ah, well, yass, of course." Bishop MacFarlane folded his hands and bowed his head. "Let us pray," he intoned.

The two prospective witch burners, torches lowered along with their heads, closed their eyes obediently.

"Dear God in Heaven," began MacFarlane.

Jenks wasn't listening. He gave a nod to McGwyn to handle Vern. Like a bird pouncing on a nice, juicy worm, Jenks placed one hand on Angus's shoulder. He held his knife across the man's throat with his other hand.

"You, my lad," he whispered into Angus's ear, in order not to disturb the bishop in his prayers, "had best pray with everything you've got. Pray you don't move. Pray you don't even twitch, or you'll never live to tell the tale. Drop the torch. Drop it. Now."

For a moment, Jenks wondered if the man might try to resist. He pressed his blade against Angus's throat with more force. "Drop it," he repeated. "And that's the last time I'll say it."

The torch hit the pavement. Jenks stomped it out with a booted foot, a cloud of acrid smoke rising to the heavens to join the bishop's prayer. "Good lad," he said, glancing to make sure McGwyn had Vern under control.

"Corporal Donovan, to me," Jenks called once the bishop completed his prayer.

"Sir." Donovan stepped out of the crowd and tossed off a smart salute.

"Take a couple of constables and escort these two 'gentlemen' to the Watch House. Lock them up. I'll be there in a bit to do the paperwork and get them in front of a magistrate. On a charge of conspiracy to commit murder, and whatever else I can dream up on the way. You lads," he said, addressing Angus and his stricken partner in crime, "are for it. Take 'em away, Corporal."

Jenks turned to McGwyn. "Henry, why don't you release these ladies and help them away from that—thing, eh?"

"Right on it, Captain," McGwyn replied. If his salute was much less textbook than Donovan's, Jenks didn't mark it against him. He and McGwyn had been together for a long time, and through a lot.

Bishop MacFarlane nodded in appreciation. "Well done, Captain. I must admit, I am impressed."

Jenks gave him a wan smile. "All in a day's work, unfortunately. And I'm afraid we're going to see more of this type of thing."

MacFarlane crossed himself.

CHAPTER FOUR

McRobbie House, Caerfaen

"Morgan?" Marissa said from her place in a chair by the sun-filled window of his study.

"Mmm?" He glanced up from the letter he'd been reading.

Though he resided in Caerfaen, he was still Duke of Westdale and had responsibilities for the lands there. The report from his seneschal detailed the current year's harvest, which would be of major import to the many farms and villages in the duchy.

"Do you believe in fate?"

"What?" He set down the letter and regarded her with more interest. "Fate? How do you mean?"

"Fate," she said. "Prophecy. Destiny. Whatever you care to call it."

He smiled at her, sitting in an armchair with a cup of tea at her elbow and a kitten in her lap. "No."

"Truly? You don't believe, for example, we were fated to be together?"

This, he sensed, was treading on dangerous ground. Even so, his instincts told him being honest was, overall, better than spouting some platitude. He leaned back in his chair and gazed into her brown eyes with their intriguing gold flecks. "Fated to be together? No, I don't believe it. We came together through a series of remarkable coincidences, beginning with you walking alone in the forest and being captured by a dragon. Was that fated? I'd have a mighty hard time believing any soothsayer or higher power wrote such a tale and forced you to follow it."

She smiled and stroked the kitten.

Morgan relaxed his guard. "Here's the thing," he went on. "Chance, or a dragon, or fate if you wish to call it such, brought us together in the first place. Our choices—happy ones, for my part—led us to where we are. Not some mysterious hand, not some prophetic vision. Not even God, if you want to know my honest opinion of the deity's workings in the world. I made choices. You made choices. As simple, and as difficult, as that."

He rested his hands on his knees. "Does it mean I can picture a life in which you don't figure? No. But that's because I adore you, and cherish you, and want you to spend the rest of your life with me." He grinned. "Even though you do have a penchant for finding trouble."

She stuck her tongue out at him. Well, at least she hadn't flung the cat at him, so he went on. "But regarding to the staying with me bit? That, my love, is a choice you have to make. We make it each day, don't we?"

She took a sip of tea and assumed a contemplative expression. "D'you know, I don't think I've ever uncovered this philosophical side of you before. I rather like it."

He shrugged. "I do have a thought or two going round my head on occasion."

"Oh, I know you do. Don't get me wrong, I wasn't saying that at all. I just meant you don't often let them out into the daylight for others to see. You have deep waters, Morgan McRobbie, and I intend to explore them."

"Again, it's a choice you are making," he said. "Because you're curious. You know what they say about curiosity and cats…"

"Mrow," put in the kitten, taking umbrage at this sentiment.

Marissa provided a spate of reassuring ear scritches while appearing deep in thought. "Because I want to know everything about you," she countered. "If I choose to spend my life with you, I want to know exactly who it is I've linked my lot with."

"Fair enough. Good heavens, Marissa, what's brought this on, anyway?"

She grimaced. "Oh, I don't know. This whole nonsense with the church and the witches. And of course the blasted prophecy. I don't fancy being a plaything of fate."

"I don't see how you are," he said. "Whatever you do, you will do because it's the right thing. Not because of some mysterious prophecy or because it's your fate to do it. Because you choose to do it."

"You think so?" She sounded dubious.

"It comes back to choices, Marissa." He ran a hand through his hair. "Sometimes we make the right ones. Hopefully most of the time. But we don't always manage it. When we choose the wrong course, we end up paying for it. The price, I've seen much too often, can vary widely. A poor choice can mean you lose something or someone you love. Often it means you live with sleepless nights and regrets. But it all comes back to choice."

"What of your instincts?" she asked.

"What about them? There's no fate involved there. My gut, or my heart, or whichever part of me is in control at the moment, tells me what it believes would be a good idea. A lot of it is based on experience. Often it's pure intuition or guesswork. Overall, it's worked out pretty well for me. Once in a while I end up stubbing my toe. If I make the wrong choice, people can get killed. But I can't say there's any destiny or fate involved."

She nodded.

Morgan thought of conversations along these same lines with his oldest friend, the Bishop of Caerfaen. "You should talk to Randolph," he suggested. "If anyone has a cause to believe in destiny, or fate, or whatever you might call it, it's him. And he doesn't."

"Perhaps I will." She scooted the kitten off her lap and set down the teacup. "Thank you for talking to me, Morgan. You've helped to relieve my mind."

"I'm glad. But I will say this: there is one fate you can't escape."

"Oh?" She arched a brow. "What might that be."

He grinned. "The one which says I'm going to kiss you."

Her eyes shone at his words. She spoiled it by saying, "Ha. That will be by my choice, I'll have you know."

"Drat. And here I thought I was fatefully irresistible." He struck a dashing pose. "Are you finding me irresistible yet?"

Her lips curved into a lazy smile. "Well, perhaps."

He hastened to her.

CHAPTER FIVE

Avern Square, Caerfaen

An older man, a shopkeeper by Jenk's estimation, stepped forward from the ring of spectators. "Forgive me, Captain," he said in a loud voice, "but I find myself confused. Those men your constables hustled off claimed the Church sanctioned their actions. So weren't they acting in accordance with the law?"

Jenks opened his mouth to reply. After a momentary pause he closed it again. He stared at the man and said, "I'm going to ask Bishop MacFarlane to answer."

The bishop gave a quiet "Harumph," and turned to address the crowd. His voice boomed out over them. "My friends, certain members of the clergy have been advocating for the punishment of women like these." He gestured toward the pair McGwyn and several of the constables were helping away from the pyre which Angus and Vern intended for their fate. "Poor things, who've done no harm to anyone."

"My question stands," the man said. "The Church, so I hear, has determined witches to be anathema. So shouldn't they be punished?" Several others echoed this sentiment.

"It's a fair question," MacFarlane admitted. "But here's the thing. Because a few clergymen say a thing don't mean it's so. Of course every one of us, clergy or not, hate to admit it, but we're all fallible. Only God is perfect. And my friends, when he looks at what we get up to, often in His name, I fear he wonders if he might have made a mistake or two along the way. But that's a topic for a different sermon."

A few of the onlookers chuckled. Bishop MacFarlane's sermons were known far and wide. They were often filled with messages of hope and love. They were also, quite often, extremely long. But the fact the crowd was at least laughing was a good sign. Jenks nodded his approval.

The bishop went on. "Some members of the clergy, some of my fellow bishops in fact, have decided amongst themselves to instigate this war on witchcraft. They term it evil. They say these witches are profane, say they act in direct opposition to God's laws and commandments."

Several heads nodded at this. MacFarlane smiled. "And yet, my brothers and sisters, is it not written in scripture how we are each given different talents? I would submit to you that those who have the gift of magic, have this gift from a merciful and benevolent God. It is not the talent itself which is evil, but what one does with it. Consider a man of great physical strength. If he becomes a blacksmith, we say, 'God gave him such strength so he might work to craft things from iron, for the benefit of his fellow men.' Yet if he uses his strength to beat his neighbor and rob him, we call the Watch on him. Do y' see?"

Jenks glanced around. The crowd was hanging on his words, and Jenks breathed a silent prayer of thanks. "Now consider this, my friends," MacFarlane went on. "These women, these witches, what are they doing?"

"Well, they're doin' magic, ain't they?" someone shouted. A general laugh met this astute comment.

"Yes, they're using their magic—the gift God gave them, remember. Tell me, who else does magic?"

This question stumped his audience. At last some fellow, a bit brighter than his neighbors, got it. "The wizards, eh?" he called in triumph.

"Spot on. Well done." MacFarlane beamed, like a teacher conferring praise on a dense student who's gotten a breakthrough. "Both wizards and witches use their magic to cast spells. There's a single difference between them in what they do. Anyone want to take a guess what the difference is?"

Heads were scratched. Brows furrowed; beards were tugged. Then a hand went up near the back of the crowd. The bishop said, "Yes, my good fellow. Have you deduced the answer?"

"Um. The witches do black magic?"

MacFarlane's mouth pursed. "No," he said. "I'm afraid that's not it. Anyone else?"

A woman in the center of the throng spoke up. "It's 'cause they're women, ain't it?"

The bishop nodded. "Well done, madam. These misguided priests who, I might note, speak for themselves and not the entire Church, have issued their decree in order to control and harass these witches, simply because they are women. If they used their magic for evil purposes, well, no one would take issue. But this is not the reason, and not the substance of the bishops' decree. They declare the witches of Kilbourne—not wizards mind you, who also use their power in the exact same way—are anathema."

"It ain't right," the woman who'd spoken up before said in a disgusted tone.

"No," the bishop agreed. "It ain't right at all. If you ask me, it's because these women dare to possess a power—a gift from God, we've established—which these priests do not have. They see these women who they believe are beyond their control, and they are jealous and fearful. And mark this well, my friends. Jealousy and fear are abhorrent to the Lord. Is it not written how we are to love God, and love one another? This false decree fails on both counts. Thus the king, in his wisdom and mercy, has declared protection for any women who pledge to use their powers for good. And so Captain Jenks here, along with his valiant constables, acted as they should, in the sight of the law, the king, and God, to provide assistance when those misguided men attempted to harm them."

Jenks stepped forward to stand beside the bishop. "Thank you, Bishop MacFarlane, for clarifying this matter for everyone. The Watch will continue to protect any women who are targeted by such men. If you see something like this happening again, you run tell the nearest constable. He'll pass the word, and you can be assured we'll deal with it like we did today."

Jenks noted several of the men in the crowd seemed disappointed. "Listen up, you lot," he boomed. "What you saw here today, what those two attempted to do? Such actions will not be tolerated in Caerfaen. There is no open season on witches. They are under the protection of the king, right? They are also under my protection, and of the entire Watch. Best remember it, and don't try anything stupid. You don't want to end up like poor Vern and Angus here, do you? Right, move along, and spread the word. And…" he paused for a moment and decided to end things on a positive note. "Have a nice day."

The bishop's chuckle sounded like distant thunder.

CHAPTER SIX

McRobbie House, Caerfaen

"Your Grace," said Kevin Jacoby, Morgan's valet and man of all work. "Mr. Barlbent has called and would like to know if you can spare him a few minutes."

"Barlbent, eh?" Morgan rubbed his chin and gazed up at the ceiling. Finding the view unhelpful, he muttered, "Somehow, I've a feeling I'm not going to like this. Very well, Kevin, show him in."

In short order, the chief clerk and general factotum of Lord Holman Barzak, head of Kilbourne's Office of Spies, was seated in Morgan's study. A cup of tea in his hand, Barlbent lounged back in his chair, crossed his long legs and inhaled the aroma of the tea. He smiled in approval and took a sip.

Morgan mused, not for the first time, what an unobtrusive fellow Barlbent was. Tall, lean, bespectacled, with a mop of sandy hair which tended to flop into his eyes. Yet people never noted his features. Instead, Francis Barlbent managed to fade into the background wherever he was. Which was an excellent trait for a man working where he did.

"How are things in the Office of Spies?" Morgan asked. Not that he had the notion his guest might provide him with any actual information. But he figured he had to start somewhere.

"Busier than normal, Commander," Barlbent replied, somewhat to Morgan's surprise. "Something appears to be up in Rhuddlan."

Morgan's brows rose. "Oh? Anything specific? Or merely a general sense of up-ness?"

Barlbent waved a languid hand. "Oh, it's all quite vague, I'm afraid. Our agents can't seem to find anything to get their teeth into. But

His Lordship wanted you to be aware."

"I'm surprised he didn't summon me to his office instead of sending you here."

Barlbent grinned. "His Lordship," he said, "has decided to designate me special liaison to Kilbourne's Knight-Commander and Royal Enchantress. He said since I manage to get entangled with your doings so much, it ought to be, um, semi-official."

Morgan laughed. "I'll admit, you do turn up in the midst of things, and at the most opportune moments. Marissa will be pleased. I think she's grown rather fond of you."

"I'm honored."

"All right, liaison, can you tell me anything else?"

Barlbent said, "All we know at this point is King Varsil has been calling in his nobles, two or three at a time. Private audiences; none of our chaps have been able to get into the room or find out anything once they come out again. Everyone's quite close-lipped when they emerge."

"Test of loyalty?" Morgan ventured.

"Possibly. His Lordship suspects there's more to it, but he doesn't know what. Not yet, at any rate."

"It's too late in the year for them to be considering any kind of invasion. Maybe Varsil is making plans for a Spring campaign and wants to prepare his nobles for the notion. Though I imagine they'd none of them be any too happy with the idea after what happened last time."

What happened the last time had been the complete rout of the Rhuddlani army. After King Llewellyn, Rhys's father, had perished with a Rhuddlani crossbow bolt in his heart, Morgan had led the enraged Kilbourne troops in a sweeping massacre of the invaders. Not a single Rhuddlani soldier had escaped the resulting carnage.

"Quite so," Barlbent agreed. He took another sip of his tea. "Still, we know full well King Varsil is rather single-minded, and doesn't brook any waffling on the part of his nobles."

"No, he certainly doesn't. Of course it's easy for him, sitting nice and snug in his palace while everyone else is out doing the fighting. I wonder what would happen if a bunch of his barons stood up and said, 'Sorry, Your Highness, but we're not going off to fight an unprovoked war again'."

"I imagine Varsil's headsman would be a busy chap, were they to take such a course."

"Mmm, that bad, eh?"

Barlbent shrugged. "Quite. He is rather a tyrant, after all."

Morgan said. "All right, we've disposed of Varsil Jarek for now. Anything on the clerical front?"

"Cleric—oh, you mean the rebel bishops? Well, I imagine you know as much, if not more, than we do, since you get your information from Bishop MacFarlane. His sources are better, and His Lordship is not best pleased."

"Does it strike you as convenient," Morgan mused aloud, "the Rhuddlanis are making unusual noises at the same time these renegade bishops are instigating a civil war within Kilbourne?"

Barlbent uttered a low whistle. "Now you mention it, it does, doesn't it? If His Lordship made the connection, he hasn't mentioned it to me."

"It might be nothing," Morgan said. "Simply my nasty, suspicious mind putting two and two together to get twenty-two."

"It's worth looking into." Barlbent's brow furrowed. "If there's anything to it, odds are someone got paid. I know you're well aware we have some smart chaps to check into the financial end of things. Let me run this by His Lordship and get a couple of them in motion. It can't hurt."

"It might also be worthwhile to have your agents in Rhuddlan poke around on that end. I know you can't risk them exposing themselves. But transfers of large quantities of gold tend to get noticed."

"Especially if the gold is going from Rhuddlan to someone here." Barlbent nodded. "A lot of men in Varsil's court might take umbrage at the notion of large chunks of the treasury being sent off to Kilbourne."

"The idea being it would be much nicer in their own vaults?" Morgan grinned. "But we're getting ahead of ourselves, I'm afraid. It's a theory, nothing more. Run it past Barzak, why don't you, and see if he thinks it worth investigation."

"Oh, be assured I will." Barlbent set down his empty cup. He rose and turned to go, saying over his shoulder, "Thank you, Your Grace. This is why Lord Holman appointed me liaison to you and Her Ladyship. I can always count on you for suggestions. Don't bother your man, I know my way out." And with cheery wave, he departed.

Morgan sat for a few minutes, lost in thought. A wry smile crossed his lips. His vaunted instincts, working overtime again. Even so, the notion was a dashed lot to swallow as coincidence. And there was another source of information he could tap, ready to hand. Or near enough.

Rising, he opened the study door to find Kevin in the hallway, polishing a pair of brass candlesticks. "Kevin, I'm going out. If Marissa asks, tell her I've gone to attend noon mass at the cathedral."

Not waiting for a reply, he thrust open the door and jogged down the steps. Two soldiers stood watch, and they straightened to attention when he passed. After the recent assassination attempt on Marissa, Morgan was taking no chances. He gave them a brief salute and headed for St. Basil's.

CHAPTER SEVEN
St. Basil's Cathedral, Caerfaen

Morgan strode along the streets of Caerfaen toward the cathedral, which was only a few blocks away. Overhead, a brilliant blue autumn sky was being overshadowed by heavy, black clouds. Underfoot, colorful fallen leaves skittered across his path, driven by sporadic gusts of wind. A storm was on the way. Morgan caught a hint of the acrid scent of impending rain and quickened his steps.

As he hastened towards the cathedral his mind returned to Barlbent's enigmatic words: "Something appears to be up in Rhuddlan." The "something" would be more martial than political in nature, which meant it would end up being his problem. Wonderful. One more thing to worry over. Like he didn't have enough already. Well, that was one of the reasons why Rhys had appointed him Knight-Commander of the Legion. Because he was an excellent worrier. Any commander who rested easy and didn't worry didn't last long.

Well, the Rhuddlanis could wait. Morgan couldn't picture Varsil making any significant moves this late in the year. His troops would have to cross the Devil's Teeth, the rugged mountain range which separated the two kingdoms. There would be snow on those mountains soon, if the higher peaks weren't covered already. And snow and the movement of large numbers of soldiers and their gear and supplies were not a combination any commander would favor.

No, his immediate concern was the renegade bishops. They were much more a threat to the kingdom's security than a nebulous "something" in Rhuddlan. Thus, he was on his way to talk with the one person who might be able to provide some reliable intelligence on where those prelates were holed up, and what mischief and mayhem they might be getting up to: Bishop Randolph MacFarlane, Primate of the See of Caerfaen, and Morgan's oldest friend.

Their friendship had begun when they were boys. He and Randolph, like their fathers—the Viscount and the Vicar—had been friends back in Westdale. While they'd grown through adolescence, each already secure in the path their lives would take, Randolph stood by Morgan, siding with him against those who taunted the Viscount's son for the color of his skin, courtesy of his mother's Orskan heritage.

The bells of St. Basil's Cathedral tolled the hour of noon, and Morgan broke into a trot. Their sonorous "bongs" echoed through the bustling streets, not only announcing the time but also calling the faithful. He hurried up the steps of the church two at a time, slipping in through the massive oak doors carved with intricate designs of religious scenes.

The mass had begun, so he tiptoed into an empty pew in the rear of the cathedral. The opening prayer concluded, and a beam of sunlight shone through the stained glass window across the aisle, painting the floor in colors as vivid as the leaves outside. Peering toward the apse, he saw Randolph was indeed the celebrant. He professed to relish presiding over the daily noon mass.

"Keeps me more in touch with folks," he'd explained to Morgan one night over a convivial glass of claret. "The upper classes turn out on the Sabbath, for the most part. But the hoi polloi will show up for a noon mass if they're able. Then I can chat 'em up afterward. It's bad form to sneak out during the final hymn, y'know, without greeting the priest."

Though Morgan slipped into the routine of the mass, his mind was distracted by a dozen other thoughts. Closing his eyes, he took a few deep breaths to center himself and regain his focus. He managed to lose himself in the prayers, and especially the hymns, which he tended to sing with a great deal more gusto than pitch. So, to his dismay, did most of the parishioners present, and he found himself thinking of a chorus of cats. His full attention was drawn when Randolph began his message by saying, "My brothers and sisters, we are commanded to love one another."

Morgan's brows rose. Randolph went on, "Our task is this simple, and this difficult. We're told to love more than our families and our friends. Everyone we encounter is deserving of our love. Those who look like us, think like us, act like us, of course. But here's the important bit—also those we meet who don't."

Morgan found himself nodding, even while his mind flashed to memories—more than he could count—of people who'd looked down on him, or snubbed him, or ignored him, because of his own appearance. His dark-complexioned status—a 'half-breed' mix of Kilbourne and Orskan heritage—made him an easy target of those who loathed those who didn't look like themselves.

Randolph went on. "How do we manifest this love? Again, it's as simple, and as difficult as this: we are told to heal the sick, care for the poor, welcome the stranger, and give comfort to those in need. It doesn't matter if someone doesn't agree with the way you do or see things. It doesn't matter if someone has different gifts than you. What matters is this: love one another and treat them the way you wish to be treated. So go forth, love your neighbors as yourself, and do God's work in the world. Amen."

A few minutes later, after the benediction and the final hymn, the congregation began its egress. Sure enough, most of the parishioners stopped to greet the priest and comment on his message, for good or ill. Morgan joined the end of the line.

"Ah, I thought I caught you sneaking in," the bishop said, taking Morgan's hand.

"And the roof is still standing," Morgan replied with a grin.

"'Tis a miracle indeed. Come along, join me in the sacristy. I need to get out of these robes."

"Thanks, I will. I want to ask you a few things."

"Yes, I suspected you weren't here solely for the good of your soul." Randolph headed back into the church and led the way to the sacristy.

"No, I did have an ulterior motive for showing up, but attending the mass didn't hurt any. A timely message, by the way. Well done, you."

Randolph nodded. "I decided I'd found a good time to present it, in light of what happened yesterday." He gave a quick precis of his encounter with the would-be witch burners. "Not to mention, I've been hearing some worrisome rumblings even among my own parishioners. I wanted them to have good guidance. I've also asked the other priests in the See to give a similar message over the next several days. It can't be stressed enough, when certain elements are doing their best to divide us."

"And where are these 'certain elements' holed up?" Morgan asked, while Randolph removed his stole and began to pull off his formal robe.

"Cormaine," came the muffled reply. The bishop's head emerged from his robe like a turtle from its shell. "The five of them, with outriders and hangers-on. Including some pretty nasty guards, I've been told. They're sequestered at St. Humbert's. McAdoo's church, if you'd care to know."

"Cormaine," mused Morgan. "It's not that far away, is it?"

"Not far enough," Randolph replied. "The lot of 'em can take a long walk off a short pier."

Mogan grinned. "Not exactly taking your own message to heart, are you?"

"Mmm." Randolph grimaced. He hung his robe on a hook set into the wall and shrugged into a less formal cassock. "I'll have to leave the sorting out of them to the Lord, who says 'Vengeance is mine'. But rest assured, if there's anything I can do to help things along, I'm all for it."

"You told me you have someone keeping an eye on them," Morgan said.

"Yes, I do. This bunch bears watching. I have Brother John with them. A good man, and an excellent spy. Holman Barzak has tried to steal him away any number of times. John used to be one of my clerks quite some time back. He's managed to take on a new identity, and gotten a position as Llachnahn's chief clerk. Poor fellow, I hated asking him to do it, but he said he was game to take on the challenge."

"And what does he report?"

Randolph harrumphed. "Oh, more of the same. Llachnahn and McAdoo are pressing the others to start stirring things up even more. Llachnahn, he says, is a real fanatic, and practically foaming at the mouth at the idea of burning some witches."

"The man's mad," Morgan said.

"Starkers," agreed Randolph. "And it's rather odd, since it turns out his own sister might well be, shall we say, of the witchy persuasion."

"Oh? That's interesting. I hope—"

"She's gone into hiding," Randolph said. "It took a good bit of convincing, but she saw the light and acknowledged she'd be much safer if she made herself scarce."

"Brother John's work?" Morgan guessed. Randolph didn't answer, but his smile was confirmation enough. "You and Barzak could be twins," Morgan said. "You both play everything close to the chest. But do me a favor, will you?"

"If I can. I can't promise. You know many of the things I hear I can't discuss."

"I know. But if you come across anything I should know—since this does affect the security of the kingdom, for which I'm at least partially responsible—let me know, will you?"

"Don't worry," Randolph said. "I'll tell you anything I believe you might find useful."

And with this, Morgan had to be satisfied.

CHAPTER EIGHT
Somewhere in The Devil's Teeth

Toby Fanshawe, former pirate and now nominally in the service of Knight-Commander McRobbie, shifted his weight in the saddle. It didn't make the least bit of difference. The horse jounced like a ship on a storm-tossed sea, and Toby's rear continued to send aggrieved messages brain-ward, indicating extreme discomfort and displeasure.

He heaved a sigh and shifted again, to no avail. *Give me a ship any day,* he mused in grim silence. *Leave the blasted nags to the chaps in the Legion.* Oh, he knew how to ride. He just didn't like it. He glanced to his left, where the reason for his clambering onto a horse rode placidly beside him.

Antonettia Radivan, who insisted he call her Toni, flashed him a brilliant smile. He smiled back, making a manful effort to emulate her carefree spirit. He failed with flying colors, for she drew closer, concern showing in her blue eyes. She asked, "Is something wrong, Captain Fanshawe?"

"Fine, I'm fine," he lied. Then winced when his mount performed an intricate dance step.

Toni reached over to place a hand on his arm. "You hate this, don't you?"

"No, of course not," Toby protested. "I—I just need to get used to riding again. Don't see too many horses aboard ship."

"You're a terrible liar," she said, and the liquid laughter bubbling up in her voice was music to his ears. An answering laugh welled up inside him.

"All right, you win. Yes, my rear end aches like there's no

tomorrow," he admitted with a cheerful grin. "I'll get used to it in a couple more days. I'll be fine."

Toni's expression grew thoughtful. She pushed a cascade of red hair back from her face. "You would much rather be sailing on your ship, wouldn't you?"

Toby shrugged. "It's pretty much the only thing I've ever known. This"—he swept an arm out to encompass the horses, the stone-strewn landscape through which they rode, and the convoy of brightly painted Tzigani wagons spread out along the trail— "is something new and foreign to me."

"So I see. But I don't understand why you're doing this. Why you're here with us."

"Don't you?" He gave her his most winning smile. "Time for a change, I guess. I mean, I no longer have a ship, so…"

"But you could if you wanted, couldn't you?"

He shrugged again. "I'd always feel like I was missing something."

"Oh?" She arched one delicate brow. "And what might you be missing?"

"I've already told you," he reminded her.

"Yes, I know. Perhaps I just wanted to hear you say it again."

He grinned across at her. "Minx," he said, but there was no trace of rancor in his tone. Far from it, in fact. "I'd be missing you."

"I think," she said, speaking more to the air than to Toby, "you must be quite mad."

"Oh, there's no doubt. Even so, I remind myself I'm being eminently sensible. I was a pirate, remember? If I saw something I wanted, I went after it. In this instance, I'm less pirate, and more like a bee drawn to a lovely flower…"

Toni giggled, pressing a hand to her heart. "A pirate and a poet," she said. "An intriguing combination. But still mad, you know."

"I know. Do you mind terribly?"

"Which?" she asked. "That you're mad, or that you are pursuing me with piratical intent?"

"Either. Both." He laughed. "Can I help it if I wasn't able to get you out of my mind?"

"Flatterer. You're just saying it."

Toby raised his hand. "Pirate's honor, it's true."

"Do pirates have honor?" she asked, but her eyes were shining.

"Oh, I assure you, they do. There are guidelines, you know, strict guidelines. There are…" he broke off the persiflage. "Here comes your father."

In an instant, Toni's mount was a good three feet or more from Toby's. *She must do it with mind control*, he thought. No tugging of reins or anything. One moment here; the next there. *Easy when you know how.*

"Good morning, Toni," Radivan said. "Good morning to you, Captain Fanshawe." His expression was hidden by his sweeping moustache, but Toby caught no trace of malice in the Tzigani chief's eyes. He relaxed a little, but remained wary. He was still a stranger among these travelers, and though he'd been welcomed readily enough, he knew he hadn't yet earned their complete trust.

"Good morn to you, Captain Radivan," he replied. "A beautiful day to travel, eh?"

Radivan gazed around, seeming oblivious to the sights and sounds of the day. A few clouds, fluffy as sky-borne sheep, dotted the blue meadow of the sky. Birds chirruped cheerfully in the underbrush, in counterpoint to the rumbling of the wagon wheels, and the air was clean and brisk.

"Yes," Radivan allowed. "I suppose it is."

They rode in silence for several minutes. At last, Radivan said, "Another few days and we will reach Rhuddlani territory."

Toby stiffened for an instant, but he forced himself to relax. The Rhuddlanis, he knew, maintained no quarrel with the Tzigani. They saved their enmity for Kilbourne. If they somehow discovered who he was—the Kilbourne privateer who'd captured so many of their merchant vessels and eluded the Rhuddlani navy innumerable times—there would be special gallows built just for him. After, he was certain, a great deal of the most painful torture they could devise. He shivered, and it wasn't from the chill mountain air. He managed to turn his mind to something else.

"Are we still in Kilbourne? I wondered if after we crossed over the last pass…"

Radivan barked out a laugh. "Neither kingdom lays claim to these mountains. There's nothing here for either of them. Dwarves once lived here, so it is said. But they moved away, down south, eons ago. Now these rocks are home to nothing but birds, beasts, and bandits."

Toby raised a brow. "Expecting trouble?"

The Tzigani's grin was wolfish. "Me, I always expect trouble. We are Tzigani; trouble dogs us wherever we go."

Toby considered this. When he spoke, he chose his words with care. He didn't wish to offend Radivan, but he was curious. "Do bandits attack your caravans? I mean, it's not like you're merchants transporting valuable cargo."

"And Tzigani and bandits are not so far apart?" Radivan asked with a sly grin.

"Hard astern," said Toby, flustered into reverting to nautical jargon. "That's not what I said, nor even implied. I mean, being a former pirate myself, I'm in no position to cast stones, am I? I figured they would stick to more lucrative targets, that's all."

Radivan regarded him with a keen eye, then shrugged. "No offense taken, Captain. I wanted to spar with you and take your measure. But these bandits… bah. They'll go after anything they believe they can get away with. And we have good horses, and food, and wagons."

"And no doubt a fair supply of coin hidden away in those wagons," Toby speculated.

The Tzigani's response was a brief quirk of one corner of his mouth. It was confirmation enough for Toby. "Captain Radivan," he said. "I have a good sword, and I know how to use it. Should you have need, I am at your service."

Radivan nodded. "Thank you. I will bear it in mind. So far, my scouts have seen no sign of any cause for concern. Once we're out of the mountains, we'll only have the odd Rhuddlani patrol to contend with. Nothing to be concerned about."

Toby's brows rose. "Oh? How do you deal with them?"

"We bribe them to look the other way while we pass by." He gave an expressive shrug. "It usually serves."

"And if not?"

"Oh, we put on a show for them, get them roaring drunk, and steal their clothes."

"Father." Toni spoke up, choking on a laugh. "You do no such thing."

Radivan threw back his head, roaring with exuberant laughter. "All right, daughter, you've caught me. Fanshawe, rest assured, the bribes always work. So far, anyway. But should they fail…" He exchanged an amused glance with Toby. Then, seeming to recall something important, the Tzigani slapped his forehead. "Ah, I almost forgot. I was sent here on an errand, Fanshawe. My wife, she wishes to speak with you."

Toby sucked in a breath. "I guess I'd best not keep her waiting any longer. If you two will excuse me?"

Toni nodded. "Of course, Captain Fanshawe. I shall ride with my father."

Toby shook up the reins and set a course for the wagon where Elbethesba, matriarch of the Tzigani, awaited him. And what, he wondered, did this summons portend?

CHAPTER NINE
McRobbie House, Caerfaen

Kevin Jacoby's role in McRobbie House varied, from valet to henchman, footman to butler, depending upon the circumstances and the needs of his master. Morgan had a hard time keeping it straight, but Kevin managed it with ease. Morgan was grateful. He was used to Kevin and would have been reluctant to take on someone else. Moreover, he liked the young man who'd hitched his own star to Morgan's several years ago.

Kevin was in total butler mode today, standing at rigid attention in the door of Morgan's study. "Your Grace?" he intoned.

"Yes, Kevin?" Morgan set aside the ledger he'd been perusing.

"Your Grace, Captain Jenks of the City Watch is at the door. Are you at home?"

Morgan wasn't used to being a duke of the realm yet, and found some of the trappings odd. "Well, I seem to be," he allowed. "Um. Does the good captain appear intent on arresting someone?"

"He did not say so, Your Grace. He did say he would be obliged if you might spare him a few minutes, in connection with a recent incident in the city."

Kevin's manner of speech was sometimes hard to follow. This was, Morgan surmised, due to the fact he'd been a scholar prior to entering Morgan's service. He parsed out the substance and nodded.

"Hmm. Oh, all right. My conscience is clear. Well, relatively so. Bring in this keeper of the law. And once you've got him ensconced, please arrange for the provision of some strong black coffee."

"Is coffee Captain Jenks's beverage of choice?"

"Not to my knowledge. But I've a strong suspicion I'll be needing it before we're done." Morgan rubbed a hand through his hair. "No, I'm sure of it."

"Very good." Kevin departed, returning in short order with Jenks. He sidled out again, in what Morgan hoped was a mission to procure the coffee.

Jenks removed his helmet, twisting it in his hands. He appeared uncomfortable, Morgan noted. Interesting. "Thank you for seeing me, Commander," the Watchman said.

"I figured I was safe, for once. I couldn't come up with anything in my recent past which might put me in your sights. Have a seat, Jenks. Kevin should be bringing in the coffee tray for us."

"Ah, awful decent of you. Not many go out of their way to pour a cup for a thirsty Watchman these days."

A rattle of wheels in the hallway heralded the arrival of Kevin with the tea cart, converted to coffee service. Two cups, a steaming pot, and a plate of ginger biscuits were on offer. Kevin poured, handed a cup to his master, one to Jenks, and placed the ginger biscuits at Morgan's elbow. The aromatic fragrance of the spice was heady and enticing, almost intoxicating. Morgan savored the tang in his nostrils while he regarded the Watchman.

"All right, Captain," Morgan said, settling back in his seat after taking the first scalding sip of coffee. He snaffled a handful of biscuits and passed the plate to Jenks. "How may I assist the Watch in their inquiries? I've got the right term, eh?"

"No inquiry, Commander."

"No?" Morgan's brows rose. "Surely this isn't a social call. Kevin mentioned something regarding an incident in the city…"

Jenks snorted out a laugh. "Social call? Hardly. I reckon I'm here under what you might term false pretenses. It's the duchess I'd like to speak with."

Morgan's brows rose to even more precipitous heights. "Oh? What has my bride managed to do to garner the attention of a Captain of the Watch?"

"Nothing I'm aware of. And I'd prefer to keep it that way, if it's all the same to you. No, I wanted to speak with her on the subject of witches. In her capacity as Kilbourne's Royal Enchantress."

"I see. At least I think I see. Your encounter with those two fools attempting to burn some witches the other day?"

Jenks nodded. "I reckon you must have learned of it from Bishop MacFarlane, eh?"

"I did. He was most indignant. He did, however, sing your

praises for how you handled things. Well done, Captain. I can't say I'm surprised; you're a clever fellow. I imagine I'd have barged in, swinging a sword, and gotten those poor women burned for my troubles."

Jenks took a sip of coffee, marshalling his thoughts. He set the cup down with enough force to slosh some of the contents over the rim. "Those women were damned lucky. If it happens again, and I'm mortally certain it will, we might not get there in time to prevent a tragedy. Thieving and killing and such, those are bad enough, but I expect them. Part of the job, you know. This, though…" He quivered with quiet fury. "Those women never harmed anyone. And those two young idiots would have burned them and been pleased with themselves for doing so. All because they thought the church decreed it the right thing for them to do."

Morgan grimaced. "Over the years, an awful lot of horrible things have been done in the name of God. Some were well intentioned, but utterly stupid. Others, like this current debacle, are evil disguising itself as religion."

"Damned right," Jenks said. "Commander, I don't want this kind of thing happening here in Caerfaen. But the truth is, my men and I are stretched mighty thin. I'm not sure how we're going to manage if we get a rash of chaps itching to do the same thing."

Morgan nodded. "Before I ask Marissa to join us, can I ask what you have in mind for her to do?"

Jenks drank more coffee, then munched a ginger biscuit. Once he'd swallowed, he said, "Commander, I've no idea. But she's the Royal Enchantress, right? The king's proclamation says the witches of Kilbourne are under her protection." Jenks shrugged. "I'm grasping at straws here. I'd hoped she might have some ideas of how to protect them."

Morgan leaned forward, elbows on the desk. "I'll have her in, of course. But I have to warn you, she's at a loss over this whole mess too. Sure, Rhys put the bit about her protecting the witches in his proclamation. But unless she's come up with some brilliant scheme I haven't heard of…"

"Blast. That's what I was afraid of." Jenks scowled. "Commander, I don't want to bother the duchess, but…"

"No, not at all. Let's have her in. You know me, Jenks, I'm a pretty direct kind of fellow. My notion was to round up the rebel bishops and toss 'em in a nice deep dungeon somewhere. Rhys doesn't care for that, and no doubt he's right. It would make martyrs of them and wouldn't solve the underlying problem." Morgan stood and stepped to the door. "Kevin, please ask Marissa to join us if she's available?"

"Of course, Your Grace," came the reply.

Morgan returned to his seat, grabbing another ginger biscuit on the way. "While we await my wife's pleasure, I have a suggestion. Or actually, an offer. I can deploy a couple of squads of Legion soldiers, in groups of twos or threes, to help patrol around the city, keeping an eye out for trouble. Might help you and your chaps to focus more on your normal thieving and killing, as you so blithely put it, and not be stretched quite so thin."

Jenks eyes widened, and he managed a smile. "I'd be most grateful," he said. "It would make some of these fellows with bright ideas think twice before trying something stupid."

"All right, consider it done. I'll have to set things up with my captains, so the patrols won't start until tomorrow. I'll have Captain Poldane coordinate with you?"

"Perfect." Jenks managed a full on, if weary, smile this time. "I reckon we can manage to muddle through today. I've got my constables working double shifts now. Having your men out there would let me get them back on regular rotation, which would be most welcome. Thank you. I couldn't have wished for better."

Marissa appeared in the doorway. "Why, Captain Jenks, how nice to see you. Unless you're here to arrest one or the other of us?" She flashed him a dazzling smile.

Jenks, Morgan noted, had the good grace to blush under her teasing. He made a quick recovery, though, saying, "Nay, Your Lady— um, I mean, Your Grace—"

"Pooh," said Marissa, with a dismissive wave. "We're old friends here, so to speak. I've always been Lady Marissa to you, and I see no need to alter things."

Jenks smiled at this. "Thank you," he said, and Morgan could tell he was pleased. "So no, Lady Marissa, I've not come to arrest either you or Commander McRobbie. I've come seeking your help."

Marissa cocked her head like an inquisitive sparrow. It was, Morgan thought fondly, one of her more adorable traits. He wasn't surprised when she leapt to the correct conclusion. "Since I'm the Royal Enchantress, and so-called protector of the witches of Kilbourne?"

"Yes, I'm afraid so." Jenks reprised his recital of the attempted witch burning. Marissa shuddered in horror.

"Those poor girls," she said, shaking her head. "What have you done with them?"

"Done with them? Why, nothing. A couple of my constables saw them home safe and sound. Nothing more."

"Hmph. Captain, please have one of your men go to those girls and ask them, most politely, if they might escort them here to me. I'd like to talk with them, and to do my best to reassure them of their future safety. Such as it is, under the current circumstances."

Jenks nodded. "Of course. I'll do so straight away. I reckon I didn't think. I wanted to get them away from the pyre right away."

"Yes, quite right. But you were thinking like both a man, and a Watchman. Neither of which you can help being, of course. But if something like this should happen again—"

"God forbid," interjected Jenks.

"We can hope so. However, the circumstances seem to require us to give Him some assistance. So if it does happen again, consider the victims, and what you'd feel, and do, if your wife or daughter was in the same situation."

The captain's eyes went hard and obsidian. Apparently Marissa struck the right chord. Jenks nodded, unclenching hands which had tightened into fists. "My Lady, you have given me wise counsel. I will keep your words in mind and pass them on to my constables and sergeants too. Most of them have wives or sweethearts, and I want them to feel like I did."

"Always happy to help," Marissa said. "Tell me something, Captain. Are there no women among your constables?"

Jenks's eyes widened in surprise. Not a question he'd anticipated, Morgan was certain. "No, My Lady, I'm afraid not. It's a dirty, dangerous job, and…"

Marissa's smile was brittle. She said, "And of course, in the long history of our world, no woman has ever put her hand to a dirty, dangerous job."

"Well—"

"Captain Jenks, we are not all delicate flowers. You know me, you know I'm not. We butcher pigs and kill chickens. We deal with husbands who drink to excess and lash out in anger. I don't mean Morgan," she added in a quick aside. "We birth children, for heaven's sake, and if there's a dirtier or more dangerous undertaking, I'd like to hear about it."

Jenks opened his mouth to protest. Morgan gave him full marks for closing it again. At last, Jenks said, "Some even chase after spies, murderers, and assassins, eh? And hobnob with dragons."

Marissa favored him with a grin, and Morgan found himself grinning with her. How in the world had he been so lucky, to have a woman like this fall in love with him?

"You see my point, Captain?" Marissa said. "Now mind you, I'm not saying to up and inundate the Watch with female constables. But you might do worse than to let it be known such a thing is possible. I've a hunch you'll have more applicants than you know what to do with. And in these uncertain times, it might not be such a bad thing."

"I shall take it under serious consideration," Jenks said. "In the meantime, I'll have one of my constables ask the women we rescued the other day if they would call on you. And if you have any notions of how to prevent another incident like this, I'd be most grateful to hear it."

Her mouth tightened, and her eyes narrowed. "I wish I did, Captain. I know Rhys named me their protector, but I don't see what I can do. Of course, I'm not going to say I shan't come up with something brilliant at any moment. If I do, I'll let you know straight away."

"Thank you, My Lady." Jenks rose to his feet and sketched a nice bow. "I could ask nothing better. If you'll excuse me, I'll leave you folks alone."

Morgan stood, reached across the desk, and shook Jenks's hand. "I'll get those soldiers out patrolling as soon as I can," he said.

With a grateful nod, Jenks took his leave.

CHAPTER TEN
Erkarna's Cavern

Storm clouds hung over the jagged mountain peaks toward which Wyvrndell led his party. His companions were the same group who had flown to Arvindir to retrieve Sir Morgan, Lady Marissa, and their companions. This time with the addition of Donathyr of the king's guard. He seemed a sturdy and unimaginative dragon, but would be good to have around if anything threatened their mission.

A jagged, sizzling bolt of lightning lit the sky, brighter than a dragon's flame. Perfect. The storm matched his mood. A crash of thunder shook the sky, and they were into the deluge. Wyvrndell wrapped the storm around him. With the unwelcome quest Petrandius had set him, it seem fitting to embrace and revel in the tempest.

He wasn't afraid to enter Erkarna's cavern again. Not afraid. But the memory of his mentor's betrayal was difficult to come to terms with. This was the reason for his reluctance.

"Are we getting close?" inquired his sire. Another bolt of lightning singed the air nearby.

"We are," he replied, winging onward through the pelting storm. The rain lashed in sidewise sheets, so visibility was at a minimum. "Over this next ridge."

"There it is," said Aireantha. They flew into a somewhat sheltered area between two peaks, which rose up to block the teeming sky from view.

"You were here?" Donathyr asked. "I understood Wyvrndell was alone—" he left the question hanging in the air, rather like another sizzle of lightning.

"I came after… after Erkarna was dead," she replied. "Wyvrndell needed me to bear the humans back to their home."

"While I was busy sealing the place up," Wyvrndell said, lest there be any mistake. He banked, gliding toward the ledge. Fortunately there was a large enough space, set partly under a rocky overhang which lent at least a modicum of shelter from the pursuing storm.

"Wyvrndell, I seem to find it my lot to follow you into unpleasant weather," Wyzandar said. "I wonder why?"

There was either nothing, or entirely too much, required as a reply to this. Wyvrndell chose the former and landed, folding his wings to make room for the others.

Aireantha dropped beside him, starting when another streak of lightning rent the sky fifteen yards away. Wyzandar landed next. Donathyr remained aloft. "I will keep watch," he said. "Though I cannot imagine any sensible dragons being out in this."

Sensible dragons? Wyvrndell braced himself, preparing to enter the place which held such grim memories for him. There was nothing sensible about any of this, was there?

Wyzandar interrupted his reverie. "I thought you said you sealed the place," he said, scanning the face of the cliff. "There are no rocks around the entrance. Has someone already been here?" He stepped forward to enter the cavern and was brought up short.

"I did not seal it with rock, Father. I did so instead with a spell."

His sire blinked. "I understood from Petrandius you did not know how to cast any spells."

"No," Wyvrndell said. "What I told the king was I had not yet determined how to use my magic for the benefit of dragonkind. I know many spells, both from studying with Erkarna, and from my instruction of Lady Marissa."

"And can you reverse this spell you have cast?" Aireantha asked.

"We shall see. No more chatter please. I am new to this, and need to concentrate." With this admonishment, he called up the form of his original spell. Once he fixed it in his mind, he began the process of reversing it.

A shimmer appeared around the outline of the cavern's entrance. With a sudden 'pop' which sent Wyzandar scrambling back a few steps, the way was clear. The barrier he'd set in place was gone.

"Impressive," murmured his sire.

"I did tell you I was able to do magic," Wyvrndell pointed out.

"So you did. Yet, hearing you say it, and seeing you do it, are two different things, my son. You are doing something no dragon has ever before accomplished, though countless numbers have dreamed of it."

"Can we enter?" asked Aireantha, her voice plaintive. "The storm is getting worse, and if I'm not seared by lightning, I'll be too wet to fly."

"Very well," Wyvrndell said. He'd been steeling himself to enter the chamber again, but he hesitated.

"Is something wrong?" Donathyr asked from above, where he flew in lazy circles, patrolling against any potential danger.

"N-no," Wyvrndell said. He wasn't afraid. But the thought of seeing the body of his former mentor was not something he relished. Taking a deep breath, he let it out slowly—sans hiccoughs—and stepped through the entrance.

"*Lumious accandio,*" he said. Lights flared into life in sconces along the walls.

He stepped further into the chamber. Once inside, he stopped so abruptly his sire ran into him from behind. Wyvrndell stared around in dismay.

"What's wrong?" asked Aireantha, glancing around.

"Move over," directed Wyzandar.

"Erkarna," Wyvrndell said, his voice trembling. A hiccough forced its way out, acrid and smoky. "He—he's gone."

The mad dragon's body had remained where it fell when Lady Marissa's terrible spell wrought its work. Wyvrndell had been too drained, and too reluctant, to move it. Now there was nothing. A single gray scale, winking dully in the flicker of the lamps, was all that gave any hint of what transpired here. It was silent inside the cavern, silent as the tomb it had been, though outside he could still hear the rumbles of thunder from the storm.

"Are you certain he was dead?" Wyzandar asked. "Perhaps—"

"Yes, he was dead," Wyvrndell said with assurance. "Believe me, if Erkarna had still been alive, none of us would have left this chamber."

"Might someone have reversed the sealing spell, like you did, to enter and carry his body off?" Aireantha asked with a little shudder.

"It is possible, though I don't know how. Or why. No one without magic of their own might have done so. I am the only dragon who possesses magic. The other possibility is a human wizard, but I cannot imagine any of them know the location of this cavern. Even if they did, why remove Erkarna's body? It makes no sense."

"Well, no matter how, or why, it does not change our mission," Wyzandar said.

"No, Father, it does not. You are correct. Let us gather—" he stopped, staring, once more.

"What is wrong?" Wyzandar's tone was brusque. Wyvrndell couldn't blame him, but…

"Erkarna's notes, his scrolls, every piece of his research." Another hiccough escaped him. "They are gone. Everything is gone."

CHAPTER ELEVEN
The Devil's Teeth

Toby swung out of his saddle and onto the moving wagon which conveyed Elbethesba. How he managed this, without falling and breaking his neck, he wasn't quite sure. No matter how, he stood on the wagon's narrow back platform, with the door before him. Looping his horse's reins over a convenient knob which appeared to have been placed for exactly this purpose, he raised his hand to knock. Before his knuckles struck the wood the door opened inward. Elbethesba stood there, holding it open.

Her mouth was drawn into a thin line. Her eyes, which he'd noticed normally sparkled much like Toni's, were dark and clouded. "Come in," she said, her voice brusque. "We have much to discuss."

Toby entered, sidling around her. She pushed the door closed again. He glanced around, amazed at how neat and spacious the interior of the wagon was. The wagon, he suspected, must have been crafted by a master ship builder, or someone with similar skills. There were cabinets and drawers everywhere along the walls, a table which folded up into the wall, and a pair of beds which also folded to double as a settee.

He turned his attention back to Elbethesba. He'd needed the momentary distraction, for her expression was so forbidding he feared without it he might have fled the wagon, leaped onto his horse, and ridden away without a backward glance.

"Sit, Captain Fanshawe," she directed. Toby pulled out a chair, but instead of sitting, he gestured to his hostess to take it. She sank into the chair, a trace of a smile tinging her lips.

Toby took the other, across the table from her, and waited for her to speak. Her eyes, dark and hooded, bored into his as if examining his very soul. Toby did his best to meet her gaze without flinching, but found the job rough sailing.

She ceased her examination of him and nodded once. *Did she see what she'd expected?* Whether this boded good or ill, Toby wasn't certain. "Give me a coin," she said. "We must adhere to tradition, you see."

Toby pulled a coin from his pouch and handed it to her. "Now, give me your right hand," she said. Toby rested his arm on the small table, palm up. Elbethesba took it between her two hands, her fingers tracing the lines of his palm. She closed his hand into a fist, then opened it again. The lightness of her touch made him squirm a little. She flashed a quick smile of understanding and said, "Hold still, I'm nearly done."

"Sorry, it tickled," he said. She didn't reply, focusing instead on tracing the lines with her long, elegant fingers.

When she released his hand, Toby fought the overwhelming urge to rub it where her fingers touched him. "Go ahead," she said, her laugh low and liquid. "Everyone does."

Instead, Toby folded his hands together on the table. "So, what did you see?"

"You doubt?" she asked.

"Oh, no, not at all. Because I don't know how to do something—magic, for instance—doesn't make it any less real. You don't know how to sail a ship. At least, I don't imagine you do. Doesn't make it any less real."

She nodded. "Well said. And no, I could not sail a ship. Nor do what you'd call magic, like witches or wizards do. What I can do is tell where a person has been, and sometimes get a glimpse of where they may be going."

She paused, waiting for him to comment. Toby kept silent, and she went on. "When we met before, I told Lady Marissa I saw no evil in you. I told her you had a good heart."

Toby sat up straighter at her words. She said, "I also told her you were impulsive, and a regular rogue."

He slumped back in his seat again. Elbethesba's eyes crinkled with amusement. "Tell me, Captain. Can you deny any of what I've said?"

"No," Toby mumbled.

"My dear Captain Fanshawe, to be impulsive, and especially to be a rogue, is nothing to be ashamed of. Look at Radivan. A rogue if ever there was one. To be Tzigani is to be a rogue, in fact. It is part of who we are, no?"

"All right," Toby said. The tightness in his chest loosened, if only slightly. "Why are you telling me this?"

"So we might understand one another. I know you, Toby Fanshawe. The good and the ill of you. I need you to realize this."

"I've a strong suspicion," he said, "you know me better than I know myself."

"Perhaps. Many of us deceive ourselves. To truly know yourself for who you are? It takes a great deal of courage. It is never easy."

"No." Toby mulled this over for a moment. "So, what now? I'll admit you know me, inside and out. Will you tell me what my future holds, for good or ill?"

"Ah, well done, Captain." Elbethesba's mouth quirked up at the corners. "Most people, they wish to know the good but not the bad. Very well, I will tell you what I see ahead for you."

She hesitated, seeming to choose her words with care. "When we met before, I told Lady Marissa I was certain our paths would cross again, you and I. And lo, here you are."

Toby waited. She said, "I sensed even then you were attracted to Antonettia. And she to you. You are from two very different worlds, so this was no great surprise. Opposites often attract, no?"

"I would be lying if I said I found her less than lovely, exotic, and enchanting. She is a rare jewel indeed."

"And pirates, it is said, love to capture rare jewels, eh?"

"Now wait a darned minute," he protested. "I—"

She waved him to silence. Locking her gaze on his eyes, she said, "Tell me this. Do you love her?"

He bristled at first. The nerve, asking such a question. But even though Elbethesba was matriarch of this band of Tzigani, she was also Toni's mother. So he caught himself before he snapped out a reply. "I'm sure you already know the answer as well, if not better than I. But how can I answer you? I've known Toni for such a short time. I find her fascinating, and I would like to get to know her better. Do I love her?" He shrugged. "Much, much too early to tell, don't you think?"

"I'm glad you are wise enough to understand this."

Toby gazed into her eyes again. It was like staring into a darkened night sky, with no moon, and clouds covering the stars. Taking a deep breath, he said, "There is something else. Toni is your daughter. If I understand your ways, this means one day she will be in line to take your place, to become matriarch of this clan. Is this not so?"

Elbethesba's eyes widened at his words. "You are even more astute than I gave you credit for, Captain. Go on."

"This means Toni's place is here, with her people. It would be unconscionable for me to even consider taking her away from this, into my world.”

“And so…?”

“And so…what do you see? What does my future portend? Even if I did come to love her, it would be an impossible situation, wouldn’t it? She belongs here, and I, despite your gracious hospitality in allowing me to ride along with your caravan, do not. I am not Tzigani, and even for Toni’s sake, your people would never consider me a suitable suitor for her.”

Elbethesba’s eyes were clouded again. With anger? Or even, perhaps, pity? It didn’t matter. He barked out a harsh laugh. “I’ve been making a right fool of myself, haven’t I?”

“Why did you come here, Captain Fanshawe,” she asked, “if you understood the situation?”

He stared at her, incredulous. “Why? Good Lord, how could I have kept away? My nights are haunted, my days not much better, and…” He took a deep breath, steeled himself, and spoke. “I came here, I suppose, out of hope. Hope someone wiser, oh, much wiser than I, might see the way.”

She gave a slow nod. “I do see. I am sorry, Captain Fanshawe. You are a good man, with a great heart. I believe you might well make Toni happy. But you are right in what you say. For her to leave here, to leave the Tzigani, would be for her to lose too great a part of herself. She would wither and fade. And much as I would like to say you might be accepted by the Tzigani… No. They would never, especially not as Toni’s consort. In another time, perhaps it might be possible. But here, now? No. Your future, I’m afraid, does not lie with Toni.”

Toby heaved a sigh which came up from the vicinity of his boot soles. “I knew it all along. I’d just hoped…”

“It gives me no pleasure to say these things, Captain. Please believe me. I like you. I like rogues, and think the world is a much better place for their presence. Toni likes you too. She has spoken often of you. But though I wish it might be otherwise, some things are not to be.”

Toby nodded and started to rise. She waved him back to his seat. “I’ve remembered something,” she said. “You recall, when we met before, how I read your hand?”

“Yes? So?”

“I told you when we met before you would face a choice. Two paths: one leading to fortune and renown; the other leading to despair.”

“Thanks for the reminder,” he said, his voice bitter. “I reckon we know which one I’m on. No need to —”

“Captain,” she snapped. “When I read your palm before, you

gave me your left hand.”

“Well, yes, I reckon I did. It’s the one I tend to favor, so…”

Elbethesba’s breath was rapid, her eyes sharp, “But today,” she said, “today I examined your right hand.”

“Well, you did ask for it,” Toby pointed out, unsure where this was leading. “What’s the difference?”

“There is a tremendous difference, my dear Toby Fanshawe. Here—give me your left hand. Let me see…”

Toby offered her his hand. The left this time. She grabbed it, once again tracing the lines while she hummed to herself, eyes half closed. After an interminable time, she released it. When her eyes met his again, he sensed a weather change in her demeanor.

“I think,” she said, her eyes crinkling, “I can see the way.”

Toby’s heart leapt within his chest at her words. Before he could form a reply, a cry rang through the air.

“Bandits!”

CHAPTER TWELVE

Erkarna's Cavern

"Gone?" echoed Aireantha. "How? I mean…why? I—"

"Taken, I suspect, by whoever removed Erkarna's body," Wyzandar replied. "There must be another way into this cavern. We need to search for it."

Wyvrndell shook himself out of his shock and bewilderment. In their place, anger rose within him. He needed those scrolls and books and notes if he was to fulfill the king's directive, and to help Lady Marissa discover the effects of Thundermist. Going back without them was unthinkable. He glanced from Aireantha to his sire.

"You are right, Father. Airie, search around in here, will you? Perhaps you will find something I cannot see. Father, come with me. Erkarna's sleeping chamber is back through here." He indicated a passageway leading off the main chamber and started down it.

An odd scent permeated the passage. It grew stronger the further they traversed its length, becoming more and more unpleasant the closer they got to the sleeping chamber. "Blech. I don't like this," Wyzandar muttered.

"Nor do I," Wyvrndell agreed. The scent was of decaying flesh, putid, sulfurous, and even more revolting than one of his juicier hiccoughs. "I think we may have found Erkarna after all."

The stench was overpowering. Wyvrndell steeled himself once more and edged into the chamber.

"Ugh." The smell coming in collided with an outgoing hiccough. It was not, all in all, a happy meeting.

"We have found him," Wyzandar said.

"Indeed we have." Wyvrndell winced. "But why?"

"Is it possible he was alive after all, and dragged himself back here after you sealed the entrance, since he could not get out?"

"No, Father. Another brought Erkarna to this chamber. Observe the floor: there are the marks of his passage. You can see where he was dragged along. Besides, Erkarna, even had he been alive, would not have removed the books and scrolls from the main chamber."

"Can you conceive of an explanation?"

"Let me think… All right, I have an idea. Someone, human or dragon, found another way in. They wanted Erkarna's research but did not want to go through it with his body lying out there in the main hall. They dragged the body here, gathered up what they came for, and left by the same way."

Wyzandar cocked his head. "Your theory makes sense. I can't come up with anything better. Shall we search for the other entrance?"

"You go on. We need to know if there is another way in. With no evidence we have a theory, nothing more. I want to search in here. Perhaps some of Erkarna's research remains."

"Very well." Wyzandar made no delay in departing the chamber. Wyvrndell couldn't blame him. He conjured up another sphere of light, set it floating above his head, and began his search. It didn't take him long. Except for Erkarna's corpse, the chamber was bare and empty. He made his way into the outside passage and found Wyzandar waiting there, a pinched expression on his face.

"Father? You said you were going to search for the other entrance."

"I was. I decided to wait for you instead. I am sorry, my son. I know this has been difficult for you. This—scales and stars, this entire mess."

"Thank you, Father," Wyvrndell said. "I am glad you waited. But before we continue the search, there is something I must do."

"What?"

"Seal up this chamber," replied Wyvrndell, preparing himself to cast the spell. "There is naught in there but Erkarna's body. If any of his notes were stored in this chamber, they were taken with the rest."

"Do what you must," said his father.

He wrought the spell, and soon the chamber entrance became opaque, hiding from view the grim sight within. The opening appeared to fill with stone, until it became just another part of the passage wall.

"The stone is an illusion," Wyvrndell explained. "It should suffice to serve for his tomb, where he will lie undisturbed."

"Well done. Quite impressive, in fact. Shall we search for the second entrance?"

"I am ready." Wyvrndell led the way farther down the passage. They approached what appeared to be the end. Instead, the corridor angled to the left, creating the illusion of a solid wall. Coming closer, he observed the passage slanted upward at a steep angle.

"It must come out somewhere on the mountaintop," Wyvrndell speculated. "We should follow this the rest of the way, to be certain."

"I will explore it," Wyzandar said. "You go back and help Aireantha search the main hall, in case our thief missed anything of importance."

"Are you sure, Father? I will go with you if you wish."

"I can manage. I assumed you understood I was capable, after our journey to Arvindir and back."

Wyvrndell chucked, for what felt like the first time in ages. "Of course, Father. I merely wondered if you might like the company. I meant no offense."

"None was taken. But I would like to get out of this benighted tomb and be on our way. Petrandius needs to know what has transpired here. Go, and I will meet you on the ledge, if this comes out where I expect it does."

"Very well." Wyvrndell started back down the passage. When he glanced back, Wyzandar was already gone, making his way upward. Wyvrndell hurried on.

"Oh, good," said Aireantha when he emerged into the main cavern. "I was going to come after you. I have found something."

"What?" Excitement coursed through Wyvrndell at her words.

"I am not sure," she said. "I left it where I found it. It appears to be a scroll. The bit I saw looks quite ancient. It's over here, half buried beneath this rubble."

She led him across the center of the cavern, toward the far side. Wyvrndell paused for a moment. Here was where Erkarna ripped a good portion of Lady Marissa's magic from her. There, Francesca made her final stand, buying them time to rally and defeat Erkarna. At the cost of her life. Wyvrndell gave a sad hiccough.

He straightened and struggled to shake off these bitter memories. There was work to be done. "Yes, I am coming," he said, in answer to Aireantha's query.

"Are you all right?" she asked. "I know this must be difficult for you. Being here, I mean…"

"Yes, it is," he said. "We found Erkarna. Someone moved his body, dragged it back to his sleeping quarters."

"Ugh. Why would anyone do something so horrid?"

He related what he and Wyzandar deduced. "Now, show me what you've discovered."

"Here." She aimed a talon at a pile of rubble, blasted from the stone wall during the final battle. The tip of what appeared to be a scroll protruded from the rocks.

"Oh, well spotted," he said, brushing away some of the stones. With his talons, he gripped the end of the scroll and attempted to work it loose.

"Careful," she cautioned.

"I am," he replied. "At least, I am trying to be. Brush away some more of the rubble, will you? I do not want to let go of this…"

She edged around him and shifted the stones away. Wyvrndell wiggled the scroll, until at last it came free. "Got it," he said, holding it up.

"Good—oh, wait, there is another one under here."

"Airie, I am glad you are here. I would have never spotted this one, much less the second."

Together, they cleared away the remainder of the rubble, until Wyvrndell was able to take hold of the second scroll. Once he'd extracted it and placed it next to the first on one of Erkarna's stone benches, he turned back to find her digging through the stones.

"That appears to be the lot," she reported.

"We are lucky to even have these. If the thief had searched more carefully…"

"Are you going to open them?" she asked.

"Well, perhaps a quick examination. Wyzandar will be waiting for us on the ledge."

"How did he get there? I know we were busy, but I am sure I would have seen him go by."

"There is a second entrance," he said. "Or so we assumed. He went to check." While he spoke, he unrolled the scroll, a tiny bit at a time. He didn't want to risk damaging it. At times like these he envied humans their dexterous fingers; a dragon's talons were not ideal for such delicate work. It was indeed ancient, and extremely brittle.

He unrolled a little more and began to read what had been written so long ago by who knew what scribe. The words swam before Wyvrndell's eyes, and he stared, speechless. His talons clenched on the umbilicus. What he saw revealed froze him into immobility.

"Wyvrndell?" Aireantha asked. "What is wrong?"

He took a few moments to regain his reeling senses. Holding up the scroll, he said, "Not now. I will not speak of it in this place. Come. We need to get this back to Ervantium right away."

"Will the rain not damage the scrolls?" she asked.

"Practical as ever," he said. He glanced around. "There should be—ah, here it is. These metal cylinders were wrought in ages long past. They are what Erkarna used to store his scrolls. They will keep them protected from wind and rain while we fly."

"Wyvrndell," his sire bellowed from out on the storm-swept ledge. "Are you two done in there?"

"We are coming," he called back. To Aireantha he said, "Be still, will you? I want to scan and try to detect any other magical items before we go."

She waited, still as stone, while he opened his senses, searching for any trace of residual magic, no matter how small.

"Nothing," he reported. "Let us go."

With the scrolls in their protective cylinders, they joined Wyzandar on the ledge. "You found something," he said. It was a statement, not a question.

"Airie did. It is important, Father. We need to get to Ervantium right away so I can examine them further."

Before Wyzandar could reply, Donathyr reported, "We have company. Three dragons are approaching, from the west."

CHAPTER THIRTEEN
The Devil's Teeth

Toby threw open the wagon's door, stepped out onto the little platform, and slammed the door closed again. "Secure it," he called over his shoulder. He heaved a sigh of relief when the bolt slammed home. He jumped to the ground, drew his sword, and did a quick reconnoiter. The bandits were pouring out of the woods to his left. Radivan, who had remained astride his horse, was directing his Tzigani men into a defensive formation. Their short, curved swords flashed in the sunlight. These would have to be some extraordinarily determined—or desperate—bandits, to test the Tzigani's' wall of steel.

Or sneaky. By habit, Toby took in the entire scene. As former captain of a privateer vessel, he'd learned the hard way that in battle, the enemy wasn't always accommodating. Ofttimes they'd cheat by sneaking about, lurking in places one didn't expect and coming up from behind. So...

First he checked on the oncoming line of bandits, pouring out of the trees, brandishing their own weapons. Those were, he saw, the main force, attracting the whole of Radivan's attention. *There must be at least thirty of 'em. Is that all?*

Turning his attention from the oncoming melee, he scanned the other side of the caravan, where no attackers should be. The rules, if there were such things, dictated that all members of the attacking force stayed together, under the theory that massed strength was superior. From that direction he saw Toni, on her chestnut mare, heading for the security of her mother's wagon. *Good. Get to safety.*

A flash of movement caught his eye, and Toby stiffened. At least one of the bandits had indeed been sneaky. He'd managed to work his way around, flanking Radivan's defenses, and made his way to the far side of the caravan. There he was, lurking in a shrub like a dodgy songbird, with a short bow and an arrow nocked and ready. And he was aiming it right at Toni.

Even years later, he was never able to explain how he managed it. As the bandit loosed his arrow, Toby leapt into the air with a wild yell, startling Toni's mount, which reared and bucked. His blade swung in an erratic arc, somehow connecting with the speeding arrow, to send it veering off into the air. And away from Toni.

He crashed to the ground, managing to keep his sword from slicing off any of the bits he might wish to use at some later date. If he'd landed flat, Toby would have had the wind knocked out of him and been incapacitated for the rest of the melee. Instead, he managed to tuck his head in and hit the ground in an ungraceful but effective roll. He came out of it on his feet, forward momentum carrying him right toward the bandit in the bush. Who was setting another arrow to let fly.

Toby brought his sword up. He careened into the marauder and ran him through, gullet to gizzard. The nocked arrow took flight, piercing the fleshy part of Toby's right arm and right on through. Except for the acrid tang of blood in his nostrils, he barely noticed. More bandits were emerging from the trees on this side of the caravan, and Radivan and his men were distracted by the frontal assault.

"Toni." he shouted. "Get to the wagon."

Instead, she swung from her mount and ran toward him with a fierce grin. "No," he cried, but she kept coming.

The bandits, faces alight with anticipatory glee, were closing in on them. Toni swept out a short sword from somewhere on her person—Toby hadn't noticed it before, and wondered where she concealed it—and set herself ready beside him.

"Radivan." Toby yelped over his shoulder. "Bandits behind."

And then they were surrounded. Back-to-back, he and Toni fought off the marauders. Parry, block, thrust, Toby's blade flew of its own volition, keeping off the bandits. Behind him Toni snarled, and her steel rang against the bandit's weapon. There was nothing for it—all he could do was dispatch the one in front of him and take on the next, trusting Toni to do her part. They moved in unison, a whirling, deadly dance where one misstep would mean death.

Toby ran another foe through. This one was obstinate. Pull though he might, Toby was unable to free his blade from the man's body, and another bandit was approaching with an evil grin.

"Around," Toby called. It couldn't have gone smoother if they'd practiced it together for years: he and Toni executed a neat half circle, so she faced the incoming assailant with her weapon.

The bandit she'd been fighting was so startled by the maneuver he stood staring, his mouth hanging open. Toby kicked him in the crotch. The bandit clutched himself in agony, dancing about and gibbering. Toby brought up a left hook which started about eight yards back and connected with the man's jaw. He went down as if poleaxed, but Toby managed to grab his sword from nerveless fingers before he sank to the ground. Stolen weapon in hand, he was fighting again.

One of the bandits, less patient than his comrades, decided to forego his turn in line. He came at Toni from the side. "Definitely cheating," Toby muttered. He pulled a dagger from his boot and hurled it at the rushing bandit.

He'd thrown with his right, or off hand, so he wasn't surprised when the dagger didn't puncture his target. He was surprised, and so was the bandit, when the hilt end struck him between the eyes. The attacker gave a happy little sigh and sank to the ground.

"Oh, well flung," called Toni from between teeth clenched with exertion. "But here comes another one. Got any more knives?"

"No, damn it," Toby replied, parrying his current opponent's steel. "Um…swing left."

She stepped in unison with him once again in their wild dance. Toby sliced the newcomer across the throat. "Right again," she said, and they returned to renew the battle with their bemused attackers.

And finally, here came Radivan and four of his men, storming to their aid. Caught between the two forces, the bandits threw down their weapons and legged it.

"After them." Radivan shouted, and three Tzigani pursued them into the woods. Toby lowered his sword and swayed. A good breeze, he was certain, would topple him right over.

"Toby. Captain Fanshawe, I mean. You're wounded." Toni touched his right arm.

Toby looked at his shoulder, which was protesting in no uncertain terms and leaking copious quantities of blood.

"This?" he said with distain, sticking a finger right through the wound. "Ah, 'tis but a scratch." Then he collapsed

CHAPTER FOURTEEN

Erkarna's Cavern

Wyvrndell glanced at his companions. "The thief, returning?" he murmured.

"We will find out soon enough," replied Donathyr. "They are flying fast and should be here any moment."

Looking up, Wyvrndell observed the approaching flight of dragons. With a sinking sensation, he said, "One of them is Jakarian."

"Scorch me," snarled his father. "Not the thief, then. We doubtless would be better off if it was."

"Seal the chamber, Wyvrndell," Aireantha suggested.

"No, leave it," Wyzandar counselled. "To do so would make him even more suspicious."

"Is such a thing even possible?" Wyvrndell said.

"I wonder how he knew we were here?' Aireantha mused.

"An excellent question," said Wyzandar. "Though I doubt we will get an answer. All right, here they come."

Donathyr flew out a short distance from the ledge to confront the intruders. "Keep back," he said. "We are on a mission from His Majesty. Do not dare to interfere."

Wyvrndell had never seen a dragon sneer before. Jakarian managed it handily. He backwinged to perch upon a nearby boulder protruding from the cliff, while his two outriders took up positions near the top of the peak. "None of your insolence, Donathyr," he snapped, shaking the rain from his wings. Silhouetted against the sky, he exuded an air of dreadful menace which chilled Wyvrndell more than the storm.

Turning to Wyzandar, Jakarian said, "Well, what have you to

say for yourself? Stooping to tomb robbing?"

"What do I have to say?" Wyzandar's tone, Wyvrndell noted, was controlled and even. He could never have managed it, and was grateful to have his sire take the lead. "I say we have business here, which is more than you can claim."

"Business, eh?" Jakarian's gaze fell on the cylinders clutched in Wyvrndell's talons. "Was it not bad enough for your spawn to get caught up in Erkarna's schemes, Wyzandar? They drove Erkarna to madness, did they not? Will this hatchling be next? Or you?"

Wyzandar swelled up in wrath at this. Before he was able to flame, Wyvrndell said, "Lord Jakarian, my father has always said you were rich in both years, and wisdom. Will you not trust the king's judgement in this matter?"

Jakarian turned a gimlet eye on him. Flicking his tail in dismissal, he returned his regard to Wyzandar. "You have trained him well," he said. "He speaks with the same honeyed words as his sire. Words meant to soften an opponent, for the killing slash."

To Wyvrndell, he said, "Trust the king's judgement? How…amusing. Petrandius has been in his dotage for ages. Magic? Treaties with Dwarves and humans? Whoever heard of such nonsense? The whole world has gone mad."

Wyvrndell determined to make one final effort. "Lord Jakarian," he said. "What if I could give you magic?"

The old dragon reared up on his perch and sent a gout of flame into the air. "You think to tempt me with your heresy? Dragons were never meant for magic. Any fool knows that."

"So it would seem," Wyvrndell replied, striving to keep his voice level, like his sire had done. "It would be best if you leave us to our delusions, before I succumb to a fit of madness and turn you into a salamander." He held up one of the cylinders. "I happen to have the spell right here."

A crash of thunder drowned out Jakarian's cry of fury. He spread his wings wide, and Wyvrndell was certain the old dragon was going to attack them. A jagged gash of lightning reflected in Jakarian's fey eyes. *It is he who is deluded, after all,* Wyvrndell said to himself. *Will he kill the bunch of us in a fit of madness?*

At last, Jakarian managed to bring himself under control enough to speak again. "Wyzandar, I told you. I said you were raising a monster. You see what he has become."

"Be gone, you old fool," Wyzandar replied, "before I encourage him to turn you into a lizard."

Jakarian rose into the air, his mouth opening and closing in ferocious snaps. "This is not the end, Wyzandar." His voice, cold and hard as stone, called to Wyvrndell's mind a conspiracy of ravens. "Beware," the old dragon croaked.

Wyzandar opened his own jaws in a convincing imitation of a yawn. "Leave us," he said. "Or I will not be responsible for the outcome."

With muttered imprecations, Jakarian banked and flew away into the storm. The two dragons who accompanied him took wing and followed.

"Stones and scales," muttered Wyzandar. "Wyvrndell…"

"I am sorry, Father," he said, hanging his head. "I should not have said what I did, goaded him so."

To his amazement, Wyzandar chuckled. Wyvrndell never recalled witnessing such a thing, and it left him speechless.

"Could you have turned him into a salamander?" his father asked, dissolving into another bout of chuckling. "Do you have the spell there?"

"No, Father. It was a bluff."

Wyzandar roared with laughter. "Brilliant," he said at last. "Being insignificant is the thing Jakarian fears most. A salamander…" He was off again, lost in guffaws and fiery snorts.

Wyvrndell exchanged a glance with Aireantha, who shrugged in bemusement. "Are we done here?" she asked. "I would like to go home." She looked so forlorn with the rain lashing down on her, Wyvrndell almost regretted dragging her out on this mission. But she was the one who found the scrolls he bore, one of which, at least, was vital, and he was glad of her company.

"Wait," he said. "I want to seal the entrance again." Ignoring his sputtering sire, he cast the spell. It took form as he'd envisioned, and he gave a satisfied nod. He was finding it easier each time.

"You should seal up the other entrance too," Wyzandar said. He appeared to have regained his composure again.

"Show me where it is. It seems rather pointless, but I suppose it cannot hurt."

"Salamander," muttered Wyzandar, and was lost in another series of snorting, fiery chuckles. He winged an erratic course toward the top of the peak. Wyvrndell and Aireantha followed.

Once they arrived at the second entrance to Erkarna's cavern, Wyvrndell made quick work of sealing the opening. "Unless there is a third way in, this place should be safe from intruders," he said.

Wyzandar didn't reply, instead stepping off the ledge and spreading his wings to catch the air. Soon Wyvrndell and Aireantha were airborne, wings beating to keep themselves aloft in the sodden air which felt more sea than sky. Donathyr joined them, and they began the rain-soaked flight back to Ervantium, bearing a prize which, Wyvrndell hoped, might be the answer to his hopes and dreams.

~*~

Ervantium

Wyzandar sighed. "Will you tell me what you found, and are bearing back with such care? It would be good to know our mission was not a waste of time."

Wyvrndell glided toward the main entrance to the fortress of Ervantium. "Something the thief missed. Aireantha found them," he replied. "And I will say no more until we are secure inside."

"Very well. I shall keep my curiosity in check. At least I do know there is not a spell to turn a dragon into a salamander." He snorted, emitting a little puff of smoke, and followed Wyvrndell and Aireantha to the ledge. Two sentry dragons stood aside while they landed. Clutching the cylinders, Wyvrndell acknowledged their greeting and passed into the fortress.

"Father, may we use your cavern?" he asked. "It is more spacious than mine, and I need room."

"Yes, of course. Get on with it, will you?" Wyzandar led the way down the stone corridor. Wyvrndell followed, the cylinders tight in his grasp. Aireantha hurried along beside him.

Once they reached Wyzandar's chambers, he set the cylinders upon a stone bench. "Before I tell you anything," he said, "I want to set a ward in place, so no one can overhear us."

Ignoring his sire's astonished expression, he began to create a shielding ward. It didn't take long. He'd gone over this particular spell numerous times with Lady Marissa. There," he said, once he was done and the ward was activated. "Now no one will be able to overhear what we say."

"And what are you going to say?" Wyzandar's tone was a mixture of bemusement and impatience.

Wyvrndell gathered himself and said, "Airie, bless her, managed to locate two scrolls the thief, or thieves, missed. I have inspected one of them so far, but wonder of wonders, it contains the ritual Erkarna devised."

"What?" Aireantha gasped. "But Erkarna's ritual is what caused all the problems. Nearly got you and your human friends killed."

He looked from her to the scroll. "Yes, it is." He unrolled it. "But that is because Erkarna twisted it, perverted it, into something evil. The ritual itself, in its pure form, is fine. If I can figure this out, it could be the key."

Her eyes were doubtful. "The key? What key?"

"The key to gaining magic for dragons," Wyvrndell said, thumping his tail on the stone floor. "And by good fortune you found it. This is what Petrandius sent us to do. I cannot believe it. When I first saw Erkarna's cavern, with his notes and scrolls gone..." He bowed his head, then said, "I was sure the task was hopeless."

"What do you intend to do?" Wyzandar asked.

"I will need to study the ritual in detail. Once I fully understand the mechanics of the spell, I will attempt to do what Erkarna convinced me he was going to do—to give magic to the entirety of dragonkind."

"Well, maybe not every dragon," Aireantha said. "Remember Jakarian's reaction when you offered the possibility of magic to him. I am certain there are more like him, who will respond the same way."

"Perhaps." Wyvrndell mused. "I shall have to take such a reaction into consideration. I should not wish to force magic upon any dragon who found it objectionable."

"I suspect the king will have an opinion on your path forward," Wyzandar said. "As one of his councilors, I urge you to tell him of your discovery at once."

"Yes, of course. But first, I should learn what the second scroll contains." Wyvrndell removed the top from the other cylinder and eased out the scroll. He spread it out upon the stone bench and inspected the scroll. Then, with a steam-laden sign, he set about rolling it back up again.

With a steam-laden sigh, he set about rolling the scroll back up again.

"What is it?" Aireantha asked.

Wyvrndell glanced up from his task, shaking his head as if in a daze.

"Wyvrndell, what is wrong?" demanded Aireantha, her patience wearing thin. She stared at him, eyes wide and wisps of smoke curling from her nostrils.

Without speaking, Wyvrndell replaced the scroll into the cylinder. "I am not sure," he said at last, "if I should put this on display in the great hall, or burn it now, and forget I ever saw it. I am leaning strongly toward the second option."

"Wyvrndell, you are being annoyingly mysterious." She huffed out another smoke-laden breath, a sure sign of her agitation. "What is in this scroll? Some new, horrible spell?"

"Nothing quite so prosaic." He sagged under the weight of his discovery and glared at the cylinder. He was ready to open it again and char the contents into ash. But no, those contents were far too important.

He met Aireantha's eyes, which were filled with a mixture of concern and dread. "This scroll," he said, "is history. Dragon history."

"Well, how bad could it be? I know dragons have done some awful things in their day, but…"

"No," he said. "It is not that, Airie. It—" He hesitated in order to steady his own tormented emotions. "You know, do you not, the legend which says dragons are creatures of magic? Were, in fact, created by magic?"

"Yes," she said, cocking her head. "It is a legend, nothing more."

"Airie, think. If dragons were created by magic—who cast the spell?"

"I—" She blinked, an expression of bewilderment crossing her face. "You are telling me the legend is true? This scroll proves it?"

A shudder passed through Wyvrndell. His gut, which he had managed to keep under control, betrayed him. An acrid hiccough erupted from his jaws, sending blue smoke and sulphur into the air. "This scroll," he said, fighting down another hiccough, "says the legend is true. Airie, dragons were created by magic. It is why magic cannot be used against us. You witnessed this yourself, when the mage Azim hurled his killing spells at us when we brought the humans out of Arvindir. You know this part is true."

"Yes, I saw," she said. He sensed she was replaying the scene in her mind. "But what is so terrible about our being created by magic?"

He took a deep breath, steadying himself to deliver the awful news. "Airie, we were created, creatures of magic, by Dwarves."

She stared. "What? I—no, you are wrong. Inconceivable. We have always been taught dragons are the oldest beings in this world. So how—"

"The teachings were lies, Airie." He held up the cylinder containing the awful truth. "This scroll was crafted by Grythorn himself. Airie, he was the first of the dragons, created by a spell of the Dwarf mage D'rz'mn."

"The Dwarf whom Grythorn fought when they were both destroyed?"

"The same. In the scroll, Grythorn tells how D'rz'mn boasted of his creation to him. How he did not believe, until the Dwarf cast a second spell, and brought forth another dragon. A female this time, so their line might continue."

"Margalenza, the mother of dragons," Aireantha breathed in

wonder.

"Yes. Grythorn wrote everything down, but he vowed the secret would never be revealed. He taught his offspring how dragons were the oldest of creatures. Eons later, when D'rz'mn learned of his deception, he challenged Grythorn. This was the root of their epic battle."

Wyzandar said, "Not some silly theft of gold, as the legends have it."

"If the knowledge is such a deadly secret," Aireantha asked, "why did Grythorn write the truth?"

"Only he knows—well, knew—the answer. Whatever his reason, it is here in my possession."

Wyzandar heaved a sigh. "I can understand why you considered burning it," he said at last. "I am not certain it is not the best course."

"Can you imagine," Wyvrndell said. "If it were revealed we were created by our ancient foe?"

"Who is foe no longer," Wyzandar said. "But the treaty Petrandius crafted with King K'var'k would be broken in an instant if this got out." He shook his head in dismay. "There would be all-out war. Not mere skirmishes over who stole whose gold, but a battle to the end of the world."

"I fear you are right," Wyvrndell said. "And by chance, and our good fortune, the thief who robbed Erkarna's cavern missed it. And you found it, Airie. Can you imagine if Jakarian had found this?"

"Unfortunately, I can," Aireantha said, her voice bitter. "Wyvrndell, you have to tell the king."

"Do I?" He gazed into her worried eyes. "I am not so sure…"

"But he needs to know," she protested. "He might know what to do."

"Airie," he said, "I believe he already knows. I am certain this scroll is the real reason he sent me back to Erkarna's cavern. Petrandius sent me, not to bring back his notes and research on magic, although it would serve us well to have them. No, he knew, or at least suspected, the existence of this scroll."

"He was aware it was in Erkarna's possession? I do not understand this at all. If Erkarna had the scroll, would he not have made use of the knowledge for his own designs somehow?"

"Erkarna's library was vast," Wyvrndell said. "He even confessed to me once there were many items in it he never found a chance to examine."

"Well, I say you should discuss this with the king."

"Oh, rest assured, I will. I am eager to hear what he has to say. But Airie, Father… There is one more thing contained in the scroll…"

She closed her eyes in dismay. Opening them again, she said, "What else is there? Is this not bad enough?"

"Dragons were not created by normal magic," he told them. "We were created from wild Thundermist magic."

CHAPTER FIFTEEN
McRobbie House, Caerfaen

Marissa bestowed ear scritches on the little black kitten nestled in her lap. Francesca—namesake of the former witch turned feline, who had sacrificed her own life to save Marissa's—purred happily.

Marissa gave a contented sigh. With the hand not occupied in petting Francesca, she picked up her tea cup and took a sip of the fragrant beverage. Close at hand lay a book: a thrilling, if fanciful, tale of a dastardly villain, a noble hero, and a beautiful, if rather brainless, damsel in distress. She had pretty much decided to root for the villain, who was the single interesting character in the bunch.

The kitten gazed up at her with bright, intelligent green eyes. "You agree, Francesca?" Marissa asked. In reply, the kitten emitted a huge yawn, stretched, and clambered to the floor in search of some other entertainment. Marissa watched her, then returned her attention to the exploits of Lady Daphne, Sir Frederic, and the Faceless Fiend.

But she wasn't able to concentrate. How could she sit here and focus on her own comforts—tea, book, and cat—when out in the world women lived in fear of what the church, or rather those who acted in its name, might do to them?

Of course, she was subject to those same fears. After all, two men had recently attempted to assassinate her, in order to earn the bounty the rebel bishops had placed on her head. Still in all, her position and privilege provided her much more protection than most. And she was supposed to be protecting those other women who possessed magic. A fat lot of good she was doing sitting here at her ease. But that was the problem, wasn't it? She sat here, not doing anything constructive, because she had no idea what to do.

Captain Jenks and his constables were doing their part, patrolling the city day and night, in an effort to prevent another incident like the one Jenks had described. Marissa shivered. It was horrible to envision the prospect of being burned alive. Such a thing was unthinkable. Yet men like Angus and Vern viewed burning witches to be their sacred duty, directed by the church.

Morgan and the Legion were doing their bit too. Small teams of soldiers were patrolling the city in conjunction with the Watch. She alone sat idle and helpless, shirking her responsibilities.

"All right, let's figure this out," she muttered aloud. "I told Captain Jenks I'd come up with something clever. Time to deliver."

"Mrwow," chirped the kitten, which had managed to materialize in her lap again. Marissa stroked the so-soft fur, luxurious under her caress. If there was anything more sensuous than the feel of a contented cat, Marissa couldn't fathom what it might be. "What a muddle. Francesca, what am I to do?"

"Mrwow. I'm sure I don't know," replied a familiar, if unexpected, voice.

Marissa stared, hardly daring to hope. "Fr—Francesca. Is it you?" She stared at the kitten. "I tried and tried, but when you never spoke, I assumed you were only a cat after all."

Francesca sniffed disdainfully. "There is no such thing as 'only a cat'."

Marissa pulled the feline into an ecstatic hug. "Oh, I am glad to see you. Well, hear you. Oh, you know what I mean. But what happened? Why now, and not before?"

"I'm not quite sure," Francesca admitted. She placed a paw over Marissa's hand and purred softly. Gazing up into Marissa's eyes, the kitten said, "Your magic is different somehow. Much more erratic than before. And, to be honest, you didn't have the best control then."

Marissa allowed herself a fierce scowl. "The dragon, Erkarna, stole a great deal of my magic when—when you sacrificed yourself to save me. Oh, Francesca, if not for you, I wouldn't even be alive. I owe you my life."

Francesca butted Marissa's hand with her head. "You may repay the debt with fish. Lots and lots of lovely fishes."

"At every meal," laughed Marissa. "I shall have the fishmonger on retainer."

"Good. Since we've settled the matter of fish, what are you moping for? You're wedded to a perfectly luscious man, for heaven's sake. You've been jumpier than a dog in an alley full of cats."

"Um. Isn't it supposed to be the other way 'round?"

"Not where I come from. Tell Francesca."

"It's the church," Marissa said, her voice bitter. "A group of bishops have split off and declared witches in Kilbourne anathema. They're calling for a war on women with magic. They've even offered a special bounty on me."

Francesca's tail bristled and she gave a menacing hiss. "Yes, I recall. Well, what are you doing about it?"

"Ah, you've hit on my problem at the first go. I don't know what to do. Rhys has appointed me the protector of witches, since he's named me Royal Enchantress. Well, we both know what the position is worth at the moment. That and two shillings might get you a cup of tea. Of course, they're also under the protection of the Crown, so anyone who attempts to harm a woman because she's a witch will be charged and brought before a magistrate…" she trailed off, mind racing.

"You've thought of something." A statement, not a question. Marissa nodded, lost in thought.

"Perhaps." She hesitated. "It hinges on how far the king is willing to go."

"Well? Are you going to tell me?"

Marissa shook her head. "No, not yet. I need to think on it first. Later we can discuss it, and you can tell me the multitude of reasons it's an awful, terrible, horrible idea."

"Hmmm. Does it involve taking the war to these blasted clergymen? A good dose of magic, perhaps a turn as a toad or a stoat, might change their perspective, don't you think?."

Marissa sighed. "No, Francesca. Satisfying though it sounds, doing so would validate the bishops' contention witches are evil."

"Hmph. My way sounds like much more fun."

"Of course it does. Morgan proposed much the same idea: ride in with the Legion and round up the rebels at sword point. Both of you have neglected to consider the aftermath."

"You mean the part where they're toads, or locked in a dark, dank dungeon?"

She laughed, but then her expression became serious. "No, I mean the part where they're considered martyrs, and those people—well, men, actually—rise up and begin to start a real war."

"Oh. Well, perhaps you're right. What do I know, I'm merely a cat."

"I thought there was no such thing as merely a cat."

"Ah, you were paying attention. Well done, you. Now, about those fish…"

McRobbie House, Caerfaen

Morgan stared at his duchess, his mouth agape. "You're not serious."

Marissa stroked the kitten snuggled in her arms. "Yes, I am," she said at the same time the kitten said, "She's serious."

"But how?" Morgan got his errant jaw under some semblance of control, but realized he was staring in disbelief. "Not to put too fine a point on it, but we saw you—um—die."

"Cat. Nine lives, remember?" Lady Francesca wriggled under Marissa's caress. "It's part of the arrangement. I must have had at least one left."

Morgan's brows went up. "You don't keep track? I'd think it's something I'd jolly well be aware of."

The kitten butted her head against Marissa's hand. "To tell you the truth, after the first two or three? They kind of run together. You don't think about it much, you know?"

"No, I can't say I do." Morgan reached over to scratch Francesca's ears. "Since I'm allotted a single outing, I find the whole notion, well, inconceivable."

The kitten's reply was a loud, contented purr. Marissa said, "Francesca tells me the memories of her last life are a bit fuzzy."

"Rather like Francesca, eh?" Morgan grinned.

"Hoy. That was uncalled for," protested Francesca. She scrambled out of Marissa's arms to scale her way up to Morgan's shoulder. "True, perhaps, but nevertheless uncalled for." She clouted Morgan's ear with a paw. With no claws extended, for which he was grateful. "Let this be a lesson to you."

"You laughed," Morgan challenged. "I heard you."

"I did not—oh, very well, I did. You surprised it out of me. You're so stodgy most of the time, I wasn't expected a pun from you."

Morgan found himself flaring up in righteous indignation. "Stodgy? Me?" He turned to appeal to Marissa. "Am I stodgy?"

"You're arguing with a cat, Morgan," she pointed out. "And I'm not certain you're winning."

Hmph. She hadn't answered the question, which was concerning. No matter; the issue of his stodginess, or lack thereof, could be better pursued under other circumstances. "Has anyone ever won an argument with a cat?" he asked.

"No." Marissa and Francesca spoke with one voice. Morgan heaved a long-suffering sigh and began the process of disentangling himself from the kitten.

"See if you get any more ear scritches from me," he muttered.

Francesca's liquid green eyes regarded his hands. "Hmm. Perhaps I was hasty. Upon due consideration, you are the soul of joviality, a bon vivant, and the life of every party."

"Liar," Morgan said, but he scratched the kitten's ears anyway. "We'll call it a draw. Now, I'd best retire from the field of verbal combat while I have a few shreds of my dignity left. I have work to do."

CHAPTER SIXTEEN

Knight-Commander's Office, Kilbourne Palace, Caerfaen

Morgan glanced up as the door of his office was thrust open. "Arthur," he began, but the chiding he'd been ready to deliver to his clerk died on his lips. He shot to his feet, chair caroming off the wall behind.

Rhys Gwynfallis, King of Kilbourne, lounged against the doorframe. His thin face was tinged with a sly grin. "It's not Arthur's fault you hate doing paperwork," he said.

"Nooo." Morgan shrugged, unconvinced.

"However, in an effort to protect Arthur's delicate sensibilities—" Here twin snorts sounded, one from Arthur and another from Morgan. "I've brought you this batch myself." Rhys beamed at his Knight-Commander, offering a flourishing pile of files.

Morgan rolled his eyes. Rhys dropped the files onto the corner of his desk, where they attempted to slither off onto the floor. Morgan made a grab, managing to capture them in the nick of time. He settled the files into a more secure position and glared at his liege lord.

"Sit, Morgan, and stop scowling," Rhys directed, pushing the door closed. "You know full well these are nothing compared to the piles I have to deal with."

Morgan sank into his seat. Rhys commandeered the one chair in the room not piled high with stacks of paperwork. Crossing his long legs, he leaned back and laced his fingers behind his head.

Morgan waited in silence. The skill was something he'd become rather adept at during his recent dealings with Ian Taggart, former criminal overlord, now Baron Swansea. Rhys opened his mouth to speak, closed it again, and cocked his head. Morgan ignored him. He opened a folder and perused its contents.

Rhys heaved a hearty guffaw. "All right, Morgan, you win. I'll tell you all."

"Oh, you wanted something? I thought you dropped by to deliver these files. Most kind of you, Your Majesty. Taking time out of your busy schedule like this." He grinned. "What's up, Rhys?"

The king's mouth turned down at the corners. "It's this princess you've brought me," he said, huffing out a long-suffering sigh.

"Oh, no." Morgan held up his hands. "Princess Saia was none of my doing. You'll have to lodge any complaints on that score with your Royal Enchantress."

"Mmm." Rhys's expression was grim. "Perhaps I shall. What was the idea, Morgan? Bringing her out of Arvindir, I mean?"

Morgan shrugged. "Saia discovered us in the midst of pinching the blasted ruby. She was ready to sound the alarm, bring every guard in the palace down on our heads, and have us tossed into a nice, cozy cell in Azim's dungeon. Marissa managed to talk her out of it. With time slipping away on us, Saia agreed to let us escape, but only on the condition we bring her out too."

Rhys drummed his fingers on his knee. "I see. A bit of judicious blackmail."

"Mind you, we'd never have gotten out of the palace without her help. And she did manage to keep Azim from murdering us and dropping our bodies into the Thundermist Sea."

"Mmm, so I gathered. She killed him, she told me. And with no remorse, either."

"I wouldn't have expected any. Azim was a real rotter, I'm afraid, and I imagine Saia had a pretty thin time of things there. Besides, he was trying to slaughter the lot of us, remember. Anything she did was in self-defense."

Rhys stroked his beard, his mouth creasing into a frown. "Yes, that does explain a few things."

"Has her father been pestering you concerning her?" Morgan asked.

"No, not a word. Which is rather odd, when you stop to think about it."

Morgan shrugged. "There's no reason for him to even suspect she's here, is there?"

"Well, if you take the fact she vanished at the same time as a party from Kilbourne…"

"True. Between the disappearance of his eldest son and his only daughter, you'd think King Radagav would have at least been making some rather searching inquiries."

"Yes, you would. But Radagav isn't my concern at the moment."

"All right," Morgan said, not wanting to ask, but knowing he had no choice. "So, what's the problem?"

"Well…what do we do with her?"

Morgan cocked his head, considering. "Well, the way I see it, you have two options. One, send her back to Parthane—"

"Good luck with that," Rhys muttered. Which Morgan took to interpret the king had broached this plan and been soundly rebuffed.

"Or find her something useful to do."

"Something useful? Hmm. I'm open to suggestions."

Morgan shrugged. "Oh, I don't know. She is a sorceress, after all. What if you set her the task of finding out how the Thundermist affects those with magic? Both she and Marissa have been somehow infused by it. No one knows anything about how, or why, or what the long-term effects might be. Marissa and I were discussing this with Master Sebastien the other day."

A gleam of interest lit Rhys's eyes. "D'you know," he said, "as ideas go, this one is not so moldy. It would make sense to have her research the phenomenon. She and her young archivist chap—"

"Alain," Morgan supplied.

"—could search both the palace archives and the wizards' records. M'yes, such a task should keep her out of mischief."

Morgan's brows rose. "Is the princess getting into mischief? I'd have thought I would have heard."

"No, she's just always underfoot somehow."

"Well, there you are." Morgan waved an airy hand. "Solutions supplied upon demand. Your problem is solved. Now, what about mine? Well, ours, since you're here."

Rhys leaned forward, hands on his knees. "What problem?"

"Problems. First, the rebel clergy who are threatening excommunication, and worse, to a significant portion of your citizens. Including my wife, curse them."

Rhys's response was a glower which could have soured ale. Morgan went on. "I've dispatched a number of small squads of Legion soldiers around the kingdom, from anywhere we have a garrison. Their orders are to stay in the background, but to protect any women who need it, in case the bishops get people riled up enough to do something stupid. They're working in conjunction with the constabulary. The local chaps will know better who and what to watch out for, but they don't have the manpower to deal with it."

"Well done," Rhys said.

Morgan slapped the top of his desk, causing both files and king to jump in unison. "It's fine, but it's a bandage, not a solution. All we can do is react to problems when they arise. It doesn't solve anything."

"The bishops," Rhys growled.

"The bishops," Morgan echoed. "Can't the archbishop do anything with them? Threaten them with excommunication themselves if they don't stop this nonsense?"

"The archbishop," Rhys muttered, "is too afraid of his own shadow to act. I've pressed him on several occasions, to no avail."

"And the other, more direct approach?"

Rhys opened his eyes wide. "Why, Knight-Commander, whatever might you mean?"

"Storm their cathedral, round up the renegades, and quash the rebellion," Morgan offered. "Simple. Direct. Effective."

Rhys shook his head. "No. Not yet at least. Not until every other avenue has been exhausted."

"Or until women start getting killed. You can't let that happen, Rhys."

"Damn it, Morgan, do you think I don't know? I said 'not yet.' Not 'never.' We're early in the game, and nothing's gotten out of hand yet."

"No?" Morgan pierced the king with a glare. "What about those thugs who attempted to kill Marissa, in broad daylight, in front of our home? On orders from the bishops, I might add. Assassination seems out of hand to me. She didn't sign up to be a target for killers. Whenever she leaves the house, I have to send a couple of soldiers with her. Which, I have to say, neither of us is best pleased with. Well, except the guards. I gather she takes them to tea shoppes and stands them pastries."

Rhys chuckled. "Why am I not surprised? But know this: I'm doing the best I can under the circumstances. I repeat, not now, not never."

"All right, if you say so. I'll refrain from riding in and lopping off any heads, no matter how tempting it sounds. For the time being…"

"Your forbearance is appreciated, Morgan. Believe me, I want to get this problem settled too, though I'll grant you have more of a personal stake."

Morgan leaned back in his chair. "Yes, I have a personal stake. But I'm not sure if you realize how much of one you have."

Rhys's furrowed his brow. "What do you mean?"

"From what I've heard, the rebel bishops intend to declare as anathema not only those who are witches, but those who harbor witches. Rhys, that would include you."

Rhys's curses turned the air blue. When he halted, Morgan said, "Welcome to the club."

"Oh, I knew it was coming. Including me, or Gwyn, doesn't change a damned thing. They're in the wrong, and somehow we'll manage to put an end to this nonsense."

Morgan didn't bother to try and hide the scowl creasing his face. "I damned well hope it's not too late when we do," he muttered.

If Rhys heard his comment, he didn't acknowledge it. Instead, he said, "What's the other problem?"

"Mmm? Oh, yes, the other problem. Well, according to reliable sources, the Rhuddlanis are up to something. Unfortunately, no one seems to know what. But whatever it is, I'm damned certain it won't be anything for our benefit."

"No, I imagine not. Still, this sounds like something we can, if not ignore, at least keep in abeyance. Until we know more. I assume your source is Barzak?"

"Yep. According to his aide, Barlbent, they're looking into a few things. He'll let me know if they turn anything up. I can't see the Rhuddlanis mounting any kind of attack at this time of year, but I'm going to get the Legion busy with some extra training exercises, at the very least."

"All right." Rhys scowled at the vagaries of their northern neighbors and sometime enemies. "Let me know if you learn anything more specific. I'll speak to Barzak too." The king rose from his seat and shook his head. "That's all we don't need."

With this less than helpful comment, he was gone.

CHAPTER SEVENTEEN
The Devil's Teeth

"Ow." Toby jerked, grunting in sleep-addled pain.

"Hold still," said a familiar female voice through the fog of his brain. "You'll rip out my excellent needlework."

Toby managed to crack open his crusted eyes. "Toni?"

"Yes, it's me. Lie still, will you? I need to change this dressing."

"Dressing? Oh…" Memories flooded back. Bandits. He and Toni, back-to-back, comrades in arms, fighting off the marauders. The arrow through his arm… "Ouch," he said again.

"I shouldn't wonder," Toni replied. "You've got a thumping big hole in you. You can pretty much see right through."

Toby winced at this mental picture, and at the pull of the dressing being removed. "Beast," he said, but his voice was tempered with fondness.

"Hmph. I might have left you to the tender mercies of Auntie Mirabel. She'd have sawed your arm off to save everyone a spot of bother."

"I suddenly feel much better," he said, managing a weak grin.

"Hmph," she said again, but a mixture of mirth and concern mingled in her eyes. "I wasn't sure you were going to make it for a bit there."

"Um. How long is a bit? Toni, how long have I been out?"

"The bandits attacked yesterday morning. So, a day and a half?"

"And I've been unconscious this whole time? From an arrow through my shoulder?"

"Not only because of the arrow," she said, packing a poultice of sweet-smelling herbs around the wound. "The arrow—well, the arrow was poisoned."

"Oh." He met her eyes, which were dark and concerned. And angry.

"Oh, indeed." She wrapped another bandage around his arm. "Fortunately, Mamma realized why you were in such a bad way and concocted a potion to counter the poison. Otherwise…"

"Otherwise," he finished for her, "the angel I'd have been seeing would not have been the one tending to my wound."

She swatted his arm. Not the one she had been bandaging, for which he was grateful. "You seem confident it's angels you'd have been seeing," she teased, "and not the other."

"It doesn't matter," he replied. "I've already got one here. I'm quite content with this one, no matter what happens later."

This was the correct response, for she leaned over and kissed the top of his head. "Mamma was right," she said. "You are a rogue. And a shameless flatterer, to boot."

"And a scoundrel," he admitted with good humor. "I'll fit right in."

Her eyes went shuttered at his words.

Damn. I've sailed too close to the wind there.

"I'd best finish this up and leave you to rest," she said, her voice becoming brisk and business-like. "Can't be tiring out the patient." She tucked the end of the bandage in.

Toby caught her hands in his, stifling a wince against the sharp stab of pain which shot up his arm. "Toni," he said, his voice low and urgent. "Your mother… she said she saw something. Something which might make this work, you and me."

Her eyes went wide. "Truly?"

He nodded. "She was going to tell me when the bandits attacked. She didn't say anything to you?"

"No, not a word." A slow smile spread across her face, and he basked in its warmth, like a cat lazing in a pool of sunlight. "We fought well together, didn't we?"

"You were brilliant," he said, and meant it. "Like we'd practiced together for years."

"I think," she said, "perhaps I should go and speak with Mamma."

"Yes, why don't you?" said another voice from the wagon's doorway.

Toby started, and Toni gave a little shriek of surprise.

"Pappa, you startled the wits out of me," she chided.

Radivan stepped into the confines of the wagon. "How is your patient?"

"Awake, finally," Toby answered. "Sore as a boil, but I'm in one piece. Well, with a hole knocked out…"

"One might say," Toni said with a sly grin, "he's hole."

Both men groaned.

"Enough of that, young lady," Radivan said. His stern expression was belied by a twinkle in his eyes. "Go and report to your Mamma."

"Yes, Father," Toni replied, her eyes demurely downcast. "I hear and I obey."

"Ha," said Radivan. He turned back to Toby. "So, how are you feeling?"

"Lucky to be among the living. And ready to chew hunks out of this wagon. Yes, my arm hurts like hell, but it beats the alternative six ways from Sunday."

"No doubt." Radivan chuckled. "Six ways from Sunday? An interesting expression. I've never heard it before."

Toby shrugged, winced, and said, "Something my grandsire used to say. I'm not sure myself what it means, but it somehow fits the circumstance. You're welcome to use it if you'd like."

"I might. Hold on a moment, and I'll see to some food for you. Can't have you chewing up the wagons, can we?" He went to the door, opened it, and called out, "Arnot. Bring me a bowl of stew."

"Were any of your men injured in the attack?" Toby asked.

"A couple of minor wounds. Nothing serious," Radivan said. "Nothing like what might have been, if you hadn't been where you were, and acted so in so bold a fashion."

"Instinct, pure and simple. When I saw the bandit aiming his bow at Toni…"

"Yesss…" said Radivan. "My wife, she kept an eye on you from the wagon. You flew through the air like a hawk, she said, to deflect the arrow which would have slain our daughter."

He paused. Toby said nothing.

Radivan went on. "After that, she said, you fought off at least a dozen of the bandits."

"Only with Toni's help," he said. "She was amazing."

"Yes, Elbethesba regaled me with Toni's exploits. A fine tale. I reckon my lessons were not in vain after all, eh?"

"I believe you could say so." Toby grinned at the memory of fighting back-to-back with her in that whirling dance of mayhem. Then he grew serious. "Poisoned arrows? Who the devil uses poisoned arrows,

Radivan?

The Tzigani shook his head in bemusement. "None I've ever encountered."

"I hate to ask this," Toby said. "But is it possible they were waiting to ambush your caravan in particular?"

Radivan's frown was ferocious. "I never considered the possibility, no. What makes you think this might be so?"

"A nasty, suspicious mind. Comes from years of being a pirate. You said yourself, bandits would be after horses, wagons, women, and gold. Your daughter is, not to put too fine a point on it, young, beautiful, and an exceptionally worthy prize. So why try to kill her? And with a poisoned arrow…"

Radivan's eyes went dark and storm-laden at Toby's words. "Fanshawe," he said, "what you say makes sense. It also chills me to the bone. This was no random bandit attack. Someone planned and carried it out for a purpose. But—why?"

"I've no idea," Toby admitted. "And I might be off the mark, you know."

"I don't think so. I wish to heaven you were. This means I have an unknown adversary, after—what?"

Toby shook his head. "Did you capture any of the bandits alive?"

"No, curse it." Radivan tugged on his moustache. "If we had… But no, there was no way to know, at the time. A few of them escaped, but most of them were killed in the fray."

"We'll have to be sure to catch a few next time," Toby said.

"Next time?" Radivan exploded.

"They failed," Toby said. "So yes, there might well be a next time. I would keep your scouts and sentries on high alert if I were you. But I'm sure you've already done so."

"No," Radivan growled. "But I certainly will." He stepped to the door, put his finger to his lips and gave a shrill whistle. A faint, answering whistle came to Toby's ears.

In a couple of minutes a giant of a man leapt up onto the wagon. Radivan conversed with him in undertones. The giant sent a sharp glance in Toby's direction, nodded once. He swung to the ground and loped off.

"Jovan will attend to the scouts and the sentries," Radivan said.

"We're camped for the night?"

"Yes. Fortunately, we're in a defensible spot here. But I don't like this. If you're right, and I fear you are, we're in for more trouble. Sooner rather than later."

"It matters how much of a force your enemy is fielding," Toby pointed out. "After all, we did manage to account for quite a few of them.

Whoever it is may not have enough reserves on hand. And they'll have to assume you'll be on your guard against further attacks."

Radivan nodded, his expression thoughtful. "You have given me much food for thought. I must consult my wife. She may have some augury to reveal what is happening. I will leave you to rest. Get well, Fanshawe. I have need of you. Both your steel, and your brain. Ah, here is Arnot with the stew."

The enticing aroma of herbs, vegetables, and chicken wafting from the bowl distracted Toby's attention. By the time he put down the spoon, Radivan was gone, and he was alone again.

CHAPTER EIGHTEEN
Royal College of Wizards, Caerfaen

Sebastien started, sending the feather in his old hat, pulled low over his eyes, dancing. He hadn't been dozing off, of course not. He'd simply been resting eyes weary from an excess of research.

"Princess Saia," he said, rising to greet the unexpected visitor to his study. Well, in truth the Chief Wizard's study; Sebastien occupied it on a temporary basis, until a more suitable candidate could be found. Which would be soon, he hoped.

"What a, um, welcome surprise," he went on, straightening out his rumpled robe.

"You mean 'what an interruption,' don't you?" asked the Parthanian princess, with a wry smile. She stepped through the doorway, accompanied by the archivist chap who'd fled Arvindir with Lady Marissa and company, all a-dragonback. "This is Alain," she went on. "My very good friend. We've come to request a boon."

"Umm…" Sebastien glanced between the pair. "I think what you want is a priest, not a wizard."

Alain flushed crimson. Saia laughed and said, "No, no, you misundertake me. Archives, not matrimony, is our goal. At least for now," she added. Her eyes smoldered when she gazed at the young man beside her. Alain flushed, if possible, an even deeper red.

"I—archives?"

"Yes, archives. Your King Rhys, not knowing what to do with me, has decided to put me to work. Alain and I, we are to search through the palace archives and the records held here, in the hopes of finding some reference to the effects of Thundermist."

"Thundermist, eh?" Sebastien drummed his fingers. "Yes, I recall. Lady Marissa said your powers were activated, or enhanced, or whatever, by the Mist. Much like hers were."

"Yes, but no one knows what it does, or how it affects things. Our mission," she hooked her arm through Alain's, "is to find out, and report back to His Majesty."

"And also to the Royal Enchantress, I trust?"

"Of course. She needs to know, since she is also affected by the Thundermist. And I owe her a debt, since she is my reason for being here."

"From what I understand, you are her reason for being here too," Sebastien murmured.

"Ah, well—" Saia waved this away. "So. Do we have your permission to search?"

"By all means. I will escort you to the archives myself. Many a happy hour I've spent there. And many more a frustrating hour."

Alain chuckled. "It is always so, is it not?"

"Indeed, indeed. All right, come along. Though first, I have a request of you, Princess."

"What kind of request?"

"If you are willing, I would like to examine you." The princess shied away, and he said, "Not a physical examination. I would like to be allowed to enter your mind, so I may examine your magic."

"Will—will it hurt?" she asked, sounding more like a nervous child than a royal princess.

"No, it will not hurt," Sebastien replied, keeping his tone gentle. He didn't want to scare her off. "It may feel odd at first, even a trifle uncomfortable. If you are uncertain, consult the Royal Enchantress. I have done the process twice with her, once a few days ago."

Saia took a deep breath and let it out again. "I will do so," she said. "Tell me one thing, though. If I were to refuse, what would happen?"

Sebastien blinked. "Why, nothing, Your Highness. I would simply know less than I might hope to regarding the effects of the Thundermist. You and Lady Marissa are, to the best of my knowledge, the only two people to enter the Mist and have their powers affected by it. My examination is intended for the purpose of trying to understand this phenomenon."

"I—yes, I see. Let me consult with the duchess. I will give you my answer once I have done so."

Sebastien bowed his head. "Of course," he said. "I am not in any way trying to coerce you into doing something against your will. But it might serve to help us understand the effects of the Mist firsthand. Such knowledge would, I think, augment your research in the archives, eh?"

"Yes, I suppose it would. Very well, I will let you know. In a day or two?"

"Of course," he replied. "Come along. You shall have free rein of the archives, within limits."

"Limits?" Saia sent him a searching gaze.

"Princess, some of the volumes in the Wizard's archives are dangerous."

"Like the book Lady Marissa brought with her to Arvindir? The one my brother coveted so?"

"Yes, I'm afraid so. But also, books of even greater power and—well, ill-intent. They are bound by strong spells, known to a select few of the archivists. If you need to study any of those, you will require assistance, and supervision. They are not to be treated lightly, I'm afraid."

"I understand, sir," Alain said. "There were quite a number of dark tomes in the archives in Arvindir. They were secured in much the same way, wrought with binding spells known to the senior archivist and one or two others."

They reached the sub-basement that housed the archives. Sebastien stopped before opening the door. "So you understand," he said, gazing into Alain's eyes. "Do not let the Princess put herself into danger, by rambling unsupervised through those types of books."

Saia appeared ready to protest. Alain put his hand on her arm. "I will protect her, as one would a rare treasure," he said.

Now Sebastien observed a warm glow light the Princess's eyes. "Good lad," he said. To himself he added, *You're going to be wanting that priest pretty soon, I'd warrant.*

He thrust open the door of the archives and ushered them inside. "Before you begin your research, there is one more condition I need to mention."

Saia bristled. Sebastien ignored this and focused his attention on her companion. "Alain, I know you are, or were, an agent of Lord Holman."

"I still am," Alain said.

"I'm afraid nothing you view here may get back to him. Report to me, His Majesty, and the Royal Enchantress. Your reports should contain items relevant to your inquiries into the Thundermist and its effects, nothing more. I'm sure Lord Holman knows plenty about what's contained here. We won't trouble him with what he doesn't know. It can, shall we say, remain a closed book. Do I make myself clear?"

"Yes indeed." Alain came near to saluting.

Sebastien gave him a wan smile. "Very well. I will take you at your word. Enter the archives of the Royal College of Wizards." He ushered them through the door, and the scents of paper and ink and ancient words rose up to greet them.

Alain and Princess Saia gazed around. Saia, Sebastien observed, with simple curiosity, likely wondering how long it would take her to complete the task Rhys had set her.

Alain, on the other hand, appeared awestruck. His mouth hung half open and his eyes were wide and staring. "It—it is magnificent," he breathed. "Oh my. I thought Arvindir's archives were something special. This—it puts those to shame."

Sebastien's brows rose. "Truly? I'll confess, I'm surprised. The archives there are much older, aren't they?"

Before Alain replied, Saia cut in. "Enough with the mutual archives-admiration society. We have a task to complete and…" she glanced around. "It is not going to be a simple one."

Alain's tone, when he replied, was drier than the sands of Arvindir's desert. "No, Your Highness, it will not be easy by any stretch of the imagination."

A clerk came strolling over to greet them. *At last*, Sebastien said to himself. *I was beginning to wonder.*

"May I be of service?" The man's tone indicated such a possibility was doubtful.

"Please present my compliments to the Head Archivist," Sebastien said. "And ask him to join us here."

The clerk sniffed. "I do not believe he is available."

For the likes of one such as you. Sebastien finished the sentence to himself. He counted to five, then favored the clerk with a crooked smile. "Indeed? You might deign to mention to him, even though I'm sure such an important individual is exceptionally busy, the Chief Wizard begs a mere moment of his most valuable time."

The clerk's eyes widened, and his gulp was audible. "At once, Chief Wizard. A thousand pardons. I did not recognize you. I—"

Sebastien waved him away. "Scat. Fetch the Archivist."

The clerk turned tail and came a hair short of sprinting away through the crowded room. A couple of heads turned to regard this unusual sight with a tinge of surprise. Once the excitement was over, dismissing the interruption from their minds, they returned to their work.

"That boy needs to get out more," Sebastien chuckled.

"We archivists do tend to insulate ourselves from the rest of the world," Alain said. "Books and scrolls are much more interesting. And less bothersome." He sent a glance toward Saia. "Well, not always."

She beamed at the compliment.

The clerk bustled back, stopping in a flurry of flapping robes. "The Archivist will receive you in his office,"

Sebastien shook his head. "I've seen his office. There is so little room in there, what with the piles of interesting scrolls and books strewn around, if he turns around he must bump into himself coming and going. Inform the Archivist we would like him to emerge, like a cautious turtle from his shell, and come out to greet," he paused, raising his voice to say, "the Chief Wizard."

The man fled. This time every head turned to regard the intruders. Well, all but one. An elderly scribe, chin resting on his chest, snored while he dozed, an illuminated scroll lying ignored on the table before him. One of his comrades reached out to shake him awake.

Sebastien shook his head. "Let him rest," he said.

The slap, slap of hurrying sandals heralded the return of the stricken messenger. A slower, more measured tread from behind him announced the arrival of the head archivist. He was, Sebastien admitted, the classic picture of what one imagined an archivist to be: tall, lean, with a hawklike nose, hooded eyes, and a pursed mouth which gave the impression its owner had bitten into a lemon.

"What's all this nonsense?" he inquired. "Chief Wizard? Bah. You're not Foxwent."

"Neither, at the end, was Foxwent," Sebastien pointed out. "But he, I'm afraid, is no longer among the living, so you have me to deal with instead. I reckon you'll have to update something. I am the Acting Chief Wizard. I seem to recall you were at my installation, Wizard Darvish."

Darvish closed his mouth, which had fallen open at Sebastien's words. "Um. Hmph. Yes, yes, I was, come to think of it. I beg your pardon, Chief Wizard. We don't often get anyone but hoary old scribes down here."

"No doubt. Well, we must move with the times, eh? Allow me to present my companions. This is Princess Saia of Arvindir." Saia essayed a minimalistic curtsey. "And this young chap is Alain, former Head Underarchivist in Arvindir."

Alain bowed before the Archivist, who gave him and Saia the briefest of nods. "To what, may I inquire, do we owe the honor of such auspicious visitors?" Darvish inquired, managing to convey a realm of derision into the two final words.

Sebastien ignored this. "King Rhys has set Princess Saia and Alain a task, one which requires access to the archives. Full access."

"I see," said Darvish.

"No, I doubt you do," Sebastien replied. "But you don't need to. Your job is to provide them access to whatever documents, scrolls, or books they need to see. I know," he said, holding up a hand to forestall the Archivist's protests. "There are many things here bound up in protective spells. Someone with authority will need to be available to provide them access."

"Chief Wizard," began Darvish.

"Chief Archivist," Sebastien cut him off. "Their orders come from the king himself. This is, after all, the Royal College of Wizards, is it not? Their inquiry is urgent to His Majesty and should be neither delayed nor hindered. Please attend to it at once."

A choking noise, akin to a badger attempting to consume a recalcitrant fieldmouse, came from one of the scribes watching the scene.

Sebastien turned toward the sound. "Did one of you have something to contribute? Perhaps a volunteer, to assist these researchers?"

Silence greeted him. Sebastien turned back to Darvish. "Thank for your time, Chief Archivist Darvish. I will leave my companions in your excellent care. Have a pleasant day."

With this, he departed at speed, before Darvish lodged any further protests. Back in the stairwell he took a deep breath and tugged on his beard. "By the stars," he muttered. "I didn't know I had that in me."

CHAPTER NINETEEN
McRobbie House, Caerfaen

"What on earth?" Morgan stared, the laden fork conveying a cargo of sausage halted in mid-air. Marissa stepped into the breakfast room, laden with a mysterious burden. The thing, since he didn't have a name for it, was long, and wrapped in what to Morgan's untrained eye looked like the drapes from one of the unused bedchambers.

She held out the misshapen bundle. "It's your wedding gift, at long last."

"Um… drapes?" he ventured.

She hooted. "No, not drapes. I—well, it's such an odd shape, I didn't know what else to wrap it in. Here, take it; it's getting rather heavy. My word, I was afraid it would never be ready."

Morgan rose and relieved her of the offered…thing. "Marissa, why? I didn't get you a wedding gift."

"Of course you did." She held up her hand. "The McRobbie betrothal ring." The emerald blazed with a green fire, reflecting the flames from the hearth. "Also, you bought me—well, us—this lovely home."

"Oh. Well, yes. Not the same thing, but…" He glanced at the package in his arms. "What is it?"

"Well, open it and find out," she counseled, hopping from one foot to the other.

Morgan placed the bundle on the table, careful not to overturn any of the plates or cups, and began to unwind the concealing draperies. She must have co-opted Kevin to take down the hangings, he realized. He neared the center and touched something solid inside.

"Um, you might want to be careful with this last bit," Marissa advised. "It could be a little…well, dangerous."

"Dangerous, eh?" he repeated, gazing at the remaining wrappings. "Is this a tradition in your family or something? It's not wriggly enough to be a deadly viper or…" The last of the draperies fell away and he halted his chatter. *No, not a viper.*

On the table, in the center of the wrappings, lay a sword. The polished steel of the blade gleamed, reflecting Morgan's astonished face. An emerald, a close match to the one on her ring, was set into the pommel. Intricate designs were etched into the guard, and the grip was wrapped in a buttery soft leather.

"Do you like it?" she asked, her voice anxious.

"Like it?" Morgan stared. "I've never seen anything like it. It—" he halted what he'd been going to say, realizing *It belongs in a museum* would extinguish the excited light in her eyes. "It's magnificent," he finished. "Thank you."

He picked it up, running his hand over the blade. Not anywhere near the cutting edge, of course. He saw, from a visual inspection, the blade was honed to a razor's edge. He ran his hand over the flat of the steel, and sensed an odd frisson, almost indetectable, but there nonetheless.

"I had it made as close to the weight and dimensions of the one you use now as I could get it," she said.

Morgan's brows rose. "How did you know to do so?"

"Captain Poldane and Captain Darby were both quite helpful. How does it feel? They both said the most important thing was how the sword felt in your hand. Like an extension of your arm, I believe?"

"That's right," Morgan agreed. "If it's awkward, you're better off not even having a sword. Another fellow whose blade does feel natural will soon best you." He glanced around. "It's too crowded in here. I wouldn't want to wreck anything. Perhaps we should relocate to the morning room. A lot less breakables there, eh?"

"You're going to try it out?" Her eyes were wide with excitement.

"Well, yes, if you don't mind." He wrapped the weapon in one of its original concealing draperies. "I'll have to see to getting a sheath made for it."

"Oh, where's my head?" Marissa exclaimed. "There is a sheath, made for this blade. Both Captains Poldane and Darby were most insistent on the point. 'The sheath must fit the blade to perfection, so there's no fumbling around when drawing it'. I was so engrossed in trying to wrap the sword itself, I forgot all about the sheath. It's upstairs in my closet. I'll go fetch it."

"Later," Morgan said. He placed the sword back on the table and approached his duchess. "Thank you, my love. It is a magnificent gift." He took her in his arms, and her eyes blazed.

Later, when due appreciation had been expressed, they strolled together into the morning room. Sunlight poured in through the windows, bathing the azure-tinted walls in a cheerful light. Morgan moved chairs back against the far wall. He also placed a small, spindle-legged table which tended to leap out and trip him, with no provocation whatsoever, into the hall. The table contrived to look morose at this unjust banishment. He ignored it.

"Now," he said, unwrapping the sword again. "Let's see what we have here, shall we?" He closed his hand over the grip.

"Hmm," he said.

"Is something wrong?"

He shook his head. "Just the opposite, in fact. It fits my hand to perfection. If you'll stand back so I can test it out? I shouldn't like to risk slicing off anything I might have an interest in later." He arched a brow.

With an answering grin which augured well for "later" she took refuge behind the somewhat tenuous protection of a wing chair and accompanying footstool. Morgan raised the blade in the classic salute. With a cry of "Have at, varlets." He launched a flurry of thrusts, cuts, ripostes, and parries. The blade was a blur of flashing steel, smooth as silk and going where he intended before he'd formed the thought. He whirled again, fighting off more unseen opponents, the sword one with his arm.

He halted at last, lowering the weapon, and turned to face Marissa. Her mouth hung open in an "O." Her eyes were wide, one hand pressed to her bosom.

"Something wrong?" he inquired.

She shook herself. "Wrong? Oh, my. No, not at all. I—I guess I've never seen you in action with a sword before. Your exhibition was quite frightening. And also quite exhilarating." She eyed him with a speculative gaze. "It's like a sensual dance. Not something they'd allow at any cotillion I've ever attended."

Morgan grinned. "It is, in a way. Of course, I'm sure it looks quite different when there's another chap with a sword of his own, intent on running you through before you do him."

"All right, spoil it, why don't you?" She laughed. "But be warned. I shall keep this in mind."

"A threat, or a promise?" He struck a pose with the sword.

She eyed him as a cat might an unguarded pitcher of cream. "I'll let you decide," she purred.

CHAPTER TWENTY
Wizards' Archives, Caerfaen

"Well?" Saia gestured to the overwhelming mass of books, scrolls, and documents. "Where do we begin?"

"What are you searching for?" inquired Darvish, the head archivist.

"I am sorry, Archivist," Alain said. "We are not allowed to reveal the subject of our search to anyone. By the king's orders."

Darvish sputtered. "These are my archives, I'll have you know."

Saia favored him with a dazzling smile. "And do you wish us to relate this fact to the Chief Wizard and King Rhys?"

Darvish deflated.

Wishing to keep on his good side, since they would be using the archives for the foreseeable future, Alain said, "We will be spending most of our time going through the catalog. Our search may take several days, I'm afraid. However, I don't believe we should need any major assistance from your busy staff for at least a couple of days."

"Very well. Let me know and I will assign someone to assist you when you are ready." With this, Darvish turned in a swirl of robes and departed.

"You were most diplomatic," Saia said with approval once the archivist was out of earshot. "I would have told him to go away and leave us to our task."

"Which is why you are a princess, and I am a mere archivist."

"You are making fun of me."

"Never," he replied stoutly. "But come, let us to our work. I was serious when I told Darvish our task will take days. Days?" He stared around the room. "It may take us weeks."

"Tell me what to do," she said. "You are in your element. Me, I have no idea what to do, or even how to begin."

"Each book and document contained in the archives is recorded," Alain explained. "Otherwise this place would be sheer chaos. No one would know where anything was, or even what is here. It would be like searching for one particular grain of sand in the desert."

"This catalog you spoke of?"

"Yes," he said. "There are multiple catalogs. One lists each item by its title. Another by the name of the author. A third lists items based on their subject matter. And each entry will tell where the particular grain of sand—a book or scroll, in our case—is located in the archives."

Saia gaped at him. "It must take an army of men to keep up with such a task."

Alain smiled. "A small army, but yes. Well, in Arvindir, a small army. Here?" He gave a rueful shrug. "A much larger one here, I dare say."

"All right, our task seems straightforward," Saia said. "We need to search in this catalog for any books or scrolls having to do with Thundermist, no?"

He shook his head. "If it were so easy, someone would have discovered the connection between Thundermist and magic long ago. Chief Wizard Sebastien told me he has spent a good deal of time researching the subject, to no avail. Of course, your question is where we should begin. It is possible we may by chance find some reference no one has noticed before. But I fear we will have to be more creative."

"Oh." Saia appeared less eager.

Well, nothing for it. He squared his shoulders. "In addition," he continued, "we need to be circumspect. If we request every item which references Thundermist, someone will figure out what we're seeking. So we need to intersperse other items in our search."

"Does it matter?" she asked.

"Both Sebastien and King Rhys indicated a need for discretion in our inquiries. So yes, I reckon it does matter."

"Mmph. This is going to be horribly tedious, isn't it?"

He grinned. "Think of how much you will learn, reading through all these books."

"I was right," she sighed. "Tedious in the extreme. Very well, lead me to this catalog, and let us begin the tedium."

The catalogs were everything Alain might have hoped for. He set Saia to searching for references to Kilbourne's waterways and seas. He, in turn, scanned for mentions of Thundermist, which were in short supply.

Saia showed him several cards she had pulled. "Good," he said, adding his own meager offerings to the pile. "Let's request these. We can keep searching for more, until these are retrieved."

"What should I search for now? Magic, perhaps?"

Alain smiled. "This is the wizards' archives. You'd find enough references to magic to keep you reading for a lifetime."

"Oh."

She was so downcast, he took her hand. "Your Highness, I didn't—"

She interrupted him. "No, Alain. Here, I am not 'Your Highness.' I am Saia Varenzi, nothing more."

"But you are a princess," he protested.

"In Arvindir, yes, I was. I left any claim to royalty behind me when we fled with the duchess. And when I killed Azim. There is no going back, Alain."

"What about your father?"

Saia shrugged one eloquent shoulder. "What about him? He will wonder, of course, what became of Azim. He was a son, a most powerful mage, and ruler of the city of Arvindir. But my father, he will never know for sure. Azim is at the bottom of the sea, with none but the fish for company. No one besides we few who were there will ever know the truth. And me? I do not think my father will concern himself. I am— was—a mere daughter, something to be bargained away in an arranged marriage to solidify an alliance. Nothing more."

Alain squeezed her hand. "You are much more. And if I call you 'princess,' it is because to me you remain a princess, a woman of great worth."

"You are sweet, Alain. If there were not all these musty old archivists around us, I might even kiss you."

He grinned. "By all means, let us hasten to complete our task, and remove ourselves from the prying eyes of these 'musty old archivists'."

Grabbing the stack of cards, he handed them to a nearby clerk. "Bring us these, if you will," he said. Once the clerk departed on his mission, he led Saia to an open table away from the bustle of the room. When he was certain no eyes were turned their way, he bestowed a kiss upon her hand.

CHAPTER TWENTY-ONE

Ervantium

"Well, now, Wyvrndell," Petrandius rumbled, sounding like the end of a distant avalanche. "Did you manage to retrieve Erkarna's notes?"

"No, Your Majesty," he replied. "Someone—human or dragon, I do not know which—was there before us. Almost everything was gone by the time we reached the workshop."

"Indeed? Most unfortunate. However, I note you said 'almost everything.' I take it you did find something of use to you?"

"Oh yes. The thief missed what I have to consider the most important thing of all: the scroll containing the ritual Erkarna devised for the acquisition of magic. Aireantha discovered it half buried among the rubble, from when Lady Marissa defeated him."

"Good, good. This will aid you in your quest to grant magic to the rest of dragonkind, will it not?"

"It will. It is my belief Erkarna perverted his own ritual, in order to wrest Lady Marissa's powers from her. I will need to study the scroll in great detail. If what I suspect is true, the ritual itself should be safe to use."

"Excellent. You have done well, Wyvrndell. I was sure you would."

"Thank you, Your Majesty. It is not a certainty, but I am hopeful I shall be successful. It will take some time, of course. I do not wish to make a mistake with the ritual."

"No, of course not." Petrandius nodded. "Is there more you wish to report?"

Wyvrndell sensed a rogue hiccough rise within him. He was unable to control it and a loud "Urp" escaped, along with a puff of blue smoke.

"I beg your pardon, Your Majesty," he said, mortified. I—"

"No matter," Petrandius replied. "Tell me what agitates you so."

Wyvrndell drew himself up and gazed into the king's eyes. "We found one other scroll, an ancient one. I examined it when we returned to Ervantium. It is a history of the early days of dragons. I believe it to have been crafted by Grythorn himself."

The king regarded him with a speculative gleam in his eyes. "A treasure indeed, if true," he said. "And you have read it, you say?"

"I—I have." The words came tumbling out, running into each other. "It—" he fought down another hiccough and lost. It hung in the air between them. "You knew, didn't you?" he said at last.

"Knew what?" The king's tone was mild, but Wyvrndell did not mistake the keenness of his interest.

"Knew the first dragons were created by Dwarf mages," Wyvrndell blurted.

Petrandius sighed. He appeared even older somehow, as if the weight of centuries had crashed down upon him. At last, he spoke. "Yes, I knew," he said in a voice so soft Wyvrndell could hardly hear it. "I have known for ages untold, Wyvrndell. Grythorn himself, my sire's sire, told me. I have always kept the knowledge a secret. Now…"

Wyvrndell shook his head. "Only Aireantha, Wyzandar, and I know the contents of the scroll, Your Majesty. No one else. If you say so, we will destroy it, and never reveal its existence to any dragon. This I vow."

"You understand why, do you not?"

"Yes, I believe I do. To unleash such knowledge would in all likelihood set off a conflict from which there would be no turning back. It would, if I am correct, spell the end of the world."

"I fear you are correct." Petrandius's voice was tinged with sorrow. "But tell me, young Wyvrndell. Why did you come to me with this knowledge?"

Wyvrndell took a deep breath and let it out again. "Because, Your Majesty, if I was wrong, and you were not aware of the contents of the scroll, you needed to know. You are our king. Knowledge is your most valuable tool, and your most potent weapon."

Petrandius gazed upon him with ancient, unfathomable eyes. "You are wise to recognize this, Wyvrndell. There is more to it, though, is there not?"

"Yes, Your Majesty. Because I was certain you did already

know, and I needed you to understand I also possessed this knowledge. You needed to be aware, in order to decide your course of action. So you could, if you deemed it necessary to preserve this secret, decree my death, and Aireantha's. And my sire's."

"And you were willing to take this risk? The three of you?"

"We are," Wyvrndell said, staring into the king's eyes again. "We have discussed the matter at great length. We understand how important this is."

"Do you indeed? I wonder..." Petrandius closed his eyes and lowered his head. Wyvrndell waited, not daring to speak. What would the judgement be?

After a time, the old dragon opened his eyes again. Wyvrndell observed in them a glint which hinted at a younger, stronger Petrandius. He took a deep breath and asked, "What is your decree, my lord?"

"I do not think such drastic actions will be quite necessary, Wyvrndell. I can find no reason to do away with you or the lovely Aireantha in order to maintain this secret. Nor your sire, either, annoying as he can be at times."

Wyvrndell let out a steam-laden breath he hadn't realized he was holding. "Thank you, Your Majesty," he said.

"You may not thank me, Wyvrndell." Petrandius gave him a toothy smile. "I have another fate in mind for you."

This time he didn't even try to control his hiccoughs. "What is your decree, my king?" he asked through the cloud of blue fog.

"All in good time," Petrandius said. "All in good time."

CHAPTER TWENTY-TWO
The Devil's Teeth

Toby's sleep had been sporadic at best. He'd woken often due to the throbbing ache in his shoulder. Still, he was lucky. The arrow hadn't severed anything vital, and he was able to move his arm, albeit with a bit of judicious cursing and wincing. At least the arrow pierced his right shoulder, for which he supposed he should be grateful.

At dawn Toni arrived to change the bandage and re-apply the poultice of herbs to his wound. Its scent, while both soothing and refreshing, didn't do a thing to negate the pain. Still, he'd done what needed to be done. Toni was alive, and Radivan considered him a hero.

"It is getting much better," Toni reported. "Another day and you should be able to go without the poultice. Would you like some tea?"

"What I would like," he said, "is a cup of strong coffee the size of this wagon. Failing coffee, yes, tea would be wonderful, thank you."

She laughed, and the sound was like water chuckling over rocks in a stream. "Tea is much better for you. I tried coffee once. It tasted like someone tossed the ashes from the fire into a cup, added hot water, and sprinkled a bunch of dirt over the whole thing to give it a little extra flavor."

It was Toby's turn to laugh. "Very well, tea it shall be." She set about brewing it over a tiny brazier, and he asked, "What did your mother say?"

"She said I should have stuck with tea, and it served me right."

He barked out another laugh. "No, I meant what did she say concerning you and me? Her telling me she'd seen a way forward."

Toni's mouth quirked down at the corners. "She was most

evasive. When I pressed her, she said there was nothing I needed to know. Things would happen in their own time, or they wouldn't."

"Hmm. Less than no answer at all, if you ask me."

"That's what I told her. But she smiled in the infuriating, enigmatic way she has and refused to speak any further on the matter."

"When she read my hand the second time, she claimed she had the answer. Have you ever known her to be wrong?"

"No, I haven't. Although I don't know if she would tell me if she was…"

"Well, we'll have to be patient, and wait for whatever manages to present itself, eh?"

She handed him a steaming cup. "I don't want to be patient. I—oh, perhaps we could run off together or something."

"What?" Toby squawked, nearly spilling the cup of tea. "Are you mad? Better you call back the chap with the poisoned arrows, will you? He'd be much preferable, I'm sure, to your father if we tried such a thing."

"Hmph." She gave a fierce scowl which soon melted into a fond grin. "Oh well, perhaps you are right."

"Trust me. In this, I'm right. I have faith in Elbethesba. If she says she saw a way, there is a way. That notion alone cheers me no end. I was certain I had no hope at all."

Toni sighed. "I suppose."

Toby set the teacup down and took her hand in his. "Toni, we barely know each other. I may have been a pirate, but even in those days I did my level best to act with honor. So let's wait and see what develops. Who knows? You might meet some dashing young Tzigani with flashing eyes and a sweeping moustache and forget all about me."

"Ha," she replied. "Now, drink your tea."

Later, after she departed, the sounds of the camp being struck filtered through the open window. Soon Radivan stuck his head in through the open door. "Ah, good, you're awake."

"And feeling human again. Although I'd fight another band of bandits for a chance at a bath."

Radivan roared with laughter. "Tonight, perhaps, but we will hope without the bandits. The place we are bound for has a nice stream, good for washing. It is, however, a mountain stream, mind you."

"So, ice water is what you're telling me." Toby grinned. "Just you let me at it."

The Tzigani nodded. "My wife, she says some clean mountain air and sunshine would be good for you. Can you manage clambering onto your horse?"

"I can try. I might need help, but I'm not too proud to ask for it. It sounds marvelous to be somewhere besides this bed."

"Excellent. I'll leave you to get dressed and be back in a few minutes."

Toby was never quite certain how he managed to get out of the nightshirt—who it belonged to he had no idea—and into his pants. He found a clean shirt which some thoughtful soul had taken from his saddlebags, and shimmied into it. The prospect of bending over to pull on his boots was daunting, but he was able to stomp his feet into them after a couple of tries.

"Hmm. I feel like a new man," he muttered. His arm twinged in pain, reminding him he was the same idiot, with the same hole through him.

Emerging from the wagon onto the back platform, he found his horse saddled and tethered there. "Brilliant," he said, and from his position on the platform, he heaved himself, with no grace whatsoever, into the saddle.

Radivan cantered up on his coal-black mount. "Well done, Fanshawe. My wife, she says a bit of movement will be good for your shoulder, so it doesn't stiffen up on you. Can you manage it?"

"Oh, I'll be fine," Toby lied. His shoulder ached like mad, but it was good to be up and around. "We'll see how long it lasts."

"Not past lunchtime," Radivan said with firm assurance. "So I was instructed."

"Eminently sensible," Toby agreed.

"Elbethesba, she is always sensible. Which is why she married me, eh? For what could be more sensible?" He uttered a hearty laugh, shook up the reins, and trotted off toward the head of the line of wagons.

A young Tzigani rode up. It took a moment, but Toby recognized him. "You're Arnot, right? You brought me stew the other day."

Arnot's teeth flashed white in his swarthy face. "I am," he said. "Captain Radivan instructed me to ride with you, and make sure you do not overtax yourself this first day out."

"I shall be pleased to have your company."

"Good. Ah, we are starting." A loud whistle went up from the head of the column of wagons, and the first one set off. Toby edged his mount out of the way as, one by one, the wagons rolled out. The final one, he noted, contained the large, shaggy shape of the Tzigani's dancing bear.

"They tell me," Arnot said while their mounts plodded along next to the caravan, "you sailed a ship upon the sea. What was it like?"

Toby whiled away a pleasant morning regaling Arnot with tales of life aboard ship. There wasn't much in the way of scenery to distract them: merely rocks piled upon more rocks, with a bare tree tossed in here and there to break the monotony. A chill breeze whistled through the fissures in the rocks, similar to the wind through the rigging of a ship, and while many might have found the sound mournful, to Toby it was comforting.

"In a way, this life isn't so different," he said at last. "Except your vessels have wheels instead of sails. Even so, you go wherever the winds of fortune take you, no?"

"Well, yes…" Arnot didn't sound convinced. Toby glanced up. Radivan approached them.

"How is your arm?" asked the Tzigani.

"Sore, but otherwise fine."

"Good. Ride up with me, will you? I want to show you something, get your opinion."

"Of course." Toby nodded farewell to Arnot and followed Radivan toward the front of the caravan. He couldn't fathom why the Tzigani chieftain would want his opinion on anything whatsoever. Regardless, he was game to give it a go if Radivan wished it. He brought his horse to a halt when the other man did, then glanced around.

"Two peaks westward," Radivan said, pointing. Toby squinted, trying to see what he was supposed to be looking at.

He blinked, trying to clear his vision against the distant mountains. He sucked in a breath when he comprehended what Radivan was showing him. "Oh, my lord," he muttered, reaching into his saddlebag. He hauled out his old spyglass—one of the few things he'd brought along from his previous life—and put it to his eye.

"Rhuddlani troops," he said when the scene came into focus. His chest went tight, and his heart was racing.

"Yes. The scouts alerted me to their movements a little while ago."

Toby put the glass to his eye again, watched for a moment, and offered it to Radivan.

"This is marvelous," said the Tzigani, once Toby had given him a quick course in how to use the glass. "It's like being right among them. I shall have to get myself one of these." He scrutinized the soldiers for a bit longer. "There certainly are a lot of them," he said. "Not a scouting party." He handed the spyglass back to Toby.

"Not a scouting party," Toby agreed. "Coming south like this? On the march through the high pass, at this time of year? An invasion force, or I'm a Dwarf. They're heading for Kilbourne."

"Yes, that's what I thought. I'm glad to have you confirm my opinion."

Toby swore. "I've got to get to Caerfaen. Warn Commander McRobbie…"

"You, my friend, are not going anywhere," Radivan said. He placed a restraining hand on Toby's arm.

Toby tried to shake it off, but Radivan's grip was not to be budged. "But—"

"Captain Fanshawe, listen to me. You are in no condition to make such a journey. Besides, I have an agreement with McRobbie, against such an eventuality. One of my men will go to deliver this unwelcome news."

Toby brought the spyglass up again. The line of Rhuddlani soldiers appeared to stretch on into infinity. "Tell him to hurry," he growled.

CHAPTER TWENTY-THREE

Wizards' Archives, Caerfaen

"Alain," Saia called. "I've found something. I think."

He'd been flipping through an interminable number of references to shipping. Thundermist was mentioned a few times, but when he'd scanned the actual documents, they were notes regarding merchant vessels lost to the vagaries of the mist. Interesting, but unhelpful for their purposes.

Abandoning this fruitless line of inquiry, he hastened to her side. "What have you found?"

She pointed a slim finger at the card lying before her on the table. The writing was ancient, faded, and more illegible than not. "If I am reading this right, it might have something to do with the Thundermist."

Squinting, Alain held the card up. Illumined by the lamp, he was able to make out the words: "Magical Mist."

"Hmmm." He strained to make out the rest of the words scrawled on the card by some ancient archivist. "It appears you have. Well done, princ—my lady. If I can manage to decipher the rest, we can request this record…"

"It is so old," Saia said. "I'm amazed I was even able to recognize it."

Alain nodded, though he was distracted by trying to decipher the words swimming before his eyes. He turned the faded card this way and that, in an attempt to make out any further details. Like the title, or at the least, part of the reference number. "I think—no, it's too faded, I can barely make it out. Hmm. 'On', the first word is 'on.' The next word starts with a 'D,' then something indecipherable. Next, I can make out 'fish.' The final word is—" he squinted again, trying to focus. "Magpies? No, that can't be right."

"Here, let me see." Saia took the card from him. Closing one eye, she focused in on the scrawled words. "I think the last word is 'mages,' Alain. Which would make sense, if this document does refer to the magical Thundermist."

Alain peered at the card. "I believe you've got it," he said. "I knew it couldn't be magpies, although it did make for some interesting conjectures. All right, what about the middle word? Can you suss that one out too?"

"Mmm, it's so very faded. I—I think, 'Dwarfish', perhaps?" Saia suggested. "On Dwarfish Mages?"

"Why not? Makes as much sense as anything else. The only other word I could come up with was 'dogfish,' and I'm certain they don't have mages among them."

"Are you sure?" Saia's glance was sly. "Perhaps they go to school for it?"

Alain groaned. "I refuse to acknowledge you even said such a thing. 'School for it,' indeed. Horrible, simply horrible. I thought better of you, my lady. Are there no depths to which you will not sink?"

She grinned at him. "You will have to wait and see. In the meantime, can we request this most interesting—what is it, a book, a scroll?"

"I'm not sure," he said. "But between the title, and the little bit I can make out of the reference number, we'll see what the clerk delivers."

The clerk, when summoned, took the request without comment and went in search of the document. "We should keep searching," Alain said. "We still have a few million cards to review."

"I'm certain King Rhys was merely trying to keep me occupied and not bothering him," she replied. "It's working. But I'm glad to be doing something useful. I've never been useful before. Also, I am glad be doing something with you, Alain."

Alain's reply was cut short by the advent of another person. The clerk, with their book already? He glanced up to observe the Chief Archivist approaching, his beard quivering. "Oh bother," Alain muttered. "We may have a problem." The Chief Archivist was waving a slip of paper clutched in his hand. Most likely the request slip Alain had filled out. "Brace yourself," he muttered to Saia. "He doesn't appear happy."

"Hmph," she snorted. "Neither am I."

"Well, this should be fun." Alain rolled his eyes.

"What is the meaning of this?" Darvish rattled the request slip at

Alain.

Alain took a breath, steeling himself, then let it out. Though he had no standing here, he did have the backing of both the king and the chief wizard, and so was prepared to assert himself. *Which will do me no harm in Saia's eyes.* "I thought it fairly obvious, Chief Archivist Darvish. It is an archival request. One of several we have submitted. Is this item, perhaps, missing from your archives?"

Alain allowed himself an internal grin. He'd presented Darvish with a pretty dilemma. He was certain the archivist would love to proclaim the item they'd requested was unable to be located. This desire would be at odds with his instinctual need to prove the accuracy and efficiency of the archives. He'd seen this before.

Darvish scowled. "No, it's not missing. At least I don't imagine it is. No one has gone searching for it yet."

Alain folded his arms and attempted to look down his nose at the archivist. This was difficult, since Darvish towered over him by a good five inches. Still, it was all a matter of attitude. "Whyever not?" he demanded imperiously.

"Josiah, who took your request, saw from the reference number this title is housed in the secured area. The enhanced security area, in fact. He brought the request to me to authorize. Which I do not. Not without an excellent reason."

Alain opened his mouth to argue, but Saia beat him to the punch. "Chief Archivist," she said. "Do you recall who I am?"

He turned a disdainful eye on her. Alain was certain the man loathed having a woman in the archives. He'd seen similar reactions before. "Yes, I do," Darvish snapped. "Some minor royal from across the sea. You have no standing here in Kilbourne. Certainly not in my archives."

He returned his attention to Alain, dismissing the pesky princess. Who was not about to be dismissed in so cavalier a fashion. "Minor royal?" she said, her voice tinged with a mixture of pity and amusement. "My good archivist, I am Princess Saia of Parthane, only daughter of King Radagav. I was dispatched to Kilbourne on a mission for my father. Your own King Rhys was gracious enough to agree. He in turn sent me to Master Sebastien, your Chief Wizard."

This last part, at least, was nothing less than gospel truth. Alain smiled to himself again, enjoying Darvish's obvious discomfort.

"My mission," Saia went on, practically nose to nose with the archivist, "was of some importance to my father. Important enough for him to convince King Rhys of its urgency, so he dispatched Duke Morgan and the Royal Enchantress to bring me here on the back of a dragon. Important enough for King Rhys, through Chief Wizard Sebastien, to explain to you we were to be given free access to anything we needed contained within your archives."

She tapped him on the chest with a slim finger. "And despite all this, you say you need good reasons before you consider allowing us to view this book, or scroll, or whatever this particular document may be."

Darvish, grasping at his one chance to save face, said, "Ha. You don't even know what it is you've requested."

Saia wasn't going to allow herself to be sidetracked. "Because you are refusing to produce it, you officious toady. I shall have to report to the Chief Wizard, who will report to the King, who will be forced to tell my father my mission was a failure, all because you determined to thwart me."

Darvish's scowl deepened. Alain figured he must have concluded he held a losing hand, and it didn't take the archivist long to acknowledge the fact. "Your Highness, if this is of such import to you, of course you may view this item. Though you will have to be accompanied by a senior member of my staff."

"Is this item laden with dire spells?" Alain asked.

Darvish shook his head. "Not to my knowledge. It is simply too rare to be allowed free usage. It is the sole copy of this work in existence."

Saia appeared ready to reply, but Alain got in first this time. This was, after all, his field of expertise. "Chief Archivist, I am not inexperienced in such things. I was Head Underarchivist in Arvindir. Our archives there could never rival yours in terms of size. Even so, we did possess a great many rare and ancient documents. I understand your concerns and can assure you we will treat this item with due care and reverence."

Darvish knew when he was beaten. "Very well," he sniffed. "I will assign someone to escort you to the secure storage area."

"Thank you for your kind consideration." Saia proffered a smile to the archivist, but Alain recognized the smile of a wolf who has made a tasty meal of its prey. He managed to keep from laughing aloud, but it was a close thing.

Darvish turned on his heel and strode off.

"You Highness, you were magnificent," Alain said.

"Bah. I am used to dealing with overbearing boors like him."

He took one of her hands in his. "I meant,' he said, eyes crinkling with mirth, "you are a most magnificent liar."

"Who, me? Why Alain, you wound me. Every word I spoke was true. Well, except the bits I told him regarding my father." She shrugged one elegant shoulder. "I won't tell him if you won't."

"My lips are sealed," he promised.

At the mention of lips, hers curved into a lazy smile, and her eyes glittered. She leaned toward him…

…As a clerk bustled in. They jerked apart, and a flush rose to Alain's hairline. "Follow me," the clerk directed. Alain turned to pick up paper and pencil, but their guide said, "No, leave it here. You are not allowed to bring anything with you into the secure areas of the archives."

Saia appeared ready to argue the point. "He is right," Alain said. "The rules were the same in Arvindir, for items in secure areas. We will simply have to remember the things we see and read."

"I will bow to your expertise," she said, and together they followed the clerk through the archives proper and into a stairwell.

"The secure archives are three levels below," their guide said.

"Thank you," Alain replied. "If it's not too presumptuous, what is your name?"

"Willum," he replied, and led them downward.

To Alain's surprise, the stairway was well lit. In Arvindir, no one bothered to waste time or oil to keep lamps burning in a little used area. One carried one's own lamp. But on a closer inspection, he noted the lamps used no oil. They were, in fact, burning with no source of fuel: magical lamps. Which made sense, considering this was the archives of the Royal College of Wizards.

"How often does someone have to cast a spell to keep the lamps lit?" he asked.

"Three times each day," Willum replied, seeming eager to impart information at the least prompting. "A junior wizard in training to become an archivist sees to it. Once at six bells in the morn, another at two in the afternoon, and again at ten in the evening. Not the same one each time," he added. "There are a fair number of junior wizards in residence, and they are assigned according to their own preferences. Some, like me, are early risers; others prefer to labor long into the night."

"Thank you," said Alain. "I myself was an archivist in Arvindir, across the sea. Though in Arvindir there were few wizards in residence, and we resorted to using normal lamps or candles."

Willum clucked his tongue in sympathy. "Open flames and soot are terrible for the books," he said. "That's the marvelous thing about these lamps. They give off a lovely bit of light, but there's no actual flame. The glow is generated by the spell."

"Incredible," said Alain, and meant it. "A marvelous advancement."

They arrived at last at the bottom of the stairs. A door blocked their way. Willum uttered words too low for Alain to hear. It must have been a spell of some kind, for the door shuddered, and bolts clattered as they retracted on the other side. When all was quiet again, Willum pushed the door open and ushered Alain and Saia inside, to a small alcove, where another door barred their progress.

"Now I must leave you," Willum said. "Someone else will escort you from here. "Oh, you will need this." He handed Alain the archival request slip.

"We will be allowed to access what we need?" Saia asked.

Willum nodded. "The fact you have gotten this far means you are authorized to be here. Also, your request has been initialed by the Chief Archivist himself. You should encounter no obstacles." He turned to go, but over his shoulder said, "May your quest be fruitful."

"Thank you, Willum," they replied in unison.

He exited the little antechamber. The door closed behind him, and the bolts began to slide inexorably back into place. Alain found Saia's hand in his, warm and trembling.

"I don't like this place," she said. "What if no one comes to let us out. What if—"

Alain took her other hand and gazed into her eyes. "No matter what, at least we will be together."

She squeezed his hands, and her voice, when she spoke, was throaty. "Who knew?"

"What?"

"One expects archivists to be dry and dusty, like the tomes they care for. Not to be…well, romantic." She arched a brow.

This required either much too long a response, or none at all. And anything he might have said or done was forestalled by a grinding noise which announced the opening of the inner door. He settled for lifting both of her hands and kissing each of them. This had apparently been the correct response, for her eyes shone like stars.

With a thud, the bolts in the inner door ceased their movement, and the door swung open.

Within, there was total darkness.

CHAPTER TWENTY-FOUR
The Devil's Teeth

Toby groaned. At Elbethesba's direction, he made another effort to lift his arm above his head. The healing wound protested, but he made it.

"Good," said Elbethesba. "Again."

He did it again, and once more at her urging. "If the wound doesn't open up, you should be fine." She examined his shoulder and nodded to herself. "It is holding. Toni did excellent work."

Toby struggled back into his shirt. It made him uncomfortable to be in such a state of undress before this woman, though she appeared to take no notice. Once he was fully clothed again, Elbethesba said, "Well, Captain Fanshawe."

"Yes, My Lady?"

"I am certain Toni informed you of our conversation regarding you."

"She did," Toby acknowledged. "Although she believed, like I do, you could have been much more forthcoming."

Elbethesba smiled. "I had my reasons."

"Oh, I don't doubt it in the least. I imagine there is little you do which does not have a good reason behind it."

Her smile remained, but he sensed a hint of something else in her eyes. Pain, perhaps? Unease? "What?" he asked. "What's wrong?"

She shook her head. "Nothing, Captain Fanshawe. I understand both you and Toni would like me to explain what I saw in your hand which gave me hope for your future. I'm sorry, but I cannot. Or at least, should not."

Toby huffed out a sigh. Elbethesba's smile was wan. She said, "Know this, Captain Fanshawe. Were I to tell you, it might alter things I have seen foreshadowed. I do not imagine you would want to take the chance."

"No," he replied. "I wouldn't." *Any chance at all, no matter how slight is better than none.* This was the way he'd operated as a pirate, and he saw no reason to change his ways. *Seize the opportunity when it's before you.* Wasn't that why he was here traveling with the Tzigani in the first place?

"Very well, Captain."

Toby sat in silence, considering the Tzigani woman's words. "Elbethesba," he said at last, "I understand the best thing I can do is trust in your vision and understanding. If I may, I will continue to travel with you, and hope for the best."

"A wise decision," she replied. "You cannot run from fate. In one sense, you are not so unlike us, Toby Fanshawe. We Tzigani call no place home. And here you are, a man also without a home, eh?"

"How—how did you know?" Toby asked. There was a sudden catch in his chest at her words.

"I told you before, I know you better than you know yourself. Your father, he is the reason for this, is he not?"

Toby clamped his jaw, not wanting to answer. Not wishing to acknowledge the pain her words brought crashing into his memory. "He is," he said when his throat loosened enough to speak. "He banished me. He was Royal Navy, and it was impossible for him to countenance my becoming a pirate."

"You never told him the truth?"

"What? Told him I was a privateer, with a letter of marque from the king himself? I don't see how it would have mattered in the least. No, not him. He would have still felt I dishonored him and his legacy. He couldn't bear the sight of me. Nor I him, truth be told. It was not a pleasant leave-taking." His mouth tightened at the memory, and his hands clenched into fists of their own volition.

She nodded, steepling her fingers. "No, I think you are right. And your mother? What of her?"

Toby managed a rueful smile. He forced himself to relax, flexing his stiffened fingers. "She came to visit me several times after my father and I had our little disagreement. She was forced to sneak out of the house to do so. She told me how she called him a right fool, to his face. She, at least—well, she understood why I charted the course I did."

"Are both your parents alive?"

"My father is. He'll likely live forever. Heaven doesn't want him, and I imagine Hell is afraid he'll take over."

"And what of your mother?"

"She got her fill of his bullyragging, told him to go to the devil, and left. She went back to her people, in Cormaine. I've not heard from her in a couple of years, but I have to assume she's still among the living."

"Cormaine, eh? Hmm. What was her name, your mother? Her name before she married?"

Toby's brows rose at this. He didn't know why this mattered to Elbethesba in the least. His family troubles were none of her business. He didn't know why he'd told her even this much. But he credited her with having good reasons for her questions. He relented, and said, "Her name is Magdalyna. Magdalyna Rabisi. She went by Maggie, though. She never liked to have her given name used."

"And I'm sure your father must have hated it." Elbethesba's smile, when it spread across her lips, was unreadable. "Thank you, Captain," she said. "I know you believe me impertinent in the extreme. So be it. Now, go and find Radivan. I sense he wishes your company and counsel."

Toby rose from his seat. He bowed to his hostess and went in search of the Tzigani chief.

CHAPTER TWENTY-FIVE
Ervantium

Wyvrndell craned his neck to glance around the cavernous chamber. Along with a host of other dragons, he awaited the arrival of King Petrandius. The scent of dragons permeated the cavern, sooty, sulphureous, and comforting. Wyvrndell had learned, to his surprise, his human friends often found the smell of a dragon off-putting. Morgan McRobbie and Lady Marissa had both come to tolerate, if not necessarily enjoy, his scent. He'd noticed the noses of other humans he'd come into contact with wrinkle at his presence. Ah well, no accounting for taste. He didn't think much of human's scent either. Even so, he counted several of them friends and was willing to make allowances.

Wyzandar, his sire, was standing at attention to the right of the king's stone bench. Observing protocol, of course, since Wyzandar was Petrandius's most senior and trusted councilor. The other councilors also waited on the dais.

Including Jakarian, Wyvrndell observed with a stifled growl. The old dragon had fought fang and talon against his every effort to help bring dragons into a new place in the world. Wyvrndell hadn't seen or heard mention of Jakarian since his return from Erkarna's cavern. Which, Wyvrndell decided, was all to the good.

As if he sensed the force of Wyvrndell's gaze, Jakarian turned to stare right at him. The older dragon's eyes held a gleam of malice.

"He hates you," Aireantha murmured. "You can tell, by the way he glares at you."

"I know." Wyvrndell sighed, returning Jakarian's stare unflinching. The older dragon turned away at last, and Wyvrndell tried to calm himself. The comforting presence of Aireantha was the one thing keeping him from turning tail and dashing out of the great hall. She twined her tail around his for a moment, and some of his anger and frustration faded. Petrandius entered the chamber, heralded by bugles from his accompanying guard dragons. Wyvrndell focused his attention on the ancient king.

The black-scaled dragon ascended to the dais, seeming to struggle to make his way up the stairs. Foregoing the stone bench which was the king's place of honor, Petrandius stood, surveying the assemblage crowding the hall.

"He looks so old," Aireantha said. "And so very tired."

"Father says he's unimaginably ancient," Wyvrndell replied. "Petrandius himself told me he is a direct descendant from the line of Grythorn. His sire's sire, he said. So it's no wonder—"

He halted his comments, for Petrandius had begun to speak. "My dragons, I grow old," the king said, and even his voice sounded weary. "I have been your king for countless ages. Now, my time draws to a close."

A rumbling from the assembled dragons shook the cavern. Protestations, affirmations, and even a few muffled cheers. Petrandius ignored them all. He went on, "Yet even as my reign nears its end, I have come to realize something of vital import, which I have left undone."

He paused, and a hush fell over the dragons. Wyvrndell glanced at Aireantha in confusion, but she appeared as baffled as he was. At last, the king spoke again. "I have no heir."

A gasp echoed around the great hall, bouncing off the stone walls in waves of consternation. The dragons stared at their king in wild surmise. A low muttering began, dragon after dragon coming to realize what the king was saying.

Petrandius spoke over the din. "Yes, I have failed you in this regard. However, I intend to remedy the situation. It is much too late for me to take a mate, even had I a mind to do so. My days draw short, I fear, and time is slipping away. I have thus decided, for the good of the kingdom, I must name my successor to the throne of Grythorn."

The hubbub continued unabated. Petrandius gazed around at the assembly, searching with clouded eyes from dragon to dragon. He rested his gaze upon Jakarian and halted his survey. Wyvrndell sighed in disgust, a covert plume of smoke issuing from his snout when the old Councilor began to preen under the king's regard. "No surprise there," he muttered to Aireantha. "Although he'd be better off picking Wyzandar."

Aireantha shushed him, for Petrandius had begun speaking

again. "I have deliberated at great length to determine who is best suited to lead us into the new age we face," the king said. "There were many excellent candidates among my councilors." Petrandius's head swiveled to regard the dragons flanking him. Jakarian, Wyvrndell noted, continued to preen mightily.

"Who do you think he's picked?" Aireantha whispered.

"Wyzandar, I hope," Wyvrndell murmured back. The king continued to survey his councilors. "But look at Jakarian. He's sure he'll be the new king."

"Ugh," was Aireantha's response. It was, to Wyvrndell's way of thinking, the correct one.

Petrandius spoke again. "My people, this was a difficult decision, and not one I undertook lightly. Whoever rules once I am gone will need to be both cunning and wise. For the world is changing, is it not? And dragons must change with it or lose our place. Thus, I have at long last decided my course."

Bile filled Wyvrndell's throat and his gut rumbled in rebellion. Jakarian edged forward from among his fellow councilors. Wyvrndell fought the urge to belch forth a hiccough. To succumb would be the supreme embarrassment. He concentrated on controlling himself and missed the king's next words.

"Wyvrndell!" squealed Aireantha.

"What? What did he say?" He sent his gaze around the chamber, though he was focused on controlling his rogue hiccoughs. Throughout the great hall, the dragons erupted in exclamations of confusion and wonder. *What did I miss?*

Petrandius was looking in his direction. Perhaps he sensed the onset of Wyvrndell's hiccoughs? Jakarian stared at the king, his jaws opening and closing in fury. A blast of steam emerged, and he bugled, "No, Petrandius, you cannot. This is madness."

"I am king, am I not?" Petrandius inquired. "I have made my decision, and I shall abide by it, as shall any dragon under my leadership. I have chosen Wyvrndell to be my successor, to lead my people into this new world. My decision is final."

Petrandius's words penetrated Wyvrndell's scrambled brain. He stared at the king in disbelief. "Me?" he squeaked, feeling like he'd been caught in a sudden whirlwind, tossed asunder and disoriented. "You want me? To be king?"

"Yes, Wyvrndell," Petrandius said, coming to the edge of the dais to regard him. "Who better? You are wise in the ways of men and Dwarves. Long have you sought to better the lot of dragonkind. And, you have one thing which no other dragon has."

"Magic?"

"Yes, young one. Magic. For now, you alone possess the power. I am certain, under your reign, you will manage to find a way to bestow this gift upon the rest of dragonkind."

"This is madness," snarled Jakarian again. "Petrandius, you have taken complete leave of your senses at last."

"If it is madness," the king replied, his voice calm, "perhaps it is because a bit of madness is what is needed to navigate the days ahead. We will get nowhere by hiding in our caverns and ignoring the wide world out there. Young Wyvrndell was instrumental in securing peace with both the Dwarves and the humans. He has managed to obtain magic, something no other dragon ever even ventured. I am confident in my choice, Jakarian. I know you are disappointed I have not named you. I am sorry, but I am firm on this."

"We will see about that," Jakarian snapped. "I cannot stay and be party to such foolishness."

"By all means, leave, if you believe you must," Petrandius rumbled. "But know this, Jakarian. If you leave, you will not be welcome in Ervantium again. It is your choice to make, as this was mine."

Lashing his tail, Jakarian strode off the dais, disappearing into the corridor. Wyvrndell, along with every other dragon in the hall, heard him snarling and muttering, his fury echoing off the stone walls of Ervantium.

Petrandius gazed around the crowded hall. "If there are others among you who wish to follow him, rather than abide by my long-considered decision, do so now. But, like Jakarian, know exile awaits you if you fly this course."

A number of older dragons, contemporaries of the old councilor, slipped away down the corridor. A smattering of younger ones followed in their wake and left the chamber, to accompany Jakarian into exile. *Where will they go?*" Wyvrndell wondered to himself. He watched, stupefied at this turn of events which sundered the dragon realm. *What will they do? This has never happened before.*

Every other dragon in the hall appeared rooted to the stone floor, though whether in shock or dismay, Wyvrndell wasn't certain. He stared up at the king. "Your Majesty, are you certain of this? For I am young and inexperienced. I do not know how to be a king."

Petrandius smiled at him from his position on the dais. "Wyvrndell, scion of Wyzandar, I was once young myself. I also was thrust into the kingship unlooked for, when my sire was slain. Many and long were the days when fear came close to besting me. Yet ever did I seek to do what I could for dragonkind. I was, I think, destined to be a caretaker king, holding the place for one who would bring dragons back to greatness. I declare, before this assembly, I foresee a bright future for dragons with you to guide their course."

Wyvrndell bowed his head. "Thank you for your confidence, Your Majesty. I shall do my best to live up to your expectations."

"No," Petrandius said. "Instead, live up to your own expectations."

CHAPTER TWENTY-SIX
Wizards' Archives, Caerfaen

From out of the darkness, a quavering voice muttered, "Curse the boy, he's let the dratted lamp go out again. What's the world coming too, when they keep sending you incompetent apprentices, I ask you…"

This was more a soliloquy than a request for comment, Alain surmised. He held one of Saia's hands in his and kept silent.

The voice drew nearer. "Every day the same thing. Six hours, and the benighted lamp goes out. I've told 'em, oh, I've told 'em, but do they ever listen?"

"*Illumios,*" said Saia, and flicked the fingers of her free hand. Light flared, and the passageway beyond their antechamber was filled with a golden glow.

There wasn't much to see, with the exception of an elderly man—a most venerable wizard, if the length of his beard was any indicator—dressed in the robes of a senior clerk. He cocked his head in appraisal.

"Now why in blazes didn't I think of that?" he asked. He regarded Alain. "Thank you, wizard."

"Not me," he replied. "You can thank the lady. She has the magic, not I."

"Lady? Lady?" The old man stared at Saia, as if he'd never contemplated the possibility a woman might intrude upon his domain, much less light his lamps for him. "How in blazes did you get here?"

"Willum was good enough to escort us," Saia replied. "We are here to examine a book in the secured area."

"Willum? Willum?" The old man tugged on his beard. "Oh, you

mean Willum. But—a book in the secured area? Nonsense. Can't be done. Go away, you shouldn't be here."

"She did light your lamps for you," Alain pointed out. "Which ought to count for something, shouldn't it? Besides, we have this." He displayed the archival request slip. "See, the Chief Archivist himself has initialed it."

The old man took the slip, regarded it with suspicion, then held it up to his nose and gave it a sniff. He handed it back. "Oh, it does smell of Darvish. Very well, why are you standing there like a pair of statues? Come in. Mind you don't step on Myrvyn."

A large snake uncoiled itself from a position behind the man and slithered down the hall.

"Oh, a speckled mironi," exclaimed Saia. "He's lovely. My brother had one, but Myrvyn is ever so much more handsome."

"He is, ain't he? And wicked useful, too. Keeps the mice down, y'know." Turning, he shuffled down the passage. "Come along, don't dawdle."

Exchanging a bemused glance, they followed. "So you're a sorceress, eh?" the man observed. "Don't get many of those down here. You're the first, in fact. All I ever get are hoary old wizards with food in their beards." He eyed Saia with an approving gaze. "You make a nice change."

"Thank you, Wizard…" She let the question hang in the air.

"Arbell," he said. "Senior Archivist Arbell. I've been here longer than anybody, y'know. Practically grew up here. My old Da was an archivist, and his before him. It's in the blood, I reckon. Come along."

Arbell led them into the archives proper. The snake, Myrvyn, was draped over a table, but raised his head when they entered, regarding them with a jaundiced eye. There were, Alain was happy to see, other tables. He wasn't afraid of serpents. He simply didn't care to fraternize with them. Myrvyn might be fine in his place, but to Alain, it was fine if his place was someplace else.

Saia, for her part, hastened to Myrvyn and began to stroke him. The snake's tail swayed to and fro, and little ripples undulated along its body.

It's like a dog, Alain thought, watching her. His own skin crawled at the notion of touching the serpent, but there was no accounting for tastes.

"Well, now," said Arbell, watching the princess caress the serpent. Alain was certain he was pleased with her attention to the creature. "What do we have here, eh?"

He took the request slip from Alain again and perused it with interest. His brows knit together and his lips pursed into a soft whistle. "A curious selection," he said at last. "I don't recall anyone having ever requested this particular volume before. May I inquire why you want it?"

"Research," Alain said.

"Mmm, well, yes, young feller, but I mean, when you get right down to it, it's all research, ain't it? What particular line of inquiry are you pursuing?"

"I'm afraid we're not at liberty to say." Alain experienced a slight pang of regret, but it was unavoidable.

Arbell grinned. He produced an apple from the pocket of his robe and took a bite of it. When he'd chewed and swallowed, he smacked his lips and said, "Well, I hope you can read Dwarfish."

"Dwarfish?" Alain's eyes widened.

Arbell chuckled. "I reckon that means you can't. Unless you can read it, I don't expect you're gonna get far in this mysterious research of yours."

Alain's heart sank to his toes. "No," he said. "No, I can't read it."

"What about your lady here?"

"She's her own lady," Alain said. "But no, I doubt it. Saia?"

She turned her attention from Myrvyn. "Yes?"

"Can you read Dwarfish?"

Her mouth fell open, then she uttered a laugh tinged with bitterness. "Alain, you know where I come from. I'm lucky I can read anything at all. But Dwarfish? Not on the best day I ever had."

"No, I didn't suppose you did. Well, that tears it. I reckon we're stymied. The book is in Dwarfish."

"Oh." She left off stroking the snake, who butted his head against her hand. "Well, how rotten. We retreat, routed at the first engagement."

Arbell grinned. "Too bad. After you got so far, too."

Alain heaved a resigned sigh. "We might as well leave. There's nothing for us here."

"Not quite so fast," Arbell said. "If you was a bit more forthcoming, I might be inclined to help you out."

"Oh? And how would you be able to help us?" He was unable to keep the skepticism out of his tone. He regretted it, but the words were loosed, too late to call back.

"Hmph. You think I'm a doddering old duffer, no good for anything but sitting here by myself, with Myrvyn for my sole company. It so happens," the old archivist went on, "I do read Dwarfish. And six other languages. But I reckon in this case, the Dwarfish is the one to mention." He chuckled. "Gotta do something with my free time."

Alain exchanged a glance with Saia. Her expression gave nothing away. "Princess?"

"Master Sebastien said we were to be circumspect."

"Yesss, he did."

"Yet I do not imagine he expects us to give up at the first obstacle. He wants results. So do I. This is important to me, Alain."

"Of course it is. To me too, for your sake. But I fear what might chance, if we find the answers we seek, and unscrupulous wizards learn of it."

She waved a hand. "Alain, the knowledge is right here, where anyone could find it, if they cared to search. Or at least it may be. We won't know unless we press on. We can't do so without Arbell's assistance. Thus, we must trust him, and trust to his discretion."

The archivist, who'd been following their conversation with open interest, said, "If I didn't know how to be discrete, I wouldn't have lasted out my first week here."

"You see," Saia said. Myrvyn hissed in agreement.

"All right." Alain's lips tightened, but she was right. "Arbell, if you will fetch the book, and assist by translating, we'll explain what it is we're seeking."

"It'll take me a few minutes," Arbell replied. "Lots of wards on this book, y'know."

"Are there?" Alain's brows rose. "Chief Archivist Darvish said the book was housed in this area because of its rarity."

"Darvish? Bah. What does he know? He's the chief archivist, that's all. He doesn't spend any time among the dangerous books. Yes, my young friend, the volume you seek has a great many protective enchantments laid on it. For you see, it is not only written on the subject of Dwarf mages, but by Dwarf mages. It's rife with power, and dark power at that. It'll be a right struggle to keep control of the book while we examine it."

"I see." Alain grimaced. "Well, if you think you're up to the challenge…"

"I reckon we'll find out, won't we?" Arbell gave a harsh laugh. "But look ye, I didn't survive these many years down here amongst these dangerous books, by being soft, did I?"

"No," Alain replied. "I don't imagine you did."

"All right, follow me," the old man said. "You can wait in the special reading room."

"What makes it special?" Saia asked.

"Ah, well, this room has its own enchantments laid on, to contain the books when they've been unbound and opened. Otherwise, the books tend to get…" he waved a dramatic hand… "a bit expressive, you might say."

"In that case, by all means let us make use of the special reading room. Lead on."

Arbell brought them down a dark corridor which smelled of paper and ink and dreams and magic. The scent of magic, Alain had come to learn in Arvindir's archives, was akin to the tangy odor of blood. Which, he assumed, was likely why so many dire spells required blood in the first place.

Opening the last door on the left, the archivist said, "*Lumos,*" and lamps flared into life. The room, thus revealed, was sparse, with thick stone walls, bare of any ornamentation, and several of the marvelous magical lamps. A battered wooden table and four heavy oak chairs were the sole furnishings. The air was fusty, and tinged with the faint odor of magic.

"Wait here," Arbell instructed. "I'll be back." Without waiting for a reply, he exited the room, closing the door behind him. Alain heard the soft 'snick' of the lock engaging.

He met Saia's eyes. "You think we can trust him?"

She shrugged. "Do we have a choice?"

"No, I don't think so. Even if we left without seeing the book, Arbell could read it on his own. He's no fool. He'd figure out what we're after in no time."

"I thought the same thing. So it's not too much of a risk to have him translate for us. Besides, he seems trustworthy."

"Oh? How do you figure?"

"My instincts. Alain, I've dealt with palace intrigues from the time I was a young girl. I've developed a skill for reading people. I've managed to stay alive this long, so I must have learned something."

Alain choked out a laugh. "Yes, you must." He turned his head at the sound of the lock retracting. Arbell opened the door and stepped into the room, bearing a metal box wrapped in heavy chains. Beneath the chains the box was etched with intricate designs which drew the eye but were almost impossible to process. Protective runes, Alain decided.

The archivist placed the box in the center of the table, pulled the door closed again, and locked it. Using a small key, he opened the lock securing the chains. He uttered a spell, and with a creaking sound, the lid of the box lifted. Arbell removed a small, tattered volume.

He placed the book on the table before them. Saia's face went pale, and she reeled in her seat. Alain put out a hand to steady her. Arbell's voice was raspy, like a saw cutting through steel. "Aye, you can sense its power, eh?" he growled.

She nodded, staring at the book and hunching her shoulders like a fighter entering the ring. "It's…strong," she said in a choked voice. "So very strong." She closed her eyes.

Arbell muttered something under his breath. Saia gulped in a deep breath and opened her eyes again. "It's better," she said. "It's not beating against me. Well, a little, but not like before."

"Aye, but I don't know how long I'll be able to last," the archivist said. "So we'd best get on."

Alain said, "Very well, Archivist Arbell. We will trust you with our task. We seek the secrets of the Thundermist. We need to know how it affects magic wielders. Princess Saia herself has been infused by the Mist, and her magical abilities enhanced by it."

Arbell narrowed his eyes. "By Thundermist? I've never heard the like. Ridiculous. I don't believe it."

Alain's smile was tight. "All the better," he said. "But it doesn't matter. Will you translate this text for us?"

Arbell appeared to lose himself in cogitation. Alain feared he was going to refuse after all. At last, the archivist said, "Why not? Not like I have much else to do, and at least I'll be able to practice my Dwarfish. And perhaps I'll learn something. Thundermist, huh?" He shook his head. "Who would have thought?"

Alain glanced at Saia and was surprised to find her lower lip caught between her teeth. "Your control," she said. "It's slipping."

At last even Alain sensed the power emanating from the little book. His mouth went dry and his eyes stung. He felt like he was facing a bitter winter gale, unable to close them against the force of it. If he was affected like this, he couldn't imagine how Saia, being so much more sensitive to the magical realm, managed to bear it.

Arbell's expression was grim. At last he uttered another phrase in a tongue Alain didn't recognize, and the pressure subsided. Not altogether, but enough to be manageable. He still sensed it, like a dull, throbbing headache, but no longer was it quite so debilitating.

"I did warn you," Arbell said. "You're sure you want to go through with this?"

"Want to?" Saia barked out a humorless laugh. "No. Have to? Yes. Anyway, you seem to have it under control again."

"For the moment." The old man appeared nervous. He reached out to pull the book toward him, and Alain realized he had donned heavy gloves.

"Can't touch this without 'em," Arbell explained. "It'd singe my fingers right off." He opened the book with care, and the pressure against

Alain's eyes begin to build again. Saia winced, and the little room was filled with a sound like rushing wind as Arbell began to read.

"I, G'x'ln, do set down these words. Whoever reads them, beware, for here are many puissant spells and workings. Here also is the history of dragonkind, its beginning, out of the mist."

CHAPTER TWENTY-SEVEN
Ervantium

Wyvrndell halted. The pair of dragons guarding the king's chambers stepped forward to block his path. A hiccough flared within his belly, but he managed to squelch it before it erupted.

"The king is at rest, and wishes not to be disturbed," said one of the guards. Arvintine was a rheumy old dragon, his once-blue scales now gray with age. His position was, Wyvrndell suspected, a sinecure, out of respect for his long years of service to the king.

His companion, Vazerak, was closer to Wyvrndell's own age and was, at least by reputation, a ferocious brawler. Wyvrndell, who felt no urge to confirm this, ignored his glare. In a neutral tone he said, "I understand. I shall await the king's pleasure."

"Why don't you wait somewhere else?" Vazerak growled. He puffed out his chest, stretching out his neck until he was snout to snout with Wyvrndell.

"Vazerak," exclaimed Arvintine. "You forget yourself. Wyvrndell is the king's chosen successor."

"Not if Jakarian has anything to say," replied the younger guard, his voice sour. He sent a ferocious glare at Wyvrndell.

Before Wyvrndell could respond, the older dragon raised up and cuffed Vazerak across the snout. "Young fool," he growled. "Do you wish to be banished from Ervantium, like your hero Jakarian?"

Wyvrndell worried Vazerak might go on the offensive. Either some semblance of sanity prevailed, or Vazerak decided to bide his time. Yet even though the younger dragon stood down, he sneered, "It might be preferable."

Before either Wyvrndell or Arvintine could respond, a stirring from within Petrandius's chamber alerted them to the presence of the king. He peered out into the passageway, blinking like a day-struck owl. Yet Wyvrndell caught a glimpse of something in the king's demeanor which made him suspect Petrandius had heard more than he was letting on.

"Ah, Wyvrndell, you are here," the king said, appearing to focus at last. "Good, good. I was going to send for you."

The two guard dragons stood back to allow Wyvrndell to pass. Arvintine lowered his head in respect. Vazerak gave a barely audible snort. Wyvrndell pretended not to hear. Petrandius was not so subtle.

"Vazerak, did you wish to speak?" the king inquired. His tone was benevolent, yet underneath lay a hint of ancient stone.

Vazerak lowered his gaze. "Nay, Your Majesty."

"Ah, I must have been mistaken. It is my age, you know. Sometimes I even imagine there are…well, dragons of questionable loyalty…in our midst." Petrandius favored the young guard dragon with a toothy smile. "Now, come, Wyvrndell, my heir. We have much to discuss."

Wyvrndell followed his king into the inner chamber. From out in the passageway came the sound of Arvintine giving his junior a rousing dressing down. Petrandius heaved a steam-laden sigh.

"Perhaps I have made an error in judgment," he said at last.

"Your Majesty," Wyvrndell hastened to say. "If you wish to change your mind and chose another in my stead…"

"No, Wyvrndell, I did not mean I made a mistake concerning you. You are my duly chosen successor. You will lead my dragons into the new world, whether they like it or not. No, I meant perhaps I made a mistake about Jakarian."

"By banishing him?"

"Well, yes, in a sense. I wonder if I might have been better served to have executed him as a traitor."

Wyvrndell stared. Petrandius shrugged. "It would have solved the problem right away. Now, I fear, Jakarian is free to cause every manner of mischief. And you may take it from me: he is an expert at it. Unfortunately, you will have to bear the brunt of it."

"Not for some time yet, Your—"

Petrandius shook his hoary black head. "Nay, Wyvrndell, I fear my time draws near. Too soon, you will have to assume the kingship. I am afraid I leave you with a bitter legacy."

"I do not fear Jakarian," Wyvrndell said, with a forced bravado he wasn't sure he could claim.

"Well, you should. Jakarian is wily and cunning, and his heart, I have seen at last, is blacker than the stones of this mountain." Petrandius sighed again. "Never did I think to see the day when dragon would be pitted against dragon."

"But you will remain king. It will be long before I ascend to the throne. You can weather this storm."

"No, Wyvrndell. Even if I were to continue, what then? Jakarian knows I have grown weary and weak with age. He would seek to wrest the kingship to himself. Such an outcome would be ten, nay, a hundred, times worse. For he would seek to lead dragons into war with both men and Dwarves. The world would be thrown into chaos and peril. In the end, everything would be lost."

"You Majesty, I fear I am not strong enough, nor wise enough, to prevent such a terrible fate."

"Wyvrndell, my heir, listen to me. You will prevail. I have seen it in the stones of augury, and I believe it to be true. For you have something Jakarian does not."

"Tell me, my lord. What do I, so young and foolish, have which might save our people?"

Petrandius smiled. "You possess a noble and caring heart, Wyvrndell. And magic. With these, you shall defeat Jakarian."

"But—"

"Listen, young one, for even now my time is drawing to its close. Gather councilors to yourself whom you can trust. Wyzandar, your sire, of course. He can advise you on others. But know this. The heart and the magic which you bear, these will be stronger in the end than the hate and jealousy of Jakarian and his ilk. For you strive not only for yourself, but for every good-hearted dragon. And also for men, and Dwarves."

"I am young, and I know so little."

"No one said saving the world would be easy, my son." As he uttered this last, Petrandius gave a long, hissing sigh, and the light was extinguished from his eyes.

Wyvrndell, new king of the dragons, sent a mournful bugle echoing through the chamber. Tears fell from his faceted eyes, hot as the fire burning within him, to score the age-blackened stones of the floor.

CHAPTER TWENTY-EIGHT
Wizards' Archives, Caerfaen

Arbell read aloud, translating the text of "On Dwarfish Mages," while Alain scribbled notes. Arbell had scoffed at the 'no writing implements' rule. "Doesn't matter in the least," the old archivist told him. "Bring whatever you want. Or I have paper and pencils here you can use."

"This is unbelievable," Alain muttered, more than once. Saia sat in silence, listening while the archivist read, and straining against the influence of the magical tome.

Once he completed reading the third section Arbell closed the book with a quiet 'thump'. "I need to stop for a bit," he said. "Put the book away, and let it settle down. Besides, from what I can see, the next few sections deal with actual spells, rather than history. Probably not relevant to your research, eh?"

Saia's voice, when she spoke, sounded dark and hollow, like something echoing from a tomb. "No. No more. I feel its tendrils pressing against my mind, searching for a way in. Take it away, please."

Alain exchanged a concerned look with the archivist. "Yes, put it away," he urged. "The book is agitated, and I don't think it likes us much."

"We have woken the book from its long slumber," Arbell said. "I fear this was perhaps not such a good idea." He placed the book back into its container and secured the chains around it. "*Embar librosi*," he muttered. The metal casket glowed an ugly shade of green. The light flashed once and winked out.

Arbell muttered soothing sounds while he fastened and locked the chains back around the box. Alain wasn't certain if they were intended for Saia, or the book, or Arbell himself. "I'm going to put it back in the vault," the archivist announced. "I don't reckon we'd best disturb it any more today." With this dire proclamation, he hefted the box and carried it out of the reading room.

Once he'd removed the book from their presence, Saia appeared to recover from the ordeal. "Well?" she asked. "Are we any forwarder? Have we learned anything of importance?"

"Have we learned anything?" Alain gaped at her, incredulous she could even ask such a question. "I think you could say so. We learned something hidden for centuries. I'd always been taught dragons were creatures born of magic. But Dwarf magic?"

"Thundermist magic," Saia said. "Which means the Thundermist must have extraordinary powers."

"And we've learned the Dwarves are able to make use of it. Or at least, they were. Perhaps we're on the wrong track. Perhaps we should be consulting the Dwarves instead." He hesitated. "Hmm. Yet, I wonder..."

"Wonder what?" she asked.

"Eh? Oh. Sorry. I wonder if either of them—dragons or Dwarves—retain this knowledge anymore."

Saia shook her head. "I don't know how they could have managed to keep the secret for so long. I imagine the knowledge must have faded from memory ages ago. Otherwise, there would be much less enmity between them."

"Or more," Alain mused.

"What do you mean?" she asked. Then, shook herself and muttered, "What I wouldn't give for a cup of strong coffee. That was...difficult."

"Perhaps Arbell can provide some sort of restorative. But to answer your question. The legends tell us dragons are the oldest creatures of this world. If what this book posits is true, the legends are lies, Saia. The Dwarves were here first, oldest of all, not dragons. Don't you think dragons would be upset to find their entire existence, or what they assumed was their entire existence, was a lie?"

"Perhaps," she said. "I do not know. What I wonder is, do the Dwarves retain any knowledge of how to utilize the Thundermist? They went away, to lands far removed from the mist, which leads me to believe they may not."

Alain shrugged. "We'll have to find out somehow. Perhaps we can learn more from the book. We have but scratched the surface. In the meantime, what do we do with this knowledge?"

"We tell King Rhys and Master Sebastien what we've learned, of course. And the Royal Enchantress."

"Yes, you're right. Good. I would not want to be the one to have to make the decision on whether or not to tell dragons or Dwarves what we've learned here today."

The door opened and Arbell entered enough to say, "I've gotten the book settled and secured. You'd best go and come back another day. It will not be safe to try and read more from it today."

"Of course, Arbell," Saia said. "We will come back tomorrow."

Arbell held up a hand. "He can come back," he said, indicating Alain. "You, on the other hand, should stay away."

"But why?" demanded Alain. "This is her task to complete."

"That may be, young feller, but I have to insist. The book we're reading is rife with power, and seeking more. The lady's magic is too tempting for it. I was able to control the book today, but it was a close-run thing. I doubt I can do it again if she's present. It's too damned strong. And I don't reckon you want another wizard here to help, eh?"

"No," Saia said. "You are right, Arbell. I could feel the book testing my defenses. Which, to be honest, are non-existent. I have power, yes, but no training in how to use it. And I know well what happens when magic is wrested away from one." She shivered. "I will stay away, since you direct it. Alain can tell me whatever he learns tomorrow."

~*~

Ervantium

The guards rushed into the chamber in response to Wyvrndell's call. Arvintine took one look and bowed his head. Vazerak, however, glared at Wyvrndell with malice. "You killed the king," he declared.

Wyvrndell's jerked his head around to stare at him in astonishment. "What?"

"You killed the king," repeated Vazerak. "I heard it from where I stood guard."

"You heard no such thing," snarled Arvintine. "Get out, you great ninny, if you cannot show respect for the fallen, and for our new king."

"I know what I heard," Vazerak muttered, turning to leave the chamber. "Foul deeds shall not go unpunished."

Arvintine stared after him. Once the younger dragon departed, he shook himself and turned to Wyvrndell. "Command me, Your Majesty," he said. "The king is dead. Hail the new king, Wyvrndell."

Wyvrndell, still lost in sorrow at the passing of Petrandius, almost failed to register his words. He managed to say, "Thank you,

Arvintine. You have been a good and faithful servant to Petrandius. I will remain here with him. I need you to act for me, if you will. First, find dragons you trust, and send them to help watch over the king. Next, find Wyzandar, my sire. Tell him—but him alone—what has happened and bid him come to me at once."

"Yes, Your Majesty," said Arvintine, bowing his head.

Wyvrndell's head snapped up. "No. Do not call me 'Your Majesty.' Not yet, at any rate. Petrandius may be gone, long may his spirit soar. But I am not yet king, Arvintine, and I am loathe to come close to the kingship so soon."

"Petrandius was ancient as these very stones, my lord," Arvintine said with great reverence. "He was, I warrant, ready to take flight with his ancestors, since he had at last named his successor. He bore great hopes for you, my lord. He spoke of this while I kept watch over him. I will go and do what you command. But know this—to me, you are king."

Wyvrndell nodded, but his attention rested on the unmoving figure of the king. "So soon, Petrandius," he murmured. "So soon. And I am so young. Yet I will do my best to be the dragon you wished me to be."

Soon enough he caught the click of talons in the outer chamber. The dragons entered in silence, four in number, heads bowed in sorrow.

"Lord Wyvrndell," said their leader after several moments had passed. Arvintine must have cautioned them not to address him by the royal title, for which Wyvrndell was grateful. *It is too soon. I am not ready. I do not know if I will ever be ready.*

"Arvintine has sent us to stand honor guard over King Petrandius," said the dragon. "Command us."

In their eyes he noted grief, along with a stern resolve to serve with honor. He set aside his own misgivings, for he could show no weakness before them. Lifting his head, he directed, "Two of you stay here to watch over the king, The other two, go into the outer chamber. Let none save Arvintine, and Wyzandar my sire, enter here. Speak to no one else of Petrandius's passing. They will know soon enough."

"By your order, my lord," replied the leader, whom Wyvrndell finally recognized through his grief. He was Donathyr, the dragon who had accompanied him to Erkarna's cavern. "Bezyndir and I will watch over the king. Luvrantis and Grynal will stay in the outer chamber to prevent any from entering here."

"Thank you, Donathyr. I will remain here to mourn the king, until Wyzandar comes."

Donathyr and his companion took up their places, one on each side of the fallen king. Wyvrndell remained where he was, near Petrandius's head. *Oh, Petrandius,* he said so none would hear. *I hope I may be worthy of the trust and honor you have set on me. May I lead your dragons justly and with wisdom, as you have done for these many long years, to bring us into this new era of the world you envisioned.*

"My lord," Donathyr broke into his reverie. "Arvintine has returned with Wyzandar."

"Bring them in," Wyvrndell said. "No, I will go out instead. You two continue to keep watch over the king. Let none disturb him in this hour of mourning."

"Yes, my lord. And know this. We of the guard were loyal to Petrandius. Now you, his heir and successor to the kingship, will also have our loyalty. Arvintine has told us you do not yet wish the title of king, and this is good and proper. Yet king you are, by Petrandius's decree, and we will serve you as we served him."

"Thank you, my friends," said Wyvrndell, humbled at his words. "Now, I must speak with my councilor Wyzandar, so he may help to guide me though this time of grief and turmoil."

Wyvrndell went to the outer chamber, where his sire waited with the guards. Wyvrndell said to Arvintine, "Take Grynal and Luvrantis and stand watch in the corridor, so none may enter. Speak not of the king's passing. Say naught but that he is at rest and is not to be disturbed."

"It is truth itself," Arvintine said. "For Petrandius is at rest at last." With this, they left Wyvrndell alone with his sire.

"So it is true," Wyzandar said, shaking his head. "Petrandius has at long last gone to fly with his ancestors. And you are to be king."

"Yes, Father. I was with him when he died. Greatly do I mourn his passing. For me, it came much too soon. It appears the kingship is to be my destiny, thanks to him. It is not one I would have ever dreamed of, nor asked for if I did. Yet it seems to be my fate."

"Do you regard your lot more curse than honor?" Wyzandar asked.

Wyvrndell snorted. "Curse? No, Father. I would never denigrate so the honor bestowed upon me by Petrandius, to name me his heir. No, I worry I am not up to the task he has set me. I need your counsel and guidance, Father, to navigate these troubled skies."

"And you shall have them," Wyzandar said. "From me, and from those on the council who revered Petrandius, and will serve you in his stead."

"Thank you. Father, tell me, what must we do in this hour? Should we not proclaim the passing of the king to Ervantium."

"Indeed, we must. He should be borne to the great hall, to lie in honor, so any who wish may come to revere him, and mourn his passing. Five days should he remain thus. And on the sixth day, I, and others we may choose between us, shall install you as Petrandius's heir, the new king of Ervantium."

"So soon?"

"Aye. And I would it could be sooner. But it would not be proper to act in too great a haste. Still, we dare not wait any longer, for you must be sealed and acclaimed, so none may challenge your right to rule."

"Jakarian?" The name left a sour taste like a rogue hiccough in his mouth.

"I am afraid so. Already tales are spreading, saying a fair number of dragons have followed him into exile. We must set you upon the throne before they arise to challenge you. Far easier will it be for you to say, 'I have the acclamation of my people, by the command of Petrandius. But you, Jakarian, are naught but one sent into the darkness by your own enmity'."

"Very well, Father, I will follow your guidance. Let us go out and proclaim Petrandius's passing, and the days of mourning to come."

Thus Wyvrndell, heir apparent to the kingship of Ervantium, led his sire from the king's chambers, which would be his once he claimed his throne, to spread the mournful news.

CHAPTER TWENTY-NINE
The Devil's Teeth

Toby rode next to Radivan while the Tzigani caravan traversed the final mountain pass before they began the long descent towards Rhuddlan. Storm clouds roiled across the sky, and the acrid promise of a soaking filled his nostrils.

"Your arm, it is healed?" Radivan inquired.

"Enough." Toby flexed the arm in question. Other than a slight twinge, he noted no ill effects from his injury, and said so.

"Good, good." In the distance, a rumble of thunder sounded. "You were fortunate, eh?"

"Thanks to a good deal of luck, and the efforts of both your wife and your daughter. If not for them…" He shrugged. "I doubt I'd be among the living."

Radivan nodded. "Luck, it is what keeps us Tzigani going. Of course, having the care of two such women never hurts either."

Changing the subject, Toby asked, "Have you given any more consideration to who might have planned the attack on the caravan?"

Scowling, the Tzigani chief said, "Much thought, with little in the way of answers. It's mad to think anyone would specifically target us, or attempt to slay Toni. To what purpose? This, I ask myself over and over, and I am no closer to the answer, I'm afraid."

"I hate to say this, but to my mind, the entire episode appeared intended to accomplish one thing: the death of your daughter."

Radivan stared, a mixture of horror and shock clouding his face. "What on earth makes you say such a thing?"

Toby spread his hands in a placating gesture. "It gives me no pleasure, believe me. And to be honest, it's merely a hunch on my part. With none of the bandits taken prisoner, there's no way to prove it. But the notion one of them decided, out of the blue, to show up to the party with poisoned arrows, and loose them at your daughter and no one else, is difficult for me to swallow."

"He also fired one at you," Radivan reminded him.

"Well, yes, there's that. But I was in the way. Both those arrows were intended for Toni, not me."

Radivan was silent for a couple of minutes. Chewing, Toby was certain, on this unpalatable notion. Thunder rumbled again, much closer this time, and the air was suffused with the sharp tang of impending rain. At the caravan's current elevation, they were right among the clouds. Toby's weather eye, developed over years at sea, suggested to him the storm, when it broke, would be a deluge of epic proportions. He secured his brimmed hat and snugged his cloak around his shoulders.

Radivan broke their silence. "Fanshawe, I hate to admit it, but what you say makes sense. Unfortunately. And so," he huffed out a breath, disturbing the sweeping moustache, "I have a proposition for you."

Toby's brows rose. "What is it? I'll help however I can."

"Good. If what you say is correct, it may well be I have a traitor in my camp."

Another ominous crack of thunder punctuated this statement. Toby stared. "One of your own men?"

"It pains me to believe it might be so. Yet it's the only thing which makes any sense." Radivan's hands were clenching and unclenching around his reins.

"What would you have me do?" Toby asked.

"First of all, I want you to act as Toni's protector. You have already proven yourself in the role, and she trusts you."

Toby bowed his head. "I would consider it an honor," he said. "Although, even though Toni may trust me, I'm not sure she will listen. She is…rather headstrong."

Radivan snorted. "You have a way with understatement, Fanshawe. She is stubborn as a mule, and more independent than any cat." He grinned, confessing, "God help us, we raised her to be so, Elbethesba and I. And now see what a harvest we reap, eh? However, I will set her mamma to have a little chat with her. I think that might be of some benefit."

"An excellent idea," Toby agreed. He didn't envy Toni that 'little chat'. He hoped it might serve to temper, at least slightly, her impetuous nature.

"There is something else, though," the Tzigani went on. "And it will be an even more dangerous task, I'm afraid."

Toby waited, not speaking. What in the world did Radivan want of him?

Radivan rode on, apparently lost in contemplation. At last, he said, "Captain Fanshawe, I want you to wed my daughter."

It was a close-run thing, but Toby managed not to fall off his horse. When he was finally able to form a coherent thought, he sputtered, "You—you can't be serious."

"I was never more serious, Fanshawe. Elbethesba and I have discussed this at great length, and we are agreed."

"But…" Toby spread his hands, shaking his head. "It's impossible."

"Captain," Radivan said, straightening in the saddle to glare at Toby. "Are you telling me you do not wish my daughter's hand in marriage?"

Toby sucked in a breath, trying to figure how to handle this. He couldn't afford to offend Radivan, not when he was presenting Toby with a golden opportunity he'd only dared to consider in his dreams. But it would never work. "That's not what I said," he protested. "But none of the Tzigani would accept such a match. I am not one of you."

"Ah, but you see, it turns out you are," Radivan replied, his smile enigmatic. "When she first met you, Elbethesba declared you impetuous, and a rogue, remember?"

"I think it takes more than merely being a rogue, doesn't it?" *What the devil is he talking about?*

"Well, yes, it does. But there is also the fact your mother is Tzigani. My wife, she discovered you must have some of our heritage when she was reading your hand. Once you told her your mother's name, she knew for certain. Magdalyna Rabisi? Elbethesba, she knows the Rabisi clan; they are distant cousins. You, my friend, are part Tzigani."

Toby stared. "I—no, it can't be."

"Is it such a dreadful prospect, to be Tzigani?" Radivan asked. "In truth, what could be better, eh? Um. Do you think you can grow a mustache?" He stroked his own luxuriant one.

Toby laughed. "I don't know, I've never tried. But as far as being part Tzigani? It explains quite a number of things. I simply can't believe I never knew. My mother never said anything."

"Married to a man like your father? A pompous officer in the Royal Navy of Kilbourne? I'd be amazed if she did."

Toby's laugh was bitter. "You've got the right of it, I reckon." He shook his head, amazement warring with excitement. "So, back to your previous subject…"

Radivan's smile was grim. "It may not be quite what you imagine, Fanshawe. It will not be all firelight and laughter and dancing with the bear. If we announce you and Toni are to wed… Well, I would not be surprised if whoever is a viper in my bosom may decide to act again."

Toby nodded. "And this time, the target will be me?"

Radivan clapped him on the shoulder. The good one, for which Toby was grateful. "You understand," he said. "You strike me as a man who likes to court danger, Captain. Well, here is your chance."

"And if I manage to survive?"

"What I said about courting danger? Well, you will be wed to Toni…"

Toby stared into the future. Two paths, Elbethesba had said. One leading to renown and fortune, the other to despair. Here, in this moment, was the fork in the road. A slow smile spread across his face. "Dangerous indeed. Very well, Captain Radivan. I accept your challenge."

"Yes, I thought you might. May you have the luck of the Tzigani, my friend. You will, unless I miss my guess, need as much of it as you can get."

CHAPTER THIRTY

Knight-Commander's Office, Caerfaen

"Come." Morgan called in response to the rap on his office door. Arthur, his aide de camp, poked his head in.

"Commander, I know you said you didn't want to be disturbed, but…"

Appraising the unsettled expression on his clerk's face, Morgan refrained from biting his head off. "…But?" he ventured.

"There's a ragged sort of fellow out in my office, Commander…"

"Well, give him a couple of coins and send him in search of a hot meal. If you're after a contribution, I can—"

Arthur shook his head in vehement negation. "That's just it, beggin' your pardon, sir. He wants to see you. Says he was sent to see you."

"Indeed? Well, I reckon you'd best show him in, hadn't you."

"What if he's another of those assassins?"

"With you standing watch over me? I'm sure we'll be more than a match for even the most determined assassin."

With a dubious nod, Arthur retreated, returning with a man who, Morgan had to admit, looked like he could use a good meal or three. His trousers and boots were spattered with mud, his cloak was worn and patched, and his face was drawn and haggard.

"Commander McRobbie?" the man asked.

Interesting. His voice bore the accent of the Tzigani, the vagabond wanderers he and Marissa had encountered earlier this summer. When the man approached, Morgan caught the quick flash of a sash around his waist. "I'm McRobbie," he acknowledged.

"My name is Tarvin," the stranger said. "I've been sent by Radivan, with news for you."

"How can I be sure you come from Radivan?"

Tarvin grinned, and Morgan was certain he'd been expecting the challenge. "One day," the man quoted, "We must all dance with the bear."

Morgan allowed a slow smile to play across his face, recalling the night he and Marissa visited the travelling Tzigani. Marissa had indeed danced with the bear. "All right, Tarvin. You're who and what you claim to be. Can I offer you something to eat or drink? You appear to have come no little distance."

Tarvin licked his lips. "I could fair murder a meat pie or two, and a big mug of ale."

"Arthur?" After the aide nodded and departed, Morgan turned back to the Tzigani. "Please, sit. Arthur will be back in a few minutes with food and drink for you."

Tarvin plopped into a chair and stretched out his legs with a sigh of pleasure. "Feels good to be somewhere besides a saddle," he noted. Sitting up, he became serious. "Commander, the Rhuddlanis are on the move," he said. "We've been up north, ye see. Our scouts spotted whole companies of them, coming through the Kirting Pass, across the Devil's Teeth."

"Damn." Morgan scrubbed a hand across his face. "You're sure?"

"Well, I reckon they might have been a big party of peddlers. 'Course, I've never heard tell of peddlers going around quite so well armed or supplied."

Arthur returned, bearing a tray. Eyes gleaming, Tarvin fell on the food, leaving Morgan to ponder his words. Once the Tzigani gobbled one of the meat pies and washed it down with a hearty draught of ale, Morgan said, "Arthur, I need a map of the north country."

"Yes sir." Arthur snapped off a crisp salute and strode to the outer office. He returned several minutes later with a rolled map. Morgan took it and loosened the ties securing it. To Tarvin he said, "Can you read a map?"

"Aye. It's one of the reasons Radivan sent me."

Morgan spread the map out across his desk. "Excellent. Now, if you'll show me where these Rhuddlanis were spotted?"

Tarvin pointed to a spot on the far side of the Devil's Teeth, the northern mountain range separating Kilbourne from Rhuddlan. "They were just starting to make their way across," he said.

"Strength?" Morgan asked.

"They were spread out quite a bit," the Tzigani said. "But the scouts estimated three companies total."

Morgan whistled through his teeth. "All right, thanks, Tarvin.

Please give my sincere thanks to Radivan. This information, while not welcome in the least, is most helpful, and I'm grateful."

"Might your gratitude run to a horse?" Tarvin asked. "I've ridden three out from under me to get here."

"Of course. And food and drink to get you started on your way, and coin for more. A bed if you'd prefer to wait 'til tomorrow to get back on your way."

"Nay, Commander, I'd best push on. My folk are heading farther north. If I delay, I'll be even farther behind. Oh, I almost forgot. Captain Fanshawe instructed me to present you with his compliments."

Morgan sat back. "Fanshawe? What the blazes is he doing with the Tzigani?"

"I couldn't say, Commander. He's been riding with us for quite a ways. He helped fend off a bunch of bandits, and saved Captain Radivan's daughter from 'em. He seems a good sort."

Morgan chuckled. "Why am I not surprised? Fanshawe likes to be where things are happening, and it sounds like your lot is where they're happening. Well, give him my best, will you?"

"Aye. I reckon I'd best be getting on."

Morgan nodded. "Arthur, attend to Tarvin's needs, will you? Then send for Captains Darby and Poldane."

"Right away, Commander." Arthur tossed off another salute and bustled off, Tarvin in tow.

Morgan glanced at the map again, doing some rapid calculations. He dipped a quill into the inkwell and marked the pass Tarvin indicated. *Three companies of Rhuddlanis.* He shook his head. This had to be what Francis Barlbent had meant when he said things were "up" in Rhuddlan. But what the devil were they doing coming across The Devil's Teeth in autumn? It seemed a fool's errand at best.

The door opened to reveal the over-large form of Captain Byron Darby. He strode into the room, running a hand through his long red hair. "What's happened?" he asked.

Morgan straightened and stretched, releasing some of the tension Tarvin's news had brought. "Hold on for a few minutes," he said. "Aartis should be on his way, and I don't want to have to go over this twice."

Byron shrugged and propped himself against the wall, twirling his knife between his fingers. Morgan returned to his musings on the vagaries of the Rhuddlanis, until the sound of booted feet in the corridor reached his ears. Moments later Aartis Poldane entered the office.

"Sorry to interrupt your day," Morgan said to his captains. "But I've received some most unwelcome news, and misery loves company. Gather 'round."

"That's why we like you so much," Aartis said with a grin. "Always willing to share."

Morgan chuckled. He could always count on Aartis, who in counterpoint to Byron's brooding bulk, was a whip-cord bundle of joyous exuberance, taking life as one big lark. Then the reality of the situation hit home again and he grew somber once more. Directing their attention to the map, he said, "According to reliable sources, somewhere in the neighborhood of three companies of Rhuddlani regulars are traversing the Devil's Teeth as we speak."

Byron and Aartis both gaped at him. "In late autumn?" Aartis exclaimed. "They must be mad. Once the snow flies, which won't be long, those passes will be closed. They'll be completely cut off."

Byron studied the map with a keen gaze. "It won't matter," he said. "Look here. If they make it through the mountains before the snow closes them, they'll be fine."

Morgan leaned forward, following Byron's finger. "I see what you mean. With three companies of soldiers, they'll be able to overwhelm the northern garrisons before we can reinforce them. They'll control Noordstrom, and these surrounding villages. They'll have the entirety of Dunstanshire."

"And those villages," Aartis added, "will have already laid up their supplies for the winter. The Rhuddlanis will be well fed and rested by the time we can get up a force of any size up there. By spring, they'll have reinforcements starting over the mountains.

Morgan scrubbed a hand across his face. "So I guess they're not crazy." He stared at the map. "This information is already several days old. Byron, you know the country up there better than anyone. How long will it take them to get into position?"

"It'll be no small job, getting so many men and their equipment and supplies across." He regarded the map, a calculating expression in his eye. "Three days ago?"

"Four by now," Morgan said. "Not ideal, but a damned sight better than finding out in the spring."

"By my estimation, the first lot should be somewhere in this area." Byron's large, calloused forefinger tapped the map. "Sordam is the first village they'll come to after they make their way from the pass. Nothing much there. A few farms, mostly sheep. Not a lot to resupply them."

"A man can get quite a ways on a belly full of mutton," Aartis noted, his expression gloomy.

Morgan's slammed his fist on the desk. "The garrisons up there won't have any notion they're in danger until it's too late." He squeezed his eyes close. "Unless we can somehow warn them in time."

Aartis snorted. "It takes a good three days for a fast messenger to get there. And at least five full days or more for us to get any kind of opposing force sent up from Caerfaen."

"Mmm." Morgan opened his eyes, glowered at the map, and lowered himself into his seat. A grim smile tinged the corners of his mouth. "Perhaps not. I've an idea. I'll need to run it by Rhys first. It's mad, but it might work."

CHAPTER THIRTY-ONE
Knight Commander's Office, Caerfaen

Rhys swore. "I knew Varsil Jarik would never abide by the peace accord he signed. Damn the man." He frowned, tugging on his beard. This, Morgan was aware, was something he did only under extreme agitation. "All right, out with it," the king said. "What's your brilliant tactical idea?"

"Dragons," Morgan told him.

Rhys's eyes widened. "Umm. Tell me, how were you considering using these dragons? To chase the Rhuddlanis back over the Devil's Teeth?"

Morgan laughed. "No, although I wouldn't count that out. Might be a final resort. No, if Petrandius agrees, I'd like to request a few dragons to ferry some men north. They can both warn, and help reinforce, the garrison there. If we have enough dragons, with two or three trips, we could have a company of men in place."

"They'd none be mounted, though," Rhys pointed out.

"No, they wouldn't. Although I'm sure if necessary they'd manage to commandeer a few horses, at least for the officers and messengers. But you've been there. The terrain around Noordstrom isn't suited for cavalry anyway. From what Tarvin told me, most of the Rhuddlanis are on foot. A few of their officers are mounted, but it won't matter in the long run."

"No, you're right." Rhys leaned back in his chair, his eyes narrowed.

"With luck, we might even be able to get some of our men into the outlying villages before the Rhuddlanis overrun them, and prevent them from either destroying the towns, or raiding their supplies."

"Sounds sensible." Rhys spread his hands. "Are you waiting for my approval?"

"With all due respect, Your Majesty, you appointed me Knight-Commander for a reason: to get things done in the best interests of protecting Kilbourne. You signed a treaty with the dragons, which allows for mutual aid in time of need. If this doesn't qualify, I don't know what does. I intend to ask Wyvrndell to seek approval of the idea from Petrandius. However, if you have issues with my plans, we can discuss the matter further. Nothing's set in stone at this point."

Rhys stroked his beard, lost in thought. "Noo," he said at last. "You are correct. You know best what needs to be done in this instance. If we can obtain the assistance of the dragons to carry our men north, it will be a game changer. Well done, Morgan."

"Thank you."

"Are you going to Noordstrom a-dragonback?"

Morgan shook his head. "I've done more than my share of dragon riding of late. Time to give someone else the chance. I was going to send Sir Byron. He's from there, and he knows the terrain and the people better than anyone else we have. Plus, he can bring some of his Green Rangers along. They're the best at operating in a woodland environment, and they'll teach the other men along the way. The Rhuddlanis are going to be in for a surprise if we can pull this off."

Rhys flashed a tired smile. "All right, I have to ask. Do you have a contingency plan, in case Petrandius isn't amenable to providing his dragons to transport our troops?"

"As a matter of fact, I do." Morgan scrubbed a hand across his face.

"Oh? What is it?"

"Well, when I say I have a contingency plan, I guess what I mean is I have a crazy idea."

"Crazier than dragons?"

"Point taken. All right, here it is. The wizards can make use of transfer portals, you know."

"Yes. Lady Marissa and Sebastien used one to get from Vynfold to Caerfaen, in time to warn us of the plot to assassinate the Dwarf delegation."

"Right." Morgan shrugged. "I figure there's got to be a portal or two up north. If Petrandius turns down my request, I'm going to talk to Master Sebastien. Since he's Acting Chief Wizard, I hope he will agree to have the wizards use the portals to get some men to Dunstanshire."

"After what you and Marissa did, recovering the Demon's Fire, and routing the demon inhabiting Foxwent? The wizards could hardly refuse, could they?"

"No, that's what I figured. However, because the portals are only able to take a couple of people at a time—one of whom has to be a wizard—it's not ideal by any means."

"But better than nothing," Rhys said.

"But better than nothing," Morgan echoed. "At least we'd be able to get a few men in place and warn the garrisons before the Rhuddlanis showed up on their doorstep."

~*~

"Wyvrndell, can you hear me?" Morgan called.

At first there was no response, and he was ready to call again. At last Wyvrndell's voice sounded in his mind. *"I am here, Morgan McRobbie."*

The dragon's voice was subdued, so unlike his normal tone, Morgan asked, "Are you all right, Wyvrndell?"

"Yes. I am—rather busy at the moment."

"I'm sorry. I didn't mean to disturb you. I rather hoped you might request a favor of King Petrandius for me."

"I cannot," came the terse reply.

"Oh." Morgan struggled to process this. "Are you no longer in the king's good graces for some reason?"

There was a long pause before Wyvrndell answered. *"King Petrandius is dead."*

"What? Oh, Wyvrndell, I am sorry. I had no idea…"

"No, of course not. His death was…sudden."

"I see. Well, you did tell me he was very old."

"Yes, he was ancient. The whole of Ervantium is in mourning at his passing. It is the end of an era. I would ask you to give this news to King Rhys. He should know what has transpired."

"Of course. Wyvrndell, I—I'm not quite sure how to put this. It is a quite human question, so please forgive me if it is out of place. Will there be some manner of memorial service for Petrandius? If so, and if you felt it appropriate, I'm sure Rhys would wish to come and honor him. And to extend greetings to the new king."

"Petrandius will lie in the great hall for five days, for his dragons to come to praise and honor him. I appreciate your offer, but I fear Rhys's presence at this juncture might be viewed by some as provocative. Best not to chance it."

"I understand. I'll let Rhys know. But tell me, if you may, who will be the new king? Will it be Wyzandar? I know you hoped he might rule when Petrandius was no more."

Another long pause. This time the dragon sounded embarrassed. *"Petrandius named me his successor. I am to be the king in his stead."*

Morgan sat back in his chair, his mind reeling. *I didn't see that coming. I wonder if Wyvrndell did.* To the dragon he said, "Well, congratulations are in order. I'm sure Rhys will feel the same."

"Thank you. I had no notion Petrandius planned to name me to fill his place. I am honored, of course, but also daunted by the prospect. In addition, there are complications which I cannot go into at the moment. However, though I said it would not be appropriate for King Rhys to attend our farewell to Petrandius, I would like him to be present—along with yourself and Lady Marissa—when I am installed king of Ervantium."

"Marissa and I would be honored," Morgan said, and meant it. "And I'm certain Rhys will be. I will relay this news to him right away."

"Very well. What was it you wished me to ask of Petrandius?"

"No, never mind. You have enough to deal with."

"Please, tell me. I will grant your request if it is within my power. I am not yet king, mind you."

"Yes, of course." Morgan recounted the reported incursion of Rhuddlani troops into the northern reaches of Kilbourne, and his hope dragons might aid in conveying men of the Legion to spread the warning before the northern garrisons were overrun.

Wyvrndell hesitated for what seemed like an eternity. Morgan waited, his fingers tapping out a staccato tattoo on top of his desk. At last the dragon said, *"I can send four dragons to you, no more, to aid you in this endeavor. They are trustworthy, and will do this out of loyalty to me, even before I am acclaimed king. I will send them soon. Get your men ready. I will tell you when the dragons are on their way. It will not be until tomorrow, at the earliest."*

"Thank you, Wyvrndell. Your trust means a great deal. Tomorrow is soon enough, for it gives me time to get things ready here. Again, I am sorry for your loss, but rejoice in your new title. I am sure you will be a wise and just monarch. I will trouble you no further, for I'm sure you have many things to do. As well as a king to both mourn and celebrate."

Even while he spoke, Morgan sensed his connection to the dragon being severed. He rose at once, for he also found himself with a great many things to do, and little time to do them.

CHAPTER THIRTY-TWO
Royal College of Wizards, Caerfaen

Alain trudged up the long flights of stairs leading from the secure archives. Arbell had turned him away, saying he wasn't yet recovered from the previous day's exertions to cope with another round of "On Dwarfish Mages."

"Even with your lady witch absent," he'd said, "the book will be too rambunctious. I need to be in full fighting fettle to handle it. We wouldn't want things to get out of hand, would we?"

No, Alain agreed, best if things not get out of hand. The princess, Arbell reiterated, should not accompany Alain on the morrow. She was much too tempting a target for the magical tome. And so Alain made his way back toward the main floor of the archives.

He reflected while he mounted the long stairways how much his existence had changed in the last few weeks: serving as head underarchivist and agent for Lord Holman Barzak in the palace of Prince Azim of Arvindir; finding himself in a rather ambiguous relationship with a sultry princess; and finally, fleeing Arvindir on dragonback, a fugitive implicated in Azim's death. His mind reeled just thinking about it all. He'd reported to Lord Holman, who had growled, "Well done, you," and given instructions to keep himself ready should another assignment present itself.

Alain found himself at a loss without Saia at his side to banter and bicker with. Reaching the main archives, he made his way toward the exit. He barely noticed the bustle of activity around him. So focused was he on his own thoughts, he collided with another man.

Spouting apologies, he stumbled back from the impact. Through his embarrassment and confusion he recognized his victim: Master Sebastien. "A thousand pardons, Chief Wizard," he blurted. "I did not see you."

"Ah, well then, my invisibility spell must be working today," replied the wizard.

Alain's brows furrowed. "Were—were you invisible? Is that why I bumped into you?"

Master Sebastien laughed. "No, I'm afraid not. In truth, you seemed so absorbed in your ruminations, you might have walked past an entire passel of pipers and never noticed. Is everything all right? You are not accompanied by the princess today, I notice."

"I—" Alain halted his words, for the wizard held up his hand, palm out.

"I suspect," Sebastien said in an undertone, "we might be best served to retire to my office before continuing our discussion."

"Of course, Chief Wizard," he said, following Sebastien out of the archives. Once they were ensconced in the wizard's cluttered office, Alain perched on the edge of the one chair that wasn't stacked high with books and papers.

The wizard inquired, "So, where is the princess? And how does your research progress?"

"Our research has been fraught," Alain said. "We found little of real interest, until Princess Saia stumbled across a reference to magical mist."

"Indeed." Sebastien leaned back in his chair and steepled his fingers across his belly. "Tell me more."

"We discovered the tome we needed was titled "On Dwarfish Mages." The book is housed in the secured section of the archives. The Chief Archivist was reluctant to grant us access at first. Princess Saia was most persuasive, and he relented."

Sebastien smiled. "I believe I would have enjoyed witnessing their encounter."

Alain continued his tale, telling the chief wizard of their visit to the secure archives, the meeting with Arbell, and the revelation that the text they required was written in the Dwarfish language. "Fortunately for us, Arbell was able to translate. It was necessary to reveal what it was we were looking for. I hope we didn't cause any problems doing so. We had little choice if we were to pursue this."

Sebastien waved his hand. "Don't be concerned about it. I know Arbell of old. He is both trustworthy and closed mouthed. No one will learn of your quest from him. The only one he talks to is that snake of his."

Alain shuddered at the mention of Myrvyn. He hadn't been looking forward to another encounter, and the day's respite was welcome in that regard. "I'm glad to hear it. We were concerned, but Saia also felt Arbell could be trusted with the secret. The book is quite baleful, rife with power and seeking more. The archivist was barely able to control it, and after the first session he forbade Saia to return, saying it would be too dangerous for her to be present. When I went today to continue our examination, Arbell said he didn't feel up to dealing with the book again until tomorrow. The experience quite drained him to the dregs, he said, and I must confess he looked it."

"My, my. That bad, eh? Why am I not surprised? So, my young friend, what have you and your princess learned about Thundermist thus far?"

"Nothing yet which might explain how the mist affects magic wielders, I'm afraid. However, we—Arbell and I—have several sections of the book still to examine. Perhaps there will be some mention of this phenomenon."

He noted a trace of disappointment in the wizard's expression. "There was one item we found which was of great interest, Master Sebastien," he went on. "According to this text, dragons were created by one of the first Dwarf mages, out of Thundermist magic."

Sebastien stared at him, not speaking. Alain maintained his own silence. When at last the wizard spoke, it was to utter a hoarse oath. "By the stars," he muttered. "It—it's inconceivable."

Alain said, "I cannot myself speak for the veracity of this information. However, Archivist Arbell is convinced the Dwarf mage who wrote it, G'x'ln by name, was being truthful."

"Mmm." The wizard closed his eyes, and to Alain, he appeared to be in no little internal turmoil. "You realize," Sebastien said, "this raises many more questions than it actually answers?"

"I do," Alain said. "Saia and I concurred the answers to any questions about Thundermist, and the origins of dragons, will be found with the Dwarves."

Sebastien opened his eyes again, but to Alain, he appeared to be looking at something far, far away. "I fear," the wizard said, "you are correct. Alain, I would ask you to speak of this to no one. The same goes for Princess Saia."

"Oh." Alain swallowed a sudden lump in his throat. "She was planning to call on Duchess Marissa, Chief Wizard. I believe she was going to relate our findings to her…"

"The Royal Enchantress? No, no, it's fine if she knows. And of course Archivist Arbell already knows. But no one else, mind you,"

"By your order, Chief Wizard. My lips are sealed."

"Excellent. Please, Alain, continue your research with all due haste, and report what you find to me." His eyes took on a far-away look again. "Dragons, created by Dwarves," he murmured. "What a muddle that's going to be."

Alain, taking this as his cue to depart, did so.

CHAPTER THIRTY-THREE

McRobbie House, Caerfaen

Marissa sipped coffee and chased the last bit of Cook's buckle—rife with luscious berries—around her bowl. She heaved a contented sigh.

Cupping her chin in her hand, she focused on Morgan. She was certain he sensed the weight of her gaze, but he made no comment. Instead, he forked a bite of sausage, popped it into his mouth, and chewed. At last, she said, "So. You're determined to leave me?"

He held up his hands in vehement negation. "Good Lord, Marissa, you make it sound like I'm casting off my marriage vows. I'll be gone for a couple of days or so, not forever. And you understood full well I'd be having to do this sort of thing. It is my job, after all."

"I know," she said. "But I needed to make sure you realize what you're leaving behind."

He flashed her an insouciant grin. Though Morgan's smiles were much more frequent now, they still had a decided effect upon her. "I know exactly what I'm leaving behind," he said, "and I'm already looking forward to getting home again..."

"Make sure you are," she said. "I don't want it said I have a wandering duke."

"Never." He reached over to take her hand. "Once I'm back, we'll have to make plans to attend Wyvrndell's coronation ceremony."

"How exciting," she said. "I can't believe we're actually invited. Imagine being one of the only humans to ever witness such an event."

"Yes, well, I hope everything goes off smoothly. Wyvrndell was going on about some complications he couldn't discuss, whatever that means. Dragon politics, I suppose."

"Hmm. Do dragons have politics?"

"I think it's like the pox," Morgan said. "Everyone gets it at some point. Some cases are more virulent than others, that's all."

"Morgan McRobbie, that's awful," she laughed. "True, perhaps, but awful nonetheless." A thoughtful look crossed her face. "I wonder if I have time to get a new gown for the occasion."

"For dragons?" Morgan dismissed this notion out of hand. "I can't imagine they'd take much notice."

She waved away his objections. "We have to represent our species, don't we. I'm sure Rhys will be in his finery. As will you, oh Duke of the Realm."

"Hmph. We'll see. Anyway, back to the topic at hand. I want to ride partway with Farquar's company, watch how he handles things in the field. He's…well, he's untested, is the best way to put it."

"He wasn't part of the Legion during the last Rhuddlani invasion?"

Morgan shook his head. "No, he's pretty much fresh from St. Colin's. No actual experience in battle."

"You're concerned he might not be up to the task?"

"No, I'm certain he is. His training exercises have been superb, and he has good sergeants under him. Which is the most important thing; they're the ones who run things. But I should tag along and observe him in action. I have rather been neglecting my duties as Knight-Commander of late. What with one thing and another."

She favored him with a brilliant smile. Then spoiled it by inquiring, "So which am I? One thing? Or another?"

"My one thing, forever and always," he said, squeezing her hand.

"Flatterer," she said. "Very well, run off and leave me here alone, if you must. I don't want you under foot anyhow."

"Oh?" He arched a brow. "Arranging assignations already? My, what will the scandal sheets have to say?"

She pitched a muffin at his head. Morgan fielded it and took a bite. "Idiot," she said. "You'll not be rid of me so easily. But I do have plans. Today Lady Sybil is coming by for a visit. Since you won't be around, we can gossip much more freely."

Morgan chuckled. "She adores you, you know. For which I am grateful."

"Well, being taken captive by pirates together does have a way of forming a bond, don't you think?"

"Never having been taken captive by pirates, I shall defer to your broader experience in such matters. But I'd have to imagine it does. By the way, be sure to introduce her to Sir Jamie. I've a feeling they'd get along like sausage and gravy."

Marissa shook her head in bemusement. "An interesting choice," she noted. "Somehow it wouldn't surprise me in the least. But no, not today. Perhaps I'll broach the notion, but no more."

"Suit yourself." Morgan munched another bite of muffin. "What else are you planning."

"Princess Saia sent a note asking if she could stop by, and since your mother is coming today, I asked her to come tomorrow for tea. Also, I've invited Miss Taggart. I want to introduce both of them, but particularly Miss Taggart, to Catoya Alford."

His forehead wrinkled in concentration. "Alford, Alford? Oh, yes, the head witch?" he ventured.

"Head of the Council of Venerable Enchantresses," she confirmed. "I'm going to see if she's willing to take Kate—Miss Taggart to you—in hand and teach her the ways of witchcraft."

Morgan leaned back in his chair and finished the last of the muffin. From around it, he said, "You don't think you should wait until we've sorted this whole church versus witches nonsense first?"

Marissa narrowed her eyes at the thought. "Yes, well, I'd prefer to wait. Safer for everyone concerned. However, Sebastien believes it would be best to get her into training in order to avoid any mishaps."

"She's powerful?"

"Sebastien hasn't come right out and said so. Which, in typical wizardly obfuscation, I take to mean yes. So I figured it best to arrange this little gathering."

"Ah, your own coven," Morgan mused, grinning.

"Pooh. Since you'll be gone, we'll have the ginger biscuits to ourselves. So there." Her smile this time was triumphant.

"Humph. Well, perhaps I can persuade Mrs. Brand to pack me a supply for the journey."

"Absolutely not. How would it look, your men riding into danger, and you munching away like anything on ginger biscuits."

"Mmm, perhaps you're right..." He heaved an oppressed sigh.

"Don't worry, I'll save you a few for your return. They'll give you a good reason to hurry home."

He gave her hand another squeeze. "I already have a good reason," he said. "The best reason, in fact."

"That," she said, leaving her seat to slide onto his lap, "was the correct response." Then her lips were on his, and there was neither need nor opportunity for further muffins, biscuits, or conversation.

A bit later, Marissa stood watching from a window. Morgan trotted down the front steps of McRobbie House. His pack was slung over one shoulder, and he was dressed in the clothes he liked best: his black leather trousers and shirt, and a leather jacket. His new sword, in its sleek sheath, hung from his hip. His boots, gleaming from a last-minute polish by Kevin, beat a staccato rhythm on the marble of the steps.

She gave a huge yawn, made an attempt to suppress it when Morgan glanced back at her, and failed. He grinned at her. "Go back to bed," he urged. "It's beastly early."

"It won't kill me," she said, and yawned again. The sun wouldn't even be thinking of shouldering its way up over the horizon for at least another hour. "Well, perhaps," she hedged, not bothering to hide her yawn this time. "Don't get up to any mischief while you're off galivanting with the Legion. I wouldn't want to have to do anything witchy."

He grinned again. He did so much more often, but his smiles still made her insides go gooey, like a jammy tart. "I'll do my best to behave myself, Your Witchiness," he said. "I'll be back sometime the day after tomorrow." He hesitated, then added, "I love you."

"As well you might." She returned his grin. "I love you too. Go on, so I can get some more sleep and dream of your return."

"That," he said, "sounds promising." He turned, gave a final wave, and strode off in the direction of the parade ground, where Captains Farquar and Darby were assembling their troops.

Marissa waited until he was out of sight. Once he was gone she turned, pulling her dressing gown around her, and went back into the house in search of more coffee. She had too much to do, and too much on her mind, to go back to bed. She yawned again.

CHAPTER THIRTY-FOUR

Parade Ground, Caerfaen

Morgan surveyed his assembled troops.

Captain Byron Darby, huge, red haired, and radiating a quiet fury. His sergeant, Sir Ronall, whose name to this day instilled a frisson of fear in at least half the men in the Legion, Morgan included. Rhys swore he continued to have nightmares of Sir Ronall's tongue lashings, even these many years later. The rough-and-tumble old soldier had been Morgan's sergeant once upon a time, back when they'd been fighting off the last Rhuddlani incursion.

The squad was rounded out by ten hand-picked men from Byron's elite Green Rangers. They were the best in all Kilbourne at close-terrain forest operations, slipping in silent menace from tree to tree to deal out sudden death to those who would invade Kilbourne. Morgan nodded his approval.

He would have preferred to send an entire company, both to spread the warning and to reinforce the northern garrisons. However, Wyvrndell was dealing with his own issues, and was unable to spare more than four dragons. Even so, Morgan counted his blessings, for having those four was a boon beyond hope.

The Rhuddlanis, he was certain, would be counting on the snows which would soon blanket the northern highlands to prevent word getting back to Caerfaen before they'd dug into their positions. By then it would be too late for the Legion to head northward to rout them. The only reason they had any inkling of this new incursion was thanks to the Tzigani. Morgan gave silent thanks for the alliance Captain Radivan had forged with him. The fruits of it were paying off with handsome dividends. Morgan wondered what he could do to repay the debt. Well, no doubt something would present itself in time.

Each of the four dragons, Wyvrndell assured him, would be capable of bearing three men and their gear. Not much, in the grand scheme of things. But the speed with which they would arrive in Dunstanshire might make the difference. At least the garrisons wouldn't be caught napping.

In another few hours, Captain Farquar would lead a mounted company of knights and soldiers northward. The journey would take them a good four, perhaps five, full days. Even so, Morgan was confident their arrival would serve to further reinforce Kilbourne's defenses. With any luck, they might achieve a complete rout of the invaders.

It was an odd sensation to not be leading this company himself. Rhys, however, vetoed it when he'd broached the notion.

"You have excellent captains, Morgan," he'd said. "Let them do what they've trained for. I want you here in Caerfaen. There are too many things going on at the moment. Between the rebel bishops, this Rhuddlani strike, and a possible power struggle amongst the dragons, I want you close at hand."

Morgan, deeming it not politic to argue the point, dropped the subject.

Byron strolled over while Sir Ronall was making his final inspection of the squad. The dragons should be arriving any moment.

"I've had a wee notion, Commander," Byron said.

Morgan raised a brow. Byron went on, "Tell me if I'm correct. Once I've been introduced to one of these dragons, he'll be able to speak with me, right?"

"Yes, he will," Morgan concurred, baffled but game.

"And they can continue to do so, even over long distances, can they not?"

"Yesss…" Morgan's eyes went wide as Byron's idea blossomed in his brain. "Byron, that's brilliant. If you can speak to a dragon, and he can in turn speak to me…"

"We have a way to communicate and coordinate from afar," Byron finished.

"Right. And if we get Farquar in on this, you'd be able to apprise him of your situation."

"Assuming yon dragon is agreeable," Byron said.

Morgan turned to a page hovering nearby. "Conall. I need Captain Farquar here three minutes ago."

"Yes, sir." The boy was off and running before Morgan finished speaking.

"Ah, to be young again." Morgan sighed.

"I reckon you've got a bit of life in you yet," Byron replied with a grin. "For an aged duke, I mean."

Before Morgan managed to form a rejoinder, Sir Ronall cried, "Here they come. Look lively, lads. Form up, groups of three. Devin, you'll be with the captain and me."

"Aye, Sergeant." Devin tossed off a textbook salute.

Morgan glanced around the parade ground and was relieved to spy Declan Farquar loping toward them, with Conall not far in his wake. Farquar pulled to a halt before Morgan, saluted, and said, "Aye, Commander?"

He wasn't even breathing hard. Morgan vowed, not for the first time of late, to start morning training with his troops again. He was getting soft and comfortable. *For an aged duke, indeed.* A grin warred with a grimace at Byron's evaluation. Well, the duke bit he was stuck with, but he'd never been one to live a life of ease, and this wasn't the time to start.

"Declan." Morgan returned the salute. In a few words, he explained Byron's plan for keeping them in touch.

The captain's eyes widened. "Speak with a dragon," he said in reverent tones. "If it works, 'twill be a rare boon, and no mistake. To know where Byron and his men are, and their situation, from afar? And he to know our position and status? Couldn't ask for better, Commander."

The dragons were landing, a short distance from where the soldiers stood watching, wide-eyed. Morgan led his captains across the field to where they waited. Both Byron and Declan had encountered Wyvrndell before, although Declan had been subjected to no more than a strafing run by the dragon. Byron, along with Sir Ronall, had been with Morgan when he'd bested the dragon by means of a ruse and earned the dragon's respect.

One of the dragons, with scales the color of an emerald, stepped forward. *"I am Donathyr, of the King's Guard,"* he said by way of introduction. *"With me are Bezyndir, Grynal, and Luvrantis. At the behest of King Wyvrndell, we have agreed to bear your men to the northlands of your kingdom, near to the range of mountains you men call the Devil's Teeth."* He bared his own in a toothy dragon grin.

Morgan bowed to the dragons and introduced himself and his companions. Once the formalities were attended to, he laid out Byron's idea for maintaining communications under the auspices of the dragons.

Donathyr cocked his head, mulling over the plan. Morgan thought it a most human gesture. Or were men merely copying the dragons? While this incongruous thought flitted through his brain, Donathyr said, *"It is a good plan. I foresee no problems with it. It will place no undue burden on me. I would, however, suggest one improvement, if I may."*

"Of course," Morgan said.

"It might be wise to have more than one of your men from each group able to speak with me. Should some misfortune befall…"

"Wise indeed," Morgan said. "Of course, dragons are renowned for their sagacity. Let me summon Sir Ronall and—" He stopped, for no other men from Declan's company were present. Morgan didn't want to delay a moment longer than needed. A sudden inspiration struck him.

"Conall," he called, while Byron hailed Ronall. "To me, at once."

The page hustled over. "How may I serve, Commander?"

"Conall, I have a special assignment for you," Morgan said, kneeling to the boy's level. "If you're willing, I'd like you to serve as aide de camp to Captain Farquar when he and his men ride north to rout the Rhuddlanis."

Conall's eyes shone like stars.

"And," Morgan continued, "you will learn to speak with the dragon Donathyr. This way, should some misfortune befall the captain, the company has another who can communicate with him, to get messages to myself and Captain Darby. I must warn you, this is not a jolly outing. You ride into danger. Are you willing?"

The lad's eyes were wide as saucers. He swallowed once, then snapped off a perfect salute. "By your order, Commander. I am ready to serve."

Morgan clapped him on the shoulder. "Good lad. Come, and I'll introduce you…"

CHAPTER THIRTY-FIVE
Over Northern Kilbourne

Sir Byron sat astride a dragon, the wind whipping through his long red hair, and a huge grin on his face. At first he'd thought Morgan's scheme a wee bit daft. Now he was certain this was the only way to travel.

Of course, the dragons would have a much different perspective on the matter. Unlike horses, which were smart enough in their own way, the dragons were in truth their own people. As intelligent, or perhaps more so, than he was, and able to communicate. He found it rather mind-boggling.

Byron normally wasn't given over to introspection. Yet here, riding the wind upon Donathyr's back, he experienced a sensation of being rather insignificant. He wondered what the dragons' opinion of him and his kind would be. Donathyr didn't appear to be surprised when he inquired.

"Dragons are the oldest of the world's races," he said. *"Next came the Dwarves, and finally you, youngest of all, men. Dragons and Dwarves are more alike than either of us care to admit. Not in appearance,"* he added in response to Byron's startled exclamation. *"But of a certainty in temperament and cunning. Petrandius believed this, and I deign he was right. You men are something altogether different."*

"How do you mean?" Byron asked.

"First off, you men live such short spans, compared to either dragon or Dwarf. You have no real sense of history, of the world's turning, and of your own place in it. You slaughter each other in your

thousands, and for what? For a piece of the world which neither you nor your enemy can in good conscience lay claim to."

Before Byron could object to this less than flattering assessment, Donathyr said, *"Yes, I know: we bear you northward toward such a conflict. This was Wyvrndell's decision, for he counts some among your number allies. Yet most dragons consider you men to be ephemeral beings who leave little mark upon their passing."*

Byron spoke up, curious how he might manage in debate with this creature. "So if another dragon—or worse, a Dwarf—were to attempt to take by force something you have long strived to possess, would you allow them to take it? Or would you not fight for it?"

"Well—"

"Long have we men heard the tales of the conflicts between dragons and Dwarves, over gold. Centuries have you contested this, have you not? Is it not the same? For I would learn the difference, to my benefit."

Donathyr was silent for several wingbeats. At last he said, *"It is said of men you are fiercesome brawlers. I, Donathyr, do say you are also wily debaters. It is as you have said. We are the same, for we will fight for what we believe to be ours. The one difference is this—where men strive against other men, and Dwarf against Dwarf, dragons do not fight among themselves."*

Byron's brows rose. "An excellent point, good Donathyr. I myself, by your courtesy, do go to engage in battle with those of my kind, who seek to wrest from my king and country a piece of what we consider ours."

"Whereas we dragons have one king over all. Perhaps this explains it. We have no disputes of territory like you do."

"An excellent system, if it works," Byron replied. "Yet in our short history, there is always another who believes a piece of land, or a crown, should belong to him instead. Do dragons never encounter this problem?"

"Our histories, which go back practically to the crafting of this world, report no such strife. Only now—"

"Only now?" Byron prompted. He found himself fascinated to be in a discussion with a being so alien to him, and was eager to learn what he could in the short time they had together.

Donathyr blew out a spurt of flame. It appeared to Byron a gesture of frustration, much as he might heave a great, resigned sigh. *"King Petrandius had no heir. To assure a smooth succession upon his passing, he selected Wyvrndell to be the next king."*

"Yes, Commander McRobbie told me of this. Go on…"

"One of the king's councilors, Jakarian, was angered by the king's decision. He was certain he would be Petrandius's choice. When Wyvrndell was named, Jakarian vowed he would never acknowledge him as king. Petrandius cast him out of Ervantium. Jakarian left the great hall, taking with him a contingent of like-minded dragons, and went into exile."

"An old story in the world of men," Byron said, his voice sad. "And it grows no less bitter through the long years."

"Never has this happened in our realm before. The king, or so history tells us, has always met with the acclaim of all dragons."

"Tell me," Byron urged, for he was certain this information was important enough to report to King Rhys. "The fact this other dragon left in anger, taking his retinue with him—it will not affect Wyvrndell's ascension to the throne, will it?"

"No, it should not. Jakarian is banished, by order of Petrandius. There is aught he can do."

"Ah, but will he stay exiled? If your old king is gone, and Wyvrndell not yet crowned, will there be any to enforce this banishment should he decide to return?"

"You have a twisty mind, Byron Darby," Donathyr said. *"We dragons tend to think in much more of a straight line. I would never have contemplated such a possibility."*

"It's the reason I'm going north," Byron told him. "After Rhuddlan's last attempt to invade our lands, their king signed a peace treaty. You see how well that's working out for us."

"Hmmm. I wonder," Donathyr mused. *"Would Jakarian be so deceitful and treacherous?"*

"It depends how much he desires to be king," Byron replied. "And what he would do to achieve his goal."

"Yes, I see—" Donathyr's head jerked up. One of the other dragons in the formation had bugled a call of some sort. Byron sent his gaze around, wondering what—if anything—was wrong. Who knew what these creatures, even intelligent as they obviously were, were doing? He might well have been announcing it lunchtime.

"A flight of dragons approaches," Donathyr reported. His voice in Byron's head sounded both puzzled and a bit wary.

"Perhaps Commander McRobbie was able to arrange for more dragons to bring our men north," Byron suggested.

"I think not. Those would be flying up from the south, and would be coming from behind us. These dragons are coming toward us, from the northwest. I have a foreboding, Sir Byron. Make sure you and your companions are secure."

"Trouble," Byron said. Not a question, a statement of fact. Turning to Ronell and Devin, he said. "There's a possible attack force incoming. Be prepared."

"Prepared?" demanded Ronell. "Beggin' your pardon, Captain, but how the hell are we supposed to be prepared? We're up in the middle of the wide blue sky, no offence to the dragons, and like to fall off as not."

Byron grunted. "Then I reckon you'd better bloody well make sure it's 'not', hadn't you?" This left Sir Ronell speechless for once in the entirety of Byron's acquaintance. Under other circumstances, he might have spent some time savoring it. Now, there were too many other things to worry about.

"Have your companions given the bad news to the rest of my men?" he asked Donathyr.

"Yes." The answer, when it came, was terse. The dragon craned his neck, scanning toward the approaching flight of dragons.

"I feel qualified to answer your previous question, Sir Byron," Donathyr said. *"Jakarian wants the kingship badly. This is his opening gambit toward attempting to claim it."*

"By attacking you?"

"Yes, I am afraid so. I do not expect this will be an exchange of pleasantries. This venture is Lord Wyvrndell's first act as Petrandius's successor, and Jakarian will not wish it to succeed."

"Perhaps it would be best if you set us down somewhere?' Byron suggested.

"If we did so, Jakarian and his cohorts would char you out of existence. At least if you remain with us, you have a chance of surviving. Jakarian may be old and cunning, but he is no fighter. Nor are many of those who went with him. Yet we four, we are the king's own guard, tested in battle and fiercesome. Be of stout heart, Byron Darby. I have not come to this age to be bested by the likes of these."

Then the other dragons were upon them.

CHAPTER THIRTY-SIX

McRobbie House, Caerfaen

Marissa had spent a most enjoyable afternoon and evening with Lady Sybil the previous day. The Dowager Viscountess had arrived bearing an unexpected gift, in the form of a pair of new sword parasols. Though uncertain she'd ever have a need for quite so many weapons, since Lady Sybil had given her a brace of five for a wedding gift, Marissa accepted them in the spirit in which they were given. They'd taken tea, toured more of the house—without meeting Sir Jamie along the way, for which Marissa was grateful—and then gone out to an excellent dinner and a play. If Lady Sybil had taken note of the Legion soldiers who followed in their wake, she made no mention of the fact.

Today Marissa would, as Morgan so blithely had teased, meet with her own little coven of witches. She wondered, while she prepared to receive her guests, how Morgan was getting on. Though they'd both jested about his accompanying Captain Farquar, she knew he was torn between his need to deal with the Rhuddlanis' challenge to Kilbourne's security, and the threat from the rebel bishops. The Rhuddlanis seemed a very distant menace at the moment, but one he couldn't neglect. If the invaders established a base in Dunstanshire over the winter, he'd explained, the Legion would have a difficult time chasing them back over the mountains again.

The rebel bishops, she realized, seemed more of an imminent danger because they were a threat to her personally. And to the women coming to tea today. She glanced at the clock in surprise when the bell sounded at the front door. Someone was very early.

"Good afternoon, Princess Saia," Marissa said when Briana

showed the Parthanian woman into the parlor. "I am delighted to see you again. Though I wasn't expecting you quite yet. Please, sit. Would you care for tea, or perhaps coffee? Nothing like you have in Parthane—my, that was strong— but it's quite good. I've just been having a cup myself."

Saia sank into a chair. "Coffee would be welcome," she said. "I am becoming used to the style here and am learning to enjoy it. Tea, I can take or leave."

Marissa stood and poured her guest a cup of the steaming beverage, savoring the nutty, smoky aroma rising up from the pot. Saia took an exploratory sip, nodded her approval, and drank some more.

"I must apologize for descending on you without warning like this", Saia said. "There is something I needed to discuss, and since you mentioned you had other guests coming, I deemed it better for your ears alone."

Marissa regarded her with a speculative eye. She turned to the maid and said, "Thank you, Briana, that will be all." Once Briana departed—no doubt to dust the keyhole with her ear—Marissa took another sip of her own coffee and waited for Saia to speak. The princess set down her cup with a decisive clatter.

"I don't know if you are aware of how your King Rhys set me the task of researching the effects of Thundermist. He sent me, with Alain, to Chief Wizard Sebastien, who sent us to Chief Archivist Darvish, who... Well, you get the idea."

Marissa's brows rose at this. "No, I wasn't aware. Although I haven't spoken to His Majesty or Sebastien in several days. Have you found something?"

"Nothing yet which would explain what happened to you and me. Alain is continuing the search alone."

Marissa asked, "Have you already given up the hunt?"

Saia's laugh was tinged with bitterness. "Yes, but not by choice. I was requested—ordered, in fact—to stay away from the wizard's archives. The book which Alain and I were investigating was similar in temperament to the one you brought with you to Arvindir. The archivist said my presence, or rather my magic, was proving too intriguing to the book, and requested Alain return alone. And since you invited me here today anyway, I agreed."

"I see." Marissa shivered at the memory of the grimoire she had brought to Arvindir. The book had made every attempt to ensnare her, and it had taken the entirety of her resources to resist it. "But you did find something of interest, I assume. Otherwise you wouldn't be here at this hour."

Saia nodded. "Yes, we did. We discovered the Dwarf mages

made use of Thundermist magic.”

“Dwarf mages? My word. I didn’t realize there was such a thing. And—” she paused, her brow wrinkling— “they are nowhere near the Thundermist Sea.”

“No, they’re not. But from the little I was able to glean from the histories, the Dwarves didn’t move their kingdom to the southern reaches until a couple of centuries ago. Before this, they made their home in the mountains of the north.”

“And those mountains,” Marissa said, “meet the sea.”

“There is more. According to what Arbel read to us, since the text was in Dwarfish, well…”

“What?” Marissa demanded after a pregnant silence hung in the air.

“I’m sorry. I am having a difficult time believing this. You know of the legends which say dragons are creatures of magic?”

“Yes, of course. Because of this, dragons are impervious to magic. It’s why Azim’s spells didn’t harm the dragons, when we escaped from Arvindir.”

“Duchess,” Saia said, her voice strained. “According to the book we read, which was written by a Dwarf, dragons were created out of Thundermist magic, by the Dwarf mage D’rz’mn.”

Marissa mouth dropped open. “Oh,” she said at last. “I’ll admit, I did not see that coming.”

“No, neither did I. However, interesting though it is, this information gets us no forwarder toward learning how Thundermist affects a magic wielder. But it raises a whole host of other questions.

“I wonder,” Marissa mused, “if the dragons are aware of this.”

“Alain and I, we wondered the same thing. You, however, might be able to obtain the answer to this question, since you are on speaking terms with a dragon.”

“Hmm, yes. Though I’m not quite sure how I’d approach broaching this particular subject. ‘Oh, by the way, did you know everything you thought you understood regarding your existence is wrong?’ Not the done thing, is it?”

Saia laughed. It was the first time Marissa witnessed such a reaction from her, and it made her seem more a real person. “No, I suppose not,” the princess said. “Also, when Alain and I discussed this, we wondered if the Dwarves were aware of it either?”

“An excellent point,” Marissa said. She paused, lost in contemplation. “So the answers we seek may well lie with the Dwarves.”

“So it would seem. Since this affects us both, I felt it important you know.”

"Thank you, Saia. Your news is most intriguing. I'll have to discuss the matter both with the king and Sebastien."

"Speaking of Master Sebastien," Saia said, "he asked if he might examine me, or rather my magic. He said you have undergone such an examination, and suggested I discuss it with you before deciding."

Marissa frowned, and said, "I don't know where my head is. Sebastien asked me several days ago to broach the subject to you, since you're the one other person besides myself whose power is known to have been affected by the Thundermist. I hadn't seen you until now so it slipped my mind."

Saia sipped more coffee. "Should I do it? Is it painful?"

"Painful? No, not at all. I will admit, it wasn't the most enjoyable thing I've ever done. That being said, it wasn't onerous. It is odd, having someone traipsing around in my head, but once you get used to that, it's fine. So I would say do it. It might help Sebastien figure out how the Thundermist magic works."

"Yes, he said the same thing. All right, thank you. I'll consider it."

The bell sounded, and in a couple of minutes, Briana was ushering in Marissa's other guests. The information Saia brought would, she decided, have to wait for another day to pursue.

Rising, Marissa went to greet her guests. "Miss Alford, thank you for coming. I hope my invitation didn't sound too much like a summons. And Kate, thank you for coming too. It's lovely to see you again."

"No, not at all." Miss Alford's gaze went to the other occupants of the morning room. "I was happy to attend you. How may I be of service? And may I be introduced to these other ladies?"

"Allow me to present Princess Saia, of Arvindir. She is a newly minted sorceress. Like me, she has at least a portion of her powers courtesy of the Thundermist. And this," Marissa gestured toward Kate, "is Miss Katherine Taggart. She has also recently discovered she is a witch."

Catoya Alford regarded the two women with a speculative gaze. "I...see. Very well, ladies, it is always a pleasure to meet fellow practitioners, novice or not. We each have to begin somewhere, eh?" She turned back to Marissa. "So, Duchess Marissa, I repeat: how may I be of service?"

Marissa found herself for some reason at a loss for words. She marshalled her thoughts and spoke. "I was hoping you might be amenable to giving Kate some tutelage. I can't do it. I'm in training myself, and I'm not qualified to teach anyone else. I don't know any other witches to even ask." Her words came out in a jumbled rush, and her agitation grew and flourished.

Catoya arched one elegant brow. "It might be useful for you to attend some of our meetings, Marissa. After all, since you are the Royal Enchantress, and protector of witch-kind, you should get to know who it is you're protecting."

Marissa flushed a bright crimson. "I—yes, of course, you're right. I'm sorry. I—it's been so busy, so hectic—"

Catoya spread her hands. "Please, don't fret. I wasn't attempting to chastise you. You have, from everything I've heard, had quite enough to deal with over the last several months. And yes," she turned to regard Kate, "I'd be happy to give Miss Taggart some training."

"Thank you. I'd be most grateful," Kate said, with an appreciative smile.

Saia, who had heretofore remained silent, watching their exchange from the periphery, spoke up. "Me too?"

All three women turned to her. "Princess?" said Catoya.

"Bah. In Arvindir I was a princess. No longer. Here in Caerfaen, I must make my own way, my own place. If I have this magic in me, I'd best learn what to do with it, eh? So. Will you teach me too?"

Marissa waited, twisting her hands together while Catoya considered the request. A sense of relief washed over her when Catoya nodded and said, "I think your suggestion most sensible, Princ—Saia."

The princess—former princess, Marissa amended—inclined her head. Well, perhaps not quite as "former" as she claimed. Marissa smiled to herself. It might take Saia quite some time to actually wean herself away from her royal habits.

Catoya returned Saia's nod with one equally regal. "Very well. Marissa, if you have no objection, may we get started?"

She blinked in surprise. "What? Now?" She hesitated for a moment, and said, "Of course. But on one condition."

Catoya eyed her, curiosity showing in her visage. "Your condition?"

"That I be allowed to join you."

It was the other woman's turn to blink in surprise. "Are you sure? I understood you were being tutored by the dragon."

"Oh, I have been. Although at the moment he's quite busy with other things, so there hasn't been much time for instruction." She shrugged. "And though he's an excellent teacher, all he knows is the theory behind magic." She refrained from mentioning how Wyvrndell now possessed magic of his own. It wasn't her place to tell this tale, at least not yet. She went on. "Training from someone who is versed in the more practical aspects would be helpful, I think."

"Mmm, I see your point. Well, I have no objection. Shall we begin?"

Marissa said, "Yes, but one thing before we do. I have something I need to discuss with you."

Catoya sent her a questioning gaze. "What, Marissa?"

"I'm trying to figure out what I—we—can do to counter the bishops' decree. To protect all those women who are at risk. I mean, here we are, with a lot of magic at our disposal…"

"Speak for yourself," Kate put in. "Well, I may have it, but I've not the least idea what to do with it. Or how to do anything with it, for that matter."

Catoya cocked her head. When she spoke, her words were addressed to Kate, not Marissa. "Miss Taggart, sometimes simple, raw power is all one needs. If you are willing, and able, to allow others to make use of your power, it might make a tremendous impact. To lend extra energy to their own spells, you see. It might make the difference."

Marissa nodded. "Yes, I know what you mean. I've seen it happen. Master Sebastien, the acting chief wizard, utilized my father's power to aid him in doing a portal transfer."

"Indeed?" Catoya's eyes were bright with interest. "I've never experienced something quite so involved. Was it… No, never mind, I'm allowing myself to be distracted. Focus, Catoya," she directed.

"Is there no way to gather up these churchmen, and turn them into toads or something?" Saia inquired. "Wouldn't this solve your problem."

Marissa barked out a laugh. "It would, Saia. However, perhaps we should try for something less…toadlike?"

"Hmph." Saia grimaced. "Chickens, perhaps?"

"I'm afraid not," Marissa said. "I wish it was quite so easy. A couple of days ago, I met with two young women, at the Grey Dove. They didn't want to come here, which I can understand. Anyway, these women, both of whom have some power, were taken captive by men who intended to burn them at the stake, because the church directed it. The Watch managed to save them, and I felt it my duty to at least try to speak with them, to reassure them…"

She glanced around at her audience, then said, "I explained about how the Watch is making constant patrols of the city, to keep an eye out for just such incidents. And how the Legion also has patrols out, to make sure something like that doesn't happen again. I don't know how much I was able to reassure them of their safety. I mean, they both said they felt better, but…" She shrugged helplessly.

Catoya said, "Marissa, you are too focused on that prophecy, I fear. I've been giving it some thought. I'm not so certain you're intended to do everything yourself. I mean, when you think about it, you may be the conduit through which things happen. Like the Legion working in conjunction with the Watch. It's not something which would have happened if your husband wasn't the Knight-Commander of the Legion. Do you see what I mean?"

Marissa's reply was cut short. She whirled as something crashed through the window. "What in the…?" *A rock?* No, a glass bottle, she saw, right before it hit the floor and shattered.

Miss Alford and Princess Saia both stood rooted in place, mouths agape. Kate Taggart caught up a shawl from the back of a chair, tossing it toward the bottle. She wasn't quick enough, for once the bottle smashed, a noxious green mist swirled up from it and filled the room. "Run!" Marissa croaked. Her throat began to close from whatever had been released from the phial. She made an effort to reach one of the sword parasols Lady Sybil had brought yesterday, which were leaning tantalizingly close in the corner. If someone was forcing their way in, perhaps she could repel boarders. But already she was becoming lightheaded, and while she attempted to move on legs grown leaden, she recalled the phial which had been flung into the coach to incapacitate her and Lady Sybil when they'd started off to rescue Morgan what seemed like ages ago.

"Drat," she muttered. Her legs betrayed her and she sank to the floor in a most unladylike heap, still struggling toward the parasols. It seemed important she reach them, even if she'd be unable to put the weapons to any use. The other women were likewise slumping to the floor, though Miss Alford was waving her arm, attempting some sort of countering spell. But whatever she tried wasn't working.

Marissa moaned in frustration. There came the heavy tread of booted feet, and the darkness took her.

CHAPTER THIRTY-SEVEN
Ervantium

Wyzandar stared. "You did what?" he growled.

Wyvrndell returned his stare, with interest. "I agreed to provide transport for several of Morgan McRobbie's men," he repeated. "Four dragons. I told him I could spare no more."

"And you did not discuss this with the council? Not even with me?"

"No, Father, I did not." Wyvrndell heaved a steam-laden sigh. "I am to be king, if you recall." He ignored his sire's snort. "I shall be required to make many decisions. Very well—I made one. Not such a big one, in the grand scheme of things."

Wyzandar remained silent, watching him with a keen eye. Wyvrndell forced down a rogue hiccough and went on. "We have a treaty with the humans. One drafted by Petrandius himself. It specifies mutual aid at need. Morgan McRobbie, as agent of King Rhys, requested my aid. He wished me to ask Petrandius, but he had flown beyond."

"So the humans are aware of Petrandius's death?"

"Sir Morgan is. I am certain at the least he has informed King Rhys. I do not imagine it is general knowledge among the people of Kilbourne. Not yet at least."

"I see. Very well, tell me: for what reason did this human make such a request?"

"He received a report of an invading force from Rhuddlan, coming over the mountains they call The Devil's Teeth into Kilbourne territory. The soldiers the dragons bear will bring a warning to their northern defenses, so they are not taken unaware."

Wyzandar nodded in appreciation. "Clever," he said at last. "A bold stroke on his part. Petrandius, I think, would have approved."

"Thank you, Father." Wyvrndell forced back another hiccough which threatened to erupt. "I am glad I have your blessing."

"I did not say you had my blessing. And my approval is beside the point. Others on the council may well take a less favorable view of your actions. You do not yet wear the crown, my son. Do not let your head grow so big it does not fit."

"Have I acted rashly, my sire?"

Wyzandar rumbled out a chuckle. "Wyvrndell, when have you ever not acted rashly? Yet fortune appears to favor you. Let us hope the council does."

"And if they do not? What can they do?"

"To begin with, they could act to undermine your policies and decisions at every turn. They could even—" Wyzandar halted, shaking his great head. "No. Even they would not do …"

"What, Father?"

Wyzandar grumbled and steamed before answering. Finally, he said, "They might, if roused, refuse to perform the coronation ceremony. Refuse to install you as king."

The hiccough got the best of him. Wyvrndell belched out a cloud of acrid blue smoke. "Is such a thing even possible?" he asked warily, the remnants of his belch floating between them. Perhaps his actions had been too rash after all.

"Possible? Of course. Likely? I—well, let us hope not. Perhaps some preemptive smoothing on your part might be appropriate."

Wyvrndell hesitated, thinking hard. At last he said, "If I go to Pendrake, Zavrym, and Barantine, and explain my reasoning, they will be more inclined to accept my decision to send dragons to aid the humans. Is that what you mean?"

"Now you are thinking more like a king to be, and less like an impetuous hatchling. Tell me, why did you name those three?"

"Because from what I have observed, they have been more willing to align themselves with Petrandius. Also with you. Jakarian is gone, banished by Petrandius, and good riddance. Which leaves Tryndon and Molgyr who would be more inclined to raise a fuss. With your support, the council would be four to two in my favor."

Wyzandar gave a slight, satisfied nod. "Once you are officially acclaimed king, one of your first acts must be to name a new dragon to council, to fill Jakarian's place."

Wyvrndell turned to stare into his sire's eyes. He said, "I shall have to name two new councilors, Father."

"Two? Why do you say two?"

"Because you will have to step down. It would be too great a conflict of interest for you to remain on the council. I am sorry, but I can envision no other way."

"You are learning, my son. I hoped you would realize this. Well done. No, it would be impossible for me to remain a member of the council."

"Do not think you will get off so easily," Wyvrndell said. "Though you will no longer be on the council proper, I desire your wisdom and advice. I need you, Father. I am young, and experienced in little but youth. Yes, I have magic, and I have friends among the humans and the Dwarves. But I know so little of dragon politics and policy. Petrandius had no time to teach me the things I should have learned. I am afraid this task will fall to you. You shall be my chamberlain, if you will. You will guide me, and I shall listen to your counsel."

"Are you sure?" Wyzandar asked.

"I am. You would have made a much better king than I, Father. But since it appears to be my lot to fill the kingship, if I can hold it, you will be the King's Chamberlain and advise me when I go astray."

The older dragon bowed his head. "I shall consider it a great honor, my son. I will confess, when Petrandius named you his successor, I was sure he was mad. But now, hearing you, I think perhaps he was right all along. You will indeed bring dragons, kicking and flaming, into this new world we find ourselves inhabiting. A world of men, and Dwarves, and dragons, to make of it what we will."

"Thank you," Wyvrndell said. "I hope I am up to the challenge. I—" he stopped, listening. "Stones and flame," he said at last. "Donathyr says they are being attacked. By dragons."

Wyvrndell turned to his father, eyes wide with concern. "All right, Councilor, counsel. What should I do?"

"Nothing, I fear." Wyzandar's voice was hard as stone.

"Nothing?" Wyvrndell echoed. "But—"

"My son, you have dispatched four dragons of the king's guard. They are wily and tested in battle in ages past. They are also eager to earn favor in the new king's eye. They will not let dragons of the caliber Jakarian took with him best them. Trust me. They will prevail."

"I beg forgiveness, Father. I know nothing of battle, nor do I wish to. Dragons fighting dragons? Blast and scorch Jakarian."

"Long has he coveted the kingship, Wyvrndell. He knew full well Petrandius was failing. He sought to sway the king in his favor, with whispers in the dark, and honeyed words, which masked his true goal: to rule over all."

"Like Erkarna," Wyvrndell mused.

"Aye, my son. Each, in his own way, but yes. Both desired to rule over dragons. But even more, they both sought a return to the old ways, when we were at enmity with the other races."

"But why? Such a course would bring needless war and destruction upon the world."

"Because neither Erkarna, whom you defeated, nor Jakarian, who seeks your downfall, has learned the secret you have," Wyzandar said.

"What secret? Magic?"

"No, my king who shall be crowned. Not the secret of magic. It is a secret much simpler, but much harder to learn. It is one even I am having to learn, difficult as it sometimes seems. Erkarna and Jakarian would never understand it is possible for dragons to have friends. To rule with fire and talon, this is all they know or understand. And so, Jakarian seeks to displace you, so he may unleash his own policies of rage and terror against any he considers inferior."

"I see. Thank you, my trusted councilor, for your insight. You have opened my eyes to the realities which face me. There is but one thing to do."

"What must we do, Wyvrndell, heir of Petrandius? What would you command?"

"Father, we must move up the coronation ceremony. We should have it tomorrow. Or the day after, at the latest."

Wyzandar's stared at him, steam curling from his nostrils. "Move up—Wyvrndell, you cannot be serious."

"I have never been more serious. Jakarian will find it much more difficult to oust an acclaimed and acknowledged king than he will a pretender to the throne, which is what he considers me. Tell me, why should we wait?"

"Tradition—" began his father.

"Exactly." Wyvrndell pounced upon the word like a dragon upon a succulent sheep. "Because it has always been done so. I think, loyal councilor, we are going to break a great many traditions during my kingship. I have a suspicion Petrandius expected thus. So I intend to rule, to fulfill his wishes. I will bring his dragons, kicking and flaming and wrangling the entire way, into this new world in which we find ourselves flying. Or die in the attempt."

Wyzandar gazed at him. Wyvrndell wasn't sure if sorrow, or pity, or pride filled his sire's eyes. It didn't matter. "I will be crowned within the next two days, Father, or not at all."

"By your order," Wyzandar replied. "The king has decreed it. Let it be so."

CHAPTER THIRTY-EIGHT

McRobbie House, Caerfaen

Francesca lay sprawled on a wide windowsill in Marissa's room, wrapped in a luscious late afternoon sunbeam. Her witch was having other witches to tea, and she'd intended to eavesdrop on their conversation. And, perhaps, cadge a saucer of cream. However, the lure of the sunbeam was too strong to resist.

But she wasn't sleeping, not by any stretch of the imagination. She'd merely been…drowsing, with visions of mice flitting through her head. But now, with no warning or apparent reason, Francesca found her hackles rising of their own accord. She raised her head, alert, and scanned for signs of danger. Nothing obvious came to her. Yet there was something…

She rose, sniffing the air. There. A scent of something ancient, foul, and malevolent reached her twitching nostrils. Francesca wrinkled her nose and found her whiskers tingling.

The sound of glass breaking from below sent her into a full feline frenzy. Leaping to the floor, she streaked out of the room and hurtled down the stairs like a furry missile. From the corner of her eye she noted Kevin, sprawled on the floor of the hall. He wasn't moving, but she had no time to stop and investigate. The door to the morning room was closed, but her senses told her the danger lay in there.

Closed doors are no barrier to a determined cat. Especially a determined cat who was once a powerful witch. Once inside the room—which stank to high heaven with some type of noxious fumes—she found intruders, men who had no business there. They were cloaked, hooded, and masked, all in black. Her witch, along with the three guests, lay crumpled on the floor, succumbed to the fumes.

One of the intruders bent to pick Marissa up from the floor. With a snarl, Francesca leapt, claws extended, and landed on his woolen cloak. She scrambled upward, claws raking at his eyes, which were barely visible between the concealing hood and mask.

Her claws found their mark and the villain let out a satisfying screech. One of the other intruders rushed to the man's rescue, grabbing Francesca and pulling her off her victim. He soon discovered his mistake, for he found himself holding a slashing, squirming, snarling fury of a cat. She scored his arms and hands and was going for his throat when he managed to get a grip once more and flung her across the room.

She landed with a bone-jarring 'whump' against the far wall and slid to the floor. She lay there, dazed and blinking, while the men gathered up the four witches, slinging them over their shoulders. Francesca struggled to her feet as they made for the door and out into the hallway.

"Fire! Thieves! Murder!" she cried aloud, but no one answered the call. She started after them, but her left foreleg chose this inopportune moment to collapse under her, and she toppled ignominiously to the floor again with a piteous, mewling whimper. Undaunted, she dragged herself after the kidnappers.

From out in the hallway, the stentorian voice of Sir Jamie, the home's resident spirit, rang out. He, at least, had heard her call. Unfortunately, in his disembodied state, the intruders ignored his demands to stand and deliver.

Cursing as only a cat can curse, Francesca staggered out into the hall and toward the open front door. Her foreleg hurt like blazes, and she vowed if she caught the one who'd injured her, she'd rip him to shreds.

From a vantage point on the front stoop, she spied the cloaked men loading the four women into a black, unmarked coach. Sir Jamie continued to wave his spectral sword and utter dire oaths, but the kidnappers kept on with their dreadful work. Two of them clambered into the interior of the coach; the third scrambled up to the driver's seat. The fourth, glowering at Sir Jamie, pulled a vial from within his cloak, opened it, and flung the contents at the spirit.

The ghost gave a mournful wail, and his form began to wobble and collapse. The last kidnapper swung up onto the rear of the coach, the driver cracked his whip, and the team of black horses set off at a gallop.

Francesca made her painful way down the steps and halfway across the walkway, but she was too late. The coach, the men, and the witches were all gone.

"Damn and blast," Francesca growled. She turned back toward

the house, noting the inert forms of the two soldiers McRobbie had left to guard the place, lying in the bushes. A quick investigation assured her they were unconscious, not dead.

She stared up at the stairs leading to the open front door. The climb seemed daunting, and there was nothing she could do here anyway. The servants, assuming they were among the living, would have to deal with the aftermath of the attack here. Her mission, Francesca determined, lay in summoning the one man who might get her witch back.

She needed to find, and fetch, Morgan McRobbie.

Gathering her strength and her wits, Francesca closed her emerald-green eyes, uttered a challenging yowl, and stepped sideways into the void known only to cats.

~*~

Somewhere in Northern Kilbourne

Morgan, astride Arnicus, rode next to his newest captain. So far, he approved of the way Farquar was handling his soldiers. The first day had gone smooth as silk, and the company had made excellent time. Now, on the second day out of Caerfaen, he watched Farquar's interactions with his sergeants. The young captain was handling things well, Morgan thought. He'd made the right choice in assigning him to lead this mission.

Even so, there was a long journey ahead, and though Morgan didn't plan to ride the entire way, he did intend to accompany Farquar while he made camp tonight, then turn back in the morning.

The sky, which had started off a brilliant blue, was filling with clouds. Morgan sniffed the air, and though he couldn't detect the unmistakable acrid scent of rain, one never knew. Out here in the hill country, storms could blow up out of nowhere.

Good. Another test for Farquar. Morgan smiled to himself. He was too old a campaigner to be bothered by wind and weather, and he hoped his new captain would prove himself of a similar disposition.

The day was drifting into evening, the sun sliding towards the horizon, and Morgan wondered if Farquar would call a halt soon to rest for the night. Then his mind drifted to Marissa, and he wondered what she was doing. Probably entertaining her fellow magic-wielders, he recalled. And snaffling all the ginger biscuits…

"Commander," said Farquar, breaking into his reverie. "Did you hear that noise?"

Morgan cocked his head, wondering for a moment if perhaps Farquar had heard thunder, which he hadn't. An odd sound came to his ears, and his expression turned puzzled. "It sounds—well, like a cat," he said.

"Aye, it does. Which is strange, out here in the back of beyond. But what's truly odd is…" Farquar's voice was strained as he said, "Commander, it's coming from your saddlebag."

"Hmm. Damned if it isn't." Morgan twisted around to unfasten the strap securing his saddlebag closed and reached in. His hand encountered an unexpected, very soft, very squirmy object.

"Don't keep fumbling around, damn it," said a familiar voice. "Get me out of here."

Morgan withdrew the form of Lady Francesca, Marissa's kitten and familiar. "What the devil possessed you to hide out in there?" he asked, setting the kitten before him on Arnicus's back. "And don't use your claws to hold on, or we'll every one of us regret it."

"Um… Commander?" Declan Farquar was staring, mouth agape. "Did—did the cat speak?"

"I'm afraid so. Long story, trust me, you don't want to know. Francesca?" He turned his attention back to the cat.

"I didn't stow away," Francesca replied. "I—well, let's say I followed you, and leave it go. That part's not important. What's important is, you've got to return to Caerfaen, right away."

The cat's tone brooked no argument, and Morgan gave her his full attention. "What's happened?"

"Four men broke into the house. I tried to stop 'em, and so did Sir Jamie, but to no avail. They rendered the witches senseless and carried them off."

"What?" Morgan roared. "But—"

"No time for buts," admonished the cat. "We need to figure out where they've gone and go get them back. So you need to get back to Caerfaen, right away. Now, move."

A shudder ran through Morgan. *The rebel bishops. It must be them behind this.* He stared into Francesca's green eyes for a moment and gave a curt nod. The terror which had gripped him at her words was replaced by a cold resolve, hardening him into steel, dangerous as the sword he bore. He brushed his hand over the pommel of the sword. It tingled at his touch, seeming eager to be put into action.

"Captain Farquar," Morgan said, his voice terse. "I'll be returning to Caerfaen. Continue your mission. In fact, it may be more important than ever."

Farquar saluted, but Morgan didn't acknowledge the gesture. He'd already turned Arnicus southward. He scooped up Francesca and placed her inside his leather jacket. "Hang on," he said. "Though not with claws, if you please."

"I'm not a fool," came the muffled reply. Morgan shook up the reins and kicked the horse's flanks. Arnicus broke into a gallop, speeding like an arrow back toward the capital. It would take him until late the following morning, at least, to get back to Caerfaen. Had the men who'd planned this counted on him being this far removed from home? Or was it coincidence? Either way, he had to get back as soon as humanly—and horsedly—possible. He was reliant on Arnicus's endurance to make the journey with all possible speed.

Morgan swore, and from his jacket, he could hear the cat swearing with him. He had a feeling if Arnicus could speak, he'd be swearing too.

CHAPTER THIRTY-NINE
Somewhere Over Dunstanshire

Byron cast a wary gaze at the approaching dragons. Unencumbered by passengers, they would no doubt prove much more agile in battle than Donathyr's group.

"True," Donathyr replied, in answer to this observation. *"Yet they are not experienced in battle. We shall soon singe their tails for them if they attempt to attack."*

"It appears,' Byron said, his tone drier than the stones of the hills below them, "your chance is here." The largest of the opposing force veered off the formation to head straight for Donathyr. The incoming dragon belched out a spurt of flame, but Donathyr sideslipped off to the left, managing to avoid it. Now the attacker found himself faced with Grynal and Luvrantis, who each basted his scales with their own gouts of flame. The attacker screamed, though whether in defiance or agony, Byron was uncertain. He knew from his own observation the dragons' scales were impervious to men's weapons of swords and spears. Would they serve to protect from another dragon's fire? This wasn't, he reckoned, the time to pose such a question.

The other dragon dove toward the ground, hundreds of feet below. Grynal wheeled and set off in pursuit, the three men of Byron's squad hanging on for dear life.

"Ha," snorted Donathyr. He and the two other dragons of his patrol resumed their wedge formation. *"It is as I said. They have no skill in battle, nor any real appetite for it either. They intended to frighten us into setting you men down. They shall have to revise their strategy."*

"Their new strategy," Byron pointed out, "looks to be an attack from the rear.”

Donathyr craned his long neck around. *"It does, does it not? Well, we shall see what we can do. You had best hold on tight. This might get a bit...exciting."*

Two dragons roared behind them, and the heat of their flames passed right over Byron's head while he relayed the dragon's words. When the pair of attackers opened their jaws to flame again, Donathyr folded his wings against his body. His forward momentum carried him on for a few seconds, but to Byron's surprise the dragon then dropped like a stone for a distance of fifteen or twenty yards. He spread his wings wide again, catching air with a snap which jolted Byron and his companions off their seats. The three men scrambled and scrabbled to hang on. The dragon flapped his wings, gaining altitude again. The attackers flew onward in a straight line, caught by surprise and unable to change course to compensate for Donathyr's maneuver. He was positioned behind his former pursuers and his flame, like the roar of a hundred forges, lashed the two dragons. They attempted to take evasive action, but found themselves hemmed in by Luvrantis and Bezyndir, whose flames basted them from each side.

"Oh, well played," cried Byron with a tactician's keen approval. "A brilliant maneuver, Donathyr. You have them on the run."

Indeed, the two dragons dove toward the ground, emulating their predecessor. Donathyr scanned the sky for further threats. *"Jakarian alone is left to confront us. I do not imagine he will deign to risk his own neck in combat. He lets others do his dirty work for him."*

The remaining dragon wheeled away, streaking back northward, abandoning his cohorts.

Donathyr and his fellow guards resumed their formation once more. *"Yet I do not expect we have seen the last of Jakarian,"* Donathyr said. *"He may have no fight in him, yet he is crafty."*

Byron stared after the retreating dragons. "You anticipate they'll be back?"

"Not if they value their miserable hides," the dragon replied, a thrill of triumph marking his tone. *"Now I must report to Wyvrndell and tell him what has happened here."*

"Well?" Sir Ronell asked once Byron was done speaking with Donathyr.

"It appears the battle is over. And, to our fortune, our side has prevailed."

"Good," the crusty old sergeant said. "These creatures routed 'em quite well, but I shouldn't like to go through another engagement. I thought for certain we was to be charred into little black bits, like what you'd scrape off the bottom of a frypan."

"Lovely," Byron muttered. Gazing ahead, he was able to make out the peaks of the Devil's Teeth looming in the distance, shrouded in mist. Closer to hand, the land below them swept upward, turning from lowland plains to forested highlands. He smiled to himself. This was home.

Well, it had been home, he amended. For now, his home was Caerfaen, with Clarise. But perhaps, he mused, after they'd dealt with this latest incursion by the blasted Rhuddlanis, and he and Clarise were wed, he might bring her back to this country. See if she liked it as he did, the high hills and rushing streams and sun-dappled forests…

He was yanked from this pleasant reverie by the voice of Donathyr in his head once more. *"We are coming close to the land you men call Dunstanshire. Where would you have us bring you?"*

"The fortress at Noordstrom," Byron said. "Can you bring us there?"

"We can," rumbled the dragon. *"Though it might be wise for us to land some distance from the fortress itself. I should not like to have borne you this far, to find you filled with arrows by your own kind, 'til you look like a hedgehog. This way, you will have a chance to explain things to your comrades."*

"An excellent plan," Byron said. *Damn, I should have thought of that myself.* A flock of dragons descending on the city would of course be viewed with alarm, and the soldiers of the garrison would do their best to protect it.

"Very well," Donathyr said. *"We will land outside the walls of the city, close enough for you, but at a safe enough distance so you do not get skewered."*

"You are wise, Donathyr," Byron said. "And most kind to bear my men and I hither. Yet I wonder if your good will might run to one further small endeavor."

"What might this small endeavor be?"

"I hoped, once the others have been dropped outside the fortress, you might consent to bear me a bit further."

"Reconnaissance?" said Donathyr, and Byron noted an approving tone in his voice. *"To learn where the enemy force is located?"*

"Yes," said Byron. "To know where they are, and how they are situated, would be a boon beyond telling. Would you mind?"

"Your request is not unreasonable, and is in keeping with Wyvrndell's command. You and I alone shall go, Sir Byron. We will fly high, so none from the ground spot us, and you may observe what you

can."

"Thank you, Donathyr." Byron's words were heartfelt. "This is good news beyond imagining." Turning to Ronell, he outlined his plan. "You'll need to enter the city and alert the garrison. Bosquet is there, he knows you."

"Aye, he does," Ronell replied. "Now whether he'll believe me is another thing."

"He'll believe this," Byron said, handing him an oilskin pouch. "This contains orders signed by Commander McRobbie. Show them to Bosquet and take charge of the muster 'til I return. I doubt I'll be too long. A few hours, at best."

"Aye, by your order, Captain," Ronell said.

Ahead and below them, Byron saw the spires of Noordstrom. The last time he'd been here was during the final rout of the Rhuddlanis, when King Llewellyn, Rhys's father, had been slain in battle. It seemed like so long ago.

In another twenty minutes the dragons had landed and offloaded eleven men and their gear. Sir Ronell led them at a trot toward the city gates. The three other dragons took wing, banking to head eastward.

"Now we will go, you and I," Donathyr said. *"And I say to you, Byron of Kilbourne, this is the most excitement I have had in a century."* He leapt back into the air, turning to wing his way westward, where the sun was just beginning to consider easing its way towards the horizon.

"How old are you?" Byron asked in wonder. The dragon's shadow swept over the city, and men below on the guard towers pointed up toward them. Horns rang out, faint but full of challenge. Donathyr ignored them.

"By men's reckoning, you would count me eight hundred and more of your years. Yet I am in my prime by dragons' figure. Petrandius, our king who was, he was ancient, even by a dragons count. Four times my years did he live, and though his body was frail at the end, his mind was clear as any dragon I have ever met."

"He must have seen the world begin," said Byron in awe.

"Nay, though his sire's sire, Grythorn the Black, is said to have flown soon after the world saw its first light."

"Incredible," Byron breathed. They swept up near the clouds.

Donathyr fell silent, and Byron scanned the land below, his keen eyes searching for any sign of the Rhuddlanis. Over trackless forests and small plots of cultivated land they flew. Ahead, a shimmering river cut a swath across the landscape, and small villages clung here and there to its banks. Far over all this they flew, so the figures of men below were like tiny insects to Byron's bemused gaze.

They crossed over the river, heading farther west. At last, Byron spotted far beneath them the column of marching soldiers, like a line of ants. "There they are," he cried.

"I see them," the dragon replied. *"Do you wish to go lower?"*

"No, we'd best not," Byron said, though he felt an urge to make a closer observation of the enemy. In the end, good sense prevailed. *No need to let the Rhuddlanis know they've been spotted.* "But let me mark their position." He pulled a map from his belt pouch. Unrolling it against the wind, he gazed at the line of troops below, spread out across the landscape like an infestation of insects, trying to match their location with the map.

"Got it," he said. "And it is interesting. They're bypassing most of the villages along their route. At least I can spot no clouds of smoke nor scorched earth. I wonder…"

"If you would like," Donathyr suggested, in what sounded like an eager voice, *"I could swoop down on their leaders, and with flame fright them into panic and disarray."*

Byron chewed on this for a moment. He shook his head. "An enticing prospect, but better they remain unaware we have marked their presence."

"Very well," replied Donathyr, banking eastward again.

"Would you be able to relay a message to Captain Farquar? Tell him we have arrived at the garrison at Noordstrom and give him the position of the Rhuddlanis."

"I can indeed," said the dragon. *"Tell me all you would have him know."*

Byron did so. By the time Donathyr was finished speaking with Farquar, they arrived back at the city.

"Noble Donathyr, dragon of the king's guard, I thank you," Byron said, bowing to the dragon. "It has been a pleasure to fly with you, and even more to converse with you. May your return to your home be swift and safe."

Donathyr gave no reply, but nodded his huge head. He leapt into the air once more, his great wings lifting him above the treetops. Byron kept his gaze on him until he was out of sight. With a shake of his head, he shouldered his pack and headed for the gates of the city.

CHAPTER FORTY
Somewhere in Northern Kilbourne

Conall rode pillion behind Sergeant Dannay. At first, Captain Farquar put him behind himself. Once he'd realized having both members of the company who were able speak to Donathyr together might endanger the entire mission, he'd relocated Conall.

Conall basked in the notion of being a vital part of the mission. Then, he offered up fervent prayers nothing would happen to the captain. Even assuming nothing untoward occurred, the other boys in his cadre of pages would be victim to unbridled envy at his being chosen to accompany Farquar and his men to help guarantee the safety of the northern provinces. And even more jealous he'd been picked to speak with the dragon, Donathyr.

"All right back there, lad?" Sergeant Dannay's voice pulled him from his reverie.

"Aye, Sergeant, I'm fine."

"Good, good. Say, hand me a meat roll from my saddlebag, will you? And snag one for yourself."

"Thank you, Sergeant." Conall opened the bag and extracted two meat rolls. He handed one forward and took a bite of the other. His stomach rumbled in appreciation, and even though he longed to finish it right away, he forced himself to savor every mouthful.

The meat roll was flaky, sending a shower of crumbs onto his tunic with each bite. Within lay a mixture of spiced mutton, parsnips, and onions, and taken altogether, Conall thought it one of the most wonderful things he had ever put in his mouth in his twelve years. When he mentioned this to Dannay, the sergeant laughed.

"Enjoy it while you can, Conall." He wiped his mouth on his sleeve. "We'll eat pretty well for the first day or two, with what we can carry with us. After our supplies run out, we'll have to forage. We're moving fast and traveling light. No supply wagons, and no cooks on this jaunt."

"Forage?" This sounded much too much like digging for grubs and picking berries. The tone of his reply set Dannay off into another round of chuckling.

"Don't worry, lad, it's not so bad. Mayhap we chance across a generous farmer, we might end up with a couple of sheep to roast. If not, some of the archers might bring down a few pheasants. Or, we might chance upon a nice brace of coneys. Mighty toothsome, coney 'tis, cooked on a spit o'er the fire. At any rate, we'll make sure you don't go hungry, eh?"

Now it was Conall's turn to laugh. "Yes, Sergeant," he said.

"After all," Dannay went on, his voice turning more serious. "We have to keep you well fed and healthy, don't we? You're an important part of the company, in the event something happens to the captain."

"God forfend," Conall replied, crossing himself.

"Indeed so. Tell me, lad. What was it like? Speaking to the dragon, I mean."

Conall hesitated, trying to figure how to explain. "First off, Commander McRobbie brought me to stand in front of him. The dragon, I mean. He was enormous, big as a house, almost. The commander told the dragon my name, and next thing I knew, there was this voice inside my head. Well, you could have knocked me down with one finger, Sergeant."

He paused. Dannay said, "Aye, lad, what happened next?"

"The dragon said, 'Greetings, Conall of Kilbourne. I am called Donathyr.' His voice was as big as he was. Not loud, like, but... big. Kind of like the sea, when it's crashing on the rocks. You know?"

"Ach, an excellent description indeed. You've a bit o' the bard in you, 'twould seem."

Conall dismissed this out of hand. "Naw, I want to be a knight, like you and Commander McRobbie. And Captain Farquar," he added, giving loyalty where it was due. He wasn't Farquar's page, though the captain had quite willingly taken him on when Commander McRobbie asked him to. No, he'd been the Commander's page for well over a year. But being Farquar's aide-de-camp sounded even more important than a mere page.

"A worthy ambition indeed," Dannay said. "At the rate you're going, you'll have your spurs in jig time, I'd wager."

Conall beamed at this and popped the last bite of meat roll into his mouth. While he chewed, the sergeant said, "So, what else can you tell me about yon dragon?"

Conall swallowed. "Well, he said, 'If you have need to speak to me, you only have to call my name, and I will hear you'."

"Amazing," breathed Dannay. "I wonder how they do it."

"I don't know," Conall admitted. "They say Commander McRobbie, and the duchess, talk to dragons all the time. Someone even said there was a dragon who was a guest at their wedding feast."

"G'wan wit' ya. Now you're spinnin' tales out of pure moonshine," the sergeant objected. "A dragon for a wedding guest? Whoe'r heard o' such a thing?"

"Honest, Sergeant," Conall avowed. "That's what I heard. Course, I don't know myself if the tale's true. But I bet Captain Farquar knows. He was there."

Well, I'll not be asking him such nonsense, will I?"

"No? Well, maybe I will…"

Dannay snorted. "Now, don't you go pestering the captain, lad. He's got enough to worry himself."

Conall mulled this over. The sergeant's statement didn't bode well, and he asked the obvious question. "Are there problems, Sergeant?"

"Nay, lad, not…not to mention. Nothing to trouble you, like. It's a real rough push, getting this lot all the way up north to Noordstrom, in time to make a difference. It's Captain Farquar's first real mission, and he wants to do it right and proper."

"Is that why Commander McRobbie accompanied us?"

"Aye, I'd imagine so. I expect he wanted to take the captain's measure, watch how he handles things in the field.

"I reckon he must have been happy, huh? He sure left awful quick, didn't he?"

"He did, for certain." Dannay remained silent while they rode along. Then he said, "Word has it he was summoned back to Caerfaen. Um… by a cat."

Conall stared, waiting for the older man to finish the joke. When Dannay remained silent, he said, "Now who's making up tall tales?"

"Nay, Conall, 'tis no tale. Sergeant McTavish was right there and saw it with his own two eyes. He said the Commander pulled this little kitten out his saddlebag, and the beast spoke to him. McTavish said the Commander went white as a ghost, turned his horse around, and took off like every devil in hell was after him, back toward Caerfaen."

"What do you figure was wrong, Sergeant?"

"Other than a talking cat, you mean? I dunno, lad. But I saw him when he rode by, and I'll tell you true: the look in his eye was fey indeed. I don't envy whoever he might be after. I don't think their fate will be a pleasant one."

CHAPTER FORTY-ONE
Somewhere in Northern Kilbourne

Conall shook out his borrowed bedroll and set it on the ground near Captain Farquar's. The captain was off to oversee the making of a rudimentary encampment. Which, Conall observed, was unnecessary, since things were well in hand thanks to Dannay and his fellow sergeants. Even so, since this was the captain's first mission on his own, of course he'd want to make his presence known among the men.

Conall stretched his legs and back and rubbed his protesting rear. He'd never ridden this long before, and his lack of experience was doing his body no favors. A chuckle sounded from behind him, and he spun around to learn who'd been watching.

Sergeant Dannay, holding his own bedroll, stood in the fading light of the sun. A smile tinged his lips. "It takes a bit of getting used to, eh?" he observed.

Conall nodded in silent agreement. "Ah, don't fret, lad," the sergeant said. "You did fine, just fine. Couple of days and you'll be an old hand at life in the mounted Legion. There ain't a man among us, no matter his rank, who didn't come away with an aching bum his first couple of days out on the trail. So consider yourself in good company." Dropping his gear, he clapped Conall on the shoulder and gave him a conspiratorial wink.

A reluctant grin spread across Conall's face. "'At's the lad," Dannay said with approval. "I'm off to make the rounds of the sentries. Want to come along?"

"Oh, yes, please." Conall beamed, but then hesitated. "Unless you think Captain Farquar will be wanting me. I am supposed to be his aide-de-camp, after all.”

“No, don’t worry, lad. The captain’s got plenty to keep him occupied at the moment. I doubt he’ll miss you.” Dannay laughed. “Besides, I already cleared it with him. So let’s go.”

Conall tossed off a crisp salute. “Right you are, Sergeant.”

Dannay led him off toward the first sentry post. Conall heard him mutter, “Ach, I’ve seen actual soldiers give worse salutes.” Conall allowed himself a grin at this.

It took them close to an hour to make the rounds of the sentries, for Dannay stopped to chat with each man. The sun was sliding toward the horizon when at last they made their way back to the main encampment. Dannay stopped, gazing up at the sky, his head cocked. Conall was sure the sergeant sniffed the air.

The older man nodded in apparent satisfaction. “Clouds are rolling in,” he said. “Should make for a good night.”

Connal gaped at him. “You want it to rain?”

“No, not at all. I don’t smell rain in the air. But clouds, now, clouds are your friend at night. If it’s fair, you’ll get a lot of dew in the grass overnight, and wind up with a soggy blanket in the morn. Clouds mean no dew, and good sleeping.”

Conall filed this bit of arcane knowledge in the part of his brain marked, “Good Things To Remember.” Dannay nodded and led him toward the center of camp, where a crackling fire blazed. A large group of men clustered round it. Conall recognized one of the other sergeants, who called out in greeting.

“Dannay, where’ve you been? We’re after having a brew-up. You want your share?”

“Now what do you think, Garvin?” Dannay replied. “Conall, be a good lad, will ya, and hustle off to my kit. In my saddlebag, you’ll find a couple of tin cups. Fetch ‘em both, if you please.”

“By your order, Sergeant.” Conall saluted again and sprinted off. Behind him, the men chucked, and Dannay said, “Aye, he’s dead keen, our Conall.”

After the brilliant light of the fire, it took a couple of minutes for Conall’s eyes to adjust to the darkness enveloping the rest of the camp. Once his vision cleared again, he hurried to where he and the sergeant had set their things. He found the saddlebag, opened one side, and felt around. No cups met his searching fingers. Opening the other side, he reached in and encountered something hard. He pulled it out and found a battered tin cup. While he fumbled for the second, a flash of movement on the outer perimeter caught his eye.

He peered out into the darkness. Whatever he’d seen, it was too big to be one of the sentries. But shouldn't one of them have sounded the alarm if there was anything out there?

Conall stared hard, trying to make out the shadowy form. The clouds parted, enough for a sliver of burgeoning moonlight to illumine the landscape. His heart caught in his throat, and he fought to control the rising sense of panic flooding through him. The panic won.

"Ogres" he shouted at the top of his lungs. "Ogres"

The hulking figures shambled out of the darkness toward the encampment. From behind him came the shouts of the soldiers hurrying toward his position. "This way," he called and thrilled at their answering cries.

Conall stared in horror, rooted to the spot. Four—no, five—ogres lumbered toward him. Each was more than twice his height, with legs like tree trunks and arms to match. In the pale light of the moon, he was able to make out glinting, beady red eyes, set under deep brow ridges. Their noses were wide and flat, more akin to a boar's than a man's. Their hair was lank and stringy, and their beards were bushy and wild. They were clothed in ragged skins, and each of the ogres bore a mighty battle club big enough to knock down a house.

The soldiers were upon him now, rushing past toward the approaching danger. Conall spotted Captain Farquar leading the charge, his sword bright and gleaming in the moon's light.

"Get back, lad," said a rough voice, and an unseen hand propelled him away from the coming fray. Conall needed no more encouragement. Being caught between the ogres, with their huge clubs, and the soldiers of the Legion, with swords and spears, held no attraction for him. Conall legged it.

Once at a safe distance, he turned back to watch the battle. Farquar was directing his men into smaller squads of a dozen each. Conall noted the tactics, nodding in approval. This way each team could tend to their assigned opponent and keep them separated. A sound strategy, he thought. While several of the men kept an ogre occupied from the front, others from the squad slipped behind and darted in for unexpected attacks. The soldiers' swords flashed, the polished steel reflecting the distant firelight and looking to Colin like the men bore weapons of flame. It was the most exciting thing he'd ever witnessed. Soon the left-most of the ogres toppled and crashed to the ground like a great tree felled in the forest.

A second was soon vanquished, and Conall cheered with wild abandon from his position in the rear of the melee. The remaining ogres, becoming more wary, lashed out with their clubs, sending wild blows in every direction in an effort to keep the men of the Legion from getting too close.

Conall gave another rousing huzzah when the third of the attackers fell under the soldiers' swords. In the distance, Captain Farquar led a small group in another flanking attack against one of the remaining adversaries. As they dashed in to strike their target from behind, the fifth ogre whirled, bulling his way out of the press of men hemming him in. He swept his club around, catching some of the men, including the captain, in its devastating path.

"No" cried Conall, horrorstruck. Farquar and two of his comrades went flying. The club was so huge Conall couldn't imagine anyone, short of perhaps the dragon he'd met, being able to withstand its force. The ogre raised his club for a final, killing blow, but the enraged soldiers came at the creature from every side, hewing at its limbs with their bright swords.

It took another, interminable ten minutes before the final attacker was dispatched. Dannay and several others bore Farquar and his fallen mates off the field of battle. Conall, with tear-filled eyes, prayed, harder than he ever had, hoping they were rendered unconscious, rather than dead.

"Are they…" He trailed off, unable to speak. His heart was pounding and his head felt like one of the ogres had thumped it. On leaden legs he stood watching the procession carrying the fallen.

"Nay, not dead," Dannay replied, shifting his burden to keep the captain from falling. His voice was brittle as cold steel. "But not good, either. Hustle off, lad, and ready the captain's bedroll."

Conall shook himself out of his funk and sped off to get the blankets ready. The sergeant and his companions arrived to lay the captain on his bedroll, and Conall pulled the rough blanket over the still form.

"Watch over him, Conall," Dannay instructed. "The surgeon will be by soon. Do whatever he tells you."

'Aye, Sergeant." Conall wiped his brimming eyes on his sleeve. He sniffed, making a manful effort to get himself back into control. He was in the Legion, and needed to act it. Then he succumbed again, the tears streaming down his cheeks. Though his grief he pleaded, "He— he's going to be all right, isn't he?"

"I hope so, laddie." Dannay's voice was rough and full of despair. He strode off to help with more of the fallen. "I hope so."

Conall blinked back the next round of tears, adjusting the blankets more snugly around the captain, and swore under his breath. The words were ones his mother would have tanned his hide, had she ever heard. He didn't care. Sometimes you just needed a good curse. This was that time.

CHAPTER FORTY-TWO
A Dungeon Cell, Noordstrom

Marissa opened her eyes. If she was honest, there wasn't much difference from having them closed. She couldn't see any better, she noted, waving a hand in front of her face. Nothing. It called to mind the night Xavier had held her captive in a barn. She was getting rather tired of being taken prisoner and dumped into dark, dank places to molder away.

Bother, she said to herself. She didn't think she could manage actual speech at the moment. Her head rang like a Dwarf was pounding away with his hammer on her temples. The room, or cell, or whatever she was stuck in, danced a minor jig and her stomach threatened dire consequences. She made an effort to call out after all, but all that emerged from her parched and cracked throat was a slight croak, rather like a bullfrog essaying a sonnet. She attempted to swallow, wincing when her throat rebelled. She tried again, and was able to swallow this time, clearing the pipes a bit.

"Hoy," she managed. Not much, in the grand scheme of things, but better than nothing.

There was no answer. In fact, there was little sound at all, with the exception of the susurration of her own voice, echoing back to her in spectral whispers. Off stone walls, perhaps? Wherever she was, it was damp and chill. It called to mind when, at ten years of age, the cellar of her parents' house had felt when she'd gone adventuring and locked herself in. No one looked for her for hours, and Marissa never felt so chilled to the bone before or since. Until now.

She shivered. She wasn't dressed for this. She'd been dressed to receive visitors. She hadn't been expecting kidnappers to come to call. That's what happened, wasn't it? The memories were stirring in her scrambled mind, and she recalled the sound of the bottle crashing through the morning room window, glass exploding everywhere, ringing like a dozen bells set off at once. The cloud of fumes released from the bottle, acrid and burning in her throat and nostrils like the smoke from a suddenly doused fire. Her futile efforts to get to the sword parasols in the corner before she collapsed. And finally, the inexorable tread of booted feet and the slow descent into oblivion.

She shivered again, not merely from the chill. She was a prisoner of men who wanted to kill her and those like her. To try them for imaginary crimes and watch them burn. She fought down a rise of bile, tasting the tangible horror of her situation. She had weathered storms before, but this might be the worst. And the last…

Sniffling, she wiped her nose on her sleeve, relegated her gorge back to its proper place, and set her jaw. She was a witch, damn it, a woman of power and dignity. She wouldn't let these mad monsters drive her into fear.

Marissa wrapped her arms around herself in an attempt to find some semblance of warmth. Perhaps if there was some light, she could find something to put around herself. Before she could focus enough to attempt the spell which would give her light, a voice sounded, close by.

"Ooooooh."

Marissa performed an excellent imitation of a frog leaping off a lily pad and found herself pressed against the wall. Which was indeed stone, and as cold and damp as she'd imagined. The voice, when it spoke again, was muzzy, like someone awakened from a bad dream. It was in the room with her. A spirit? This was worse than any nightmare. So much for being a woman of power and dignity. Those took flight in an instant, leaving her quaking against the wall.

"W-where am I?" the voice asked, in a plaintive tone.

Marissa breathed a silent prayer of relief. No mistaking it—the voice belonged to Kate Taggart.

Well, time to put on a brave face for the world to see. Or hear, since no one could see a blasted thing in this stygian darkness. "Hello, Kate," she said. "I'm glad you're among the living. Welcome to our less than happy gathering. If I've any guess at all, I'd venture to say we're in a dark dungeon cell."

"Ugh," replied Kate.

"Ugh, indeed. To further complicate matters, I'd imagine we are awaiting the rather dubious pleasure of entertaining the bishops of Kilbourne. Well, the rebel ones, at least."

"Blergh. I'd like to entertain them with a stout club."

"Yes, I agree. Bad cess to them. But bad luck for us. Since, if my recollection of history serves, we are about to undergo what were once known as the witch trials."

"You do say the most comforting things, don't you?" replied her unseen companion. "I —ouch! Oh, damn this dark."

Marissa heard what sounded like her companion finding a solid piece of furniture with her small toe—which was exactly what the good Lord seemed to have perversely designed small toes to do.

Four witches, neatly nabbed. Well, she assumed four. Were Saia and Catoya also here? If so, they might still be under the effects of whatever foul stuff their assailants had used to knock them out. How long had it been, she wondered? And where were they? She didn't think the bishops would risk keeping them prisoner in Caerfaen. Morgan had mentioned something about the rebels being sequestered at a cathedral in Cormaine. Perhaps that's where they'd been brought?

She wondered if the bishops—for it must be they who'd instigated this escapade—knew what they were getting. Or if they, or their minions, came for Marissa and seized anyone with her on suspicion of being a witch by association.

Hmm. Was she still a witch? Or rather, did she have access to her powers? If her head didn't throb so, she might try casting a spell to check. Well, time enough to test it later. Now, she needed to figure how they were going to get out of wherever they were being held, and back to Caerfaen.

No, she chided, best to test out the spellcasting first. Because it might well be their sole means of escape, by using magic. First things first: she attempted a small restorative spell aimed at settling both her head and stomach.

To no avail. Quirking a grimace, she resorted to her old standby. *"Lumios accacido,"* she muttered. The welcome little ball of light she was able to conjure at will and without thinking failed to materialize.

"What?" Kate asked. "What did you say?"

"I was trying to work a spell," she replied. "Unfortunately, it didn't work. Bother." And because in the current circumstances this felt most insufficient, she added a rousing, "Damn."

"What happened?" Kate asked. "Why didn't it work?"

Marissa huffed an aggrieved sigh. "Something's preventing me from using my power. My intent was to conjure up a bit of light for us, but I can't seem to manage it. And it's the one spell I can always do. Which means something's very wrong."

Kate's voice came out harsh. "You mean besides the obvious?"

"Yes, quite right. Well, if I count aloud, perhaps you can follow the sound of my voice," Marissa ventured. "One. Two…" She'd got to five when Kate clutched at her arm. Marissa took her hand.

"I'm sorry you've been captured along with me," she said. "But I am glad of your company."

"Me too, on both counts," Kate replied. "Although if what you say is true, we're going to be in for a rather thin time of things, aren't we?"

Marissa nodded. Realizing this gesture was wasted, she said, "Yes, I'm afraid so."

"And you've none of the magic these beasts so despise, eh? Rotten."

"Not a lick," Marissa confirmed. "I'm sure they've dosed me— well, you too, I'd venture—with witchbane. Witchbane," she went on, to forestall Kate's next question, "is a substance which, in small doses, prevents anyone with magical talent from accessing their power. In larger doses, it can prove fatal."

"Lovely," Kate said. "Fatal, as in the dead kind of fatal?"

Marissa gave a humorless laugh. "Yes, that's the one. I hope whoever administered the blasted stuff got the dose right."

"Does it wear off? I mean, the kind which doesn't kill you."

"Yes, it does, but it takes a while. Although, I'd be willing to wager any food or drink we're given will be simply loaded with the stuff."

"Oh. Yes, I see." She felt Kate's shiver. "I guess it hasn't hit me yet," Kate said. "I mean, the fact I'm subject to this too. That these fiends might want to kill me along with you and the others."

"Hmm." Marissa mused on this. "There's no reason for them to suspect you of being a witch. I mean you, along with the others, were only taken because you happened to be with me at the wrong time."

"D'you think so?"

"Well, I don't think there's any way for this lot to say with any certainty, 'This one's a witch, and that one isn't'. Do you know what I mean?"

"I suppose." Kate sounded rather dubious. Marissa couldn't blame her. "You don't reckon they'll go ahead and kill us all, to be sure?"

"Well, it would be the logical thing for them to do, wouldn't it? Damn. I do loathe the logical thing to do."

Kate snorted. "I can't say I'm any too enthused over the notion myself. Well, time, as they say, will tell the story. Say, where do you reckon the others are?"

"Another cell, I'd imagine. I—" Marissa's words were brought short. A virulent stream of invective cut through the darkness, so the air was almost luminescent. The most printable of which, she noted, began with "Infidel dogs" and soared from there into stratospheric curses upon the heads of all and sundry.

"Princess Saia, hello," she called.

Saia halted her diatribe. "Ah, Duchess, you are with us."

"Yes, welcome to our little party. Kate is here with me. Catoya, are you with the princess?"

"Present and accounted for," Catoya replied. "It's rather like being back in school, with the additional thrills of possible torture and beheading."

"Lovely," murmured Marissa.

Catoya went on. "In addition, I seem to be dosed to the gills with witchbane."

"Yes, I'd come to the same conclusion. Princess, can you access any of your power?"

Saia hesitated before answering. "No," she said at last. "There is a trace of something, but it's like a will-of-the-wisp. I can't pin it down."

"Residual effects of your encounter with the Thundermist," Marissa said. "Keep trying, perhaps something will present itself in time to help us get out of this predicament."

"If nothing else, perhaps some light," said Catoya, her voice a touch plaintive. "I believe a rat just ran across my foot."

"Blast," Marissa exclaimed. "I do hate rats. I rather wish you hadn't told me." She'd no sooner said this than she sensed something near her own foot. She kicked out, eliciting a startled "Ow," from Kate.

"I'm not a rat," Kate reminded her, her voice frosty.

"Sorry. I—" Marissa shuddered, beset with memories of being held captive by the Rhuddlani spy Xavier in a rat-infested barn. She'd hated it. Hated the dark, hated the rats, hated Xavier. She'd even hated Morgan at the time. "Sorry," she repeated.

"Well, a fine mess we're in, and no mistake," said Catoya. "And I'm certain the dinner menu will be lacking in both taste and quality."

Marissa choked back a laugh. Catoya went on. "Not to mention, I could right murder a cup of tea and a bun at the moment."

A rumbling in her own stomach led Marissa to concur with this sentiment. "Curse it," she grumbled. "Cook baked the loveliest sticky buns for our tea."

"Too bad no one thought to pack a basket for us," Kate said with forced cheer. "We might have made a jolly picnic out of this outing. But perhaps the fact the buns are still there, and we're not, will alert Duke Morgan to the fact something is amiss."

"Yes, it might well," Marissa said. "Except Morgan is off gallivanting, doing Knight-Commander-type things. Although," she said, "he did leave a couple of guards posted. I hope nothing awful happened to them. Both for their sakes, and so they can sound the alarm."

"It would be comforting to imagine Duke Morgan and Aartis riding to our rescue," Kate said, her voice wistful.

"Yes, but in the meantime, we'll have to see if we can't manage to rescue ourselves. Saia, are you having any luck with your magic?"

"I am afraid not. I shall keep trying," the princess called back.

Restless and needing movement, Marissa started to pace. She was somewhat thwarted in this by the act of walking into a wall. "Damn," she said, rubbing her nose.

Catoya said, "Unfortunately, I'd say any hope of rescuing ourselves is going to lie in our eating and drinking nothing. I'm sure anything we're given will be rife with more witchbane."

"Yes, I'd come to the same conclusion," Marissa said. "The sooner we can get it out of our systems, the better."

CHAPTER FORTY-THREE

Northern Kilbourne

"Mmmph?"

"Conall. C'mon now, wake up, lad."

Blinking like a startled owl, Conall peered through crusted eyes at the insistent figure shaking his arm. Sergeant Dannay, his face grim, bent and said, "Wake up, Conall."

"I—I'm awake." Barely, but that was beside the point. He focused on the figure of Sergeant Dannay, and the reality of recent events exploded in his brain. Conall jerked to his feet. "I'm sorry, Sergeant," he said in a voice hoarse with interrupted sleep. "I—I was watching the captain, but I fell asleep. Is he—is he all right?"

Dannay breathed a heavy sigh. "He's still out cold. The surgeon says his arm is broken, and he's got a nasty knot on his head. Bloody ogres. But he's breathin' easy, and there's no fever."

Conall hung his head. "I'm sorry I didn't stay awake. I shouldn't have dozed off. I was supposed to be watching over him."

Dannay patted his shoulder. "Ach, don't fret so, Conall. There was naught ye might ha' done, in truth. If you want to know, you saved a lot of lives when you sounded the alarm last night. If those ogres managed to get right into camp, they'd have wiped out half the company. Ye done well, laddie. And Captain Farquar, he'll recover fine. Surgeon says so. It'll take time, but he'll be fine."

Conall heaved a sigh of relief. "Good. What can I do?"

Dannay's gaze was speculative. "Well, there is one thing…"

"Whatever you say, Sergeant." Conall stood straight as a pike and came a hair short of saluting.

"We need you to speak to the dragon," the sergeant said. "Tell him our situation, so he can let Captain Darby know. With the captain out of commission, you're the only one who can do it."

Conall's eyes widened. "Oh."

"I know it's a lot to ask, but…"

"No, Sergeant Dannay, it's the reason I'm here. Commander McRobbie didn't have time to get anyone else, so he sent me. I can do it. I—well, I never thought I'd be needed. Never thought anything would happen to Captain Farquar…"

Dannay nodded. "No more did anyone else, to be honest. But fate has a way of sneaking up on you when you're not expecting, ya know?"

"Like ogres."

"Aye, like ogres. Anyhow, I'll tell you what you need to say to the dragon, so he can relay the situation to Captain Darby up in Noordstrom. Even though the captain, along with a few others, is injured, we have a mission to complete."

Conall nodded. "I'm ready, Sergeant. Tell me what you want me to say to the dragon."

~*~

Noordstrom, Dunstanshire

"Sir Byron. Can you hear me?"

The dragon's voice sounded in his head. Byron reined in his borrowed mount. He and several of his Green Rangers were riding west from Noordstrom, in order to scout out the landscape. Two of the Green Rangers, along with a couple of men from the local garrison, were even further afield, searching for signs of the oncoming Rhuddlani troops.

"Yes, Donathyr, I hear you," he replied. He waved off one of his men who'd started to approach when he stopped.

"I have news for you, from the company riding north from Caerfaen. Captain Farquar and several other men have been injured in an ogre attack and are incapacitated. The company rides on, but their progress is slowed because of this."

"Did they give an estimate of when they expect to arrive? How much will this delay them?"

"I was told this may cost them half a day, perhaps more. I know nothing beyond this. Do you wish me to relay any questions or instructions?"

Byron hesitated, thinking hard. He said, "No, it is not necessary. Nothing can be done to change things. Thank you, Donathyr, for relaying this news."

"You are welcome, Sir Byron. Good hunting."

The dragon's voice was gone. Byron shook his head and directed his mount forward. The Rhuddlanis appeared to be approaching at a rapid rate, bypassing every village and hamlet in their path. Farquar's company might not have arrived in time to help defend the city against the invading force even if they'd kept to their original timeline. A delay of half a day or more meant there was no question they'd arrive after the Rhuddlanis.

Which, he reasoned, might not result in a complete disaster. A call to muster had gone out, and men were pouring into Noordstrom to swell the garrison's numbers. If they could hold off the Rhuddlanis long enough, keeping them outside the gates, Farquar's company might be able to catch them in a flanking maneuver. Such a possibility would be where the ability to communicate via the dragons would be critical. Byron grinned to himself. It might even work to their advantage.

"Cap'n?"

Byron glanced up from his reverie. Sir Ronall was hailing him. Standing next to him was one of the forward scouts. Byron clicked the reins and his horse trotted over to where they waited.

The scout was one of the local men from the garrison. He saluted. "Captain, I'm glad to have stumbled across you. Saves me a trip all the way back to Noordstrom."

"What's the word, Danvers?" Byron asked.

"The Rhuddlanis have halted their march," the scout reported. "They're queuing up around Arvaine, a little village west of here."

"Good," Byron said. "I was beginning to wonder if they were going to quick-march the whole way, right into Noordstrom."

"I reckon their pace caught up with 'em," Danvers said. "'Course there's no telling how long they'll stay put, but I figure they'll be there at least a day, if not more. They're setting up tents, not bivouacking for the night."

"They'll need to resupply," Ronall said. "Is there enough in the village for 'em?"

Danvers shrugged. "It's a pretty small place, Sergeant. Hard to say. But there's not much else out there, so I reckon they'll have to make do with what they get. Most of the farms out there have sheep or goats, so they'll get meat, at the least. Maybe some root vegetables, and there's not a farm wife in all Dunstanshire that don't make a nice loaf of bread. They'll commandeer enough to keep 'em moving."

Byron nodded. "Even so, having to round up food from the various farms around will take time. I can't envision them moving out much before day after tomorrow. Good luck for us, for it gives us a bit of time to work with."

Danvers saluted. "Right. I'll be getting back on patrol?"

Byron returned his salute. "Well done, Danvers. Yes, best get back to it."

The scout turned and headed west. He was out of sight in minutes.

"Well," Ronall said. "Good news for a change, eh?"

"Right when we needed it." Byron filled him in on the dragon's news of the delay of the reinforcements, and his notion of how it might work to their advantage.

The grizzled old sergeant allowed himself a quick grin. "It might, at that. Reckon we'd best be getting back, eh?"

"I reckon we'd best," Byron agreed. He signaled to the others, and they turned their mounts eastward, to see to the defense of Noordstrom.

CHAPTER FORTY-FOUR

A Dungeon Cell, Noordstrom

A light flared down the passageway, jerking and bobbing toward the cells. Marissa squinted against the glare, then took stock of their prison for the first time. It did not present any salient features of interest. Well, other than a glimpse of a chamber pot beneath a sagging cot covered with what appeared to be a horse blanket so filthy even the horse might have balked at it. The chamber pot, however, was indeed a welcome sight, and Marissa vowed to avail herself of it at the earliest opportunity.

Which might be some little time, she reckoned. The bearer of the light shuffled along the corridor, mumbling to himself as he approached. Hanging his lantern on a hook set into the wall, he turned to display a small iron cooking pot, which he placed with great care on a small bench standing along the far wall. From a large pouch at his waist he produced four wooden bowls. Humming to himself, he ladled the contents of the pot into the bowls.

Marissa decided the time for silence was over. "Why have we been brought here?" she demanded. "And where are we?"

"Don't antagonize him," muttered Kate, "or he might take away the food."

The man continued filling the bowls. "I asked you a question," Marissa said. "And I expect some answers."

Instead of replying, the man extended one of the bowls through a slot in the cell door just large enough to let it pass through. Marissa took it, and surprised herself by saying, "Thank you." The man showed no indication of having heard her speak. He passed another bowl through the slot. Marissa handed the first one to Kate and took possession of the second. From his pouch, the man produced a pair of wooden spoons and offered them through the bars. Marissa took them, said, "Thank you" again, and stared at their jailer. He nodded once and repeated the process with Saia and Catoya in the next cell.

Marissa set her bowl on the floor and took advantage of the lantern's light to survey their surroundings. The corridor extended quite some distance in the direction from which the jailer arrived. In the other direction, the passageway ended in a solid mass of stone after what appeared to be one more cell. There weren't any doors on the other side of the passage.

From the other cell, Saia demanded, "Why have we been brought here? We've done nothing wrong. What right have you to lock us up like sheep in a pen?"

Again, the man ignored her. From a bag at his waist he produced two small loaves of dark bread and four apples. He again handed his bounty in through the bars, one loaf and two apples to each set of prisoners.

Marissa wondered if the guard was aware the food was being laced with witchbane. Or if he even questioned why four women were being held prisoner in his dungeon. Marissa hoped their situation was somewhat out of the ordinary. Yet with fanatical clergymen, how might one even tell?

"The bread," Kate observed in bitter tones, "is fresh."

"I know, curse it." Marissa savored the aroma of the loaf. There were, in her opinion, few fragrances better than that of fresh bread. "It's quite rude."

Kate choked out a laugh. "We'll have to be sure to speak to the management."

The guard began packing away his things, heedless of Saia's continued shouted questions. He picked up the lantern and the light illuminated a hook set into the wall opposite. Marissa gave a gasp, managing to stifle it before the guard took notice.

"What's wrong?" Kate asked. "Did you weaken and eat some of the bread?"

"No," she replied, her mind reeling with possibilities. "I saw something."

"A rat? This place is lousy with them."

"No, not a rat. A key."

"A key? Are you sure? Where is it?"

"Yes, I saw it right before the guard left with his lantern. It's hanging on a hook on the wall, to the left of the little table where he prepared our bowls."

"Are they that stupid," Kate asked. "Or cocky? To leave it out in plain view?"

"A bit of both, I'd imagine," Marissa said. "They know we can't get to it, especially if they've dosed us to squelch our magic. So it's one more way for them to intimidate us. But it gives me even more reason not to touch any of their food. If one of us can get some magic going, we could get the key."

Kate scrutinizing the apple she held. "Say, do you think they've put—what was it, witchbase—in the apples somehow?"

"Witchbane," Marissa said. "Well, remember the girl in the old story."

"Pooh." Kate dismissed this out of hand. "In the story, a witch gave it to her, filled with some kind of nasty potion. We're the witches in this tale, and there's no holes in the apple, so perhaps it's safe."

"I wouldn't risk it," Marissa said, while her own stomach rumbled in protest. "There's no telling. Me, I'd rather be hungry and have my powers back than the other way round. We need to get that key."

"Hmm. Well, perhaps you lot might manage it. I couldn't do a thing. Useless, that's me."

"Untrained," Marissa corrected. "Well, it's more reason to get you some lessons once we get out of here."

"You're making a rather large assumption there, aren't you?"

Marissa turned to regard her companion, realizing too late with the lantern gone, there was nothing to see. "How so?"

"You're assuming we're going to get out of this alive, rather than be executed for witchcraft."

"Yes," Marissa replied, with a tad more positivity than she possessed. "Yes, I am. I mean, even if we don't get our magic back, trust me when I say there's no way Morgan, or Aartis either, is going to stand by and let these foul priests do away with us."

"Yes, but they have to find us first."

"Well, yes. Oooh, I know. I can tell Wyvrndell, and he can tell Morgan. Good heavens, what a ninny I am. I should have done so straight away."

"Wyvrndell. He's your dragon?"

"Not my dragon," she said. "Very much his own dragon. But my friend, yes. Now, hush for a moment whilst I call him."

Kate kept silent, and Marissa cast her thoughts out toward the dragon. She called several times, but there was no calm, reassuring draconic voice in her head.

"Bother," she said at last.

"No answer?"

"No. I'll try again later. It's odd, because he can always hear me, even over long distances. I mean, Morgan and I were in Parthane, for heaven's sake, and we conversed with him here with no problem whatsoever."

"Perhaps he's asleep?"

"Mmm. It's possible. I wonder…"

"Marissa," came Catoya's voice from the next cell. "Did you eat or drink anything?"

Marissa turned her attention from the problem of silent dragons. "No," she called back.

"Bah," said the princess. "What a rude fellow he was."

Catoya said, "I don't think he was being rude on purpose. I suspect the truth is, he couldn't hear you."

"Oh." Marissa's heart gave a lurch in sympathy for the man's plight. "I'll bet you're right. Poor fellow. It must be awful not to hear."

"But canny on the part of our captors," said Kate. "It would be difficult to bribe a man who can't hear you talking. He's not going to be swayed by any protestations of innocence, or by offers of coin if he sets us free."

"Hmm. I hadn't thought of that. Quite sneaky, isn't it?"

"Blast," said Catoya.

"What's wrong?" Marissa asked.

"It's this stew."

"Is something wrong with it?"

"The opposite, unfortunately. It smells wonderful. Much better than I'd have ever expected."

Marissa furrowed her brow. She was still savoring the bread's yeasty aroma. According to scripture, one could not live by bread alone. Marissa was of the opinion if she had a reasonable supply of butter, she could make a pretty good stab at it. She turned her attention to the stew. It did smell most tempting, a fragrant bouquet of herbs mingling with the scent of roasted meat and root vegetables And was, she was certain laced with more witchbane.

Hunger warred with good sense, and good sense was getting the worst of the battle. "Do you think a bite or two would hurt?" Kate asked. "I'm famished."

"Much as it pains me to say it, Catoya's right," Marissa told her. "We stand a much better chance of getting out of here if we have our powers available. If we eat this, though it smells delicious, we throw away any chance of it."

"But I can't even use my power," Kate pointed out.

"No, I know you can't. But we might need to channel some of your power to make up for the rest of us being weak. In terms of magic, that is. It might make a big difference."

"Oh. Well, yes, if you say so." Kate didn't sound convinced.

"Kate, the alternative is to eat the stew, be stuck here, and be put on trial for witchcraft. And executed," Catoya pointed out.

"Yes, well, when you put it like that, the stuff smells positively foul," Kate said.

Saia said, "When the guard comes back to collect the bowls, he'll be suspicious if they're full."

"A good point," Marissa agreed. "The best thing to do is dump them into the chamber pot."

"Capital idea," said Catoya. "But leave a little bit in your bowls. I have a glimmer of an idea."

"What?" Marissa perked up. "Tell us."

"Not quite yet," replied Catoya. "I want to mull on it first."

"Oh." Marissa's sudden excitement flowed away, leaving her deflated and exhausted. Not to mention hungry. She glared at the bowl she scraped by feel into the chamber pot she couldn't see. "I do wish he'd left the lamp."

"Not much to see," Kate pointed out. "I say, does anyone know any jolly songs? We might have a sing along."

A chorus of groans echoed around the cells.

"Well, it was just an idea," she said.

Marissa smiled. "When we get out of here, we shall retire victorious to The Gray Dove, for buns and copious amounts of tea. And jolly songs. My treat."

"Oh, an excellent notion," Catoya said. The tea shop was where she and Marissa had first met. "Both The Gray Dove, and the getting out of here bit. No sign of any magic yet?"

"No, not yet. And the key is hanging right on the wall there in plain sight. Well, when there's a lantern it's in plain sight. If one of us was able to move it somehow…"

"I'm afraid neither Princess Saia nor I are able to manage it yet."

"I can sense my magic," Saia reported. "But I cannot touch it. It's like trying to catch a seed floating on the water. You can close your fingers over it all you want, but each time, when you look, it has slipped away again."

"Rotten," Marissa commiserated. "Do keep trying. I don't intend to spend my declining years here."

"Since we're on the subject," Kate ventured. "Do any of you find it the least bit surprising no one in any position of authority has been down here to check on us, or interrogate us? Or even gloat a bit?"

"Well, yes, now you mention it," Marissa said. "Although I can't say I'm especially disappointed. The taunting and gloating would be bad enough, if tolerable. As for the interrogations and such? I've done a lot of reading since this whole mess began, on how the Church treated those poor women accused of witchcraft before. The outcome was…not pretty."

"Oh," said Kate, her voice sounding small and alone in the darkness.

Marissa managed to locate her by the sound of her voice and took her hand in a gesture of reassurance. "Don't worry," she said. "I've been in some tighter places than this and made it out. I don't believe my luck has run out quite yet."

"Thanks," Kate said, squeezing her hand.

The thud of boots sounded in the corridor, and a glimmer of light danced along the cold stone walls. Marissa gave Kate's hand one final squeeze and turned toward the cell door. Bowing her head, she sent up a quick prayer for strength for them all. She didn't imagine whoever was coming this time was bringing a picnic luncheon.

CHAPTER FORTY-FIVE
A Dungeon Cell, Noordstrom

Five men in rich ecclesiastical robes gathered in the corridor outside the cells. A half dozen guards, each armed with a short, curved sword which called to mind the Tzigani weapons, accompanied them.

A couple of the guards appeared nervous. So, Marissa noted, did at least one of the clergymen. Which, she said to herself, might somehow be used to her advantage. How, she couldn't fathom. It didn't matter. She was certain something would suggest itself in time.

Now, however, the best course of action lay in taking the offensive. Better to do so instead of allowing these overbearing priests to gain the upper hand right off the bat. It didn't help that they already owned it, by virtue of the fact Marissa and her companions were locked in these dank cells, and they weren't.

"For men of God," she said, "you lot evince a decided lack of His qualities. Kidnapping innocent women. Keeping them locked away by force, in constant darkness. The qualities of charity and mercy have given over to brutish lawlessness."

"Bah," said one of their captors. "Words, nothing more."

"Yes," said the nervous one. "But shouldn't we bind their mouths, so they can neither blaspheme, nor set terrible curses upon us?"

"Their very existence is blasphemy," replied the first. "But we have no need to gag them. I have taken steps to ensure they can work no spells, either upon us, or on these locks."

Which meant whoever this priest was, he must indeed have learned of witchbane, and ordered it administered to them. No doubt through some association with the wizards. Or at least with the former

Chief Wizard Foxwent, who'd helped initiate this debacle. At least they hadn't been gagged, which was all to the good. Words were the only weapons they possessed now.

"Bah yourself," she said. "You have no cause, and no right, to treat us in such a churlish fashion."

"As to cause," replied the leader, his face imperturbable, "you are witches, and thus despised by God. As to right? We do the work appointed us by God, to scour the land of evil."

Marissa glared at him. She would have loved to be able to slap the self-righteous expression off the man's face. Even if she could have reached him through the bars of the cell door, it would have provided but a momentary pleasure, offset by some awful punishment. She shrugged and said, "Well, I can hardly deny the fact I'm a witch, since the king himself appointed me to an exalted place in his court, his Royal Enchantress. Yet you have no evidence these other women are witches. Your quarrel, foolish though it is, is with me, not them. Set them free."

"Nay, cursed daughter of night," the man snarled. "Their association with you has condemned them along with you."

"Condemned?" Marissa uttered a bitter laugh. "Better you leave any condemnation to God and be concerned for your own spiritual wellbeing. For is not murder proscribed in scripture? And this is what you plan for us, is it not? Murder most foul, carried out under the auspices of religion."

"Enough," roared the target of her verbal barbs. "We do God's work, to rid the world of such hell spawn."

"Yet is it not for God to judge? Does not scripture instruct us to judge not the speck in another's eye when there is a plank in your own?"

A smile spread across the bishop's face. It was the most evil and frightening thing Marissa had ever encountered. The assassins she'd faced, the mad sorcerer Azim, even the demon inhabiting Foxwent—none of these even came close.

"You dare to bandy scripture with me, spawn of Satan? Then hear this one: 'Suffer not a witch to live'."

Marissa blanched. This man's obsession was driving him into madness, and it was clear she wasn't helping. He was going to kill them all, and enjoy every moment of it.

A wild cry of triumph resounded from the adjoining cell. "At last," yelled Saia. A bolt of green lightning bloomed out of the cell.

"Saia, no," cried Marissa, but she was too late. The spell felled one of the guards. Yet it didn't touch the group of bishops at whom Saia's spell was aimed, instead curving around them to strike the stones of the corridor, diffusing into wriggling tentacles of shadow.

"Bloody hell," Marissa muttered. One of the drawbacks of being married to a soldier. She'd picked up a few choice oaths in the bargain. At the moment, this one felt strangely comforting. "A shield of some kind," Which meant one of these men possessed magic, and in no small supply, if he was able to counter Saia's strike.

"Infidels," snarled Saia. She went silent. The one use of her power must have drained her to the limit. *Oh, Saia, why didn't you save it for when it might have been more useful?*

The leader's expression was, if anything, even more cruel than before. "Innocents?" he snapped. "You are every one a witch, and you will all burn." He turned to one of the guards. "Dose them," he instructed. "Be sure they swallow it, each of them. And that one," he gestured toward Saia and Catoya's cell, "give her an extra dose."

"No." Marissa's voice was shrill. "You'll kill her if she gets too much."

The bishop smiled again, and her mind's eye imagined maggots and other horrid crawling things in his mouth. "Perhaps she'll be fortunate enough to escape the fire," he intoned. "You, however, shall not." With this, he turned and stalked away, his retinue trailing in his wake.

The nervous one, Marissa noted, glanced back toward the cells. His face bore an anguished expression.

"Hmm. Perhaps I played to the wrong one. I should have never attempted to sway that monster."

"I don't expect even an earthquake would shake him from his foundation of false righteousness," Kate murmured from behind her.

"No, I'm sure you're right," Marissa agreed. A key sounded in the lock. Three guards entered. Two stood with their swords pointed at Kate and Marissa. The third carried a pair of small vials.

"Drink it," he said. "Both of you. I have to make certain you swallow the stuff."

"You know he's mad," Marissa said. She took the vial. "Quite literally mad."

The guard shrugged, although he did manage an apologetic manner. "Drink," he repeated.

"Well, why not? It won't make any difference." Marissa upended the vial and drained it to the bitter dregs. "Blergh. What on earth did they add to it, vinegar?"

Kate followed suit, with a similar reaction. "Yuck. I've tasted soured ale better than this. At least put some decent wine in next time, won't you?" She fluttered her lashes at the guards.

The one who'd given them the vials went red to his hairline. His mates remained stolidly pointing their very pointy weapons. The blusher collected the empty vials, turned tail, and fled. The others followed, and the lock clanked closed again. The sounds of the guards opening the other cell followed.

"Oh dear," Kate chuckled. "The poor boy's going to go off thinking I intended to bewitch him."

"You never know," Marissa said, listening to the guards repeating the process in the other cell. "Perhaps you've made us a friend we sorely need. And no," she went on hurriedly when Kate bristled. "I wasn't suggesting you do anything untoward. I meant perhaps he'll realize you're not some kind of monster, like these foul churchmen—" she spat out the word, venom stinging her tongue "—portray us."

"Oh. Well, all right." Kate sounded mollified, for which Marissa was grateful. She went on. "What did you mean when you told the guard drinking this vial of vile stuff wouldn't make any difference soon. Because they're going to kill us soon? Or because you've figured out a way to counteract the witchbane?"

"Neither," Marissa said, pitching her voice low so the guards wouldn't overhear. "I meant it wouldn't matter because even though I can't figure out any way for the four of us to get out of this on our own— at least not yet, though I've not given up hope—I have every confidence Morgan and Aartis and a host of others are going to show up soon to put a crimp in this bishop-cum-wizard's plans."

"Oh, good. I'm not quite ready to die yet. I mean, if I'm going to be burned for a witch, it doesn't seem quite fair, does it? I've never gotten the chance to do the least thing witchy."

"Right you are, my girl. We shall have to remedy this oversight at the earliest opportunity."

Kate paused for a moment. "Marissa, what did you mean before? You muttered something about bishops and wizards…"

"Oh, right. One of those bishops managed to cast a neat shielding spell to ward off Saia's attack. There's more here than meets the eye. I don't know yet what it portends, but I intend to find out."

The echo of the guards' footsteps retreated down the passageway. From the next cell came the sound of retching. "I'm trying to get Saia to bring the stuff back up," Catoya announced.

"Brilliant," Marissa called back. "I guess we'd best do the same, eh?"

"Not pleasant, I know," replied Catoya. "But best in the long run, don't you think?"

"I do." Marissa scowled, though in the dark, no one could see it. It didn't matter. It felt good to scowl. She would have preferred to rage and swear and create a veritable tempest with her Thundermist-laden magic. She settled for scowling into the dark.

Kate asked, "Who was that awful man? If he's what a priest is supposed to act like, I think God has made a serious mistake."

"I have no idea," she said. "I wish I did. If I'm going to loathe someone, I'd prefer to have a name to attach."

"He was rather grim, wasn't he?"

"Grim? He was horrid. The foul beast wants to kill us—burn us, in fact—and gloat while he watches it happen. Oooh, what I wouldn't give for a bit of magic…"

The sound of more retching came from the adjoining cell. Catoya said, "I've managed to get Saia to bring her double dose of witchbane back up."

"Ew." Marissa started to pace. "I'm sorry you had to do it."

"One does what one must," Catoya replied, her voice calm. "I'm afraid the process was not pleasant for either of us. However, I think she should be all right."

"I'm fine," growled Saia. "Next time I won't miss." She succumbed to a fit of coughing.

"You didn't miss," Marissa told her. "One of those priests used a shield of some sort. Your spell bounced right off it."

"Yes, I noticed the shield," Catoya said. "Quite accomplished for a man of the cloth, don't you think?"

"I'm not sure what to think," Marissa replied, continuing to pace. "Of course, other than the Vicar at home, and Bishop Randolph, I can't say I've had an awful lot to do with priests. Having magical talent doesn't preclude one from taking holy orders, does it?"

More retching came from the other cell. "Poor Saia," Marissa commiserated.

"No," said Catoya in a somewhat strangled voice. "That was me. And I would encourage the two of you to void your stomachs too. This was a strong dose, and if we're to have any hope of regaining our powers…"

"Oh. Drat." Marissa grimaced. "You're right, of course. Unfortunately. Where's the blasted slops jar? Let's get this over with."

The next several minutes, Marissa decided later, were some of the least enjoyable of her existence, and she'd nearly been eaten by a dragon. The one thing which even came close was when she was twelve and contracted a particularly virulent strain of stomach flu. At least then her mother had been there to soothe and comfort her. Now there was only Kate, who she was certain felt as rotten as she did.

"Are you all right?" she inquired of Kate once her turn at the slops jar was completed.

"Oh, lovely. Let's see. I'm locked in a pitch-dark dungeon. Can't eat or drink anything, and got fed some sort of foul stuff which might kill me. To top it off, there are monsters out there who are planning to light us on fire. I'd like to go back to my tavern, if it's the same to you. At least there, the worst thing to contend with was drunks with grabby hands. It's all a bit much for this girl."

Marissa sank onto the thing which pretended to be a cot. "I—I'm sorry," she said. "I didn't expect things to end up like this."

"Oh, I know it's not your fault. Not your fault I am—well, might be—a witch. Not your fault these beastly priests decided to do this. I simply happened to get swept up in it all. I wish—oh, how I wish—we had a little light here in this cursed darkness."

Marissa opened her mouth to respond. Before she got a word out, a tiny gleam of light blossomed in the darkness. In its glow she saw Kate jump back, her mouth agape. The light winked out.

"Did—did I do that?" Kate's voice was small and scared, like a small girl told ghost stories by an older brother.

"Yes," Marissa said. "Yes, you did. You wanted light, and you got it. And you did it without even casting a full-blown spell, which I have to do. Well done."

"But…I didn't…I mean, I can't… Ooooh."

"Maybe you can't, but you did. Can you do it again?"

"No." Kate's tone was defiant. This time she sounded like a young girl who's been told it's time for bed. Marissa stood up, stepped toward where she'd last seen Kate in the so-brief glimmer of light, and managed to take the other woman's hand in hers.

"Now you listen to me, Miss Katherine Taggart. You don't want this power, I know. No more than I did when I found out it was in me. But if you can draw on it, you may be our best—our only—hope of getting out of here."

"Oh."

"Marissa? Kate?" Catoya called from the other cell. "Are you all right?"

"We're fine," Marissa called back. "Kate has managed to access her power."

"Brilliant," said Catoya. "I'm glad someone can. Saia is asleep. Between casting her spell and the fun time we had getting the witchbane out of her system, she's exhausted, poor thing. And I can't reach anything magic-wise at the moment."

"No more can I," Marissa said. "I've been explaining to Kate how she might be our way out."

"The key?"

"The key."

Kate spoke up. "Even if I somehow managed to obtain the key, what could we do?"

"We open the doors and get out of here," Marissa declared. *What could be simpler than that?*

"You don't imagine they're going to just let us walk out of here, do you?" Kate asked, incredulous. "And even if we did manage to get out of the dungeons, what do we do next? We don't even know where we are."

"Hmph. I hadn't considered the aftermath." Marissa frowned, but the gesture was wasted, since they were once again in pitch darkness. "You're much too practical. It must come from being a woman of business. Oh, you're right, of course," she said to forestall Kate's protestations. "But I don't have to like it."

"We need to make a plan, instead of rushing headlong," Kate said. "I want to get out of this place as much as anyone. But you saw what happened when Saia tried something. Next time they'll dose us with witchbane again, and have guards watching over us, so we'll have to keep it down."

"I just hate being helpless," Marissa said. "I want to do something. Anything."

"Might 'anything' include showing me how to use this— whatever it is I've got? Because, despite the fact I managed to conjure up that little gleam of light, it was by accident, and I doubt I'll be able to do it again."

"Catoya," Marissa called. "This is why I invited you both over in the first place."

"Mmm, yes, it was, wasn't it? We can give it a try. Kate, if you will…"

Marissa sank back onto the cot again and tuned out the voices of her companions. Kate was right. They needed a plan. Damn it, she hated needing a plan.

Kate had been correct. The first step was to learn where they were being held captive. Once they'd done so, then they could figure out how to get back home again.

A thought, vague and tenuous, niggled at the outskirts of her brain. She sat still, quieting her mind, hoping it would reveal itself. The sensation was similar to when she'd been a young girl, seated under a tree in her parents' back garden, attempting to coax birds to her hand with a crust of bread.

At last, the thought flittered into view. Learning their location wasn't important. If they got out of the cells, which must be warded somehow, she'd be able to communicate with Wyvrndell. The dragon could speak to Morgan, and then the two of them could come to rescue Marissa and her fellow prisoners.

But she wondered if Wyvrndell would be able to tell where they were. While she was pondering this vital question, Kate said, "Oh, I've done it." She glanced up to see the familiar little ball of light which had been her own first magical endeavor blossom in Kate's hand.

"Excellent," she said. She reached deep, trying to locate any trace of her own power. She sensed the Thundermist-laden magic, tenuous as tendrils of fog, with nothing to catch hold of.

Soon, she promised. *Soon.*

CHAPTER FORTY-SIX
Ervantium

"Wyvrndell, you didn't."

Aireantha's voice was filled with a mix of both horror and pride. "What did your father say?' she went on.

"He said, 'It will be done.' What else could he say?"

"So you are to be crowned tomorrow, the next king of the dragons. Do you think Jakarian will learn of this, and try to stop the ceremony?"

"I am counting on it," he replied, wrestling with his gut to stave off another fit of hiccoughs. He'd fought against a bad bout which had come close to disabling him after Wyzandar left to attend to moving up the ceremony. They were getting the better of him, and he didn't have time or inclination for it.

Aireantha reared back, aghast, emitting a cloud of smoke. "Counting on it? What do you mean, counting on it?"

Wyvrndell swallowed bile. Which wasn't conducive to the calming of his recalcitrant innards. "Airie," he said, "I am going to have to confront Jakarian. We both know this to be true. I would much rather do so at a time and place of my own choosing, than to allow him the advantage. So, yes, I have ordered the ceremony to be moved up to tomorrow. It will rush Jakarian, force him to act before he is ready."

"Before you are ready, either," she said.

"Perhaps. Even so, I may yet surprise you. And Jakarian as well. I have a few tricks in me, Airie, which I think will serve me well."

"I hope so," she said, but he could see the concern in her eyes.

Wyvrndell hesitated, and she turned to face him. "Nervous?" she asked.

"Yes, but not about Jakarian. Well, perhaps a bit. No, nervous about what I am getting ready to say."

She waited for him to speak. Wyvrndell squelched another hiccough, and steeled himself to his task. "Airie, if I get out if this with my scales intact, I would ask you to be my queen, oh dragon of my heart."

She didn't answer at first, and his innards churned in earnest.

Then she twined her neck around his, and murmured, "In that case, you had best come out the victor, my king."

Wyvrndell roared…

~*~

Legion Garrison, Noordstrom

"Cap'n," Sir Ronell bellowed. "The scout's back."

Byron whirled. He'd been readying the first wave of defenders to head out into the forest west of Noordstrom. He would have preferred to deploy his men in daylight, but the advancing Rhuddlanis weren't going to afford him the luxury.

He left the final preparations to the two Green Rangers he'd assigned to be squad leaders and trotted over to where Ronall waited with the scout. The bells of St. Benedict's Cathedral, in the center of the city, tolled the hour of ten in the evening.

The scout looked like he'd run the whole way from wherever the Rhuddlanis' position was. Although, Byron acknowledged, the scouts probably tethered their horses a fair distance from the enemy line, in order to get a report back to the garrison on the double.

Captain Bosquet, in command of the Noordstrom garrison, loped toward them. He and Byron arrived at the same time. The poor scout, not certain whom to salute first, compromised by aiming it between the two officers. "Report, Mallern," Bosquet ordered.

"Sir, the Rhuddlani line is no more than seven miles out," Mallern said. "At the rate they're going, they'll reach the city walls by dawn."

"We need to get our men out there and into position," Bosquet said. "A major force guarding the eastern wall of the city."

"We don't have enough men to defend the city like that," Byron said. "They have three companies. We have one, and not enough weapons for the force we can field. Rakes and hoes aren't going to be much use against Rhuddlani swords."

Bosquet's hands tightened into fists at this assessment. He took a deep breath, unclenched his hands, and gave one brief nod. "So we prepare for a siege, then?"

Byron grimaced, not liking the prospect any better than his fellow captain. "We do, but with a little something extra. I want to take a couple of squads out into the woods. We'll leave enough here to defend the walls, but if we can hole up behind the Rhuddlani lines, we can coordinate with Farquar's company when they arrive, and catch the enemy in a flanking action. And in the meantime we can pick off some of the Rhuddlanis from behind and melt back into the forest."

"They'll hunt for you," Bosquet objected. "They won't let something like that go."

"All the better," Byron said. "If they're rambling around the forest looking for me and my men, it's less of them to try to breach Noordstrom's defenses. We just have to keep loose for a couple of days, until Farquar's lot gets here. Then it's another game, one we have a chance of winning."

"I reckon we'd best get a move on," put in Ronall. "If the Rhuddlanis are advancing that quick, we don't have a lot of time to get our lads into position."

"Do it, Sergeant," Byron ordered. Ronall took off at a run, bellowing orders and curses along the way. The great gates of the fortress creaked open, and the two squads quick-marched out.

"Aren't you going with them?" Bosquet asked. Byron recognized the resentment in his voice, at having an officer from Caerfaen show up to supersede his command. Well, it was Bosquet's problem, not his. Byron had too many other things to worry about to rise to the bait.

"Sergeant DeLaMaarche will have this lot under control," Byron said. "I'll follow them soon. Tell me, Mallern, did your chaps spot any Rhuddlani scouts?"

"Aye, Captain. We took two of 'em prisoner. If there were any more, we didn't spot 'em."

"The Rhuddlanis don't know we're aware they're coming," Byron mused. "So I don't reckon they sent out a lot of scouts. They hope to stroll right up to the city gates before they're challenged."

"So what happens if their scouts don't return?" Bosquet asked. "You're the mind reader, Darby. What will they do?"

"Simple," Byron said. "Their commander will assume the scouts got lost in the forest. He'll send out a few more. But our lads will know the Rhuddlanis are out there, and be able to avoid them, or capture them. And the new scouts won't find anything to report, because the men we sent out are going to be laying low until the Rhuddlanis have passed their position."

Bosquet gave a nod of grudging acceptance. "All right, you seem to have things well in hand," he said. "What do you need from me?"

Byron gazed into his fellow Legion captain's eyes. "I need your support, Devon," he said. "If we are to weather this storm, we have to work together. I need to know I can count on you, like I want you to be assured you can count on me and my men. That's all."

The other man looked at the ground, considering his answer. When he looked up at last, he gave an affirming nod and reached out a hand. Byron took it, knowing how difficult the gesture had been for Bosquet. "Thank you," he said. "Now, let's get to work."

CHAPTER FORTY-SEVEN

McRobbie House, Caerfaen

It was late afternoon before Morgan made it home. He'd had to stop several times to rest and water Arnicus along the way. Morgan and Francesca had caught a couple of catnaps during those stops, but they weren't enough. He was running on a heady mix of fury, fear, and adrenaline, and he knew once that wore off, he'd collapse into a soggy heap. It didn't matter. He had to keep moving.

He reined Arnicus to a halt at the foot of the cobbled drive leading to the carriage house and stables. "Hmmph," he muttered.

He'd expected the place to be a beehive of frenzied activity. Instead, a placid calm hung over the house, at least from the outside. Two Legion soldiers stood sentry in a strange semblance of normality. No one from the Watch was scouring the grounds for clues or evidence as he might have expected. Morgan shook his head. Granted, it had taken him the better part of twenty-four hours to get back, but still…

Francesca stuck her head out from beneath the protection of his leather jacket and sniffed the air. "It's getting whiffy in here," she complained. "Let's go. Both of us need food and water. And you need a bath something fierce. Then, we find my witch."

Morgan rolled his eyes. Nothing like a cat to keep one's perspective on life in focus. "Things are so quiet," he said. "Maybe they've already found her."

"No," the cat replied. "I'd be able to tell if she was here."

Morgan hauled the cat the rest of the way out of his jacket and held her up to look into her huge green eyes. "Can you tell where she is?" he demanded. "If you can…"

"No, sorry, I can't. Something's preventing me from being able to tell where she is."

"Witchbane?" Morgan asked, his voice coming out a growl.

Francesca blinked. "I'm impressed. You know more than I gave you credit for. Yes, I'm certain it's witchbane. It prevents the use of magic, yes. But it also acts in a number of other ways. One of which is to make a witch magically invisible to her familiar."

"Right. Well, we'll have to figure out something else. Let's go." With this, he urged Arnicus forward, and headed for the house.

As he approached, Morgan realized things weren't calm after all. Through the open window, raised voices could be heard, and one of them… He stifled an exhausted grin. He should have known.

"Damn it, Captain, don't just stand there looking officious. Find her."

"Lady Sybil," replied the voice of Captain Jenks, and Morgan heard both fatigue and frustrated patience in his voice. "We're doing everything possible to locate the duchess. If you have an actual helpful suggestion, rather than shouting at me when I'm doing my job to the best of my ability, I'll be happy to take it. Otherwise…"

Morgan swung down from the saddle.

"I'm going to check around," the cat told him, and scrambled awkwardly to the ground.

"Are you hurt?" Morgan asked. He hadn't noticed before. Of course the kitten hadn't been moving around much on the journey back from the north, sequestered in his jacket most of the time.

Francesca gave a throaty growl, surprising from such a small creature, and replied, "Nothing to concern yourself over. I'll be back in a little while. Carry on."

Morgan found himself almost saluting. Shaking his head, he handed Arnicus's reins over to one of the guards who had hurried over to greet him.

Both sentries saluted, and one led Arnicus towards the stable. The other said, "I'm terrible sorry, Commander. Fardin and Quint, they were the ones here when this all happened. Fardin's okay, but Quint got a good knock on the head, and is still unconscious. These fellers meant business."

Morgan's eyes narrowed. He managed to refrain from pointing out their charge was to keep fellers who meant business out, instead of standing around getting knocked on the head. But it wasn't their fault, any more than it was Fardin's or Quint's. The men who'd come for Marissa were determined, skilled, and ruthless. Not to mention fanatical. A deadly combination, and not one even the most resolute sentries could hope to withstand.

He settled for saying, "I hope Quint recovers soon. Carry on." With that, Morgan strode up the steps and shoved open his front door.

The hubbub ceased when he stepped through the doorway. Everyone turned to focus on the man in black. Morgan straightened, scanning the group standing before him. His mother, Kevin, Briana, Mrs. Brand, Captain Jenks and his sergeant MacGwyn. "Well?" he demanded.

Everyone began talking—shouting, in fact—at once. The din did nothing whatsoever for his already throbbing head. "Quiet!" he bellowed.

"—and nothing's being do—Oh." Lady Sybil ceased her harangue and joined the rest of the crowd in blessed silence.

Morgan breathed a relieved sigh and said, "Captain Jenks, I'm glad to see you here. Tell me what you know, what you suspect, and what you're doing to find the men who took my wife and her friends."

Jenks mouth tightened. "You'd best have it all from the beginning." He turned to Kevin Jacoby. "You were here, why don't you tell your story, and then I'll pick it up from there."

Kevin said, "Very good, Captain." Turning back to Morgan, he said, "Yesterday, the duchess received three ladies to tea. Miss Taggart and Miss Alford, both of whom have called here before, at her invitation. Also, the Princess Saia from Arvindir."

Morgan nodded. "The meeting of witches. She told me she invited them."

Kevin resumed his narrative. "I can't tell you what they discussed, for the door to the morning room was closed."

"I can," Briana piped up. "At least, when I brought in the tea things, they were going on about how to best protect the witches of Kilbourne from those foul priests who're saying they're evil. Stuff and nonsense. I've seen a lot more hurt and pain caused by so-called men of God than ever by any witch."

Kevin picked up his tale again. "At any rate, I was doing my chores, tidying up your study. Mrs. Brand and Briana were in the kitchen—"

"I'd just finished up the loveliest batch of sticky buns for their tea," Mrs. Brand moaned. "Ach, the villains."

"I heard what sounded like glass breaking," Kevin said. "I hopped it, thinking one of the ladies dropped the tea pot or something. Hadn't more than got into the hallway when a man in dark robes, hooded like, loomed up out of nowhere. He grabbed me and slapped some sort of cloth over my face. That was the last thing I knew for a good while."

Briana said, "Mrs. Brand and I was in the kitchen, waiting for the buns to cool so we could ice them. Two more of those dark men rushed right in through the back door, like 'twas their own house. I was so startled I never even let out a peep."

"Ha," said the cook. "I'd been sharpening a knife, and I give one of the bast—fellows, beggin' yer pardon—a cut on his shoulder he won't soon forget."

"Ah, well done, Mrs. Brand," Morgan said. "Sharp thinking."

"'Tweren't no thought to it," she replied. "There he was, and I went for 'im."

"Anyway," Briana continued, "they grabbed us, like they must have done Kev, and put those cloths over our faces, and that was that."

Kevin resumed his narrative. "When I woke up, half an hour had gone by, for I'd just finished winding the clock in the hall. There was a window broken in the morning room, the four ladies were gone, and I found Briana and Mrs. Brand waking up on the kitchen floor." He shook his head in dismay. "I sent a boy off to fetch Captain Jenks here, and another to Arthur, to try and get a message to you."

Morgan nodded approval. "Thank you, Kevin. You did the right thing. And don't fret. There was nothing you could have done to prevent this. Those men were trained and determined. They would have killed you like swatting an annoying fly if you'd gotten in their way."

Jenks took up the tale. "I came off straight away with Sergeant MacGwyn and a brace of constables. From what I can make out, they first knocked out the guards posted outside. One of them is under a surgeon's care; he got a pretty good knock on the head. The other's all right."

Morgan nodded. "Yes, I spoke with the chaps out front, who filled me in."

"Right." Jenks continued. "The intruders broke the window of the room the duchess and her friends were in. They tossed in a vial of stuff to render them unconscious. We found shards of glass from the vial on the floor where it broke. With the staff out of commission, they waltzed right in and carried off the ladies to a waiting coach."

"Any lead on the coach?" Morgan asked.

"Not so far. This is a busy street, there's dozens of coaches back and forth along here, day and night. No one we've spoken with noticed anything out of the ordinary. I'm sorry to say, Commander, we have no notion at the moment where the duchess is being held. Short of a house to house search of the city, I don't know how we'd be able to find her." He had a difficult time meeting Morgan's eye as he made this dire pronouncement.

Morgan considered. "If she was able, Marissa would have

spoken to Wyvrndell, the dragon. He would have alerted me if he had heard from her. Which means she's either unconscious, or incapacitated somehow." His thoughts went back to witchbane. *Damn.*

"Hmm. You would think," Morgan mused, "someone might have noticed men in hooded black robes loading four unconscious women into a conveyance."

"Yes, you would," Jenks agreed. "I've had men scouring the area for any witnesses. So far, though—"

"I saw it," said a hollow, rumbling voice. Morgan looked up to see the spectral figure of Sir Jamie, former owner and now resident spirit of the house, materialize as if out of a bank of fog. Briana gave a shriek and shut her eyes. Mrs. Brand crossed herself. Kevin gulped but managed to maintain his composure.

"Sir Jamie," Morgan said. "Tell us all."

Jenks, he noted, was taking the sudden appearance of a specter in stride. Which, considering some of the things he'd ended up involved with during his association with Morgan and Marissa, was no real surprise. "Allow me to introduce Captain Jenks, of the Watch, and Sergeant MacGwyn. Sir Jamie is our resident spirit, and watches over the house like his own, which in fact it used to be. Sir Jamie, please give us your report."

"Ahem, yes. Well, I was puttering upstairs, inspecting the new drapes the duchess had installed in the second bedchamber. Not bad," he noted in an aside to Morgan. "Anyways, there was a commotion downstairs, and I hastened to see what was going on. By the time I got there, this young feller was out on the floor and the ladies was gone. I got outside, and there were these hooded sons of—well, ladies present, best mind me tongue. They was stuffing the ladies into this black coach. I reared up to do a good bit of haunting on 'em, see if I couldn't frighten them off. And do you know what?" he cried, indignation writ clear in his hollow voice.

The entire company was hanging on his every word. Morgan asked, "What happened, Sir Jamie?"

"The rascals threw holy water on me. Can you credit it? I've never been so mad in me life. Damn them, it discombobulated me for a bit, long enough they was able to get away. I—I'm afeared I wasn't able to tell which way they went, even…"

Jenks, the picture of politeness, inquired, "Sir Jamie, were there any markings on the coach. Anything which might help to identify it?"

The specter's expression was morose. "Nay, Watchman, no crest or any insignia. They were most canny, these villains. If ye find 'em, I'll rouse out me old squad, and we'll give 'em such a haunting they'll quake in their boots and wail for mercy. Bah. Holy water, indeed."

"Holy water, eh?" mused Jenks. "Not a lot of kidnappers would come quite so well prepared."

"No," Morgan agreed, his voice tight. "Which to my mind means they were sent by the rebel bishops, to capture the Royal Enchantress. The others were a bonus for them, I imagine."

"To what end?" Jenks asked.

Morgan swallowed hard, forcing down the bile in his throat. "To put her on trial," he said. "And burn her at the stake for witchcraft."

Jenks stared, his eyes narrowing. "Where are they?" he demanded. "Nobody gets burned, witch or not, in my city."

Morgan scrubbed a weary hand across his face, thinking hard. "I doubt they're in the city, Jenks. The bishops are holed up somewhere. Last I knew, they were in Cormaine. If they're still there, that's where they'll have taken Marissa and the others."

"Well, what are we waiting for?" the Watchman said, a fey light in his eyes. "Let's go find 'em."

"Sorry, Captain. This is out of your jurisdiction."

"Not if I'm in pursuit of a criminal who committed an offense here, it's not," Jenks protested.

Morgan shook his head. "Thanks, Jenks, but no. These men believe they are outside your laws. They make their own, and say they're given to them by God. No, I'll handle this."

"Commander, with all due respect, you can't go taking justice into your own hands. I know it's your wife they've taken, but—"

"Captain, I'm not planning to. I will be acting in my formal capacity as Knight-Commander of the Legion. The renegade bishops have kidnapped Kilbourne's Royal Enchantress, which I consider to be an act of war. I think the king will agree with me. The fact she happens to be my wife—" he waved a hand. "Well, it has no bearing on the situation."

Like hell it doesn't, he muttered to himself.

Jenks stared into his eyes, searching for truth, then gave a curt nod. "Acts of war do indeed fall under your purview, Commander. Good hunting. If I can be of any assistance, however…"

Morgan gave him a grateful, if weary, smile. "As a matter of fact, you can. I'd like you to send a few of your constables to present their complements to some men I need to see, and have them escorted here."

Jenks blinked once. "All right. Who do you want?"

Morgan gave him four names. "Don't let your men take no for an answer."

At the fourth name, Jenks face became shuttered. "Ian Taggart?"

"Yes, Taggart. His daughter is one of the women who was taken with Marissa."

Jenks stared. "His…daughter?"

"Yes, I'm afraid so. She's a novice witch, and the woman Captain Poldane is planning to marry. Assuming we get her—and the others—back in one piece. Miss Alford is the head of the witch's council. The fourth woman is Princess Saia of Arvindir, who is enjoying the king's hospitality. She's also a powerful sorceress."

Jenks swallowed. "You'd think, with so much magic between them, those ladies ought to be able to sort these fellows out on their own."

"Yes," Morgan said, with visions of witchbane dancing dark tarantelles through his churning brain. "You would think so, wouldn't you? Now, those constables?"

Jenks set to dispatching his men. "Your Grace," said the cook, approaching Morgan. "I'm terrible sorry for what's happened. I know you'll get her ladyship and those others back, safe and sound. But you oughtn't be about it on an empty stomach. If you'd like, I'll fix you a bite of something. I've got some good roast beef, and a bit of the cheese you like so, and yesterday I baked up a lovely loaf of the dark bread you favor…"

"Mrs. Brand, you have saved me from gnawing the furniture," Morgan said. "Jenks, join me for supper while we wait on my guests?"

"I wouldn't want to be in your way, Commander," he replied.

"You won't. I'd like you to stay, actually. Your men can continue to report in here, right?"

"Sure. Very well, I'd be obliged. I can't stay long, I have a lot to do back at the Watch House. But I don't remember the last time I ate, and I wouldn't turn down a bite of something that doesn't bite back."

Francesca appeared by Morgan's feet. "I've been trying to find any trace of either the witches or the men who did this," she reported. "Nothing, blast it."

"Thank you, Francesca," Morgan said. "Why don't you go to the kitchen and see if Mrs. Brand will find some fish for you."

Catching Jenks's expression when the cat spoke, Morgan grinned to himself. It had taken him some time to become accustomed to the notion when Marissa had first introduced her familiar. The Watch captain's brows rose slightly, but other than a slight narrowing of his eyes, he took a talking cat in stride. After Francesca had departed again, Morgan said, "Lady Francesca is Marissa's familiar. It's a long story, and not really mine to tell."

Jenks took a deep breath, let it out again, and said, "You know,

Commander, perhaps I'll be pushing off after all. I'm not sure my poor head can take anything else. Henry." He summoned the sergeant.

Morgan chuckled, for the first time in quite a while. "Understood, Captain. Thanks."

From out in the kitchen, Morgan heard Mrs. Brand bustling around. "Kev," she called. "I need you in here."

Lady Sybil approached him, her expression rivaling the most ominous storm cloud Morgan had ever seen. "Are you all right?" she asked.

"I will be," he replied. "Once I get her back."

"What can I do? I want to help."

"In this instance, there's not a damned thing you can do, I'm sorry to say. I wish there was."

She eyed him with a speculative gaze. "You have a plan?"

He nodded. "I do, and I'm afraid it doesn't include you." He held up a hand to stall the protestations he could see on her lips. "No, Ma, not even with your sword parasol. This is going to be quick, dirty, and dangerous, and people are likely to get hurt. I can't risk you."

Her lips tightened, and he knew damned well she wanted to argue the point. Allowing sanity to reign, she nodded, albeit with extreme reluctance. "You're right, of course. Though it hurts like the very devil to admit it, I couldn't keep up with you. Go find her, Morgan. Bring her home safe and give those bishops the very devil."

"I plan to, Ma," he said. "Oh, I plan to."

CHAPTER FORTY-EIGHT
A Dungeon Cell, Noordstrom

A light flickered in the passageway outside the cells. Marissa jerked herself out of a semi-dozing state. Even though she was stuck in the most frightful situation she'd ever encountered, exhaustion had taken its toll. Plagued by dreadful dreams which all featured fire and gleaming teeth, she struggled back to reality. Which, as realities went, wasn't a hell of a lot better.

As the light drew closer, she cocked her head, considering. "That's odd," she muttered aloud. "It hasn't been long since the guard brought us our oh-so-lovely luncheon we didn't eat."

"Don't remind me," Kate groused from the other cot. "If I can't eat it, I don't want to think of food. Hmm. I hope it's not those mad priests again, coming to torment us some more."

"Sorry, but I imagine it is." Marissa steeled herself for this unpleasant prospect. The light danced closer. "No, it sounds like one person. Interesting. Shall we put the kettle on?"

"If you even mention biscuits," Kate said, her voice grim, "I am liable to scream."

"Sorry," she replied. Their unexpected visitor hove into view. He wore a monk's robe, with a cowl pulled far up over his head, so his face was hidden in shadow.

"Hello," he said. His voice was pitched low, so only the women in the cells would be able to hear him.

Marissa went to the cell door. "Hello yourself. I don't suppose you've come to let us out of here, have you?"

"Not yet," replied the stranger. "But give me time, I'm working on it.”

Marissa blinked in complete astonishment. Kate joined her at the door. “What? Who are you? And why--?”

“We don’t have a lot of time for explanations,” he said, his voice terse. “I’m Brother Francis. I was sent here to keep an eye on Bishop Llachnahn and his cohorts. I’ll try to set you free, if I’m able. At the moment there are guards everywhere, so it’s too risky. You’d be captured again, and I’d be found out and unable to help you.”

“Where are we?” Marissa asked.

“Noordstrom. The Cathedral of Saint Benedict.”

“Noordstrom?” She shook her head. “Why in the world did they bring us all the way up here?”

“I don’t know,” Brother Francis replied. “I—blast, someone’s coming, I have to go.”

“Can you bring us some food and water?” Marissa asked as he turned to flee.

“I’ll try.” He blew out his candle and melted into the shadows. “Tonight.”

She stared after him. “Noordstrom,” she repeated softly. “Now, why Noordstrom?”

~*~

McRobbie House, Caerfaen

Many leagues away, back in Caerfaen, Morgan was asking the exact same question.

Randolph MacFarlane shrugged a broad shoulder. “I couldn’t say. They were holed up in Cormaine, last I knew. Maybe they decided it was smarter to get as far from Caerfaen, and from you, as they could manage. I would, if I was them. But that’s all I can tell you. The feller I had keeping an eye on things for me, Brother John, is no longer part of their little band of villains.”

Morgan winced. “Is he all right?”

“Yes, he got out in time. He said McAdoo was getting suspicious, and he didn’t consider it wise or safe to keep on. At any rate, my source of direct information has dried up. Now I only get things second hand.”

“Second hand? How so?”

Randolph harumphed. “Holman Barzak managed to get one of his chaps in place with them. He shares his reports with me when he’s in a generous frame of mind. Which isn’t often, I might add.”

Morgan scowled, running a hand through his hair. “Noordstrom. They couldn’t get much further, for certain, or they’d be in Rhuddlan…”

He squeezed his eyes shut, opening them again to focus on Randolph.

The bishop cocked his head. "What's so interesting about being near Rhuddlan?" he asked.

Morgan pinched the bridge of his nose, trying to make sense of his whirling thoughts. "Noordstrom… On the border with Rhuddlan. Holman Barzak's man, Barlbent, told me several days ago there were odd things going on in Rhuddlan, but none of their agents were able to pinpoint what was happening. Suddenly we have three companies of Rhuddlani soldiers coming across the Devil's Teeth right before the snow flies up there. And where are they headed? Into Dunstanshire. According to Sir Byron, they're heading straight for Noordstrom, and in a bloody great hurry to get there."

Randolph's eyes widened. "You figure there's a connection?"

Morgan threw his hands up. "Yes. No. Maybe? Damn it, Randolph, I don't know. But the timing is awfully suspicious, isn't it?" He raised a finger. "Rumblings from Rhuddlan." A second finger. "The bishops declare a war on witches in general, and on Marissa in particular." A third. "The Rhuddlanis march into Dunstanshire." A fourth. "Marissa and her friends are taken captive and hauled off to Dunstanshire."

Randolph heaved a huge sigh. "When you put it in those terms, it does strain credulity, don't it. But why? What's the end game?"

Morgan's hands tightened into fists. "Because Varsil Jarek wants to eliminate what he deems one of the biggest obstacles to his taking over Kilbourne."

Randolph sucked in a breath. "The Royal Enchantress," he said.

Morgan smacked a fist into his other hand. "Yes, damn it. Her and the witches she supposedly has at her beck and call. If Rhys has an army of witches at his command…"

"That could be a game changer, all right," Randolph allowed. "But there's something else, Morgan."

Morgan looked up to see the sorrowful gaze of his oldest friend fixed on him. "They'll be sure you'll come after her. She's bait, you know. Those Rhuddlani soldiers are coming there for you too."

"I know. It doesn't matter."

"Doesn't matter? So you're going to walk right into their trap with your eyes closed?"

"Don't be silly. I'm going to walk right into their trap with my eyes wide open."

"Oh, good," Randolph drawled. "Because that makes it so much better."

"And you," Morgan said, staring into his eyes, "are walking in right beside me.”

“Me?” Randolph squeaked, rearing back like a man who’s encountered a deadly viper. “You don’t want me along. I’d only hold you up, get in your way.”

“Perhaps so. It doesn’t matter, you’re coming with me. In fact, I can’t do it without you.”

“Hmph. Why, for heaven’s sake? Though I’m not so sure I want to hear the answer. I figure I’m big enough, you’re planning to use me for a shield. Right?”

“Hmm, I hadn’t considered doing so, but…” He appraised his friend with a calculating eye.

Randolph gave him a reproachful glare. Morgan chuckled, then grew serious again. “It’s not your bulk I need, but your brains. Or rather, your knowledge. You’re the one person I know who’ll be able to find their way around the cathedral where Marissa and the others are being held prisoners. You, my friend, are going to lead me into the trap.”

Randolph crossed himself. Morgan said, “Don’t worry, it won’t be just the two of us. Captain Jenks of the City Watch has his men out rounding up the rest of the crew. He was here most of the day, but had to leave to take care of some actual Watch business. They should be here soon.”

“Jenks?” Randolph stared at him, a thoughtful gleam lighting his eye. “Are you bringing criminals rather than soldiers?”

“Just one,” Morgan replied. A rap sounded at the door. “Come,” he called.

Kevin opened the door and stuck his head in to say, “Your Grace, there are constables on the stoop. They’ve brought Captain Poldane, Master Sebastien, and Baron Taggart.”

“Ah, excellent,” Morgan said. “Jenks made good time. Bring ’em in, Kevin. Well, not the constables, I don’t reckon we’ll need them.”

“Very good,” replied Kevin. Morgan went to stand by the door and greet his guests.

“Kevin, fetch a few more chairs, will you?” To the assembled men he said, “Thank you for coming.”

Taggart flashed him a broad grin. “Ach, like old times, it was. Watchmen showing up at my door and requesting the pleasure of my company. Although,” he went on, eyes lighting on the bottle of claret on the little table near Morgan’s desk, “the accommodations weren’t anywhere near this good.”

“Kevin?” Morgan tipped his head toward the bottle. The valet finished positioning chairs for the guests and started to pour. While drinks were handed round, Morgan said, “I’m sorry to take you away from whatever you might have been doing, but I need your help. My wife, along with three other women, has been abducted by the rebel bishops."

There were mutterings from Sebastien and Taggart. Aartis stood ramrod still, with a face to curdle milk. Morgan had spoken to him earlier in the evening and forbidden him from riding hell-for-leather after them. It had taken a good deal of arguing and persuading to convince him to stay put.

Morgan went on. "The other women are Princess Saia of Arvindir; Miss Alford, head of the witch's council; and Miss Katherine Taggart."

"What?" roared Ian Taggart, nearly spilling his glass. He glared at Aartis. "Why did ye nae tell me, lad?"

Aartis shrugged. "Because you'd have done the exact same thing I wanted to do—and was hindered." He shot a scowl at Morgan. "Gone after them."

"We are going to go after them," Morgan put in. "And we're going to bring them home again. But we're going to go about it in the right way, instead of storming the place half-cocked and with no plan."

"I presume," Sebastien said, "this means you do have a plan."

"I do. At least I have a plan to get us there. Which is where you come in, Sebastien. Tell me, does the cathedral of Saint Benedict, in Noordstrom, have one of those transfer portals?"

The wizard's brows rose, then he smiled in comprehension. "Ah, I see where you're going with this. Well, I'd be surprised if it didn't. Most of the old churches and monasteries had one, and St. Benedict's one of the oldest. How soon do you need to know?"

"Yesterday would be nice," Morgan said.

"Ah, that soon, eh? All right, if you'll lend me paper and ink, I'll send off an inquiry to the College. Might your man take it, and wait for a reply?"

Morgan was already hauling out a quill, ink, and a piece of parchment. After handing it to Sebastien, he stepped to the door. "Kevin?"

The valet came hurrying down the hallway. "Yes, Your Grace, how may I be of service?"

"Master Sebastien is drafting a note. I need you to deliver it to the Royal College of Wizards, with all possible haste, to…" He turned to the wizard.

"Journeyman Wizard Nardis Cardione," Sebastien said. "No one else. He should be there. If you'll wait, he should have a reply for you in short order." He blew on the paper, folded it in thirds and held it out.

"Duke Morgan, would you mind?"

Morgan took it and set the note on his desk. He procured wax and his seal from a drawer. He melted wax over the flame of the lamp and dripped it onto the paper, pressing the seal into the warm blob. He handed it off to Kevin. The valet sketched a bow and bustled out.

Taggart spoke up. "I understand why you'd need Master Sebastien, and why you'd want to bring Aartis. Why me?"

Morgan returned to his seat. "Two reasons," he said. "One, because your daughter is one of the prisoners, and I figured you might want to come along. Second, because we may well need to get into places, or open things, we're not intended to. Cell doors, for instance. I didn't know a better man for the job."

Taggart nodded, his smile tight. "All right, seems sensible. Thank you for including me."

Sebastien drummed his fingers on the arm of his chair. "You don't need me along on this little jaunt, do you? I mean, to get you in through the portal, assuming there is one. But that's all, right?"

"Well," Morgan said, "I do need you. Consider this: the rebel bishops managed to capture four witches. Three of them are powerful, with varying degrees of proficiency. And from what I understand, Miss Taggart also has a lot of power, though she has no idea how to use it."

Sebastien's brows furrowed. "That's correct. Go on."

"I don't know if the bishops have a wizard or two on staff, or what. But someone knows enough regarding magic, and is skilled enough, to keep those women from using their powers to level the whole place, turn the bishops into stoats, and stroll out. Someone is familiar with witchbane."

Sebastien flinched. Not so long ago an assassin had gone after him with a knife slathered in the stuff. If not for the efforts of an excellent surgeon, along with Francis Barlbent and Nardis Cardione, who'd managed to locate the antidote, Sebastien would not be alive.

Sebastien's smile was grim. Morgan was certain he was reliving those terrible days. "Yes, I get your point. You want your own wizard on hand."

"It would be sound strategy," Morgan allowed. "And since you're one of the few wizards I know and can trust, you're elected."

"Hmm. I'll hold off on thanking you for the honor until we've managed the task and made it back in one piece. If it's all the same to you, that is."

Morgan chuckled. Aartis asked, "When do we go?" His hand rested on the pommel of his sword. Spoiling for a fight, Morgan was certain.

"Assuming my hunch is correct, and there is a portal at St. Benedict's we can make use of, tonight. Late, when most of the cathedral should be in bed."

"If that's the case," Randolph said, "I'd best be going."

"Oh, no." Morgan shook his head. "You're not getting out of this."

"Of course not," Randolph replied. "Don't be daft, I wouldn't miss it. The chance to upstage and confound these—" Words appeared to fail him. Morgan chuckled to himself while he waited for his friend to find his tongue again. "But if you want plans of Saint Benedict's, I'd better go and find 'em, hadn't I? What time do you figure to go?"

"Half past one," Morgan said. "Be back here—oh, wait a minute. Sebastien, what if we use the portal at Saint Basil's?"

"Why not? There are several at the College, but at the cathedral, there shouldn't be anyone nosing around or interfering. Which is something I couldn't guarantee at the College."

Morgan nodded. "Excellent. Randolph, we'll meet you there at one?"

"I'll be ready." He gathered up his hat and strode out. Once again, Morgan was reminded how quick he was for such a large man.

In a subdued voice, Sebastien said, "Aren't you being a wee bit premature, Duke Morgan?"

"How so?" Morgan cocked his head, wondering what he'd overlooked.

"Well, we don't know for certain there's a portal at Saint Benedict's. If there's not, we're somewhat in the way of being stymied, are we not?"

"Yes, but I figured if there's not one in the cathedral, there must be one somewhere in Noordstrom. Right?"

"I expect so. I asked Nardis to check, if he found the cathedral lacking in portalness. But there's a world of difference between appearing in the midst of your enemy's stronghold, and getting near it in a hurry, but then having to force your way inside."

Morgan didn't bother to stifle his groan. "Perhaps I'd best relinquish my planning duties to you. I'm not making such a good job of it."

"You're too close to things," the wizard said. "It gets in the way of your normal objectivity."

"He's right," Taggart said. "It's much too easy to be distracted when you have a personal stake in the game."

"You do too," Morgan pointed out.

"Of course I do. So does Aartis. My point is, you can't let

emotions cloud your judgement. Save those emotions for when you need 'em later, and figure out the plan. Not only how to get to this cathedral, but what we're to do once we're inside. I've said my piece. I need to go gather up a few useful items we might need in our endeavor. I'll meet you at the cathedral at one."

"Don't eat a lot," Sebastien called after him. "Trust me."

Morgan squeezed his eyes shut against the thought of what was to come, what they were up against. Taggart was right, damn it. He'd been acting like an angry husband. Time to start thinking like the trained soldier he was. "All right," he said, opening his eyes again. "Assuming there is a portal, this is how we play it…"

CHAPTER FORTY-NINE
St. Benedict's Cathedral, Noordstrom

Brother Francis eased his head out of the pantry's doorway and scanned the corridor in each direction. No one was in sight, and he breathed a silent prayer of thanks. Getting caught with two loaves of bread, several apples, and a couple of wedges of cheese might be difficult to explain. Somehow, he didn't imagine "I was feeling a bit peckish" was going to go over well.

Especially not with everybody and his dog in the entire cathedral complex on edge. The monks Francis managed to speak with—the ones who'd not taken a vow of silence—were tightlipped and wary. The resident bishops—Llachnahn and McAdoo in particular—seemed to be viewed by the rank-and-file brothers as "overly zealous, if you get my drift." At least that was how one of the brothers Francis talked to phrased it. Overly zealous was, to Francis's way of thinking, a masterful piece of understatement.

Now here he was, once again, in the thick of things, doing his damnedest to not make a hash of it all. *How in the world do I end up in these situations*? It hadn't been what he'd signed on for when he'd taken the position of Lord Holman's clerk in the Office of Spies. But His Lordship wanted someone on the spot when Bishop Randolph's man was forced to bow out. Francis, being both available and somewhat monkish in appearance, was his choice. And that had been that.

The cathedral's bells tolled the hour of eleven in the evening. Francis calculated it best to wait until well after curfew. He didn't want to risk encountering anyone who might ask uncomfortable questions, like "Where the devil are you going with all that food?" Though he did, in fact, have an answer to the question. If pressed, he was bringing a late supper to the guards in the dungeon, poor chaps who had to be awake at this hour, wasn't it hard on them?

He scowled. Hard on them? *Bah.* It was hard on those poor women locked up in darkness, anticipating the worst, and going to get it unless he could do something to help them. Which he was doing, at least a little, by bringing them food and drink. He'd already stashed a couple of water skins in a hidey hole he'd discovered not far from the cells. He didn't expect the guards would find them. They were in all likelihood much more concerned about keeping intruders out, and in keeping the women locked in their cells, than in searching the premises for contraband.

Well, this was one intruder they were going to have a difficult time keeping out. Although his level of field experience wasn't on par with many of Lord Holman's agents, he was more resolute than any of the others might have been in the same circumstances. He was determined to free the Royal Enchantress and her friends from their durance vile, and save them from the stake he knew the rebel bishops were planning for their fate.

He slipped down the corridor, the parcel of food in his pack concealed under his cloak. He moved in silence, almost invisible, emulating his sobriquet. They didn't call him The Wraith for nothing. Well, were he to admit it, they didn't call him The Wraith at all. It was a nom de guerre he'd taken for himself. Francis allowed one corner of his mouth to turn up at the thought, then chided himself. This was no time for frivolity. He hardened himself back into a demeanor of half determination, half courage, and half bold action. *Too many halves by half. Get on with it, Francis.*

He was on his own here, in what was considered enemy territory, with no hope of outside assistance. There was no way the message he'd managed to smuggle out, destined for his chief in Caerfaen, would reach its destination for several more days. Even then, getting more agents dispatched to Noordstrom would take another week at the least. No, this was Francis's storm-tossed sea to navigate.

Lost in these less than comforting musings, he nearly missed seeing the dark figure which materialized at the far end of the passageway. It wasn't until the man unshuttered his lamp that Francis registered his presence. Francis sucked in a breath and looked for a convenient door through which to dart. The quantity of doors in the cathedral's corridors were so ubiquitous as to be overwhelming. In this instance, they displayed a singular lack of availability and helpfulness. There was nowhere to hide. Francis swore under his breath and prepared to bluff his way through if necessary.

It was necessary.

"Hoy, what are you doing about at this time of night?" demanded Bishop Dafyd McAdoo. "It's long past curfew, you know."

Francis could have pointed out to His Excellency how the aforementioned curfew applied to both brother and bishop alike. Deeming this unpolitic, he settled for muttering, "Couldn't sleep, your worship. This cough, y'know. 'Tis bad tonight. Thought I'd spend a little time in the chapel, in prayer instead." He managed to feign a rousing bout of hacking which he hoped would send McAdoo scurrying away, lest he catch something noxious himself.

To his dismay, his plan backfired. Bishop McAdoo, taking pity on the sufferer, said, "An excellent plan. I'll come with you and do a bit of praying for your relief meself."

"Damn and blast," Brother Francis muttered under his breath. But he had a sneaking suspicion the bishop was less concerned about praying for him than in having him think McAdoo was about at this hour for some clandestine motive of his own. Aloud he said, "Thank you, your worship. I shouldn't—" here he brought about another frenzied round of coughing— "wish to cause you any inconvenience."

"No, no, not at all," said McAdoo, placing a hand on Francis's shoulder. Much too close to where the pack, filled with its cargo of contraband, was concealed under his cloak. Francis circumvented its discovery by turning away to engage in more coughing.

Thwarted, he allowed himself to be led, like a sheep to the slaughter, into the chapel. In the dim flicker of the vigil candle, he sank to his knees and began to pray, with surprising ferocity for a man of his particular religious proclivities—which meant little to none, in truth— that the Lord above would send a lightning bolt, or at the very least a fast-acting plague of some sort, to strike this pesky and persistent priest, in order to allow Francis to get on with his mission. The parcel of food concealed under his cloak practically cried out to be discovered, and his excuse of delivering supper to the guards was long flown at this point.

He threw in a few faux coughs, more to keep up the act rather than out of any hope his professed malady would deter the bishop. There was no way he could leave before McAdoo. He remained in place, eyes closed. A simmering loathing burned like a smith's forge within his heart for this interrupter of noble deeds. Who, Francis hated to admit, was going out of his way to provide comfort to a sufferer. If only he'd do the same for the women he and Llachnahn had locked in the dungeon, Francis thought, the world would be a better and happier place.

After an interminable period of feigned—at least for Francis—

prayer, the bishop rose from his kneeling position. Francis heard the man's knees crack, and in an uncharitable fit of temper wished a rousing bout of arthritic pain upon him, since the requested lightning bolts never materialized. It was times like this, he mused, which tended to confirm his suspicions that the heavens were quite thoroughly unoccupied.

Once McAdoo tiptoed out of the chapel, Francis remained where he was for several more minutes. He didn't want the bishop returning with a cup of tea or a tisane to ease his cough, find him missing and raise the alarm.

Once he estimated a reasonable amount of time had passed, he rose from his own aching knees, stood, and stretched. He checked the corridor outside the chapel, found it empty, and darted toward the cells on his mission of mercy. He wondered what McAdoo had been up to, sneaking around in the middle of the night. But there were things to do, places to be, and captives to assist, so he didn't spend an inordinate amount of time worrying about it.

He navigated the rest of the journey in wraithlike silence and stealth, retrieved his cached water skins, and eluded the drowsy guards to arrive in the corridor containing the prisoners.

"Psst," he hissed through the bars of the cell which housed Lady Marissa and Miss Taggart.

"Mmmph?" came from within.

He hissed again, charry of rousing the guards if he spoke any louder.

"Wazzat?"

Brother Francis smiled. He recognized the distinctive, if muzzy, voice of Lady Marissa du Berry-McRobbie, Duchess of Westdale and Royal Enchantress of Kilbourne. Weighty titles for such an unprepossessing figure. "It's me. Brother Francis," he whispered into the cell. "I've brought you food and water."

That got her attention. Her voice brightened measurably. "Really? Food?"

"Yes, hurry up. I can't risk a light; the blasted guards might notice. But I've got bread, and cheese, and a couple of apples. Oh, and water skins. Are you ready? Don't drop it." He handed the loaf of bread through the bars.

"Hold on," Lady Marissa muttered. "Here, Kate, take this, will you?"

"With pleasure," came the voice of Miss Taggart.

Francis handed over the rest of his offerings. Lady Marissa said, "If I have anything at all to say about it, you will be up for sainthood. Thank you, Brother Francis."

"At your service," he replied with an airy wave. "I'm working on some way to get you all out of here, but it won't be easy."

"The key is on the wall behind you," Lady Marissa pointed out.

"I'm afraid it's not that simple. I wish it was, but there are guards everywhere. I'm dashed lucky I managed to sneak by them myself. The four of you trying to get past them? I can't see it. Our one chance may lie in you ladies being able to utilize your magic. I don't know, make yourselves invisible or something?"

"Being able to eat and drink without worrying about witchbane makes that a much stronger possibility," she replied. "Thank you, Brother Francis. You're wonderful."

Francis flushed with pleasure at her words. "Be sure to hide the water skins," he cautioned. "And the apple cores. If anyone learns I've smuggled food in to you, we'll all be in the soup. Now, if you'll excuse me, I need to deliver the rest of my offerings to the other ladies and get out of here before anyone comes along."

"A saint indeed," Miss Taggart said as he headed for the other cell. Francis made his final delivery and set about navigating his stealthy way back past the guards and back to his tiny room. Exit The Wraith, he thought with a grin.

CHAPTER FIFTY
Kilbourne Palace, Caerfaen

Rhys Gwynfallis stood motionless while a valet buffed his already gleaming boots. Queen Gwyndolyn fastened the heavy golden chain of office around his neck. Even though immobilized, he managed to acknowledge the arrival of R'gm'l, his page, who bowed low before him.

The young Dwarf, son of King K'var'k, had been fostered to Rhys's court for a year and a day. In exchange, Prince Robert of Kilbourne, Rhys and Gwyn's sole heir, was serving equal time in the Dwarf king's court. The arrangement was proving satisfactory to both kingdoms, although the exchange of princes had been fraught, coming near to disaster. If not for the quick actions of Morgan McRobbie, both princes might have been lost.

"How may I serve Your Majesty?" R'gm'l asked.

Gwyn stepped back and Rhys relaxed his stance. The valet retreated with his rag. "I want you to accompany me on a state visit, R'gm'l," he said.

"Of course, Your Majesty. Are we to visit Orsk, perhaps?"

Since R'gm'l was privy to Rhys's recent communications with the ruler of that island nation, this was a natural assumption. Natural, but in this instance, far from the truth. Rhys held up a finger to signify a pause in their conversation. To the valet he said, "Thank you, Orvan, I won't need you any more tonight. You may go."

Orvan bowed to his liege and departed, closing the door of the king's dressing room behind him. "Would you like me to leave too?" Gwyn asked.

"No, please stay," Rhys said. "You already know most of this. But what I'm going to say must not go beyond we three."

Gwyn arched an elegant brow. R'gm'l stood at attention, waiting for the king to speak.

When he was certain there were no listening ears outside the door, Rhys said, "You will accompany me on this journey not in your role of page, but in the persona of Prince R'gm'l, ambassador from your father. For we are to attend the coronation of the new dragon king."

R'gm'l's eyes grew wide. "Petrandius is dead?" he asked, his voice choked with emotion.

"Yes, I'm afraid so."

"Wyvrndell has said nothing to me of this. Which dragon is to be the new king?"

Rhys's smile was tight. "If Wyvrndell has not yet told you, you will have to wait and see."

"Oh, I hope it is Wyzandar, Wyvrndell's sire," R'gm'l exclaimed, bouncing with excitement. "Wyvrndell says he would make an excellent king, ruling with wisdom and justice. Like both you and my father."

Rhys said nothing, but Gwyn said, "If you are to accompany His Majesty, you'd best hurry and change into your finest clothes. Be back before the clock strikes the hour."

"At once, Your Majesties. By your leave?"

"Go," said Rhys, "and be quick about it. But remember, say nothing to anyone of where you are bound."

"Yes, Your Majesty." The prince executed a swift bow and fled.

It this wise?" Gwyn asked when they were alone. "Bringing R'gm'l, I mean."

Rhys shrugged. "The lad is here, he is friends with Wyvrndell, and he is the best representative from the Dwarf kingdom we have available."

"The ambassador?" Gwyn asked.

"I inquired. The ambassador has been recalled to R'mk'vl for consultations and won't be back until next week. His junior would not serve in this instance. No, it must be R'gm'l or no one, and to my mind it would be an insult, both to Dwarves and to dragons, not to bring him."

"I suppose." She cocked her head, her gaze focused on something only she could see.

Rhys shot a sharp glance at his queen. "Something wrong?"

"Nooo. At least, nothing I can put my finger on. Just—be careful, Rhys."

He'd learned long ago to trust Gwyn's instincts, which were on a par with Morgan McRobbie's. "I'll do my best," he promised.

"I wish Morgan was going with you."

"To keep me out of trouble?" he chided.

"To protect you from trouble," she countered. "Yes, I know, you're an excellent swordsman. I also know Morgan defeats you on a regular basis."

"All right, rub it in, why don't you." Rhys chuckled. Her words didn't rankle in the least. "I'll be the first to admit I'm not his equal with a blade. Nor will I ever be, no matter how much I practice. Which is why I'm merely a king, and he's the knight-commander of the Legion. But where we're going, swords wouldn't make a difference, you know. And anyway, neither Morgan nor Marissa is available to attend, though they were both invited. I wish to heaven they were."

Her eyes went dark with fury at this.

"Don't worry, Gwyn. I've every confidence in Morgan. He'll get Marissa, and those other women, back safe and sound."

"And what of the rebel bishops?"

Rhys's mouth formed a ferocious scowl. "Kidnapping," he said, "is a capital crime. And since they have kidnapped Kilbourne's Royal Enchantress, I believe a charge of treason is also warranted. It will fall to a magistrate to decide their fate. However, I've little doubt they will face either a very long prison sentence, or a very short rope."

"I for one hope it's the latter." Gwyn's tone was vehement. Before she could expound on her theme, a rap on the door heralded the return of Prince R'gm'l.

Rhys inspected his fosterling, noting the well-polished boots, black hose, and burgundy doublet embroidered with the insignia of King K'var'k. A circlet of silver, studded with one ruby, rested on his head, and a black woolen cloak lay across his shoulders.

"Excellent," Rhys said. "Let us go down to the courtyard. Our transport should be arriving at any moment."

"Is Wyvrndell coming to fly us to the coronation?" guessed R'gm'l.

"No, he is busy with other matters and unable to come. He is sending his friend Aireantha to bear us to Ervantium. Come, we must be ready for her arrival."

"Farewell, Queen Gwyndolyn," R'gm'l said, executing a courteous bow.

"Farewell, Prince R'gm'l," Gwyn replied. "You represent your father well."

With this, Rhys led the prince of the Dwarves down to the courtyard to await the arrival of the dragon Aireantha.

Ervantium

Rhys was glad he'd opted for his warmer woolen robe and a heavy cloak. The air was freezing here in the mountains.

"We are almost there," Aireantha announced.

Peering ahead, Rhys observed row upon row of high mountain peaks, most covered with a thick blanket of snow. The cold seeped through even the wool cloak, caressing him with icy fingers and drawing away his body heat. He shuddered from the chill.

"I believe," the dragon said, *"you are the first human—or Dwarf—to ever set foot in Ervantium. Things are changing so rapidly for us…"*

"Both R'gm'l and I are aware of the honor which has been accorded to us," Rhys told her, trying to keep his teeth from chattering. "We will do our best not to betray your trust."

"Indeed so," said R'gm'l, through his own bout of shivers. His clothes were much less warm than Rhys's.

"Even so," she said, banking toward one of the higher peaks. *"I should have made you cover your eyes, so you would not be able to divulge the location of this place."*

"Aireantha, I vow to you, such was unnecessary" Rhys said. "I'd not be able to find this spot should my life depend upon the knowledge."

"Nor I," R'gm'l affirmed. "Every one of these mountains looks the same to me."

"Very well." Aireantha side-slipped toward an enormous ledge jutting out from one of the mountain tops. Gazing down, Rhys spied two dragons, one at each end of the ledge. Guards, no doubt.

Beyond the two watchers, he observed a large entrance from the ledge into the interior of the mountain itself. Light glowed from inside. Aireantha appeared to sense his surprise. *"What did you expect?"* she asked. *"Imagine we perhaps roosted in trees upon the slopes of the mountain?"*

Rhys barked out a laugh. "Nay, Aireantha, not at all. I reckon it would have to be a mighty tree indeed to hold the likes of you and your kin. No, I have no excuse for my surprise other than sheer ignorance. The times are changing, but they change for men and Dwarves too. I just need to adjust my thinking."

She landed like a feather on the ledge and folded her wings. Rhys was awed by her grace and precision. The guard dragons stepped forward, barring the way forward. *"I bring honored guests,"* she said to them, allowing Rhys and R'gm'l to hear her words. *"At the invitation of Wyvrndell himself."*

The two guards turned their attention to her passengers. Rhys remained seated and placed a hand on R'gm'l's shoulder to signal to him to stay put. "I am Rhys Gwynfallis, King of Kilbourne, at your service," he said, addressing them. "My companion is Prince R'gm'l, scion of King K'var'k of R'mk'vl."

The guards exchanged a look and stepped back. Aireantha lowered her haunches and Rhys clambered to the ground without incident. Once on firm ground—or ledge, as the case might be—he assisted R'gm'l to dismount.

"You may enter," one of the guards said, and Aireantha led them through the opening and into Ervantium, seat of the kings of the dragons.

There was, in truth, not much to see. The entrance from the ledge led into a long tunnel, worn smooth by the passage of countless dragons over the long ages. Unlike the halls of the kings of men, his own included, there were no portraits of revered ancestors, nor displays of mighty weapons. The dragons' fortress was stark and utilitarian.

Indeed, who would paint such portraits, Rhys chided himself. To the best of his limited knowledge, there were no artists among the dragons. Hmm, did the Dwarves go in for art of any kind? Well, other than metal working? He would have to ask R'gm'l sometime. Was art, he mused, a strictly human endeavor? And if so, why?

The tunnel widened at last, and Rhys put this interesting, if unproductive, train of thought aside for the time being. Aireantha stepped aside, allowing the visitors to behold the scene before them.

"Welcome to the Great Hall," she said, and any consideration of art was driven from his mind.

Rhys managed not to stagger at the sight which met his eyes, but it wasn't easy. The hall, hollowed out from the living rock of the mountain, was immense. Lit by torchieres set into the walls, the light from the flames danced and flickered upon a veritable sea of dragons. From beside him, R'gm'l caught his breath.

"There are," Rhys said, overstating the obvious, "a lot of dragons here."

"Yes," she replied. *"A coronation is a rare event for us. For many, this will be the only one in their lifetime. Every dragon who was able to make the journey has come to witness it. Come, for your place is near the front. Since you are considered honored ambassadors, you have been given choice spots. Also,"* and Rhys detected a trill of a chuckle in her voice, *"otherwise you would not be able to see anything over all these dragons."*

Weaving her way through the throng, she led them past dragons of every size and hue. Rhys found R'gm'l's hand clutched in his. The young Dwarf was trembling. What must it be like, Rhys wondered, to be surrounded by creatures who not so long ago were your sworn enemies?

With this thought came another. He was, if he was being honest, in somewhat the same situation. Dragons and men had never reached the same levels of enmity that dragons and Dwarves had. Even so, he was walking into a fortress filled with those who a few weeks earlier might have charred him on sight.

He bore no weapons here, for even the doughtiest of swords would have done him no good. He had no guards to aid him, and likely no sense either. The only thing he did possess was faith in Wyvrndell. He wondered if even Wyvrndell could control things if a few dragons got it into their minds to rid the world of a couple of their ancient foes.

Even so, he needed to maintain an impression of stoic calm, for R'gm'l's sake. *And for my own.* He gave the Dwarf's shoulder a reassuring squeeze and followed their guide. There was nothing else to do. They were here, for good or ill, and would have to make the best of whatever came their way.

As they trundled along in Aireantha's wake, Rhys sensed the air in the hall charged like a lightning-filled summer sky. He had always been quite sensitive to the emotions of those around him, and he detected such a wide range here he was barely able to process them.

A good deal of what he noticed was directed at himself and his companion. Curiosity, surprise, and even hostility here and there. None of which was unexpected. What was surprising to him was the aura of charged expectation, anxiety, and—yes, even dread—emanating from the dragons around him. There was more to this ceremony than the installation of a new monarch. Everyone present was expecting something, for good or ill, to happen here.

Before he reached a decision on whether or not to broach his concerns with Aireantha, they broke through the final ranks of dragons to stand at the forefront of the throng.

"I will remain with you," she said, *"to tell you what is happening, and to ensure you do not get trampled."*

It took Rhys a few moments to catch the undercurrent to her statement, the thing she had left unsaid. Which was, he decided, "…to get you out if things go sour."

Well, there was nothing for it but to wait and watch and hope he hadn't led himself and Prince R'gm'l into something they might not make it out of.

"Where is Wyvrndell?" R'gm'l asked.

"He will come," Aireantha assured him. *"You must be patient."*

Rhys smiled to himself. He had refrained from telling the Dwarf that his friend was to become king, and managed to convey this information to Aireantha so she didn't slip and give away the secret.

A stentorian bugle rang out over the crowd, quieting the rumbling dragons to a muffled hush. From where he stood, Rhys gazed upon a raised dais which he presumed did duty as stage, altar, and perhaps even throne. No mere chair, no matter how grand or well crafted, would be suitable for a dragon.

From a passageway on the left side of the platform, six dragons filed onto the dais. Rhys thought he recognized Wyzandar, Wyvrndell's sire, whom he had met before when the dragons had brought Morgan and company out of Arvindir. Although, if he were being honest, this was simply a guess. He wasn't experienced enough to tell one dragon from another, save for Wyvrndell, whose azure blue scales were recognizable.

"They are the king's councilors," Aireantha said. *"They will perform the coronation ceremony."*

A ceremony, Rhys noted with bemusement, no human or Dwarf had ever before witnessed. Neither he nor R'gm'l conveyed any honor to the proceedings by their presence. The honor was bestowed upon them, to be allowed admittance to this most ancient of rituals.

The six upon the dais split into two groups of three, one upon each side of the platform. The dragon who signaled for quiet before, off the dais but right below it, let out another call which split the air. Every dragon in the hall fell silent.

The king's councilors each lifted their heads, and together uttered a soft keening sound. In response, every dragon in the great hall answered them, keening in unison.

It was, Rhys mused, much like a religious ceremony in a human church, with the call of the choir and the response of the congregation. He wondered if there were words, or if this was descant. Whatever it was, the sound was also strangely beautiful and moving. He found, to his surprise, that his heart soared at the sound, like a bird—or a dragon— taking flight.

There was movement upon the dais, and R'gm'l stiffened in shock beside him. For Wyvrndell now stood between the two groups of councilors, azure scales gleaming and his head held high. The keening increased in volume, and Wyvrndell joined the chorus.

As if at some unseen signal, every dragon in the great hall fell silent.

CHAPTER FIFTY-ONE
St. Basil's Cathedral, Caerfaen

Morgan reviewed his crew of marauders. It was not, to his eye, a particularly inspiring sight. An out-of-condition priest; an elderly wizard; and a semi-reformed criminal mastermind. Well, at least he'd have Aartis along to watch his back.

Sebastien's cadre of younger wizards waited in the wings, ready to escort them through the transfer portal. This, Morgan admitted to himself, was not something he was anticipating with any great sense of eagerness. Marissa had waxed quite lyrical on the subject after her experience with it, to the point Morgan found his hair standing on end. However, if she'd managed it, so could he.

He hoped…

Sebastien headed toward him, a questioning expression in his eyes.

Morgan nodded. "Let's get on," he said.

"Very well. This should be a good time to make the transfer. Late enough most should be abed, eh?"

"We can but hope," Morgan agreed.

"So. I'll go through first, with Captain Poldane." Sebastien said. "Vardrian will bring Bishop Randolph, and Daryl will take Mr. Taggart—I beg your pardon, Baron Taggart. Then you'll come through last, with Nardis. Each pair at three-minute intervals. No less, mind."

"It sounds easy enough when you say it," Morgan said. To the group he announced, "All right, you lot, we're going to start. Aartis, you'll go with Sebastien."

Aartis joined Sebastien at the portal while Morgan lined up the others in the order the wizard had outlined. Nardis gave him a rueful grin and said, "I keep finding myself on these little adventures. Not what I pictured the life of a journeyman wizard to be when I was in training."

"No, I'm sure it wasn't. But Nardis, you've acquitted yourself well so far. I'm glad to have you along."

Out of the corner of his eye, Morgan saw Sebastien make a gesture and utter words inaudible to his ears. He blinked, and in that instant the wizard and Aartis vanished.

Morgan blinked again. No, his eyes weren't deceiving him. The transfer portal was empty. "Amazing," he muttered. Then a terrible foreboding coursed through him. Wild-eyed, he turned to Nardis. "What if—" The words stuck in his throat.

"Don't worry, Your Grace," the young wizard replied. "I went through earlier to make certain the portal wasn't warded. It works fine. We'll have no problems."

Morgan blew out a long breath. "Sorry. I recalled what happened when Sebastien and Marissa used one of these things and ended up being trapped on the other end, here in the cathedral."

"Yes, Master Sebastien told me the tale. He said he'd never been more terrified of anything in his life. Which is why I tested it out earlier, to be on the safe side." His grin flashed, gleaming white in his dark face. "Otherwise it might start getting crowded when the next group came through…"

A low chuckle escaped Morgan. "Thanks. I needed that. This is a bit odd for me, you know…"

"It's nothing to be too concerned over. It'll feel like you've walked off a ledge—a kind of sudden dropping sensation, you know. It's why Master Sebastien recommended everyone have a light meal tonight. Otherwise, things tend to get messy."

Grimacing at this mental picture, Morgan glanced over to where Vardrian and Randolph were standing. In an instant, they disappeared from sight. Ian Taggart, eyes bright and curious, stared at the empty portal, his hands on his hips.

"Incredible," he breathed. "Who'd ha' thought it?" He turned to Morgan. "Sure beats going in through the upstairs window, eh?"

Morgan bestowed what he hoped was a quelling look. "Don't go getting any ideas."

Taggart grinned, waving this away. "Don't worry yourself, Commander. That was me old life. Wouldn't work anyways for my purposes. There'd never be a portal where you wanted one. Like in a bank's vault…"

"Except now," Morgan said, handing the old reprobate—well,

reformed reprobate, he allowed—over to Daryl's charge. "Now there's one exactly where we need it. Some good luck for a change."

Taggart gave an airy wave from the portal. "See ya in church," he said. He and Daryl vanished.

"Now we wait," said Nardis at his elbow.

"Is it necessary to wait three minutes?"

"No, it's not. A minute would more than suffice, if you want the truth. Master Sebastien prefers to proceed with due caution, though, so three minutes it is. If we came through early, he'd have my wand for disobeying orders. Well, you know how it is…"

"Indeed I do. Not following orders is an excellent way to earn an early grave." He glanced at the hourglass Nardis set each time a pair vanished from the portal. "Another minute?"

"Close enough." Nardis grinned. "I recommend you close your eyes when I give the word. It'll help. But don't worry, you'll be fine."

The last few grains of sand flowed through the hourglass. Morgan took a deep breath and steadied his nerves. This shouldn't present any terrors. After all, he'd flown a-dragonback. *Yes,* said a snarky voice in his head. *But the dragons were real. This is different. It's magic.*

Bah, Morgan replied to the voice, positioning himself where Nardis indicated.

"Ready?"

"Do it," he replied, and closed his eyes. Nardis spoke an arcane phrase and, as the young wizard predicted, Morgan experienced the sensation of being shoved off a cliff. Or perhaps more like the trap door of the hangman's platform opened up under his feet. Eyes squeezed shut, he managed to keep from stumbling through sheer willpower. "It lasts for a count of seven," Nardis had told him. Morgan counted.

As he reached seven, the world shifted again. There was light beyond his closed eyes, and the ground under his feet felt solid again. He opened his eyes.

"Well done," Nardis said with approval. "You didn't miss a beat. Not bad for your first time. Let's join the others."

"Thanks." Morgan surveyed the chamber. They were in a stone-walled room, fifteen feet on a side. Little grottos were carved into the rock of the walls, and statues of saints peered out from around candles which gave light to the room.

Sebastien herded Darryl and Vardrian toward the portal. Nardis joined them, but the Acting Chief Wizard said, "No, Nardis, I'd like you to stay. You're much better at defensive magic than I. Who knows what we might run into?"

"Of course, Master Sebastien," Nardis replied. The other two wizards vanished. "Duke Morgan, I presume you agree."

"I do," Morgan replied. "You'll be a welcome addition." He scanned the chamber again, saying, "All right, let's get ready to move out. Randolph, you know where we're to go?"

His oldest friend produced a map from a pocket in his robe. "It's been a long time since I've been here," he said. "I figured a bit of aid wouldn't go amiss."

"Well done," Morgan said, and meant it. He drew his sword.

As he did so, Sebastien uttered an oath and drew back. "What's wrong?" Morgan asked, scanning the room for signs of danger.

"Y-your Grace… Where did you get this sword?"

Puzzled, Morgan held up the blade in question. "This? Marissa gave it to me. It was a wedding gift. Why?"

The entire company was staring at Sebastien. The wizard was trembling like a leaf in a wind, and he took a hesitant step toward Morgan. His expression was a mixture of shock and amazement. "A wedding gift, eh? She simply handed you this blade?"

Morgan shook his head in bemusement. "Yes, she did. Wrapped up in an old drapery, but yes. Sebastien, for heaven's sake, what's gotten into you? It's a sword. A fine one, I'll grant you, but…"

"Have you—" Sebastien hesitated, but then marshaled his faculties. "Have you given it a name?"

"What? No, don't be daft. It's a weapon, a tool, nothing more. I don't hold with nonsense like naming a sword. It's—well, it's silly."

"Thank goodness," the wizard replied. "Your Grace, may I examine this fine sword of yours for a brief moment?"

Morgan shook his head. "Now? No, Sebastien, we're wasting valuable time here."

"It's important," the wizard replied. "Very. Please, humor me."

Morgan huffed out a breath. "Oh, fine, but hurry up. Here. Be careful, the edge is exceptionally sharp."

"I'd be exceptionally surprised if it wasn't," Sebastien said, his tone enigmatic. Morgan held out the sword, resting it on upturned palms. Instead of taking it from him, Sebastien laid his hands on the flat of the blade. At his touch, a soft greenish glow emanated from the sword.

In the brief glow, Morgan observed tiny runes etched into the steel. He blinked in surprise, but the light soon faded and the sword appeared like it had before. Had he imagined it? He shook his head, baffled. "Well?" he asked.

Sebastien didn't answer right away. His eyes were wide and unfocused, as if he was seeing something far away. He stepped back, muttering to himself, and scrubbed a hand across his face.

"What's wrong?" Morgan asked, his tone brusque. They needed to get moving. Instead, they stood around, wasting precious minutes, while Sebastien prattled on about swords.

"Duke Morgan," Sebastien said at last, "tell me something. Have you ever heard of a legendary blade called 'The Sword of Fate'?"

Morgan stared. Not at the wizard, but at the weapon in his hand. He swallowed. Hard. "Yes," he said at last. "I've heard the tales. But it's a myth, a legend. Nothing more." He glanced at the blade again. "Right?"

Sebastien's expression was wan. "Myths and legends," he said, "often have their basis in truth. But the stories told of them over the long years grow in the telling." He turned to Randolph. "You saw, did you not?"

Randolph didn't respond right away. His face was pale. Which of course might be the residual effects of the transfer portal. Finally he nodded and uttered a choked, "Yes, I saw." He cleared his throat and began again. "I saw, but I can't believe what I saw. How—"

"Me either," Morgan put in. "We're losing time here…"

Unfazed, Sebastien said, "The Sword of Fate, so it is said, only appears when the need is dire, and only in the hands of an honorable warrior."

Aartis and Taggart were both staring at the sword, wonder in their eyes. Aartis' voice was hoarse. He said, "I too saw the runes, though I'd no notion what they meant. But—"

Taggart said, "If this blade is indeed the Sword of Fate, I can think of no better man to wield it."

This is getting out of hand. "We need to find Marissa and the others," Morgan urged. "Whether this thing is or isn't some mythical blade, our mission hasn't changed. Because," he muttered, "next you'll be telling me the Hammer of Justice is real."

Randolph chuckled. "It is," he said. He produced a small hammer, the size of a magistrate's gavel, from his robe. "Dunno why I brought the silly thing along, but here it is. The Hammer of Justice, or so it's called. Handed down from bishop to bishop for ages. It's somewhat a badge of office, eh?"

Sebastien was staring again, more like a statue of a man than a living being. "Great stars," he breathed. "And you casually haul it out like it's the most natural thing in the world."

Randolph harumphed and waved the little hammer. "Doesn't mean anything," he said. "Badge of office, like I said. Someone ages ago, playing silly buggers, named it, and it stuck, that's all."

The wizard let out a long sigh. "Bishop Randolph, would you do me a favor?"

"I suppose."

"Touch the hammer to the sword."

Randolph's brows rose. "You're serious?"

"Never more so in my entire life," was Sebastien's reply.

"Oh, all right, if it'll make you happy. I say it's a lot of tripe, though…" He brought the hammer into contact with Morgan's sword.

A pulse of energy coursed through the sword. It glowed again, illuminating the chamber with a soft light, and the runes became visible once more. Morgan stared, trying to make sense of them. Of any of this.

The hammer, in turn, also gave off a luminous glow. Similar runes appeared on the handle, and the hammer swelled in Randolph's hand. Soon it doubled its original size. The bishop's face bore an expression of extreme bemusement. Sebastien's smile was a mixture of triumph and awe. "Would anyone care to argue the point?"

"It appears," Taggart said, awestruck, "you've managed to take all the tricks. Unless anyone else has another mythical geegaw they've neglected to mention?"

"There's nothing left but the Screwdriver of Time," Aartis mumbled.

"Don't be daft, there's no such thing," Sebastien said.

The soft slap of sandaled feet echoed in the corridor. Morgan glanced around, eyes wide. There was nowhere in the chamber to hide.

CHAPTER FIFTY-TWO
Ervantium

The keening of the dragons ended, and Wyvrndell straightened. Wyzandar and the three other senior members of the council, Byzanth, Pendrake and Nyrendor, approached him.

Storvold, the old seneschal, let forth another loud bugle, to call the dragons to attention. A hush fell over the hall, and Wyzandar spoke into the silence.

"Dragons of Ervantium, a new era begins today. Petrandius, our beloved king for ages untold, is gone. With no direct heir, he selected Wyvrndell to be his successor, in order he might guide us into a changing and tumultuous future."

He paused, surveying the crowd. "The Council has met. We are agreed in confirming Petrandius's choice. His goal was for the betterment of dragonkind. He believed Wyvrndell would be up to this challenge, and we of the Council concur in this assessment. Wyvrndell was instrumental in securing peaceful relations with both Dwarves and humans. He alone, for now, possesses magic, and vows to bestow this gift upon any dragons who wish it."

There was a rumble from the assembly. Wyvrndell maintained his silence. It was Wyzandar's place to speak in this moment.

"He is young, of a certainty. Yet in youth we may find new ways of looking at the world. I am his sire, and some may say I am biased. And yes, I am. I am proud of Wyvrndell and the things he has accomplished thus far. But I am also the senior member of the Council of Dragons, and I say to you I believe he will do even greater things for dragons during his reign. The entire Council has agreed Wyvrndell has the intelligence to lead us forward, and the desire for dragons to take their rightful place in the world."

Wyvrndell noted some fraught glances exchanged between several of the older dragons. His sire must also, for he said, "Our rightful place, not as oppressors or enemies of Dwarves and men, but their equals."

Wyzandar sent his gaze around the hall, daring any to challenge this statement. At last he said, "As is our custom, the Council asks you each to acknowledge Wyvrndell the rightful King of Ervantium, and pledge your loyalty to him."

Before any could respond, a furious roar erupted from the rear of the hall. In strode Jakarian, smoking and steaming in wroth. He was flanked by six brawny dragons.

"Enough," snarled Jakarian. "Equals of men and Dwarves? Never in my long years have I heard such utter madness. Dragons are oldest of all and are meant to have dominion over the other races of this world. And you would set this mere hatchling to lead us into ignominy and oblivion? Never, I say."

Even though Wyvrndell's attention was riveted on Jakarian, he noticed a few dragons nodded at his words. Wyzandar glared from the dais at the intruder. "Jakarian, you were banished, and are not welcome in Ervantium, by the king's decree," he said. "Petrandius's death does not change the fact. Go, while you are still able."

Jakarian sneered. "Banished? By a doddering old fool, who was himself taken in by this whelp. No, Wyzandar, here I am, and here I will stay. I have seen through your scheme. If Wyvrndell is named king, you will be the power behind him, guiding him to your own interests. Like you did with Petrandius."

"No!" Wyvrndell roared. "You lie, Jakarian, like you have always done."

"Do I?" Jakarian stared up at him, his expression a mixture of pity and contempt. "You are too young and ignorant to even realize how you have been used. I should have been Petrandius's successor, not you. I am here to claim my right. I challenge you, Wyvrndell, scion of Wyzandar, to combat."

"I accept, Jakarian," he replied, before anyone objected. He needed to get this done. To Aireantha, so she alone was able to hear, he said, "Get Rhys and R'gm'l away. I do not want them caught up in this battle. Jakarian would use them as pawns against me were they here."

To Jakarian, he said, "Since you are the challenger, you have the right to name the time and place of combat. Speak, if you are bold enough."

"Bold enough?" The old dragon snorted, smoke curling from his snout. "I shall not need boldness to defeat the likes of you, you sprat. Here and now," he spat, and his mouth foamed with fury and eagerness. His eyes glowed red with the madness which was on him.

"Let it be so," Wyvrndell said in reply. To the crowd, he directed. "You all should depart, so none are injured during the battle."

A few dragons trickled away. The rest remained. Wyvrndell had suspected they would. *No one likes to miss out on a good fight*, he said to himself. This would be one for the ages. Or so he hoped.

Out of the corner of his eye he observed Aireantha leading Rhys and R'gm'l out into the tunnel. At least they would be safe. He hoped she was explaining what was happening. He didn't have time to spare for them, for his attention was focused solely on Jakarian.

As the host of watching dragons edged back toward the walls of the great hall, Wyvrndell experienced the first small tremor of fear. What was he doing? He was no fighter. Yes, he had battled Erkarna, but that had been in the heat of the moment, when his friends' lives were at stake.

Is this any different? No. For now, it is not only my friends at risk, but everything I believe in.

With a silent nod, he stalked down from the dais to where his challenger waited. Jakarian wore a smug expression, already counting himself the victor. *Do not underestimate him He did not get here by being soft. He will kill you if he can.*

His gut rumbled in protest. *No. Do not betray me.* He reached the floor, and the wall of silent dragons parted to allow him to stride to the center of the hall, facing Jakarian. The crowd closed behind him again, enclosing challenger and challenged in a wide circle.

"Are you certain you wish to follow this course?" he asked Jakarian. "If you leave, no harm will befall you. This I promise."

"Insolent whelp," snarled his challenger. "When this is over, you will be dead, and I will claim the kingship, which should have been mine from the start."

Another hiccough formed in Wyvrndell's innards. He forced it back. He couldn't allow himself to show any weakness or fear. Not to Jakarian, and certainly not to the dragons watching them, waiting to see who would be their new king.

"Perhaps this is why Petrandius did not choose you," he said. "You desired the kingship too much. Like Erkarna, whom I also defeated, your desire is to subjugate others, instead of working alongside them."

"Be quiet," roared Jakarian. "I am the rightful king. Now, we fight to prove it. Yet, since you are the challenged, you have the honor of the first strike."

Wyvrndell gave him a toothy smile. "Jakarian, in deference to your rank, and your age," he said, "I waive the honor. You may have first strike."

Jakarian's eyes went red with fury at these words. "You patronize me?" he growled. "You will pay for your insolence." And with this, he charged, flame pouring from his jaws.

Wyvrndell dodged out of his way with ease, and Jakarian's momentum carried him almost into the crowd of watchers. "It that the best you can offer, old one?" he taunted. He needed to keep his opponent angry and off balance. "Try again."

Jakarian whirled, a harsh cry almost like a scream escaping him. Wyvrndell prepared himself for another blind, rage-filled charge. But Jakarian managed to bring his anger under control. This time, instead of rushing at Wyvrndell, he stalked toward him, jaws opening in silent menace.

For the first time, Wyvrndell experienced true terror. He found himself frozen in place, a prisoner of his own anxieties. while Jakarian prowled the floor watching for his chance. This was about more than Jakarian wishing to be king. The old dragon wanted to obliterate him, the symbol of everything he believed wrong with dragonkind. This would be a battle to the death. The death not only of one of the combatants, but also of their ideals.

With this knowledge, another hiccough rose within him. This time he was unable to control it, and it erupted into the air in an acrid blue cloud.

Distracted by this, he almost didn't notice Jakarian rushing him. Shaking himself out of his stupor, he managed to dodge. This time Jakarian's flame caught his left hindquarter. Pain shot through him, searing white hot, like nothing he'd ever felt before. His scales were on fire, feeling like they might melt right off, and he choked off a tortured scream. He mustn't allow himself to show weakness, no matter how he might hurt. There would be time for screams later. If he prevailed. If not…

Jakarian whirled again, pouring more flame toward him. Instead of dodging this time, Wyvrndell called upon the magic within him. He summoned up a shield against the flames of his enemy. A murmur of astonishment rippled through the crowd at this. It was one thing to be told a dragon had obtained magic; another thing to observe it in action.

Jakarian's fire broke against the shield, useless. While his challenger stared in shock and anger, Wyvrndell dropped the shield and charged him. Ignoring his injured leg, he barreled into the older dragon, ripping at his foreleg with teeth and talons. He danced away, wary, for he knew Jakarian would try to disembowel him if he remained close.

Wyvrndell limped. His leg hurt—all right, it was pure agony—but he couldn't allow it to slow him. He needed to lull his opponent into a sense of overconfidence. The older dragon charged again. Wyvrndell allowed himself to be bowled over, but when Jakarian's momentum carried him over Wyvrndell, he raked the older dragon's underbelly with his talons. He managed to get in under his challenger's scales, ripping flesh and sinew, and Jakarian screamed in pain and rage. Blood dripped from the gashes Wyvrndell scored in his hide. Jakarian righted himself, but he was moving slower. Out of caution, Wyvrndell wondered, or because he was injured? He sent a gout of flame toward Jakarian. The older dragon skipped away. Ah, so he was playing up his injury, similar to what Wyvrndell himself had done. He sent more flame at the old councilor, in an effort to keep him off balance while he decided on his next move.

Jakarian wasn't having it. Heedless of Wyvrndell's flames, he charged, biting and ripping as he crashed into him. Wyvrndell managed to fight him off and get clear, but not before his right haunch was scored deeply.

They circled around the chamber, each watching for an opening, a weakness they could exploit. A dawning of alarm, like a chill mixed with a burning hiccough in his gut, struck Wyvrndell. Jakarian was coming again, death in his eyes, and he could envision no means of stopping him.

Unless, he acknowledged, he used the one weapon available to him: his magic.

But how? He had used the shielding spell before, but it wouldn't last long before he was drained, and Jakarian would move in for the kill. What could he do?

Jakarian sent more flame at him, closing in to strike with teeth and talons. Wyvrndell scrambled backward, mind churning, searching his memory in a desperate effort to come up with some spell which might help him. Jakarian laughed, and the sound was terrible, cold as death, merciless as an avalanche. Fear wormed its way into the depths of Wyvrndell's heart and mind

I'm going to lose. His magic, his friends, his heart Petrandius had spoken of? All for naught. He would die, and all would be lost. Wyvrndell opened his jaws, determined to make one final effort, to fight fire with fire. If he was going to lose, he would at least go down fighting to the end.

Instead of the expected flame, what emerged was another acrid hiccough. Jakarian laughed again, edging closer. To Wyvrndell's astonishment, the hiccough remained visible this time, shimmering in the air between them. It hung there, yellow and bilious, writhing with—could it be—magic?

Jakarian did not notice. He gathered himself for another rushing charge, in order to overwhelm his flagging opponent. With a tremendous roar, he lunged at Wyvrndell.

Jakarian stepped into the spell-laden hiccough, borne of Thundermist magic. It bloomed out around him, encircling him like a sphere. The old dragon's eyes went wide in shock when he comprehended what was happening. He struggled to escape the spell—Wyvrndell didn't know what it actually was—as it worked upon him.

The horrible yellow sphere contracted around the dragon. Jakarian struggled harder to break free from its confines. It grew smaller and smaller, taking the dragon with it. This spell, Wyvrndell realized, was similar to the one Lady Marissa used to destroy the demon not long before. Jakarian roared, sending flame against the walls which trapped him. This served him ill, for the fire filled his prison and seared himself even as it continued to shrink.

There was fear in the old dragon's eyes at last. "No!" cried Jakarian, but the spell relentlessly compressed in upon itself, taking him with it. Smaller and smaller it became, until soon the little bubble was the size of a pebble. With a soft "pop," it winked out of sight. Jakarian was gone.

Wyvrndell sagged to the floor. After a few moments of stunned silence, the crowd of watching dragons roared his name.

CHAPTER FIFTY-THREE
St. Benedict's Cathedral, Noordstrom

"It ain't guards," Randolph whispered. "At least, I don't think it is. This chap's alone and wearing sandals. I'd warrant it's the night porter, come to tend to the candles."

"You don't look much like a candle," Morgan replied. "Nor do any of us. No matter who he is, he's bound to raise an alarm. There's no place in here to hide one man, much less six of us, some of the extra-large variety."

"Hmph. I'm well rounded is all."

"Whatever you say. Randolph, I don't want to hurt an innocent porter... Ah, got it." Moving with speed and silence, Morgan herded the others to flatten themselves against the wall by the entrance. He positioned Randolph closest to the doorway. "When he comes in," he whispered in the priest's ear, "thump him—gently, mind you—on the noggin with your Hammer of Justice."

"Right." Randolph readied his weapon. The soft swish-slap of sandals sounded right outside the chamber, and the light of a lamp preceded the figure of an elderly monk into the room. When he stepped through the door, Randolph brought the hammer down on the top of the monk's head with a quiet "Thunk."

Morgan caught the swaying, unconscious man before he slumped to the floor, managing to keep one hand on the lamp so it didn't fall and raise a ruckus or start a fire, or both.

Randolph's gaze went from the man in Morgan's arms to the hammer in his hand. His eyes were wide, but his expression was triumphant. "I did it," he said in tones of amazement.

"Yes, well done," Morgan replied. "Here, someone help me lay him down. I don't want to drop this poor old duffer."

Taggart was at this side in an instant, and together they stretched the unconscious monk out on the floor.

"I did it," Randolph repeated.

"Now don't go getting bloodthirsty on me," Morgan ordered. "I don't want to hear you've been taken in charge by the Watch for bopping random strangers over the head. Control those baser instincts if you please."

"It was fun," Randolph murmured.

"No." Even in a whisper, Morgan put a touch of steel into his voice. "No more bopping. Put the hammer away."

"Oh, all right." But there was a curious light in his friend's eyes, one which Morgan recognized, and didn't care for.

"What happens when he wakes up?" Aartis asked.

"Ah, leave it to me," Randolph replied.

"Randolph…" Morgan narrowed his eyes.

"No hammer, I promise." Randolph strode about the chamber, scanning around. "There should be a bottle of sacramental wine… ah, here it is. We'll douse the good brother with this and leave the bottle in his hand. He'll never speak of this night, and if anyone finds him, they'll draw their own conclusions."

"A bit hard on this poor chap, ain't it?" Sebastien said.

"Ah, well, no one said the religious life was an easy one, did they?" Randolph closed the monk's fingers around the neck of the bottle. "Aren't we ready to go? Why are you lot standing there?"

"Because you're the one with the map," Morgan said through clenched teeth.

"Oh. Well, yes, I suppose." Randolph retrieved the map and consulted it. "We go left down this corridor. We're after a stairway. The dungeons are two levels below this one. I'm presuming you figure to find them there?"

"I'd imagine so," Morgan said. "I don't think your brethren bishops will have installed them in the fancy guest accommodations. I'll go first. Aartis, you're rear guard. The rest of you keep between us. Nardis, you might want to have a couple of stray lightning bolts to hand, just in case."

"Right." The young wizard grinned. Morgan led them into the corridor, where candles burned in sconces set along the walls on both sides. Their flickering light sent the men's shadows dancing in a wild frenzy.

"Should be nearing the stairway," Randolph muttered. "On the left."

An opening appeared in the wall, with stone steps leading into a stygian darkness. Morgan waited for the others to join him before starting the descent.

"Sebastien, would you mind providing a light?" Morgan asked. "I'd like to keep Nardis in reserve for—other things we might have to deal with."

The old wizard gave a quick nod, sending the feather in his battered hat fluttering. "*Lumios accacido,*" he said.

Morgan recognized the same phrase Marissa used to conjure her little balls of light. He smiled to himself at this, but his smile turned into a pensive frown. She'd also used the same spell to create a flaming sword, on more than one occasion. Why hadn't she done so when they'd been taken prisoner? Or here, to fight her way out?

Because she didn't have the ability to do so, came the unwelcome thought. *Because she—and likely the others—were dosed with witchbane.* He stifled a growl.

Sebastien sent the little luminescent sphere soaring above Morgan's head. "It will follow you," the wizard said. "Better this way than me holding it."

"My own personal halo," Morgan quipped.

"Perhaps not so far off," the wizard replied. "You do bear the Sword of Fate."

"Mmm." Swords, fateful or otherwise, were not a subject he wished to explore any further. No, his only concern was to find Marissa and the others and get them out of here. He started down the stairway, the ball of light keeping pace a few inches above his head.

They made their way to the first landing. The silence, though welcome to Morgan, was oppressive. He felt like the stones of the cathedral walls themselves exerted some type of strange pressure against the intruders.

Nardis must have also sensed it. At the next landing, he edged closer to Morgan and said in a quiet voice, "There are protective enchantments wrought into these walls. They're designed to keep out those who don't belong. I'm doing my best to counter them, but they're getting stronger the farther we venture."

"I'm glad to know I wasn't imagining things. Can Sebastien help you?"

"A bit, perhaps, but he's concentrating on keeping the light going. It appears simple, but to keep it longer than a couple of minutes can be tiring and requires a great deal of concentration."

"All right. Well, do what you can. I hope we don't have too much farther to go."

Randolph, who'd been listening with interest, said, "We have to descend another whole level to reach the dungeons."

"Oh, good." Morgan rolled his eyes. "At least we should be close to the bottom of the first level. These stairs can't go on forever."

After they'd descended one more flight, he found his prediction was correct. The stairs ended. But they ended at a sturdy oak door with a strong lock which barred their way.

CHAPTER FIFTY-FOUR
Ervantium

Wyvrndell hiccoughed again, releasing another cloud of noxious fumes. This one, he was happy to note, was not imbued with magic. At least, he hoped not. The dragons nearest him edged away, on the theory of better safe than sorry. None wanted to suffer Jakarian's fate. The cloud rose toward the ceiling of the hall, fading from sight.

The vanquished councilor's supporters also faded away like Wyvrndell's hiccough. The fact they'd slipped out unchallenged was a problem, but he decided this was a problem for another day. Today, Wyvrndell grumbled, presented problems enough of its own.

Counter to every fiber of his being, which urged him to remain slumped on the stone floor, he straightened himself, gazed around the cavern at the wrangle of dragons watching him, and threw his head back to give forth a resounding roar. This one was unpunctuated by any embarrassing hiccoughs.

When every eye was directed his way, Wyvrndell said, "Now that this minor interruption has been settled, let us proceed with the ceremony, shall we?" He struggled to rise, managing the endeavor with no major mishaps.

Wyzandar nodded his approval, and began the task of shepherding the other councilors into some semblance of order, back on the dais. Wyvrndell made his way to join them. Though each step was a chore, he did his best not to let the pain show in his demeanor. For now, at least, he needed to project strength. Later, he could collapse into a quivering heap.

When the dragons were again silent, Wyzandar spoke.

"Some of you may say Wyvrndell is too young, too inexperienced, too untested, to be the next king of dragonkind. To those, I say two things. First, Petrandius himself, the wisest dragon who ever flew, chose him out of all the possible candidates. Second, you have witnessed Wyvrndell, who never aspired to the kingship, fight for his right to it, and vanquish his challenger.

"So, I ask you to, in unity, declare Wyvrndell your king, to rule with honor and dignity and justice, from this day hence."

A hush, more solid even than the mountain itself, fell over the crowd. From the rear of the hall came a shout: "Hail, King Wyvrndell." An echoing call sounded, then another, and soon the hall rang with their acclamation, until the fortress shook with them.

Wyzandar gave him a slight nod. Wyvrndell stepped forward to the edge of the dais. He bowed his head for a moment, allowing the weight of their acknowledgement to wash over him.

When the tumult subsided, he spoke. "Dragons of Ervantium, I thank you. I am humbled, and honored, and in truth nervous. For following King Petrandius is a daunting challenge. It is one I never sought, nor even dreamed of. Yet this I pledge to you: ever will I do my best to lead you justly, with honor, and with hope, taking our place in this new world we find ourselves inhabiting."

He paused, sending his gaze around the hall once more. "And now, I fear, I must get to work immediately. I know it is traditional to celebrate such an event with a great feast. It has been prepared and stands ready for you. Unfortunately, neither I nor my councilors will be able to attend. Matters of great import lie before me, which require my urgent attention."

Several of the councilors were taken aback at his words. Wyvrndell was certain they were anticipating the coming feast as much as the rest of the assembled dragons. He went on. "Thank you, once again, for the honor you have bestowed upon me. Wyzandar, if you and the other councilors would join me in my chambers?"

He turned and strode off the dais, calling to Aireantha, "Please bring King Rhys and Prince R'gm'l and join us."

"By your order, Your Majesty," she replied.

"Airie," he said in warning tones. But in spite of himself he chuckled. "If nothing else, you will keep me from getting a swelled head, won't you?"

"I shall do my best. If you don't mind, though, I would like an explanation of something."

"Oh? What would you know?"

"I thought dragons were impervious to magic. Did we not

discuss this very fact a few days ago?"

"We did. It seems the rule does not apply to magic from another dragon. This was fortunate for me, for I don't know if I could have overcome Jakarian otherwise. No, I will be honest, Airie. I would not have prevailed. Without magic, he would have defeated me."

"Did you intend to do what you did—cast that spell against him?"

Wyvrndell hesitated. Then, deciding he needed to give her his complete honesty, he said, "No. It was a complete and utter accident. In the heat of battle, and in my fear I might lose, my hiccoughs got the better of me."

"And the better, it would seem, of Jakarian," she replied. "So what you have always considered your liability was what saved you in the end."

"Airie, may we continue this discussion later?"

"By your command, my king," she said, and he could picture her smug expression. *Great stars and flames. And I asked her to be my queen. What have I let myself in for?* He would, he decided, have to have a long conversation with Sir Morgan about the vagaries of females.

But at the moment, he had more urgent things to deal with. He led the way down the corridor toward the king's chamber, calling to Donathyr. "Hold yourself and the other members of the king's guard ready. I expect to have a mission for you soon."

"At once, Your Majesty. And allow me to offer my congratulations. We are yours to command."

"Thank you. Inquire of Sir Byron their situation in Noordstrom and report it to me once you know."

"Yes, Sire."

Wyvrndell entered the chambers which now belonged to him. The scent of Petrandius lingered, a reminder of the legacy he was expected to live up to. Wyzandar ushered in the other councilors, and Wyvrndell regarded them each in turn. How would they react to what he planned to say? Well, he was about to find out.

"I apologize for the abruptness of my summons. I am certain you were each eager to partake in the feasting. However, what I have to say will not take long. Ah, one moment, please, Donathyr has news for me."

A couple of the councilors appeared relieved Wyvrndell would not keep them long away from the feast. Wyvrndell ignored them, focusing on Donathyr, who said, "Sir Byron reports their enemies have made a forced march, bypassing the towns and villages he had expected them to capture. Instead, they will soon approach the city of Noordstrom."

"Thank you," Wyvrndell said.

Aireantha entered the chamber. With her were Rhys and R'gm'l. Rhys bowed, saying, "Congratulations upon your victory in combat, and your ascension to the throne, King Wyvrndell. I look forward to a long and fruitful relationship between Kilbourne and Ervantium."

R'gm'l bowed next, saying, "On behalf of my father, King K'var'k, I also offer congratulations. Long may peace reign between dragon and Dwarf."

Wyvrndell bowed his head in acknowledgement. *"Thank you, my friends,"* he said. *"I too anticipate a productive relationship with both Kilbourne and R'mk'vl."*

Turning his attention back to the dragons arrayed before him, he said, "In order to fulfill the intent of our treaty with Kilbourne, I and the king's guard will fly to the human city of Noordstrom, to lend aid to the men of Kilbourne, who will soon be beset there by their enemies from the North."

"Nonsense," snapped Molgyr. "It is not our—" Under the force of Wyvrndell's gaze, he trailed off and lowered his eyes.

"The men of Kilbourne are outnumbered if it comes to a conflict," Wyvrndell went on, deigning to ignore the breach of decorum. "Our assistance will prove vital to their cause."

"I will also go," Wyzandar said.

"And I," chorused Aireantha.

Wyvrndell glanced around the chamber. "Well. This begins to take on the quality of a major expedition. Do any of you others wish to join us?"

None of the councilors spoke. They exchanged wary glances. His actions were not what they expected of their king. They would have a lot to learn. This almost elicited a laugh from him, which would have definitely worried them.

Before Wyvrndell continued, Rhys stepped forward. "If I understand you, your mission is in aid of my men. If it is not impertinent of me to ask, I would like to come with you."

Wyvrndell considered the request for a moment. *"We fly into battle,"* he said. *"Yet I know from my conversations with Morgan McRobbie you are no stranger to conflict. You are welcome to join us."*

Now R'gm'l stood, straight and proud, next to Rhys. "I, too, wish to join you. I believe my father would call this a 'learning experience'."

Wyvrndell exchanged a glance with Rhys, who shrugged. "Better bring him along," Rhys said. "I don't fancy leaving him here alone."

"Very well," Wyvrndell replied. Then he said to the chief of his guards, "Donathyr, tell Sir Byron seven dragons are on the way."

"Eight."

Wyvrndell started in surprise. Pendrake, one of the councilors, stepped forward. "I will accompany you, Wyvrndell."

"Are you sure you wish to? We fly into a conflict."

"Wish to? No, not at all" Pendrake replied. "But I will go anyway. The times, as you say, are changing around us. I want to see how you intend to deal with them."

Wyvrndell nodded acknowledgement. "I understand, Lord Pendrake, and will be glad to have you join our company. Donathyr?"

"I have relayed your message, Your Majesty," the guard said. "Sir Byron expressed his gratitude for your support. He says the Rhuddlanis are quite close to the city and there is a good chance their enemies will overrun them."

"Let us depart. Fortunately, it is not a long distance from here, perhaps only an hour." With this, he led his little band out to the outer ledge. Along the way he said to Rhys, *"It might be best if you are seated upon Wyzandar. I will bear R'gm'l, for he has flown with me many times, and is used to me. He will be safer with me."*

"Has he indeed?" Rhys shot a speculative glance at the Dwarf prince, who maintained an air of innocence. "Very well, if Wyzandar will consent to bear me, I will be honored to fly with him."

They reached the ledge, where Donathyr and the others of the guard waited. Rhys and R'gm'l mounted.

"Lead on, Donathyr," Wyvrndell commanded.

The dragons took wing.

CHAPTER FIFTY-FIVE

St. Benedict's Cathedral, Noordstrom

Morgan glared at the door. It remained solid and implacable in its refusal to open. He stepped back. "Taggart, this looks like your meat."

Taggart gave him a raffish grin and yanked off his pack. Opening it, he extracted a rolled chamois pouch. "Hold this, would you?" he said to Aartis. "I need to see if I still possess a couple of useful talents."

Aartis glanced at Morgan, who gave him a terse nod. Aartis held the pouch spread out across his palms, and Taggart extracted a couple of long, slim pieces of metal. "Flexible steel," he said in an offhand manner, and went to work.

It took him several minutes, three different tools, and a bit of judicious cursing—both of himself and the lock—but at last he stepped back with a flourish. "You may proceed at your leisure," he announced. "And I'll be the first to admit, I should have done the job in less than half the time. Disgraceful, to be this out of practice. I'm going to have to lock meself out of the house, I am, and burgle my way in again, just to keep my hand in. See what bein' an honest man does to a fellow?"

Morgan ignored this commentary and opened the door a crack to peer through. There was nothing to see. The next corridor, similar to the one they'd left above, was dark and empty.

Randolph consulted his map. "We need to go left, following this passage. Halfway, we should find the next set of stairs, on the right side of the corridor."

Morgan pushed open the door and led his band of marauders through and onward. His instincts were screaming to get on with the job and find Marissa and the others. He scanned the passage in both directions, but tomblike silence and darkness were all that greeted him. Those, and the oppressive sense of unease which emanated from the spell-wrought walls.

Nardis, in the dim light of Sebastien's sphere, appeared strained. He continued to mutter counterspells to help allow them to pass. "What happens if you stop?" Morgan asked him.

"I imagine we all stop," came the reply through clenched teeth. "These spells are intended to make intruders feel they can't go on any further. We use something similar in the College of Wizards. Which is good, because at least I have an idea of how to counter them."

"Remind me not to visit the College of Wizards," Morgan muttered, and walked quicker. Ahead, he was able to make out the opening in the wall which would, if Randolph's map was accurate, lead them to the dungeon level.

"What I want to know," rumbled Randolph, "is who ordered these enchantments made, and why? No offense to you wizard chaps, but this type of thing doesn't belong in a holy place. And St. Benedict's is an extremely holy site."

"I don't know why," Sebastien said, following Morgan down the stairs. "But the priests here must have requested these enchantments from a wizard, or wizards. And paid a handsome price for the job too."

They reached the first landing. "From here on out," Morgan instructed, "no more talking unless necessary, and then only whispers. We've been damned lucky so far, but we're getting close to the dungeons, and there's bound to be guards posted. We can't afford to alert them. Right?"

The others nodded agreement. Taggart raised a finger. "Yes?" Morgan said.

"As the lone professional here, so to speak, aye, we've been chattering away like a pack of schoolboys on holiday, and you're right to shut us up. But don't you think yon floating light will be a tip off to any guards who might see it?"

"Fair point," Morgan said. "Sebastien, any way to dim it, to a faint glow?"

The wizard waved a hand at the sphere of light, which diminished to mere pinpoint dimensions. "Better?" he inquired, his smile this side of smug.

"Perfect. All right, let's go."

They moved out again, navigating the stairs in silence. Morgan earlier had made a point of cautioning each of the team to place their feet carefully, so their boot heels didn't strike on the stones and alert any guards.

Down, down they went, struggling against the enchantment the entire way. To Morgan it felt like they were slogging through treacle. When they reached the bottom, another stout door barred the way.

Taggart stepped forward, his tools in hand. Prior to using them, he placed an ear against the door and remained stock still, straining to listen.

At last he glanced up at Morgan and held up three fingers. Three guards. Morgan nodded. He trusted Taggart's senses. He recalled Toniq, who had accompanied Marissa and him to Parthane. The young thief had possessed similar instincts.

Morgan motioned Aartis forward. "Three guards," he whispered into his ear. "Once Taggart unlocks the door, we go in fast and hit them hard." Aartis nodded.

Nardis made his way to Morgan's side. "Remember how the duchess took out those men in Arvindir? I could do the same if you'd prefer. No blood shed that way."

"Do it." Morgan stepped aside so the wizard could stand by Taggart at the door. At Morgan's gesture, Taggart slipped the lock.

"And go," Morgan breathed. Taggart thrust open the door. Nardis stepped through, uttering the words of his spell. He spread his hands, and a blue light blossomed out into the room beyond, encompassing the three guards who'd begun to scramble to their feet.

The guards sank to the floor, stunned, their swords falling from senseless hands. Morgan and the others entered the chamber to join Taggart and Nardis.

"Handy," observed Aartis. "That trick would be quite useful in the Legion."

"We'll bear it in mind," Morgan replied, but his mind was elsewhere. A ring of keys hung on the wall, and he grabbed it. To Aartis he said, "You, Randolph, and Nardis stay here in case any more guards show up. Taggart and Sebastien, with me."

Catching up a lamp from the table where the guards appeared to have been having their early morning brew up, he headed down the single corridor.

"Marissa," he called. There was no answer. The left side of the passage was solid stone. Cell doors were set into the right side, spaced at short intervals. He opened each door in turn.

Every cell was empty. Morgan's heart sank to his boots. They were too late.

CHAPTER FIFTY-SIX

St. Benedict's Cathedral, Noordstrom

Cursing to himself, Morgan led the way back out of the dungeons. Passing by the unconscious guards, Morgan tossed the ring of keys on the table. Aartis grabbed them. "Hang on, I've got an idea," he said.

Morgan raised a brow. Aartis grinned. "Help me lug them into a cell. If we do, there will be less of them to come after us once they wake up."

"We don't have—oh, all right." Morgan hated to waste even another moment, but Aartis was right. Any guards they got out of the way were the fewer they'd have to deal with later. He grabbed one of the guards, the burliest of the bunch, by the legs and dragged him into one of the cells. He dumped the man on the floor, and Aartis came with the second. Sebastien and Nardis brought the third one, with Taggart and Randolph following behind. Aartis slammed the cell door and locked it.

"Leave the key in the lock," Taggart said.

Randolph protested. "They'll let themselves right out again. A lot of manual labor for nothing."

"Trust me, they won't," Taggart said. Aartis looked a question at Morgan, who nodded once. He left the key in the lock. Taggart took a firm hold on the bars of the cell, raised one booted foot, and struck the key with his heel. The stem of the key snapped off, leaving the rest stuck in the lock.

"Now they'll stay put, even once someone finds them," Taggart said with a grin. "They'll have to saw the bars off to get 'em out."

Morgan laughed in spite of himself. "Incorrigible," he said.

"Now, let's go. We've wasted too much time. We've got to find those women before these madmen decide to burn them."

They headed back up the stairs again. Morgan, Aartis, and Nardis soon outdistanced the others. "Go on," Taggart said when Morgan slowed his pace. "We'll catch you up."

The stragglers were standing on a landing, next to a doorway. The door opened and a man in clerical robes, with a deep hood concealing his features, stepped out. There was nowhere to hide. Morgan was too far away to be of any assistance. It would be up to them to deal with this.

The robed figure gasped and let out a yelp when he noticed the intruders. Randolph pulled out his hammer, but before he struck the man said in an incredulous tone, "Bishop Randolph?"

Randolph halted his blow. "Who's there?" he demanded.

"Brother Francis. Lord Holman sent me here, to keep an eye on the rebel bishops. He told me he informed you of this when your man was forced to leave."

"Yes, he did," Randolph said. "By the saints, man, what are you doing here at this hour?" He turned to where Morgan was standing on the next landing. "Brother Francis is the chap who's been keeping an eye on this lot for Barzak."

"I was on my way to the dungeon, to see if there was anything I might be able to do, to help Lady Marissa and the others. Bishop Llachnahn is becoming unhinged. I'm afraid of what he might do."

Morgan trotted back down the stairs to join them. "They're not in the dungeon. We just came from there. Where would he have taken them?"

Brother Francis sucked in a breath. "The courtyard," he said, his voice husky with worry. "They've had the monks collecting firewood the entire day. But I didn't expect it would be so soon. I didn't figure they'd act until tomorrow at least."

Morgan caught him by the sleeve. "I need you to lead us there. Now."

"Follow me." Brother Francis opened the door he'd come out of, leading them into a wide passageway. He hurried along it, with Morgan, Aartis and Nardis right behind. The others followed in their wake. Sebastien and Taggart kept up a brisk pace, but Randolph puffed along in the distance.

"G'wan," he said between breaths. "Don't wait for me. You don't need me for this bit anyhow. I'd be useless, and slow you."

He was right, though Morgan hated the idea of leaving his friend alone here. "Taggart, stay with him, will you?" he said. The older man sent him a look of comprehension and slowed his pace.

"Quickest way to this courtyard," Morgan instructed.

"Take this hallway to the end, and out the last door on the right."

"Let's go," Morgan said to his team, and took off at a run. The others followed in his wake.

Wild shadows gyrated in the flickering torchlight illuminating the courtyard. A knot of men waited near the pyre which stood ready in the center. They stared in intent anticipation while servants brought more logs and kindling to toss onto the already enormous pile.

A pole jutted up from the base of the pyre, its lower section hidden among the wood made ready to set ablaze. It reached toward the star-strung night sky, angry and forbidding. Rings of iron, intended for the witches to be bound to, were set into the rough surface. Staring at the monstrosity, Morgan let out a low, feral growl. At least none of the women were chained to it. Not yet. Not ever, if he had his way.

Scanning the courtyard from their place of concealment, he spotted Marissa and the others. They stood huddled together, blindfolds covering their eyes. Their hands and feet were bound by lengths of heavy chain. He growled again, deeper and more visceral this time, like a wolf which has spotted its prey.

His body tensed in preparation for action. He would scour the earth of those who harmed the innocent to satisfy their own lust for power and control. It was his destiny. His fate.

A hand fell on his shoulder. It took all Morgan's self-control to wrench himself back to reality, to not lash out at the interruption of his righteous fury. "Not yet," Aartis whispered.

Morgan blinked, shaking his head. He felt like he'd woken from a particularly violent dream. He took several long, slow breaths, releasing the tension in his muscles. He gave Aartis a brief nod of thanks. He was glad to have someone along who would not only have his back, but also keep him from making a hash of things by charging in with reckless abandon.

Even though Morgan begrudged the delay, Aartis was right. Brother Francis was leading Sebastien and Nardis to a vantage point on the other side of the courtyard. Until the wizards signaled they were in position, he needed to wait to make his move. But knowing didn't make it any easier to wait.

Two sets of footsteps—one barely audible, the other the slow "clomp" of a weary man—sounded in the passageway behind him. Taggart and Randolph. Morgan set a finger to his lips. He wasn't concerned about Taggart, but Randolph had neither training or inclination to the arts of stealth.

Puffing and wheezing like a badly mended bellows, his oldest friend nodded in acknowledgement of the warning. Morgan stepped aside so the newly arrived pair were able to scan the situation in the courtyard.

"They're still preparing the pyre," he whispered. "Marissa and the others are across the yard, up against the stone wall."

"Well, what are you waiting for?" demanded Randolph, though he did manage to modulate his voice to something less than avalanche volumes. "An invitation?"

"In a manner of speaking." Morgan glanced up to where Sebastien was to take up his stand. No sign of him yet. He scanned further along, to where Nardis should appear, and... Ah, good, there he was. The younger wizard gave a brief wave. A few moments later, Sebastien appeared in the other window, also signaling his readiness.

"Ah, our invitation—" He broke off, for Wyvrndell's voice sounded in his head. Morgan held up a hand to forestall the others from making their move.

"Morgan McRobbie," said the dragon. *"Can you hear me?"*

"Yes, Wyvrndell, I can. I'm a bit busy now."

"So am I. But I wished to inform you I and a small force of dragons are approaching your city of Noordstrom, to lend aid to Sir Byron and his men."

"What?"

"The Rhuddlani troops have marched straight through and are nearing the city. Your reinforcing men have not yet arrived, due to a mishap to their captain. Sir Byron fears the Rhuddlanis will overrun them and take the city. We have come to discourage them."

"Marvelous. Wyvrndell, thank you for your aid. It so happens, I also am in Noordstrom with a small force of my own. We're here to rescue Marissa from the men who abducted her and her friends."

The dragon was silent. After a long pause, he said, *"This does not feel like a coincidence, does it?"*

"No," Morgan replied, his smile tight. "It doesn't. Wyvrndell, are you able to speak with Marissa?"

"No. I have tried. Something is blocking my ability to communicate with her."

"Damn. I was hoping you might let her know we're here."

"I am sorry. I would imagine she will realize it soon. There is one other thing I should mention."

"Oh? What's that?"

"Both King Rhys and R'gm'l are with us."

"Oh. I see." Not by a long shot he didn't, but it didn't matter. In this case, Rhys's presence might prove beneficial. He said, "Once you've dealt with the Rhuddlanis—for which I am more grateful than you can imagine—can you bring Rhys here? I'm at the cathedral."

"Of course. It should not be long."

"Wait for my signal before you land. I have a few things to tend to here first."

"Very well. Good hunting, Morgan McRobbie." The dragon's voice was gone.

"What the devil were you doing?" Aartis demanded.

"Dragons," he replied. "I'll explain later." He shook his head, bringing his attention back to the urgency of the task at hand. "Everyone ready?"

Three nods. Morgan peered out the window again. Sebastien and Nardis were both staring toward him, waiting for his sign to proceed. He drew his sword. It hummed in his hand, eager to be put to use. He raised his left hand, all five fingers extended, and closed it into a fist, giving the signal to the two wizards.

~*~

Noordstrom Plain

Wyvrndell scanned the countryside below. Ahead, he spied the human city of Noordstrom. Which, it appeared, was becoming an unexpected point of convergence.

Lady Marissa was there somewhere, brought by the men who abducted her and her friends. Sir Morgan was also there, dead set on rescuing her. The Rhuddlanis were on their way there. And he would, if everything went to plan, deliver King Rhys and Prince R'gm'l there too.

He spied what he assumed must be the cathedral Sir Morgan mentioned, its spire piercing the night sky. He alerted the others to give it a wide berth. He was certain Sir Morgan did not wish his opponents there to become aware of the dragons' presence until he was good and ready. Wyvrndell was not certain of his intent, but Sir Morgan was a wily tactician, and Wyvrndell was willing to trust him.

He communicated his thoughts to Aireantha and Wyzandar. Being at least somewhat familiar with humans, they were able to appreciate his reasoning. When he'd finished, Pendrake drew near.

"What is your plan, Your Majesty?" inquired the councilor.

"Thank you, Lord Pendrake, for the acknowledgement. I was not sure you believed I earned it."

The older dragon dipped his head. "I have done some hard thinking on the flight up here. To my knowledge, no dragon has ever earned the right to be called king. The kingship has always passed from sire to scion, down through the ages.”

“True enough,” Wyvrndell said. He was uncertain of Pendrake’s point, but was willing to hear him out.

“Wyvrndell, you have labored long on behalf of dragons. You have been instrumental, so Petrandius told me, in creating bonds with both Men and Dwarves. You have struggled to bring magic to dragonkind, and against all hope and belief, you have succeeded. In addition, today you have battled a challenger for the kingship, and bested him in combat to secure your place.”

Wyvrndell maintained a judicious silence. After several silent wingbeats, Pendrake said, “Petrandius was no dragon’s fool. He selected you from among all those he might have chosen. If this does not equip you to be the rightful king, I cannot fathom what would. You have my loyalty, as did Petrandius before you.”

“Lord Pendrake, I am honored by your words, and by your trust. Thank you.”

Pendrake said, “So, I ask again. What is your plan?”

“I have been discussing strategy with Donathyr during our flight. He is captain of the guard, after all, and tested in battle, and I am not. A wise leader relies upon his experts, does he not? He suggests a three-pronged offensive. Four dragons will engage the front of the Rhuddlani’s line. Two dragons will be stationed at each side of their company, to prevent them from breaking off and going around the first group. They will thus be forced to retreat back the way they came.”

“A sound tactic, I warrant,” Pendrake said. “How will you allocate our number?”

“The four dragons of the guard will be the primary force. Wyzandar and Aireantha will stand watch on the left. You and I will take the right side if you will fly with me.”

He glanced over at Pendrake, who appeared to be considering his words. At last, Pendrake spoke. “It is a good plan. I will be honored to go into battle with you.”

“Thank you, Lord Pendrake. Please bear in mind, our task is not to slaughter these men. I intend to frighten them off if possible, force them to retreat back to their own land.”

“A show of force, but not of killing force.”

“Yes, that is my intent.”

Pendrake asked, “If they refuse to turn away and depart?”

Wyvrndell sighed. “I hope it will not come to pass. Yet if it does, we shall have to be more…forceful.”

“I see you are resolved in this. Why?”

"Two reasons. The first is this: the men of Kilbourne, whom we support here, are our allies. We have a treaty with them, drafted by Petrandius."

"And the second reason?"

Wyvrndell said, "These are my friends, Lord Pendrake. Even if no treaty existed, I would be so resolved. Even were I here alone."

Pendrake was silent for several wingbeats. Finally, he said, "I see I have much to learn from you, Your Majesty. It will be as you decree." They flew on, in search of the foe.

"I have spotted the soldiers," Donathyr reported at last, scouting from an advanced position. "They are continuing their march toward the city, at a rapid pace."

Wyvrndell dipped out of the low-hanging clouds. "There they are," said R'gm'l, pointing excitedly.

"Keen are the eyes of a Dwarf," Wyvrndell rumbled. *"Ah, yes, there they are. There are certainly a lot of them. Donathyr? What is your recommendation?"*

"I can see no reason to delay our offensive, Your Majesty," the chief of the king's guard replied. "If we act now, we will catch them in the open. Wait, and they will soon be into the forest, where we will find it much more difficult to carry out your plan."

"Make it so," Wyvrndell commanded.

"Guards, form up on me," Donathyr told his fellow guards.

Wyvrndell held his position for a moment while the other three dragons of the guard shifted into formation. Once they were in position, he said, "Lord Pendrake, let us take up our station. Wyzandar, you and Aireantha on the left. And Wyzandar, mind you have King Rhys with you. Endeavor to keep him safe from the arrows these men might fire at you. I will do the same with R'gm'l."

He and Pendrake banked to hover off the right flank of the advancing army. They remained right inside the cloud cover. Even if one of the men below were to glance toward the sky, Wyvrndell doubted the dragons would be spotted before they began their assault.

"We are ready to begin, Your Majesty," Donathyr reported.

"Commence your attack," Wyvrndell replied.

CHAPTER FIFTY-SEVEN

St. Benedict's Cathedral, Noordstrom

Morgan counted down the seconds. Five. Four. Three. Two. One. A thick mist enveloped the courtyard, as if a dense sea fog had rolled in in an instant, despite this location being fifty leagues from the sea. Sebastien was giving them excellent cover.

"Go," he said. Aartis threw open the door and Morgan burst out, the others following him, charging into the fog. Men were shouting questions and orders and managing to get in each other's way, just as Morgan had hoped.

"Get those women onto the pyre," someone roared. Morgan didn't recognize the voice, but Randolph muttered, "Llachnahn" in his ear.

A flash of light came close to blinding him. Morgan shielded his eyes against it. The fog cleared slightly. One of the bishops, or a wizard they'd coopted, must have set off a counterspell against it. Through the swirling tendrils of mist, his gaze lit on Marissa, who huddled against the wall. A surge of hope, mixed with a tumultuous fury, swelled within him.

A sizzle of green energy zipped down from the window where Nardis was stationed. Mogan assumed he was sending a spell against whoever was trying to clear away Sebastien's fog. Which, he noted, was gathering strength again as the older wizard pouring more energy into his spell. He hoped Sebastien was up to the task. Through its cover Morgan sprinted on toward his goal.

"Marissa!" he shouted above the din.

A call came back to his ears. "Morgan? Well, I was beginning to wonder. You've left it late enough again, haven't you?"

Something between a laugh and a choking sob welled up in his chest. He ran on, shoving men out of his way with his left hand, his sword clutched at the ready in his right. He was reluctant to use it yet. There were too many innocents here to start slashing away, even though he felt an unaccountable urge to do so. Randolph lumbered along in his wake, brandishing his hammer.

Beside him, almost invisible in the mist, Aartis matched him stride for stride. "Kate," Aartis bawled, and Morgan heard an answering cry.

"Stop those men" yelled one of the bishops. "Don't let 'em near the witches."

No one rallied to his cry. Instead, the brothers of St. Benedict's thrashed about in the enveloping mist, unable to see and uncertain of their position or orders. Another flash of green energy spat from the window where Nardis stood overlooking the tangle of servants, guards, and bishops. A crackling answer of purple met it in midair, blooming out into a dome designed to protect those below from Nardis's spells. Sparks like fireflies danced in the air.

Through a brief break in the fog, Morgan spied Marissa, about ten yards away. He dodged around a man carrying an armload of kindling, but found the way blocked by a trio of men, garbed in the ecclesiastical uniforms of Bishop Llachnahn. A less likely looking bunch of guards for a prelate Mogan couldn't imagine. This lot was more like some secondhand ruffians hired from the grimy alley behind an unsavory tavern.

The three men raised their swords, though none appeared enthused over the prospect of facing Morgan and his oncoming companions. Morgan skidded into a crouching lunge, since if he kept on running he'd impale himself on one of their weapons. Trusting Randolph and Aartis to watch his back, he sprang back to a standing position, sweeping his sword around to meet the weapon moving toward him.

The blade was perfect in his hand, an extension of his arm, as he'd told Marissa when she'd presented it to him. But instead of the expected crash of steel on steel, his sword sliced right through his opponent's weapon, cleaving it in twain.

A gasp went up from the watchers close enough to view what transpired. Morgan was damned certain he uttered one himself. *What happened there?*

The guard's mouth dropped open, and he stared at the remnant of his blade in disbelief. "Cor," he exclaimed. He flung down the hilt end and turned to flee. His egress was halted by the simple expedient of Randolph's hammer meeting his head with a most satisfying 'thonk.' The guard, duly thonked, slumped to the cobbles of the courtyard.

The two remaining thugs—well, thugs in uniform—waved their weapons in Morgan's direction. They appeared even less enthused than before. However, they were being paid to do a job, so they needed to at least put on an appearance of resistance.

Morgan, for his part, was more than happy to oblige them. He swept his sword in a singing arc again, cutting both their blades in two with one stroke. The men exchanged a glance which seemed to say, "Yes, we're getting paid, but not near enough for this." Like their predecessor, they tossed the remainders of their swords to the ground and backed away.

Right into Randolph. Once again, he wielded the Hammer of Justice like he was striking a pair of drums. Both men oozed to the ground.

"Kill them!" screamed a voice from somewhere in the fog. Morgan was coming to loathe the sound of it. He wasn't able to spot its owner, but he intended to find the man and silence him. After he freed Marissa and her friends, of course.

"Any time, Morgan," a much more welcome voice called over the din, and Morgan pounded toward it through the mist. Marissa was barely visible through the spell-generated fog.

A crackling sound rose over the hubbub of the crowd, and acrid smoke filled his nose. *Damn it.* Someone had managed to set the pyre alight. This was no cheerful campfire, but an inferno designed for the sole purpose of destruction. Flames leapt toward the darkened sky, sparks swirling up to shine like stars. The tongues of hungry flame called to his mind the demon which had taken over Chief Wizard Foxwent, and Morgan's fury swelled in response.

The sword thrummed in his hand. The fire's glow, reflected in the polished steel of the blade, gave it the appearance of a weapon more suited to be borne by an avenging angel than a mere mortal.

A crash of steel behind him caused Morgan to glance over his shoulder. Aartis was engaging one attacker, while Ian Taggart held off another with a long dagger. Turning his attention back to his goal, his searching gaze found Marissa, manacles on her wrists and ankles, attached to chains looped through iron rings set into the stone wall. Each of the other women was bound in a similar manner. A man in prelate's robe and miter was attempting to unlock the manacles from Marissa's wrists.

"The fire is ready," said another, and Morgan recognized the voice: Llachnahn, the one who kept urging his minions to kill people. Not quite the thing one would expect of a chap in holy orders. "Get the witches onto the pyre, now," Llachnahn went on. "I'll hold off McRobbie."

Marissa, Morgan was pleased to see, was making vigorous

efforts to kick the man who was trying to unlock her chains. Her kicks weren't causing him much in the way of actual injury, but were helping to keep him off balance and distracted. Her blindfold had come off, and she was able to see who she was kicking, at least.

"Not her," ordered another of the bishops, pointing at Marissa. Llachnahn gave him a surprised look. "I want to save her for last," the first one said.

The crowd edged back, leaving an open half circle in front of the women, and Morgan got his first glimpse of Bishop Llachnahn. Tall, gaunt, and gangly, he was scarecrow-like in appearance, except for the fury which blazed in his eyes. The man was a complete fanatic, Morgan understood at last, driven by some demon within him. Not a real one, he hoped, like Foxwent had been, but even inner demons were bad enough.

"Hold me off, will you?" Morgan snarled. An answering fury surged within his chest. "And how do you expect to manage it?" The sword hummed in his hand, the blade glinting with a fey light. Silver runes appeared on the blade, and the emerald in the pommel blazed with green fire.

"It's over, Llachnahn," boomed Randolph. "Give it up and surrender peacefully. No harm will come to you if you do."

"Over?" spat Llachnahn. "We'll see about that." He raised his hand and something like lightning flashed from his fingertips toward Morgan.

"Nooo!" cried Marissa. From the window above them, Nardis was attempting a counter-spell, but it would never be in time. The crackle of the lightning buzzed in Morgan's ears, heading straight for his heart.

His hand, holding the Sword of Fate, came up of its own volition, so the sword was in the path of the spell. To Morgan's amazement, the sword pulsed once and absorbed the bishop's spell into itself. The runes blazed silver again, and the hilt grew hot in his hand.

Llachnahn stared at Morgan, his eyes narrowed. "So, you think to best me with this…this trinket?" he snarled. "Very well, let's see how it likes this." Raising both hands, he released a double jet of magical force at Morgan.

~*~

Noordstrom Plain

Wyvrndell cautioned R'gm'l, *"We are ready to begin. Hold on. I would not care to have you tumble off my back."*

"Have I ever?" replied the prince.

"No, and let us plan to keep it so."

R'gm'l huffed out an aggrieved sigh, but his arms tightened

around the dragon's neck. Ahead of the columns of soldiers, Donathyr and his fellow guards began a synchronized descent. Each opened their jaws. With a roar like thunder, the dragons poured flames toward the ground.

They'd kept enough distance so their fire didn't directly endanger the men of Rhuddlan. Even so, coming so unexpectedly, the four gouts of flame sweeping the land before the advancing soldiers resulted in utter chaos among them.

Taken off guard by the aeriel assault, they cried out in dismay, shock, and even horror. The forward part of the columns broke, the soldiers backing away from the wall of flame. Some turned tail and ran, despite the orders of their officers.

"Dragons!" The terrified cry went up from a soldier farther back, who'd happened to look toward the sky. While some of their officers tried to reestablish control of the situation, another called up a squad of archers.

Men from the middle of the righthand column broke formation and began to run. "It is time for us to convince them their sole hope lies in retreat," Wyvrndell told Pendrake. They swooped toward the ground in unison, sending blasts of fiery breath ahead of the running men.

From the midst of the column, a group of archers launched their bolts toward the hovering dragons. Most of their shots went wild. Those few who did find the intended mark bounced off the dragons' protective scales.

"There," called R'gm'l, from his perch on Wyvrndell's back. "Some more are trying to slip off in this direction."

Pendrake banked and sent another gout of flame ahead of the soldiers, driving them back toward their lines. Aireantha and Wyzandar were engaged on the other side of the Rhuddlani's line, herding a group back towards the main force. Wyzandar reported, "King Rhys has spied the man he believes is their commanding officer. Might it be worthwhile to speak to him?"

"An excellent idea," Wyvrndell replied. "Which one?"

The four dragons engaging the front lines of the soldiers renewed their assault. They were, Wyvrndell noted, taking great care not to char any of the humans. He hovered, watching while Wyzandar consulted with Rhys. After several moments, his sire described the officer. "Yes, I mark him," Wyvrndell said. "Let us see if this accomplishes anything."

He explained to Pendrake and the others what he was going to attempt. This done, he flew toward the Rhuddlani officer. The man stared up at him, and Wyvrndell made eye contact. Oblivious to the arrows of the archers which continued to fly toward him, Wyvrndell sent his words into the Rhuddlani's mind.

"Captain of Rhuddlan," he said, and chuckled to himself when the man's mouth fell open at the unexpected voice. *"I am Wyvrndell, King of the Dragons of Ervantium. We are allied with the men of Kilbourne, whose lands you have entered. We are also allied, you should know, with the Dwarves of the Southlands. These lands are under our protection. Do you understand what I am saying to you?"*

The officer's voice, when he spoke, was a mix of trepidation and wonder. "I—I hear you, King of Dragons."

"Good. Tell your men to stand down. If you obey my commands, no harm will befall you. If not… Well, you have seen what we are capable of."

"I have indeed," the officer replied. He turned and began bawling orders.

The dragons hovered, watchful and ominous, dark silhouettes against the sky. Once the soldiers began to regain a semblance of order and the archers ceased their fire, Wyvrndell asked, *"What is your name, Captain of Rhuddlan?"*

"I am named Vardan, Baron Vyrndon," he replied.

"Heed me well, Vardan of Rhuddlan. Take your soldiers and return to your own lands. If you do this, you and your men will be spared. If you continue your incursion into Kilbourne territory, well—you have seen what the flames of a mere eight dragons can do. Imagine what havoc a host of dragons as I command might wreak. We have taken great care, thus far, to ensure none of your company was harmed or killed. Unless you agree to abandon your mission and return to Rhuddlan, our next attack will not be so merciful."

Vardan said, "Your words have the ring of truth, King Wyvrndell. Though my life may be forfeit if I return to report failure, I will hazard the chance of a possible beheading over the certainty of being charred by dragon flames."

Wyvrndell held a hurried consultation with Rhys. Then, to the Rhuddlani captain, he said, *"Vardan of Rhuddlan, Rhys Gwynfallis, the King of Kilbourne, flies here with us tonight. He has authorized me to extend an offer to you. If you, or any of your men, would prefer to remain in Kilbourne rather than return to face the consequences of your failed endeavor, you will be welcomed. Providing, of course, you are willing to swear an oath of loyalty to Kilbourne."*

Vardan hesitated but for a moment. "Our company," he said, "was chosen because none of us have family who would miss us or mourn should we not return. I, for one, will accept this generous offer.

May I have some time to tell the rest of my men what you have said, so they may each decide their own course?"

"*You may, Captain Vardan,*" Wyvrndell replied. "*And let them know any who chose to return to Rhuddlan will be free to go in peace so long as they do not loot or destroy on their way. But also let them know we dragons will be watching over them, to ensure their good conduct.*"

"I understand," said Vardan.

"*King Rhys tells me any who, like yourself, chooses to remain here, should report to the fortress at Noordstrom. He will send word to expect you and treat you honorably.*"

"Thank you," Vardan said. "It has been a most unusual day—night—whatever."

"*May I ask you one question?*" Wyvrndell asked.

"Of course. I will answer if I can."

"*Why were you sent here, Captain Vardan? What were your instructions?*"

Vardan told him. Wyvrndell hovered in silent contemplation of his words. At last, he said, "*It is as we assumed. I must go. Instruct your men to make their choice quickly. Four dragons will wait here, keeping watch. Do not tempt fate, Captain Vardan.*"

He informed the others of what had transpired. Instructing Donathyr and his comrades to remain, to the rest he said, "We must return to Noordstrom. Sir Morgan and Lady Marissa have need of our aid, and of the presence of King Rhys."

With this, he banked eastward. Wyzandar, Aireantha, and Pendrake followed in his wake.

CHAPTER FIFTY-EIGHT
St. Benedict's Cathedral, Noordstrom

Morgan swung the Sword of Fate in a wide arc, catching the twin bolts of magical energy on the flat of the blade. This time, instead of absorbing the spell like before, the sword reflected it back toward the rebel bishop. Llachnahn's eyes widened and he dodged out of the path of his own spell. The energy struck the wall of the building behind him with the force of a boulder hurled from a catapult, punching a large, smoking hole through the solid stone. Shards of rock exploded outwards, and the onlookers ducked and fled.

Instead of fleeing, the bishop growled out an arcane phrase. A flaming sword appeared in his hand, and he laughed aloud.

Morgan bared his teeth. "Excellent," he said, his voice ringing out through the courtyard. "I've been wanting to test out my new blade. This little contest will do quite well."

"Little contest?" Llachnahn snarled. "You're a fool, and a knave, and a consort to witches. Thrice damned, you are. Now you shall pay the price for your many sins."

"My sins?" Morgan raised a brow and hefted his sword. "I'm not the one calling for the death of innocent women because they have a gift. One which you yourself bear, I might add. I'm not the one who kidnapped the Royal Enchantress and her friends. Your actions," he noted with a scowl fit to sour wine, "are an offense against God and the laws of Kilbourne. You are a traitor, Bishop, and deserve a traitor's fate."

"No," the rebel bishop replied, baring his teeth in a fierce snarl. "You and your devil of a wife are the ones who offend God. Enough talk." With no warning, Llachnahn charged, waving the spell-wrought sword. Morgan understood well how deadly such a weapon was. Marissa once used something similar in her battle with Augustus Rhenn, while Morgan lay bound and helpless, able to do no more than watch and pray. He was certain the weapon Llachnahn bore was even more dangerous than Marissa's had been. The man must be a trained wizard, though he professed to be a clergyman.

Llachnahn's eyes were wild and fell, like a man possessed. Was the bishop controlled by a demon from the netherworld, similar to what Chief Wizard Foxwent had been? Llachnahn gave him no further time to wonder about it. He brought the flaming sword singing through the air toward Morgan's head. He raised his own blade to parry, and the two weapons met in a clash of sparks. Though the bishop was no swordsman, the force of the blow from his enchanted blade shook Morgan right to the soles of his boots. Llachnahn's eyes took on a malevolent gleam and he pressed his advantage, raining a flurry of blows which Morgan barely managed to fend off.

C'mon, he chided himself as he and Llachnahn circled each other, looking for an opening to pounce. *You're the damned Knight-Commander of the Legion and supposed to be the best swordsman in Kilbourne. And,* he added with a grunt as Llachnahn's blade met his again with a crash and another shower of sparks, *you've damned well got a magical sword. Get on!*

Whirling out of range of another of Llachnahn's strikes, he continued to play defense for the moment, sizing up the other man's strengths and weaknesses. The rebel bishop possessed no form at all, but waved his sizzling blade with wild abandon, in evident hope it would strike a target. After a few minutes of this, while they danced back and forth across the courtyard, Morgan was certain he had seen enough.

Llachnahn was puffing, out of shape and winded, and his guard appeared to be slipping. Morgan, on the other hand, though not in the best shape of his life, was sure he could spot the priest, or wizard, or whatever the hell he was, a five-minute start and still run rings around him on the best day he ever had. Llachnahn brought his magical blade to his side for a second. Morgan raised his own weapon, and cried in a loud voice, "Behold, the Sword of Fate. It is herald of your doom, and I am its instrument."

The words seemed to come not from himself, but from some outside force, acting through him. But there was no time to wonder about the source, for Llachnahn was coming at him again. Morgan launched his own offensive, whirling and darting, thrusting and slashing. Each time their swords met, fateful steel on spell-wrought blade, sparks showered the onlookers, until the air of the courtyard appeared to be filled with a million fireflies.

Llachnahn's parries weakened and his eyes widened, but Morgan continued his onslaught. The bishop backed away, while Morgan pressed his attack further. "Help me," the bishop called, his voice plaintive, but none came to his aid. He cried, "Someone stop him."

"Drop your weapon, Llachnahn," Morgan ordered. "Do it, and I will spare you. If you continue to resist, I cannot say what your destiny may be. The Sword of Fate desires justice."

His words were meant to give his opponent a chance to save himself. But he sensed, deep within himself, the intent of the Sword. He wasn't sure he'd be able to alter it, even were Llachnahn to surrender. The hilt of the Sword pulsed in his hand, and Morgan's heart raced, his breath coming hard as he struggled to control it.

There was, he comprehended a moment too late, no way to alter fate, or to control the path it took. Llachnahn raised his own weapon to attack again, and Morgan lunged forward, the Sword of Fate swinging in a great arc. It cleaved the man's head from his torso. The whole thing was, he explained later, beyond his control. The Sword sought its own justice, and Morgan was merely its instrument.

Llachnahn's lifeless form went limp and crumpled to the cobbles, his head rolling to stare sightlessly from against the stone wall which he had blasted into splinters. The spell-wrought sword he'd borne sizzled once and flickered out of existence. Morgan stood, half dazed, staring at what was once a man of substance and import, now a mere shell.

He lowered his weapon, his breath ragged. His voice was harsh and choked when he spoke. "Fate has been meted, justice served." The words were not his own, but came from something outside himself. *The Sword?* He gazed at it, in a mixture of both awe and revulsion, and dropped the weapon to the ground.

Turning away, he stumbled toward Marissa.

CHAPTER FIFTY-NINE
St. Benedict's Cathedral

With Llachnahn's defeat, the courtyard was in complete chaos. Monks rushed to and fro, shouting orders or pleading for directions. Morgan saw Taggart, his little set of tools in hand, unlocking the chains binding Kate Taggart, Miss Alford, and Princess Saia. Randolph helped them shed their chains. Aartis, his sword at the ready, kept anyone from interfering.

One of the bishops, his cassock askew and his miter ready to fall off, was attempting to unlock the last of Marissa's chains, in order to drag her off with him. Not, Morgan noted, toward the pyre, but toward a door set into the far stone wall.

Which didn't surprise him in the least. Based on what he'd learned in the last couple of days, and in particular from Wyvrndell's recent report, he expected no less. He broke into a trot and caught up with the bishop and his struggling captive. Grabbing the man by the shoulder, he swung him around.

"McRobbie," snarled Bishop McAdoo. "Guards. To me."

Even though he no longer bore the Sword of Fate, Morgan sensed its continued influence coursing through him. The Sword was urging him on, directing him to mete out a deserving fate upon those who broke faith with Kilborne, preyed upon the innocent, and conspired with the enemy.

Marissa, no longer in McAdoo's clutches, staggered and fetched up against a stone wall. Morgan became aware of booted feet heading their way. Before McAdoo managed to call out again, Morgan punched him once in the gut. The bishop keeled over from the force of his blow, and Morgan brought a swift uppercut to the jaw. McAdoo started to slump to the ground, but Morgan caught him around the waist and held him up. Producing a knife from its sheath at the small of his back, he held it across the bishop's throat.

"I may have given up the Sword of Fate," he snarled in his captive's ear. "But the dagger of death here will do fine for what I intend." He pressed the edge against his captive's throat, drawing a tiny line of blood.

"M-Morgan?" Marissa's voice sounded far away, as if she were calling him from a deep cavern. He struggled against the hold of the Sword, emerging when she called his name again, like a drowning man desperate to reach the surface.

Taking a deep, gasping breath, he thrust McAdoo away from him. The bishop stumbled and went down on his knees. "Be glad I don't toss you on your own pyre," Morgan growled. His mind was at odds with his nature, the lingering effects of bearing the Sword of Fate thrumming through him. Fighting for control, he lowered the knife, staggered to his duchess, and took her into his arms.

She swayed there, huddling against him, while all around them chaos reigned and the fire blazed. "I knew you'd come," she said.

Morgan pulled her even tighter into his embrace, kissing her hair. "Of course I came." He resisted the urge to retrieve the Sword and lash out against those whose fates were sealed by their deeds. "Nothing in heaven or on earth could have stopped me." Quite literally, he realized with a slight shudder.

He glanced around. The guards McAdoo had summoned appeared to be frozen in place, their weapons raised but immobile. From above, Nardis gave a jaunty wave.

A monk approached them, calling his name. Morgan blinked like a startled owl and managed to recognize the voice of Brother Francis. "Your Grace," Francis said. "Can I be of assistance?"

Morgan prodded McAdoo with the toe of his boot. "Chain him up?" he suggested. "Along with the other bishops."

"At once." Brother Francis went to gather up the locks and chains used to bind the four women. Marissa gave a final, massive shudder.

"Are you all right?" Morgan asked.

Her smile was weak, but she managed to say, "I am now. I have to admit, I wasn't eager at the prospect of being burned at the stake."

"No, I don't reckon you were. Witchbane?"

"Gallons of it. At least it sure felt like it. Brother Francis did manage to sneak us some food which wasn't laced with the stuff. We appreciated it no end, believe you me. We were close to starving. But if he'd managed it again, in another day or so, I think we'd have been able to access our magic and attempt an escape."

"Instead, Llachnahn and McAdoo and company rushed things."

"And you rode to the rescue once more."

"It's my job," he reminded her. "And in this case, my sacred duty."

"My, you say the sweetest things," she said, her eyes crinkling. This, he felt, was a good sign. If she could still tease, she would be all right.

Out of the corner of his eye, Morgan noticed one of the monks pick up the Sword. He dropped it at once, wringing his hands like he'd grabbed a red-hot poker. "Later on," Morgan said, "we need to discuss where you got this sword."

"Oh? Was there something wrong with it?"

"Later," he said. "Now we have other business to take care of. Wyvrndell will be here soon."

She glanced up at him, a calculating expression on her face. "Wyvrndell, eh? Morgan McRobbie, what have you gotten up to this time?"

He laughed, and the Sword's hold over him cracked. Bending, he kissed her. "Oh, one thing and another," he said once they'd parted. "You'll see."

"Sir Morgan, are you ready?" Wyvrndell's voice sounded in his head.

"Give us a couple of minutes to clear some space for you to land," he replied.

"We are four in number."

"Four, eh? Very well, we'll need to clear out a lot of space…" Turning to Marissa, he said, "Wyvrndell and three other dragons will be here any minute. They're also bringing Rhys, and Prince R'gm'l."

Her gaze grew even more appraising. "My, my, you have been busy."

"And need to be busier yet. They need a space to land." Assuming his parade ground voice, he bellowed, "Everyone clear the center of this courtyard, unless you wish to be squashed by dragons."

This got their attention. "Dragons!" cried one of the monks, pointing skyward, and soon the milling, muttering crowd edged back, away from the center of the yard.

"Can you speak with Wyvrndell?" he asked Marissa.

She didn't reply for a few moments. When she did, her tone was subdued. "No. It must be an effect of the witchbane."

"I'd wondered. I figured if you could have done, you would have contacted him so he could let me know where you were. And that you were all right."

"Mmm. All right is a rather relative term, isn't it?"

"You're safe," he assured her. "With any luck, the witches of Kilbourne will be safe too, once we're done here."

From out of the clouds, the company of dragons descended like a flock of silent starlings. The chattering crowd of monks gasped as Wyvrndell and his companions landed, one by one. Rhys scrambled down and strode over to Morgan, with R'gm'l following close in his wake.

"Knight-Commander McRobbie, well met," the king said. "Royal Enchantress. I'm delighted to find you unharmed."

"Fancy meeting you here," Morgan said. He was still holding Marissa, and saw no reason to let go of her, monarch or no. "Nice of you to drop in."

"Yes, well, I happened to be in the neighborhood." Rhys surveyed the courtyard, complete with its ominous, still burning pyre. "It appears," he went on, "you arrived, as the stories say, in the nick of time."

Morgan glanced toward the pyre. The sight of it filled him once more with a cold fury, blazing hotter than its flames. He found himself unable to speak. Only the sensation of Marissa in his arms grounded him to reality.

With an effort, he found his tongue. "Your Majesty," he said, inclining his head. "Bishop Llachnahn is dead, by my hand. He intended to burn Marissa and the others on that pyre, for the crime of existing. I say this because magic is indeed part of the fabric of their existence."

Rhys waited, listening while Morgan continued his narrative. "Bishop Llachnahn, however, fanatical though he was, did not operate alone. The four other renegade bishops are here and have been taken into custody. Captain Poldane stands guard over three. The fourth," Morgan prodded McAdoo's prone form with the toe of his boot, "is here."

"I see. Well done, Commander. I—"

Morgan cut him off. "There is something else you need to know, Rhys. Llachnahn was encouraged in his scheme, and even urged along, by Bishop McAdoo. For McAdoo, however, none of this had to do with eradicating witchcraft from Kilbourne. In his case, it was all about money."

"You lie," snarled McAdoo, writhing on the ground in an effort to escape the chains which bound him.

"Shut up." Morgan resisted the urge to kick the prostrate prelate, but it took all his willpower.

Rhys's smile was grim. "Go on."

"I learned, through Lord Holman, of strange things going on in Rhuddlan. Holman's man, Barlbent, acting on a suggestion I made, directed their financial chaps to start checking for substantive movements of money from Rhuddlan to someone in Kilbourne. They struck gold, so to speak, with Bishop McAdoo's accounts."

"I believe I know where this is going," Rhys said.

McAdoo struggled even harder against his bonds. Morgan ignored him. "I'm sure you do. The Rhuddlani invasion force wasn't here to capture territory. They were sent because McAdoo was paid to capture Marissa, and through her me. He was planning to hand us over to the Rhuddlanis, who would then have turned around and hauled us back to stand before Varsil Jarek."

"And with the pair of you out of the way, Varsil would have been much more confident over launching an actual invasion in the spring," Rhys said.

Morgan scowled. "Yes. 'Out of the way' being a much more polite way of saying painfully, messily, and quite nastily dead."

Marissa pulled out of his embrace, an outraged expression on her face. "You mean to tell me this was all some silly political game? Nothing to do with witchcraft after all?"

"Oh, no." Morgan shook his head. "For Llachnahn, his obsession was always about the witches, even though he was himself a trained wizard. He was a fanatic on the subject. Randolph told me Llachnahn's sister possessed magic, and they had to spirit her away somewhere safe. I don't know if her having magic triggered anything to do with his fervor on the subject, and I suppose we'll never learn the answer. At any rate, McAdoo decided to use Llachnahn's fanaticism to his own advantage."

"And, turned traitor in the bargain," Rhys observed.

"Well, the lot of them are traitors to Kilbourne," Morgan said. "They conspired together to kidnap the Royal Enchantress, which to my mind is high treason. McAdoo decided to line his pockets in the bargain."

Rhys stood in thoughtful silence. At last, he asked, "How much of this can you prove, Morgan? You know I can't act on your word alone. I have to have something to bring before a magistrate."

"Well, first you have the evidence of the Rhuddlani captain, and what his mission here was." He noted Rhys's surprised expression. "Yes, Wyvrndell related that bit of news to me. And Lord Holman can confirm the bit concerning the financial end of things regarding Bishop McAdoo, and—well, you don't even have to wait until we get this lot back to Kilbourne." He turned to scan the courtyard and found the man he sought. "Brother Francis," he called. "Please come here."

"Morgan, he was trying to help us," Marissa said, watching the cowled monk hasten toward them through the aftermath of the battle. "He even brought us food."

"I've no doubt," Morgan said, resisting the urge to laugh. "He's rather fond of you, I believe, and has an interesting habit of turning up in the right place at the right time. Don't you, Barlbent?"

Brother Francis pushed his cowl back. "Ah, well spotted, Your Grace," he said. "How did you know?"

"A hunch, pure and simple," Morgan said.

Marissa, who'd been standing with her mouth agape, burst out in a peal of delighted laughter. "Mr. Barlbent, you do manage to land in the thick of things, don't you? Thank you for your kindness." Stepping to him, she bestowed a quick kiss upon Barlbent's cheek.

Blushing crimson, he said, "Thank you, My Lady. I only wish I could have done more."

"Barlbent," Morgan said, "can you confirm to His Majesty what Lord Holman told me regarding McAdoo's accounts?"

"Oh, I'm happy to," Barlbent said. "Our financial fellows are like terriers after a rat when it comes to this type of thing. And Bishop McAdoo didn't go much out of his way to conceal anything. He received a transfer of gold, in the amount of ten thousand crowns, from King Varsil of Rhuddlan."

Rhys nodded. "The Rhuddlani captain, Vardan, told Wyvrndell his contact was Bishop McAdoo."

"McAdoo ordered Llachnahn to leave Marissa until last," Morgan went on, "when they were going to start putting these women onto the fire. He couldn't risk not being able to deliver what he'd been paid for. Varsil has a definite aversion to failure and would have required he return the gold. Something which didn't fit in with McAdoo's plans."

A torrent of lurid curses emerged from the bound bishop. Rhys bent and said, "If you don't be quiet, I shall be forced to take action, Bishop. You are in a most precarious position. Another outburst from you, and I might consider allowing the dragons to tickle you with their fire."

"You wouldn't dare," snarled the bishop. "I'm a holy man."

"Not so holy as you profess to be, from what I've learned," Rhys said. He turned back to Morgan. "Very well, Commander, you have managed to storm the rebels' fortress and capture them after all. What shall I do with them?"

"Rhys, I'm afraid it will be up to you to decide their fate," Morgan said. "I know what I would recommend. The punishment for high treason is death. I've already beheaded one, but it was in self-defense." He prodded McAdoo, silent at last, with his boot again, "This one deserves a similar fate. But it's not for me to pass judgement, for which he should be grateful."

Rhys nodded, his eyes speculative.

Morgan said, "Now, I'm going to take Marissa home, if Wyvrndell will consent to bear us."

"I will, Sir Morgan," came the dragon's reply. *"My friends can also bear the other women who were taken captive here, if they would like. Also King Rhys and Prince R'gm'l."*

"Thank you, Wyvrndell," Morgan said, bowing to the dragon.

"Your Grace?" Barlbent hurried over. He carried the Sword of Fate. "I think you might have forgotten this in the heat of battle." He held out the weapon.

Morgan accepted it, with reluctance. Where once the sword was light and agile, an extension of his arm, it now hung like more a millstone. What, he wondered, did this portend? Was the Sword done with him, since he'd dispatched Llachnahn?

But he didn't have time to delve into this particular problem. He sheathed the sword. "Thank you," he said to Barlbent. "If you will, help Aartis and Master Sebastien get everyone back to Caerfaen? We arrived through transfer portals, courtesy of the wizards. You'll have to return the same way."

"Of course." Barlbent's lips curled into a grin. "I've always wanted to experience a bit of magic."

"Make sure the bishops remain chained up when they go through. I wouldn't want them to try and attack one of the wizards on the way."

"I'll instruct them to be careful," Barlbent said.

"Good." Turning to Marissa, Morgan held out his arm and said, "My Lady, your dragon awaits. Shall we go home?"

She took his arm, and together they walked toward Wyvrndell. In an undertone, so only Morgan was able to hear, she said, "As soon as ever we can, we're going to need to pay a visit to the Dwarves."

Morgan stopped in his tracks and stared…

ABOUT THE AUTHOR

Keith W. Willis graduated (long ago) from Berry College with a degree in English Lit. He now lives in the scenic Hudson Valley/Adirondack region of NY with his wife Patty. Keith's interests include camping, canoeing, and Scrabble. Keith began writing seriously in 2008, when the voices in his head got too pesky to ignore, and has penned five published novels, *Fateful Knight* being the fifth.

Keith recently retired from a career managing an eclectic group of database content editors for a global information technology firm. Keith and Patty spend much of their time exploring America, and attending Renaissance Faires across New York and New England. Keith is a member of the Science Fiction & Fantasy Writers Association, and is a Board member of the Hudson Valley Writers Guild.

Keith loves to hear from readers. You can find and connect with him at the links below.

Website/Blog: http://www.keithwillisauthor.com/
Threads: https://www.threads.net/@kilbourneknight23
Facebook: https://www.facebook.com/keith.willis.581
https://www.facebook.com/TRAITOR-KNIGHT-191368320972613/

TRAITOR KNIGHT

When Morgan McRobbie rescues a damsel-in-distress from a dragon, he expects she'll swoon, murmuring "My hero!" Instead, Marissa has only loathing for the man everyone believes will betray Kilbourne. That's fine with Morgan. A woman in his life would just complicate things.

A high-level informer threatens the kingdom's security, and Morgan is out to stop him. Posing as a turncoat himself, he's walking a fine line between honor and betrayal. A single misstep could result in disaster, and his mission is fraught with distractions: the pesky dragon, a pair of conniving courtiers, and the disillusioned damsel who's certain Morgan can't be trusted.

If Morgan's going to save the kingdom, win the girl, and manage to stay alive, he'll need to step up his game. Because the traitor is lurking in the shadows, and his scheme calls not just for the betrayal of Kilbourne, but also the destruction of Morgan McRobbie.

CHAPTER ONE

A clamor of rooks exploded through the trees, nearly drowning out the woman's scream.

Morgan straightened in the saddle. Trouble, at last. The patrol had been boring up 'til now. He set his heels to Arnicus's flanks and the big gray gelding quickened his pace along the narrow trail. The birds flapped off, their raucous calls fading in the distance. A watchful silence overtook the woods, broken only by the thud of Arnicus's hooves on the summer-dry earth.

Morgan peered through the trees, searching for the source of the cry. He knew no good reason why a woman, screaming or otherwise, should be in the middle of the King's forest. But no matter the reason, he had to find her. Help her, if possible. He'd never been one to shy away from trouble. No soldier was, or he didn't remain a soldier for long. He loosened his sword in its well-worn sheath.

Another shriek split the air. Arnicus leapt forward, nostrils flared and ears laid back. Morgan bent low over the horse's neck, scanning ahead for danger. It might be a trap. The trees thinned slightly, the mottled light of the forest replaced by brighter sunshine that heralded a clearing. Suddenly Morgan jerked hard on the reins, causing Arnicus to toss his head in equine complaint. He paid little heed.

Just ahead, the trail opened out onto a serene sun-dappled clearing. The little meadow, dotted with bright patches of wildflowers, would have been charming if not for the hulking blue dragon crouched in its center.

"My God!" Morgan whispered, half curse and half prayer. Arnicus pawed the ground nervously, suggesting a strategic retreat might not be such a bad idea. Morgan didn't blame him in the least. "Steady on, fellow," he whispered, as much to himself as to the horse.

Despite the generally accepted notion that dragons had been extinct for centuries, this one looked pretty damned corporeal. Iridescent azure scales covered the creature's enormous body. Huge green eyes gleamed with an alien intelligence from beneath bony brow-like ridges. Vast leathery wings rested on the creature's back, twitching slightly as if eager to lift off into flight. Curls of steam vented from its snout, forming delicate patterns in the air.

Blast! The standard-issue dragons had been bad enough. This was one of the fire-breathing ones. And he didn't have time to call up reinforcements from the Legion garrison at Caerfaen. This was his problem.

The dragon held a dark-haired girl in its talons, and its attention was focused exclusively on her. Which was both good and bad. Good, in that it hadn't noticed him yet, giving Morgan a brief moment to reclaim his scattered wits. Bad, in that its attention was focused on the girl in its talons. He was going to have to act at once to have any hope of saving her.

Morgan swung down from the saddle and drew his sword. The steaming nightmare inspected the girl much as a cook might a particularly savory delicacy. She strained to free herself, wriggling and even managing to land a fierce kick on its snout. The dragon didn't deign to notice. A surge of adrenaline fizzed through Morgan, familiar as the hilt of the sword in his hand. Well, he'd been looking for excitement, and he was about to get it. Likely a lot more than he could handle.

"Unhand that maiden!" he shouted, storming toward the monster and probable death. "Release her and prepare to meet your doom!"

The dragon, hissing like a brace of tea kettles, turned to face this interruption of its mid-morning snack of maiden flambé. Ominous rumblings sounded in the beast's superstructure. The girl struggled harder now, a wild hope lighting her eyes.

If nothing else, perhaps he could force the dragon to drop her. Then she might have a chance to escape while Morgan kept it occupied with killing him. He heard the deep rumbling again, herald of his own doom. With a wild yell he darted forward to strike the first blow.

The sword ricocheted back off the protective scales, nearly cleaving Morgan's head in two. His hand throbbed as if he'd just launched an attack at an anvil. Curse it, that just wasn't fair! Fire and armor, against his insignificant sword and a worse than useless shield. Definitely not fair. He stubbornly hacked again with roughly the same effect as the girl's kick.

The dragon tracked his progress, taking careful aim like an

archer sighting on a target. Well, if he had to die, Morgan thought, it might as well be in combat with a dragon. Perhaps after he went up in flames he might go down in song. Assuming anyone found enough in the charred remains to tell who he had been. But without a doubt his death was going to be quicker and messier than it was glorious. From what he'd seen on battlefields over the years, death usually was.

The dragon opened its mouth to flame. Like a fighter desperate to get inside his opponent's reach, Morgan flung himself directly toward the beast, clutching at its haunch. He scrabbled one-handed for purchase on the smooth scales, using the dragon's body as a shelter against the fiery death intended for him. A roar like a thousand forges being lit at once nearly deafened him. Then the flames came, passing just overhead. The heat slammed into him like a blow from a giant, sending him reeling.

Quitting his refuge before the dragon decided to squash him, Morgan dodged around the massive hindquarters. He spared a glance up at the girl. At least the fire hadn't harmed her. Yet. She was still trying to break free. He made another quick foray with the sword, but it was like trying to drive a butter knife into a boulder. Then a huge clawed foot lashed out, catching him in the chest. Morgan went flying.

He hit the ground with a wrenching thud, skidding on his back until he crashed against a large rock. He fumbled around for the sword. It lay halfway between him and a very smug-looking dragon. When he reached for the weapon, blinding pain shot up his arm, exploding in his scrambled brain. It didn't seem to really matter. He was going to die, with or without the sword. Morgan swore like the Legion soldier he was.

He spared a quick glance at the girl. She watched his imminent demise with an air of resignation. Her expression almost seemed aggrieved, as if she resented having her hopes raised only to see them dashed again so quickly. The dragon took careful aim once more, opening its jaws to deliver the coup de grace. Morgan struggled to his feet and raised his shield. It was pointless, he knew, but instinct was driving him now. He stared into the gaping maw and waited for death to overtake him.

But instead of deadly fire, what emerged was a little plume of steam and a loud "Urp!"

Morgan stared. The dragon stared back, as if daring him to snicker. It took another sulphur-laden breath and gave forth what was probably intended to be a mighty roar. The effort was punctuated with another series of hiccoughs and a large wisp of acrid blue smoke.

The dragon tossed its head in a gesture of what Morgan could only interpret as frustration. It made a final effort to produce a flame, but more spasms shook the massive body. Shaking off his trancelike state, Morgan made a dash for the sword. Not that it was going to do him any good, but at least he'd have made the effort.

Looking rather sheepish, the dragon hiccoughed twice more, dropped the girl, and unfolded its wings. With two flaps it began to rise, the ascent marred by its ongoing hiccoughs. Morgan grabbed his sword in his left hand—his right still felt useless—and slashed savagely at the dragon as it gained altitude. The blade bounced off its scales again, and Morgan growled in frustration.

The spiked tail lashed almost idly in his direction. Another shudder spoiled the dragon's aim, and what should have been a killing blow flashed harmlessly by. Morgan stood captivated as the dragon winged drunkenly away over the treetops. One final "Urp!" echoed back to him.

Good God, I'm still alive! And still had all the important bits attached.

A feminine voice broke in on his reverie. "Don't just stand there gawking," it commanded. "Help me up!"

DESPERATE KNIGHT

Morgan McRobbie and Lady Marissa duBerry swing back into swashbuckling action, facing old enemies, new threats, and a diabolical conspiracy—not to mention a more personal battle, one with hearts and pride at stake.

As the pair escorts Prince Robert to the dwarf king's court, a scheme intended to hurl men and dwarves into a devastating war is unfolding. Morgan ends up sidetracked by a kidnapped dwarf and a centuries-old feud, while a mysterious wizard's revelations shake Marissa to her core, throwing into question everything she thought she knew about her past and future. And the advent of a rival for Marissa's affections threatens any hope of a happy ending—if they survive.

Once again, the desperate knight and indomitable damsel must hazard everything on a single throw of the dice, gambling on untested allies and unimagined weapons to save their world.

CHAPTER ONE

The rapier slid from its sheath with a soft susurration that presaged swift and violent death.

Morgan McRobbie ignored his opponent's blade. Instead he scanned the man's eyes for the telltale flicker that signaled an attack. All around them men lunged and dodged and whirled. Cries of anguish and triumph rang out over the clash of steel on steel. But for Morgan, no one else existed at this moment.

His attacker approached, his movements tentative. From caution, perhaps, leavened with a bit of trepidation. He was, after all, facing the renowned Knight-Commander of the King's Legion. The Dark Knight of Kilbourne.

Morgan scowled fiercely at this sobriquet, and his opponent danced a hasty step back.

Then, gathering himself, the man lunged forward with a wild yell. His sword sliced the air in a hissing arc. Morgan stepped neatly back out of its trajectory, and air was all it sliced.

He acknowledged the strike with a brief nod. Maintaining his defensive posture, he watched the other man's eyes for his next move. He knew the fellow to be a decent swordsman. He was also well aware his opponent didn't possess Morgan's level of proficiency. His reaction and recovery times were definitely slower. Offsetting this lack of expertise was an attitude of grim determination.

His opponent launched a furious flurry of thrusts and slashes, but Morgan parried the attack with studied ease. He refrained from going on the offensive himself quite yet. He had plenty of time. If he finished off this fellow too soon, there'd be plenty ready to take his place.

The attacker lunged again, his blade darting like a swallow to find an opening in Morgan's defenses. The man was breathing a bit harder now, further evidence of his lack of practice. Morgan flashed him an evil grin.

"Not slowing down already, are you?" he taunted. "I would have expected better from you."

His opponent didn't answer. He just gasped a little. Likely saving his wind for the fight. He lunged again. This time he was careless, leaving his left side wide open,

It was like being handed a gift. Seizing his opportunity, Morgan went on the offensive at last. His sword sliced the air with an angry hiss as he stalked inexorably toward his foe. The man fell back into a determined defensive posture, managing to parry the first few thrusts.

Then Morgan feinted, his blade slashing low. As his opponent reacted, Morgan shifted his stance in the blink of an eye, his rapier darting in high to find its mark.

Gently he touched the point to the spot over his opponent's heart. "You're dead, Your Majesty," Morgan said.

Rhys Gwynfallis, King of Kilbourne, yanked off his protective helm. Tossing it to a waiting attendant, he pushed his long, sweat-soaked black hair back from his eyes.

Handing his sword off as well, he groused, "Blast it, Morgan. After all this time, I still fall for your tricks."

"But you are getting better," Morgan pointed out charitably. "Once upon a time I would have had you in the first couple of minutes. Your defense is much more controlled now. You just need to focus on your opponent's eyes instead of concentrating so completely on his blade."

"As you've told me time and again." Rhys gave a rueful shake of his head. "Very well, you've killed your king. Again. Gwyn won't let me hear the end of it, you know." His glum expression was at odds with his normal good humor. No doubt the thought of the teasing he'd receive from Queen Gwyndolyn rankled more than his actual defeat. Then he shrugged and quirked a grin. "Which is why you're Knight-Commander and I'm just a king. Let's go get an ale, eh? I'm parched!"

"Sounds like a royal command to me." Morgan sheathed his blade and tossed his own helm to an attendant. Doffing their protective garb, king and knight left the training ground in search of something to quench their thirst.

As they walked through the palace corridors Rhys suggested, "How about going to the Sword and Crown?"

Morgan eyed him with raised brows. "Really? I assumed you'd want to go back to your study and relax there."

"Yes, really," Rhys replied in a tone which brooked no argument. "I don't get out and about enough of late. There's a lot going on in the wide world beyond these walls, and I need to have a good feel for it. As you keep reminding me, a man can get stifled in here. Besides, you've been raving about Rajan's latest batch of ale. With such a masterful swordsman at my side, what could possibly happen?"

Morgan hesitated, but only for a moment. "By your command, Sire. Let's be off to the Sword and Crown."

A quarter of an hour later found Morgan escorting his liege lord down Montrose Street and into the tavern. Rhys had waved away his suggestion to change out of the military leathers he wore for sword practice.

He would prefer, he'd stated emphatically, to slip out of the palace incognito. Or at least as much as was possible, given that his thin, angular face was well-known to pretty much every inhabitant of the city of Caerfaen, capital of Kilbourne.

The Sword and Crown was a soldier's tavern, and the only one Morgan visited with any regularity. It exuded an air of comfortable shabbiness, along with a firm disregard for the creature comforts. No one came here for the atmosphere. They came to eat, drink, and gossip. And on occasion, to brawl.

Solidly built, well-scarred tables and chairs of dark oak were spaced about the main common room, far enough away from each other to allow a man to carry on a conversation without being overheard by his neighbors.

A massive utilitarian hearth, currently occupied by a slowly roasting boar, took up nearly one entire wall. The smell of the sizzling meat hung heavy in the air, delectable and enticing. Morgan felt his stomach growl with pleasant anticipation.

Kegs of ale and casks of spirits lined another wall. A third was taken up by the bar itself. No gleaming wood here, just a good stolid place at which to enjoy a pint or two, or however many Rajan Turksa, the barman and owner, would allow.

Only a couple of tables were occupied this early in the afternoon. After dark, there would hardly be room to move.

Rhys gazed about in royal approval as Morgan led him to a table. "It's been a long time since I was in here," he observed. "A comfortable place. Nice and quiet."

"Until a fight breaks out." Morgan chuckled. "A couple of nights ago some big farm boy wandered in after having a few too many at another tavern. He decided he'd pick a fight with anyone who'd take him on. Rajan had to use the big club he keeps beneath the bar to clean house.

Afterward they stacked the bodies out in the street."

Rhys hooted as Rajan made his way to their table with as much haste as his bad leg would allow. Normally the barmaids waited on customers while he kept to the bar. Rajan, who had served under Morgan in the Legion, made certain he attended to the Knight-Commander himself.

The barman's eyes opened wide when he recognized Morgan's companion. "Yer Majesty," he gasped, attempting to kneel. "You do me great honor."

Rhys scrambled out of his chair and steadied the barman, raising him to his feet before he toppled over in the effort. "Here now, we'll have none of that. Commander McRobbie has given me glowing reports of your ale. I decided I should come try it for myself and make certain he wasn't exaggerating." He gave Rajan a knowing wink.

The barman grinned. "Well, now, Yer Majesty, I'll admit, 'tis not bad, not bad at all. I keep a little something set aside for special customers. I'll not be but a moment." He stumped off behind the bar.

He returned in short order, reverently bearing two foaming tankards. He placed one before the king with a flourish, and then handed the second to Morgan.

"Thank you," said Rhys, taking an exploratory taste. He licked the foam from his lip and set the tankard back down on the table, regarding it with pleasure as Morgan sipped his own drink.

"Morgan's reports were accurate, as I expected," Rhys said. "Excellent, most excellent."

"Thankee, Yer Majesty." The barman beamed. "Let me know when ye needs another."

Rhys swallowed another draught. "Ahhhh," he sighed happily.

Morgan sipped from his own tankard while his mind raced. What the devil was Rhys up to? He didn't have to wait long to find out.

"Morgan," said the King of Kilbourne, wiping foam from his mouth with the back of a royal hand. "I was wondering…"

"Here it comes!" Morgan cringed in mock terror. "I knew it."

Rhys threw back his head and laughed. "You know me too well, my friend. But it's nothing too onerous, I assure you. Nothing like the last little task I set before you."

He shuddered at the recollection of Rhys's "last little task." At the king's request, Morgan had posed as a turncoat to expose a traitor on the Royal Council. It had nearly ruined his good name, and resulted in his arrest on charges of murder and treason. It had also almost gotten him killed at the hands of the ruthless Rhuddlani agent Xavier.

Of course, that adventure had also led to several encounters with

Lady Marissa duBerry. Some of those encounters had been more pleasant than others, but on balance Morgan felt making her acquaintance might have been the only good thing to come out of the whole affair.

If, he amended, he could finally bring himself to…

Realizing he was woolgathering under the curious gaze of his sovereign, Morgan shook himself out of this reverie. "So, what do you want me to do this time?" He lifted a brow. "Vanquish another dragon? Storm Rhuddlan single-handed? Go on a quest to find the Jewel of Archandyll?"

"No, nothing so formidable. Although…" Rhys's black eyes gleamed with sudden mischief. "A quest for the Jewel of Archandyll might—"

Morgan cut him off with a growl. The Jewel, a blood-red ruby reputed to be as large as a man's head, had not been seen by anyone in living history. Indeed, most scholars considered it a myth, and a particularly tenuous myth at best.

Morgan was not inclined to go chasing after myths at the moment. He had other, more interesting things in mind to pursue. Like Lady Marissa.

"Very well." Rhys flashed a quick grin. "It's really quite simple. Merely a little courier assignment. I need to you to deliver something to the Dwarf King in Rockfast."

Morgan leaned forward, his eyes widening with genuine surprise. "Something to do with the upcoming trade negotiations? Something you can't send by regular royal messenger?" He frowned. "Just what is it I'm to deliver?"

Rhys heaved a sigh. "Prince Robert."

Morgan gaped at him. "Robbie?" Of all the things he might have anticipated, this wasn't even within the realm of possibility. He sank back into the chair, running a hand through his close-cropped dark hair.

It wasn't that he didn't like Prince Robert. He did. Robert was a prince among princes, as it were. But still, it didn't make sense. "Rhys, I don't understand."

"I'm sending Robbie to be fostered with K'var'k, King of the Dwarves, for a year," Rhys explained. "K'var'k's son, Prince R'gm'l, will be coming to Caerfaen. I'd like you to serve as Robbie's escort on the way to the rendezvous, and as R'gm'l's on the return journey. To make sure nothing happens to either of them."

Morgan nodded as he mulled this over. "An interesting notion. It would certainly help to firm up our relations with the Dwarves. Don't you feel Robbie's a bit young, though? I mean, he's only seven."

Rhys shrugged. "I would have preferred to wait until he was a bit older. Ideally another two or three years. However, when K'var'k recently broached the idea of sending his son here if I was agreeable, it seemed too good an opportunity to pass up. So I jumped at it."

"How does Gwyn feel about all this?"

Rhys's grimace told the tale. "She's certainly not thrilled. Like you, she feels Robbie's too young. However, she accepts the political expediency of it. We desperately need to maintain good relations with our neighbors to the south. It'll do Robbie no harm, and I think it'll be a good thing in the long view. He'll have a much better appreciation of our Dwarf neighbors and their culture when he comes of age. Not such a bad thing for a future king to have, eh?"

"Not at all. If more folk knew something about the Dwarves besides 'they live in caverns, have long beards, and carry axes,' we'd all be better off. Not to mention some of our recent troubles might have been avoided."

Rhys's nose wrinkled as if he'd stepped in something particularly nasty. "Ramis d'Eastmond, you mean."

"Lord Ramis," agreed Morgan, his mouth tightening.

Ramis d'Eastmond, until the unfolding of recent events, had been the Marquis of Dryslwyn. He'd been unmasked as both a murderer and a traitor by Marissa duBerry.

Even after his exposure, d'Eastmond had asserted that his actions were motivated by opposition to Rhys's policy of improved relations with the Dwarves. It hadn't made any difference. He was in a dungeon cell, awaiting trial.

Personally, Morgan was convinced the greater part of d'Eastmond's incentive had been the gold paid him by the Rhuddlani agent Xavier. In exchange, d'Eastmond had provided large quantities of sensitive information to the Rhuddlanis. Varsil, King of Rhuddlan, dreamed of launching another invasion of Kilbourne, and would stop at little to achieve his aims.

D'Eastmond had also, by his own admission, been promised a good portion of Morgan's lands as a part of his bargain with the Rhuddlanis.

Eager for more land and the resulting wealth and power this would bring him, d'Eastmond had conceived a bizarre scheme intended to see Morgan executed. He'd been foiled by Lady Marissa, whose own mad plot had made d'Eastmond's seem pathetic by comparison.

Still, Morgan acknowledged, the Dwarf issue had probably been a factor as well. "He's not the only one," he told Rhys. "Lots of people view the Dwarves with disdain or even suspicion. Some with outright loathing. Which seems totally absurd, but there you are. That's people for you. All because they know nothing of Dwarves but old stories heard at their granny's knee. It wouldn't surprise me in the least if feelings in R'mk'vl run the same way toward us." He shrugged. "So yes, an exchange of princes would certainly serve to strengthen the ties between us and perhaps reduce those feelings on both sides."

"Good, you understand."

"Oh, I see the benefits all right," said Morgan. "Just not why you need me to serve as Robbie's escort. I mean, of course I'll do it, if it's what you want. But wouldn't a squadron of Royal Lancers be more appropriate?"

"Certainly, if I wished to make a grand spectacle of the whole affair." Rhys waved an expansive hand. "Actually, I want this done quietly, with as little attention as possible. No formal announcement will be made until the exchange has been accomplished and the two lads are settled in their respective new homes. Once you're back with Prince R'gm'l, we'll throw a welcome banquet or something and show him off to all Caerfaen. Until then, not a word. The only people who know about this are you, me, and Gwyn."

"Mmmm. I see what you mean. If word got out, someone might get ideas."

"Exactly. To tell you the truth, I'll feel much better knowing Robbie's under your protection. The same goes for Prince R'gm'l on the way back to Caerfaen. Gwyn and I both know we can rely on you to keep them safe."

"Right. Wouldn't look good if I were to come back and report I'd managed to lose the royal heir. Either of 'em. The hangman would be tuning up his noose for me. Again."

Rhys shuddered. "Good God, don't even think such a thing! Gwyn's nervous enough about this as it is. Please, no joking about it, at least not around her. I know you're only teasing me, and I have no problem with it. But believe me, she wouldn't take it well."

"Don't worry," Morgan assured him. "I'll be the soul of discretion around the queen. So what's the plan? When do we leave? Are we sneaking out of town in the dead of night? Or are you leaving the planning part up to me?"

"You'll need to go soon. The rendezvous is scheduled for next week. And no, it shouldn't be necessary to sneak out in the night. You'll simply leave Caerfaen without any fanfare."

Morgan considered then said, "All right, it all sounds simple enough. Where's the rendezvous?"

"Bremaine." Rhys was squirming in his seat as if beset by ants.

Morgan's eyes narrowed. This didn't bode well. "There's something else, isn't there?" He allowed an accusatory tone to tinge his voice. After all, Rhys couldn't very well have him beheaded before he carried out this mission, could he? "What aren't you telling me?"

"I've arranged for a coach and driver," Rhys continued. "Henry Dawkes, you'll be happy to know."

Morgan cocked a brow. He and Dawkes had a long history. The coachman had worked as a driver for Morgan's father before Martin McRobbie had succumbed to the wasting fever that had decimated his last years.

Now Morgan called on Dawkes whenever he needed a means of conveyance beyond his favorite horse, Arnicus. But there was something off here, something not ringing quite true.

He frowned. "Rhys, why on earth do we need a coach? Robbie's no hothouse flower. Much simpler, and less obvious, for us to go on horseback. I know he's an excellent rider."

"You should. After all, you trained him."

"You're holding something back, Rhys. Out with it."

Before he could answer, the pieces began to click into place. The Dwarves. The halfway point for the exchange. The need for a coach.

"The exchange point?" Morgan's voice was almost a croak. "It wouldn't happen to be in Vynfold, would it?"

Rhys hesitated, refusing to meet Morgan's eye. Then he nodded once.

At least he had the decency to look sheepish. Morgan threw up his hands. "Rhys," he snapped. "What the devil are you playing at?"

"Nothing," Rhys said, but he still wouldn't meet Morgan's eye. "Nothing at all. Lady Marissa is planning to visit her parents in Vynfold. I figured if Robbie went along, no one would be the wiser. Only her servant and Dawkes would have any idea, and I believe their discretion may be relied upon." He trailed off under the force of Morgan's glare.

"And you decided you'd seize the opportunity to play matchmaker as well, eh? Throw me together with Marissa for an extended journey. Damn it, I'm perfectly able to do my own wooing, thank you. I don't need any royal assistance."

"Oh, really? I certainly haven't heard the banns being read out."

Now it was Morgan's turn to squirm. "Well, no. Things haven't, uh, progressed quite as well as I'd hoped."

Rhys's mouth twitched. "Cat got your tongue?"

Morgan shrugged. "Not exactly. More like the fates conspiring against me. It seems every time I think I've found an opportune moment to tell her how I feel, something or someone interrupts us. The other night we were having dinner together and I thought the time was ripe. Suddenly, a friend of hers showed up out of the blue, she ended up joining us, and we even gave her a ride home in my coach. And," he glared at Rhys, who was unsuccessfully holding back his laughter, "it's like that all the time. There's always something, blast it. It feels like a conspiracy."

"Well, perhaps this little journey together will give you the opportunity you require."

"Right. Just me and Marissa. And her maid. And the prince. And my valet. And Dawkes. That's right, we'll be all alone."

Rhys was lost to another spate of laughter. Morgan favored him with a dark look, and then succumbed to laughter himself.

ENCHANTED KNIGHT

A storm is coming, borne on the wings of prophecy, and Morgan and Marissa stand squarely in the path of the tempest.

They should be preparing to celebrate a joyous wedding. Instead, Marissa struggles to master her newfound powers, while Morgan becomes enmeshed in an unwelcome alliance to repay a debt of honor.

As multiple cryptic prophecies unfold, the indomitable pair find themselves facing power-hungry wizards, treasure-hunting pirates, a wrangle of dragons, and an enigmatic woman driven by forbidden magic and revenge.

When Morgan vanishes under suspicious circumstances and Marissa's power unexpectedly falters, the lines between enemies and allies swirl and blur like deadly Thundermist. With threats closing in from all quarters, Marissa's only hope to save her enchanted knight lies in taming the wild magic she never wanted.

CHAPTER ONE

The dragon sizzled and steamed in the morning mists.

It paused at the edge of the clearing, scanning the area. For threats? Or more likely, for prey?

Morgan decided it really didn't matter. Other than a couple of squirrels chattering their indignation at this invasion of their domain, he was the only creature in the dragon's vicinity. He stepped out of the shadows of a concealing oak, pacing forward into the clearing. He set his lips in a grim line as he watched its every movement. *This is madness*, he told himself for what seemed like the hundredth time. Still, it had to be done.

The dragon's tail lashed back and forth. Its sulfurous odor marred the earthy scent of trees and decaying leaves. Morgan halted and stood his ground.

He likely would have felt much better with a squad of soldiers at his back. But this was something he had to do alone. Abandoning caution for boldness, he stalked to the center of the clearing, ready to face the beast out of legend. Hissing ominously, the dragon undulated serpent-like to meet him.

Morgan halted, his hand hovering by the hilt of his sword in its worn leather scabbard. He could draw it in the blink of an eye. But… a dragon's eye? That remained to be seen.

The beast regarded him from emerald-faceted eyes reflecting eternity. Its mouth curved into a draconic grin, displaying an impressive array of extremely pointy teeth. Delicate plumes of steam swirled on an errant air current and circled Morgan's head, a reminder of the deadly inferno presently banked within. A fire, Morgan knew, that could be called up in an instant to char him into oblivion before he could move.

Inclining his huge head toward the sword, the dragon blinked. *"Would you seek to skewer me, Morgan McRobbie?"*

His words, inaudible to human ears, rang in Morgan's head as Wyvrndell projected his thoughts. His tone held more amusement than menace.

Quirking a sheepish grin, Morgan removed his hand from the sword and stepped closer. "Sorry, Wyvrndell," he muttered. "Old habits die hard."

"For me as well. In other days I might have made a mid-morning snack of you. But I will refrain if you will."

Morgan huffed out a laugh. "Very well. You have my word on it."

"So if not to do battle, why have you asked to meet me here?"

"Because I need to understand what's going on. With Lady Marissa, I mean."

"Nothing is 'going on'. I am her teacher, as agreed."

"Yes, but—" Morgan heaved a sigh, running a hand through his close-cropped dark hair. "Look. I know you've committed to train Marissa how to use her magic. And I appreciate it. I don't want her to hurt herself—or anyone else—because she doesn't know what she's doing."

"Also, power such as hers must not go unchecked. This is why I agreed to teach her."

"What do your kin think of this arrangement? I mean, do they agree with what you're doing?"

The dragon tossed his huge head, sending another plume of smoke skyward. Then, giving a draconic shrug, he said, *"Actually, the matter has not yet been discussed."*

"Oh." Morgan pondered this for a moment. "Um, how do you think they're going to take it?"

Wyvrndell appeared to consider this for a moment. Finally he said, *"I do not foresee any difficulties."*

To Morgan's surprise, the dragon didn't seem as certain in this pronouncement as was his norm. "If you say so. I was rather under the impression dragons don't relish the notion of dealing with humans."

"Do not worry. They will see the necessity of my tutelage of Lady Marissa. It is for the benefit of all."

Morgan's brows rose at this statement. *The benefit of all? How would Wyvrndell's tutoring of Marissa benefit dragonkind?* But another thought crowded this one out. It was why he had arranged this clandestine meeting out in the forest, away from Marissa. He could easily have held this conversation from the comfort of his own study rather than traipsing out here into the forest. Instead, he'd felt an undeniable urgency to speak with Wyvrndell face to face. Which was, he realized, ridiculous. It wasn't like talking with another man, where you could gauge his reactions by watching his eyes. This was a dragon, ancient and unfathomable.

Which didn't change the strange imperative he'd felt. "So how are you able to teach her?" Morgan asked. "I just don't understand it. I mean, if dragons are unable to perform magic, then how can you…" He trailed off as the dragon regarded him reproachfully.

"Just because we can't do it doesn't mean we don't know all the arcane theories. I, and others of my kin, have studied magic for centuries, attempting to learn how to harness its power. I can teach her, Morgan McRobbie. And teach her well, rest assured."

"As you say. I suppose, all things considered, I don't have much choice."

"You may have choices to make, sooner than you think. As will your lady. Choose well. Now I will bid you farewell."

"What? Choices? What are you talking about?"

But Wyvrndell had already unfurled his wings and did not reply. With a graceful leap he mounted the sky, leaving Morgan staring, slack jawed, after him.

Shaking his head, he gathered his wits and started back to Bryntop House, the McRobbie family estate. As Duke of Westdale and lord of the manor and the surrounding lands, he had responsibilities now. Much more than he really had anticipated, which was why he was temporarily in residence.

Well, also because of the aftermath of the recent near-debacle with Xavier. Morgan still had nightmares of Marissa held hostage by the Rhuddlani. She'd only been rescued by a combination of extraordinary luck and the intervention of Wyvrndell. Once the smoke had settled, Morgan had suggested they remove themselves to the country for a bit, where she could recuperate in relative seclusion and undergo the dragon's tutelage.

She seemed to be doing much better since they'd come here. Of course, his mother fussed over her like a protective hen, although this was likely as much due to their impending nuptials as to her concern for her future daughter's mental state. But Lady Sybil was no fool, a lesson Morgan had long since learned. She had gone above and beyond in her efforts to put Morgan's betrothed at ease. When Marissa wasn't engaged in her lessons with Wyvrndell, Lady Sybil made sure to keep her occupied with discussions of gowns, flowers and banquets. Which was, all things considered, much better than allowing Marissa to dwell on such things as near death at the hands of vicious assassins. Morgan was grateful, and especially pleased the two women he loved most seemed to be getting along so well.

Once Wyvrndell had departed, the forest seemed to return to normal. Birds sang and small animals darted through the underbrush around him. Morgan hardly heard them. His thoughts buzzed like bees in a hive as he tried to make sense of the dragon's enigmatic intimations. The blasted creature was as bad as his friend Randolph when it came to beating about the bush. Why the devil couldn't people—yes, and dragons—just stick to the point?

Abandoning this line of inquiry as fruitless, he turned to considerations of a more immediate nature. Like what the near future might hold. For him and Marissa and their life together once they were wed.

For Morgan had indeed made a choice. He had chosen to marry a witch.

Well, a woman with magical talent. No, he amended, might as well call a witch a witch. This was how Marissa referred to herself now. An extremely powerful witch, according to the wizard Sebastien, who had first discovered the magic latent within Marissa. She had inherited the magical potential of both her mother and father, each of whom possessed powerful magic in their own right. Neither of them made use of it, but it was there. The combination of talent inherited from two such puissant parents had resulted in, as Marissa had put it, "A witch with a capital W."

Wyvrndell had confirmed Sebastien's assertion. The two of them, dragon and wizard, had come to a consensus: Marissa needed immediate training before anything untoward happened.

Sebastien had disclaimed any ability to properly teach Marissa how to harness and control her burgeoning powers. When Morgan had asked him if he thought she should attend St. Giles Academy for Magic, where her parents had gone, long years past, the wizard had hesitated several moments before answering.

"She could," he allowed, but Morgan noticed the emphasis on the word *could*.

"But?" he'd prompted.

"But I think she might be best served by allowing Wyvrndell to instruct her. He's eager to do so, and I'm certain he has both the knowledge and the capacity. And the patience." He gave Morgan a wry smile.

"You're telling me you'd trust a dragon before you'd trust your fellow wizards to teach her?"

"Well, when you put it that way…" Sebastien's eyes had glinted with a strange light. "Yes, I believe in this case I would."

Morgan had been unable to extract any more from the wizard. And with this recommendation, Marissa had agreed to accept the dragon as her tutor.

While Morgan was prepared to do everything in his power to protect the woman he loved, her heritage was the one thing from which he couldn't shield her. It was maddening. Here he was, a duke of the realm and Knight-Commander of the King's Legion. He possessed wealth, power, and skill at arms. But none of these mattered a jot. He growled at the thought.

Preoccupied as he was, Morgan was nearly at the manor gates before he realized he was being followed.

STOLEN KNIGHT

Married at last. And shipwrecked.

A storm on the Thundermist Sea has cast newlyweds Morgan and Marissa onto the shores of Parthane. This exotic land boasts ancient temples, sumptuous feasts, court intrigue…and deadly danger.

But it's all part of a plan. The dauntless pair has been dispatched to recover a priceless jewel stolen from the wizards of Caerfaen by Prince Azim of Parthane. The ruby, known as the Demon's Fire, is not merely beautiful and valuable, but is also a magical artifact which gives whoever wields it access to unimaginable power. Power which, in the wrong hands, could lead to a catastrophe of demonic proportions.

As Royal Enchantress (and possessor of an ancient grimoire), Marissa is the only hope to retrieve the jewel. There's no way Morgan will allow Chief Wizard Foxwent to send his new bride off to Parthane alone and unprotected, but he'll need to call on all his skills and instincts to keep them safe in this new world of decadent temptations and lethal double-crosses.

The book and the jewel are somehow bound together, and their confluence might turn both Parthane and Kilbourne into magical wastelands. Morgan and Marissa must outwit ghostly guards, malevolent magicians, and an impregnable palace to steal back the jewel and return it to Kilbourne. They'll only have one chance to complete their mission, and failure might just mean the end of the world.

CHAPTER ONE

The cat stalked in an angry circle, lashing her tail like a small whip. "No!" she snarled. "It is not simply a book. It's dangerous."

Morgan discreetly moved his feet away from the cat's path. He glanced over at Marissa. She stared, wide-eyed, at the furry beast.

"But—" she began.

"Wrong," the cat remonstrated. "But me no buts, witch. It. Is. Dangerous. I should know."

Marissa's sharp intake of breath made Morgan's heart unexpectedly skip a beat. She swallowed, hard. "Yes." Her voice sounded raspy, almost unfamiliar. "You do, don't you? The—the binding spell. It's in the book. You created it. You told me."

Francesca bowed her head in apparent acknowledgement. "Yes."

Morgan was still getting used to the notion of a talking cat. This one, undeniably, talked. In fact, he'd come to realize over the last few days, she was rarely silent. Then, with a start, he understood what they were talking about. He cast a basilisk eye on Francesca and said coldly, "The binding spell? The one Kiara and Rhenn used? On me?"

"Well, yes," Francesca admitted. "That's the one."

The cat's expression, he thought, was rather hangdog. Which was a bit incongruous, all in all. Morgan rose from his seat to loom over Francesca. His breath came in a hiss mimicking the cat's own response. Marissa's head swiveled between them as she gaped at Morgan and her familiar. Francesca arched her back, her tail bristling, as they exchanged glares.

"Morgan, please," Marissa said. "Not now. We have other things to deal with. Go on, Francesca," she instructed the cat. "You were saying?"

"No, wait a minute," he protested. "Enlighten me, please. This thing, this book, was just lying about where anyone could pick it up? Make use of such a dangerous spell?"

Francesca's ears were ears flat against her head. Her green eyes glittered. "No, it wasn't," she spat. "I mean, it shouldn't have been. There aren't even supposed to be any copies still in existence. They were said to have been destroyed ages ago. Well, all but one. That one was supposed to have been secured, under protective enchantments, in the archives of the Royal College of Wizards."

"Right. One copy, eh? Which somehow happened to fall into Kiara Northram's hands?"

"More likely the wizard's," Francesca opined. "Oh, I don't know. Anyway, what does it matter now? The point is, the blasted book should be destroyed. Before it can cause any more trouble."

"I'll second that," Morgan said. Marissa gave a less than enthusiastic nod. "What?" he asked.

"Nothing," she said. "No, I— Well, shouldn't we give it back to the wizards? To keep secure? I mean, destroying it sounds so… final."

"Keep it secure?" Francesca arched her back. "Like they did before?"

"Nooo," Marissa said. "But—"

The cat levitated into her lap and stared into her eyes. Marissa blinked and sat back.

"Oh, no you don't," Francesca said, her voice sharp. "You've felt the book's call, haven't you? It has power on its own, never mind the spells it contains. It's whispering to you, isn't it?"

"No!" she protested. "Don't be silly It's only a book."

"Is it?" Francesca purred. "Is it really? This is no laughing matter, witch. Books like this have serious magic. Deadly magic. I won't say they are aware, or alive, but they do have… desires."

Marissa shivered. "What kind of desires? I don't—"

"I don't think I really want to know," Morgan. Neither cat nor witch paid him any heed. He returned to his seat, anxious fingers drumming a nervous tattoo on his knee.

Francesca leapt up into Morgan's lap this time. He found himself giving her ear scritches. "No, I'm sure you don't," she said. "But you're going to. Because she—" the cat nodded toward Marissa, "—is in danger."

He blinked. Then he heaved a sigh. "All right. Tell us."

"Books of power—and make no mistake, this is a book of power—seek those who will make use of them. They want, no, need, this. Because then they absorb even more power, from those mages. As the wizard, and this Kiara woman, did.”

Marissa’s eyes widened. “So, you’re saying the book wanted me to find it? Pick it up?”

Francesca flowed back down the floor again. She paced in a circle, then sat, with her tail curled around her paws, before she answered. “I won’t say the book is alive. Still, because of the power contained within it…well, let’s simply say I won’t rule it out. Consider it like this. It has a certain awareness. So yes. When there was a choice between being stuck in that tower for ages, or coming along with you? No contest. You were the logical choice.”

“And now I have the book,” Marissa mused.

“Now you have the book. On the other hand, the book also has you. Which brings us back to my original point. I don’t want my witch caught up in this. You need to destroy the book.”

Marissa was silent for longer than Morgan thought called for. “Marissa?” he prompted.

“Yes, yes, I’m just—”

“Come on, let us destroy it.” Francesca stared at her, unblinking.

“How?” Morgan asked. “Do we just…burn it or something?”

“No!”

Morgan could see Marissa’s response was involuntary. She went ashen as the word sped from her, and clapped her hand to her mouth.

Francesca eyes glittered with a fey light. “No?”

“Yes, all right. We’ll…we’ll burn it.”

Even to Morgan’s ears she didn’t sound particularly convincing. “I’ll build up the fire in the grate,” he offered.

Francesca cocked her head, regarding Marissa. “I’m glad to hear you say it, even if only with reluctance. However, I fear attempting to burn the book won’t work.”

Marissa, Morgan noted, looked relieved. Which was not reassuring in the least. “It’s just paper, isn’t it?” he asked. “I’d think a nice hot fire… No?”

“No. If this were merely a normal book, certainly.” Francesca glanced up at him, her green eyes glittering. “But it’s not a normal book, is it? It is a magical artifact. A very powerful one to boot. It contains all manner of dark spells, woven into it by its crafters. Your little hearth blaze here? The book would snuff it out before you could blink twice. What’s worse, the book would not be best pleased. There are tales, from ages long past, of just such attempts. Objects of power, like this, which the possessors attempted to destroy in such a manner. Things did not…go well.”

"Umm. I see. At least I think I do." He considered this. "Drop it into the sea?" he suggested.

Marissa sighed. "No, it wouldn't be any better. Some big fish would just swallow it, get caught, and someone would end up with the book again. Someone who wouldn't be able to withstand its call."

The cat nodded approvingly. "You are learning, witch," she said.

"I'm learning the things we can't do," Marissa replied. "Very well, what can we do? How do we destroy it?"

The cat shrugged. "I wish I knew. Not, I realize, the least bit helpful. I shall have to consult."

Morgan glanced over at the hearth. "Francesca, you said our small fire wouldn't be able to do the job. What about something bigger? Much, much hotter?"

"You mean like a smithy's fire?" Francesca resumed her pacing again. "It's been tried. The attempt I mentioned before? The one which didn't go well? That time, it was a magical ring, if I remember correctly. It got a little…feisty, shall we say? Spread itself a bit." Her gaze went from Morgan to Marissa. "You do understand what I'm saying, don't you? The results, well, they're not something I even want to discuss."

"Actually," Morgan said, "I was thinking more along the lines of a dragon."

Francesca halted her pacing. Sitting back on her haunches, she stared up at Morgan, her eyes unblinking. The force of her gaze was so strong he only barely managed to not look away.

"You," she said at last, "are not as stupid as one might think."

Marissa choked out a laugh. Morgan merely nodded. "Thank you," he said. "I shall take that as a compliment."

"It was meant as one. Enjoy it; it's not likely you'll get another anytime soon. Hmm. I don't suppose it's ever been tried. A dragon's fire, I mean. Until now, there would have been no one who could have even asked. I wonder…"

"Should I speak to Wyvrndell?" Marissa asked.

"No, not yet. Let me do some research first. In the meantime, don't use the book." She turned her gaze on Marissa. "Don't even touch it."

Morgan rounded on the cat. "This book—this thing—is it somehow possessing her?" he asked. "Already? This soon?"

"Hello," Marissa said, waving at them. "I am here, you know."

Francesca ignored her, stalking in a small circle before she spoke. "No, I don't think so. She is rather reluctant, I'll admit. But she hasn't used the book, as far as I can tell. Which is to her benefit."

"Are you certain? I mean, certain she hasn't used it?"

"Still here," Marissa said, a bit louder this time. "And no, I haven't. Barely even opened it."

"Certain? No." Francesca was still focused on Morgan. "I believe I'd be able to tell, although I offer no guarantee. Dark magic like this generally leaves traces. Auras, if you will. The witch shows no signs of it. We'll see. If she willingly gives it up. If she allows it to be destroyed. If the book allows itself to be destroyed."

Morgan shuddered. *If the book allows itself to be destroyed?* A most unsettling notion. Even more unsettling, he suddenly became aware of Marissa marching up to him, fire in her eyes.

"Morgan McRobbie, I do not appreciate being ignored," she snapped. "Or being talked around, like I'm not even here. This affects me, you know."

"Yes, we know," Francesca said. "That's the problem, isn't it?"

"Well, then, you'd be better served to include me in your discussions, instead of being rude. Otherwise, I shall have to get witchy about things."

"Marissa, I'm sorry," Morgan said. "I just wish you'd never picked up the blasted thing in the first place." He enfolded her in his embrace, but she jerked away and crossed her arms.

"Don't you think I feel the same way?" she demanded. "I never asked for this. For any of this. Learning out of the blue I'm a witch? Having to fight off Rhenn? Getting saddled with this stupid grimoire… I hate it."

"Yes, I imagine you do," said a voice from the doorway.

~ * ~

Marissa whirled to face the intruder. "Sebastien," she said. Her voice came out a hoarse mixture of exhaustion and relief. "I—"

"I tried to stop him, Your Ladyship." Briana, Marissa's maid, pursued the wizard into the room, indignation writ plainly across her face.

"It's all right, Briana," Marissa replied. "Always delighted to welcome Master Sebastien."

Briana retreated with a toss of her head and muttered imprecations.

"Apparently I've come at just the right time. I gather the grimoire is under discussion?"

"Got it in one," purred Francesca. "We've been discussing how to destroy it."

"Yes, well, I'm not sure you can." Sebastien eyed Marissa with an appraising gaze. "How do you feel about it, my lady?"

She heaved a gusty sigh. "Oh, I don't know. Francesca says she thinks the blasted thing will overwhelm me. Use me somehow. For something horrible, naturally."

"Of course." The wizard gave her a rueful smile. "What fun would it be otherwise, eh?"

"I don't—oh, very well, have your little joke. Seriously, Sebastien, do you feel the same? Is this thing dangerous to me? To us? It's only a book, Sebastien. Isn't it?"

"Well, yes. And no. It's a book of magic, has magic woven into it. Dark magic, I fear. I think perhaps it might be best if we stored this thing somewhere a bit, well, safer. Where there's no likelihood it might do anything…suspect. Away from any temptations." He locked his eyes on Marissa's. She met his gaze at first, then hers faltered. She looked away. At the floor. At the cat. Anywhere but at the wizard.

"Lady Marissa," Sebastien said. "Please, don't fret. You did the right thing in agreeing to destroy the book. Happily enough, I feel it means the grimoire has no irreversible hold upon you."

Morgan exchanged glances with Francesca. Marissa cocked her head at them, then returned her attention to Sebastien. "Well," she said, "then that's all to the good, eh? Would you like tea, Master Sebastien?"

"Thank you, no. What I'd like, if you'll permit, is for me to take the grimoire away with me."

"Where?" she asked, as Morgan and Francesca both said, "Yes!"

The wizard smiled. "It's for the best, I believe, if the location remains secret. No offense intended."

Marissa considered his words. "Yes, I suppose you're right. Very well, I'll get it for you. It's upstairs. In my room." She headed toward the door, then turned back to add, "Where I have most assuredly not been perusing its contents. It's stuffed well away, in the back of a closet, behind a box of old boots."

"As good a place as any," Sebastien said. "Probably more secure there than it was in the wizards' archives. Please, fetch it down. I'll deal with it." He held up a hand. "Now, wait just a moment." Striding to the hearth, he caught up the tongs and brought them to Marissa. "Just to be certain, take these."

She took them, even as her brows rose. "Really? You feel it's necessary?"

"Let's just say I'm going under the theory of 'what could it hurt?' Humor me?"

"Of course." Taking the tongs, she strode from the room.

Mounting the stairs, she entered her bedroom. As she glanced over, she noticed her reflection in the glass and gave a harsh laugh. She was holding the tongs out before her, like a fencer ready to enter a fight.

"Hmph," she muttered, lowered them then opened the closet. As she did, an almost palpable sense of dark foreboding suffused the room.

"Ridiculous," she muttered, pushing aside gowns and chemises to reach the spot where the book lay hidden.

Shifting the box of boots to the floor, she finally uncovered the hat box where the grimoire reposed. She lugged the box into the room, set it on the bed, and opened it. A wave of nausea spilled over her, and she felt near to retching.

"Stop that," she ordered, both to the book and to her rebellious stomach.

The feeling passed. Marissa reached in with the fireplace tongs, lifting the grimoire from the hatbox. When she was certain it was well secured, she turned to go back downstairs. Just then, she caught sight of her reflection again. This time, the image shimmered and blurred, distorting her own appearance into something haggard and crone-like. The grimoire, caught in the teeth of the tongs, looked more like a writhing serpent. She gasped, nearly dropping the book.

A soft, sibilant whisper slithered into her ears. "Is this what your beloved sees, witch? When he looks at you, does he see the true witch you see in the glass? Or does he only see what you allow him to?"

"No!" she shouted. "You lie! I'm not like that."

"No?" The whispers were more strident. "Are you sure? There is a monster, deep within each of us. Some show more than others… Gaze into the glass, witch. See yourself as you are truly revealed."

Unwillingly, yet unable to resist, she stared into the mirror again. Her features blurred once more, until she was displayed as a distorted, repulsive old woman, bent with age and hatred.

With a harsh breath, Marissa rasped out the spell Sebastien had first taught her, when he'd discovered her magic. The spell allowed her to block out external forces. As the final word left her lips, the image in the mirror shifted again, back to her normal features. The hideous crone was banished.

"Damn you," she whispered.

Then, trembling, but resolute, she renewed her grasp on the handles of the tongs, to ensure she didn't drop the grimoire. The book appeared normal again, the serpent-like form banished as well. She squared her shoulders, marched into the hall then headed back down the stairs.

"Here," she said to Sebastien. "Take this. I never want to see it again."

The wizard regarded her with a thoughtful expression as he accepted the tongs into his gnarled hands. "It did something, eh?"

Not even daring to speak of the horror she'd just seen, Marissa simply nodded. Sebastien's smile was grim. "I wondered if it might. I'm happy to see you were strong enough to resist. Well done."

"I told you it was dangerous," put in Francesca.

"Yes, thank you for your kind concern," Marissa said. "Next time, you can deal with it."

"I wouldn't have picked it up," the cat replied.

"Yes, but that's only because you don't have any hands."

Francesca snorted. "Fair enough. Still, if you can joke about it, I supposed there's no lasting harm done you."

Sebastien held the book out before him, as she had. Marissa wondered, if only for a moment, if he could see it in its serpent form. She shuddered at the thought.

"My lady?" he said. His voice sounded strained, as if he was exerting a great effort. "If you'll bring me that little box?"

He gestured with his head. Marissa saw a small wooden casket on the table near the door. She fetched it over to the wizard. It was quite heavy for its size.

"Please open it," he said. She did so, observing the box was lined with some kind of metal. The wizard dropped the book neatly into the open box. "Now, close it, quickly."

She slammed the lid shut, uttering a low sigh. With a wan smile, Sebastien leaned the tongs against the hearth and picked up the box. Setting it back on the table he placed his hands over it and began to chant. His words rolled out, the power he poured into them infusing the very air. His voice grew stronger, the words unfamiliar, but redolent and filled with authority.

He grasped the little box as if it might try to escape. Casting his gaze to the heavens he cried, *"Fermiti signati!"*

She half expected an accompanying rumble of thunder. Instead, there was only a sound like a soft breeze caressing the leaves of an oak tree, and then a sharp click.

Stepping back, he swayed like a young tree in a stiff wind. Morgan hurried to take his arm. With a grateful nod, the wizard allowed himself to be helped to a seat. He drew a long breath and scrubbed a hand across his suddenly weary face.

"My, that took a lot out of me," he said in a tone of mild surprise.

Marissa frowned. "Are you all right?"

"Yes, yes, I'll be fine. Just some serious magic, like I haven't done in many years. I need to catch my breath for a few moments. Although I wouldn't say no to that cup of tea now."

"Of course. Wait right here." She hurried out, calling for Briana.

When she returned, Sebastien was leaning back in his chair, with Francesca curled up in his lap.

"Well, don't you two look cozy," she said.

He drooped one eye in a slow wink and chucked the cat under her chin. "I am endeavoring," he said, "to ensure I remain on good terms with Lady Francesca. One never knows when an ally might be useful."

Francesca purred. Finally, the cat stretched, then drifted to the floor. "For a wizard," she observed, "you're not so bad."

"High praise indeed," murmured Morgan. Marissa could see him struggling to keep a straight face.

"Wizard, be sure you keep the blasted book somewhere safe," Francesca added. She stared at Sebastien. "Very safe. We wouldn't want anything to happen to it."

"No, we certainly wouldn't," he agreed. "I shall do my best."

With a curt nod and a flick of her tail, Francesca stalked out. Marissa returned to her seat, making a wide detour around the table where the box stood. With the grimoire now secured, she felt lighter, somehow able to breathe easier.

As she sat, Morgan reached over to take her hand. His eyes held a question, and she nodded. "I'm fine. Still a witch, though." A mischievous smile danced across her face.

"Enchantress," he corrected.

Marissa shook her head. "Only in public. For you, I'm a witch, through and through."

"Casting spells upon your unsuspecting betrothed?"

"Hmph," said Sebastien. "Young love is all well and good, but where's my tea?"